IN TOO DEEP

What Reviewers Say About BOLD STROKES Authors

✑

KIM BALDWIN

"Her...crisply written action scenes, juxtaposition of plotlines, and smart dialogue make this a story the reader will absolutely enjoy and long remember."—**Arlene Germain**, book reviewer for the *Lambda Book Report* and the *Midwest Book Review*

Hunter's Pursuit is a "...fierce first novel, an action-packed thriller pitting deadly professional killers against each other. Baldwin's fast-paced plot comes...leavened, as every intelligent adventure novel's excesses ought to be, with some lovin'. Even as she fends off her killers,...the heroine...finds the woman she wants by her side — and in her bed."—**Richard Labonte**, Book Marks, *Q Syndicate*, May 2005

✑

ROSE BEECHAM

"...a mystery writer with a delightful sense of humor, as well as an eye for an interesting array of characters..."—*MegaScene*

"...her characters seem fully capable of walking away from the particulars of whodunit and engaging the reader in other aspects of their lives."—*Lambda Book Report*

✑

JANE FLETCHER

"...a natural gift for rich storytelling and world-building...one of the best fantasy writers at work today."—**Jean Stewart**, author of the Isis series

"In *The Walls of Westernfort*, Fletcher spins a captivating story about youthful idealism, honor, and courage. The action is fast paced and the characters are compelling in this gripping sci-fi adventure." —**Reader Raves**, BookWoman 2005

✑

RADCLYfFE

"Powerful characters, engrossing plot, and intelligent writing..." —**Cameron Abbott,** author of *To the Edge* and *An Inexpressible State of Grace*

"...well-honed storytelling skills...solid prose and sure-handedness of the narrative..."—**Elizabeth Flynn**, *Lambda Book Report*

"...well-plotted...lovely romance...I couldn't turn the pages fast enough!"—**Ann Bannon**, author of *The Beebo Brinker Chronicles*

IN TOO DEEP

by

RONICA BLACK

2005

IN TOO DEEP

ISBN 1-933110-17-1

This Trade Paperback Original Is Published By
Bold Strokes Books, Inc.,
Pennsylvania, USA

First Printing: September 2005.

Credits
Editors: Jennifer Knight and Stacia Seaman
Production Design: Stacia Seaman
Cover Design By Sheri (GRAPHICARTIST2020@HOTMAIL.COM)

Acknowledgments

My sincere thanks to everyone online who read the first draft and encouraged me to continue. Without your e-mails and support, this story would not be what it is today.

Also my thanks to the ladies at The Sandbox. Nancy and Wizzy, fellow authors and readers, thanks so much for your unrelenting support and for creating an environment in which to thrive.

To the entire team at Bold Strokes Books for all the invaluable hard work you've done to produce the best book possible. To Jennifer Knight, my editor, thanks for holding my hand and guiding me through the entire process with humor and grace. To Sheri for designing such an incredible cover. And most especially to Radclyffe, for taking a chance on me.

Thank you to my two sisters, Robin and Rebecca, for their unconditional love and support. A sister's love knows no bounds.

And to C.W.—without you, this dream would not have come true. I will forever be grateful for the feedback, advice, and heartfelt encouragement you've given me.

Thank you.

Dedication

For C.W....for everything.
Te quiero, siempre.

Prologue

Arcane, Alabama

"Come on, Lizzie, hurry!" Jay yelled as they ran through the woods. "We gotta get to Papaw's house by suppertime!"

"I'm comin', I'm comin'." Lizzie ran as hard as she could, but she never could keep up with her older sister.

The shortcut to their grandpa's house was always an adventure Lizzie enjoyed. It led deep into the woods, a good ways from their aunt Dayne's house. The house they had been living in ever since their mother left them as babies.

Jay stopped to wait for her, hands on her hips. "You better hurry up. I got better things to do than to wait for your ass." She kicked a pebble at Lizzie with her worn sneakers. Her tanned and sockless legs were covered with tiny scratches and scrapes from her rough play outdoors.

"Oh yeah? Well, at least I ain't getting boobs!" Lizzie taunted, earning herself a rough shove.

"Shut up, you little shit! I ain't getting no boobs." Jay clasped her hands quickly over her tank top, hiding the budding mosquito bites on her eleven-and-a-half-year-old chest.

"Are too. And if you ain't nicer to me, I'm gonna tell Bobbie Hollaway that you got hair on your twat." Lizzie scampered ahead of her sister, knowing she was about to get pummeled.

She ran hard and fast, glancing back over her shoulder to measure Jay's advance. A ledge loomed ahead, and Lizzie slammed to a halt, Jay gaining on her rapidly. She peered down the embankment, trying to decide whether or not she should risk the steep descent. As her eyes skimmed over the heavily overgrown area below, something caught her attention, something so out of the ordinary that she completely forgot about Jay and the impending ass-kicking.

"You're dead, dickhead!" Jay shouted victoriously as she slammed into her from behind.

Lizzie almost toppled, but turned and threw her arms around her sister to steady herself. Her eyes never left the strange sight at the bottom of the embankment.

"Git your hands off me, you freak." Jay shoved her away. "What's your problem?"

Lizzie pointed and said with a gasp, "Look."

"What?" Jay peered into the ravine.

They stood in silence for a moment, trying to see an object partly hidden by a rotting log. Lizzie walked a few yards along the ledge to get a better look. But on her final step, the soft red earth gave way and she fell with a shriek, rolling over and over until she slammed into something that stopped her momentum.

She lay there, eyes clenched shut, her brain spinning. She could hear Jay calling and coming after her, and she tried to get up, not knowing which limb to move first. Pain seeped through her body, and a terrible smell filled her nostrils, almost burning them.

"Lizzie!" Jay came to a running stop behind her. "Oh my God. Lizzie, git up." Her voice was a strangled whisper.

"I cain't." She opened her eyes for the first time.

"I said git up!" Jay yanked her up and away by the waistband of her jean shorts.

Lizzie cried out as her left arm fell limply to her side. She studied it in silence, too shocked to say a word. Adrenaline surged through her as pain registered. She looked up to speak to Jay but then, with a hoarse cry, focused on what it was that had stopped her fall.

There, amidst the dead leaves and the rotting log, lay the nude body of a young woman. Lifeless eyes bulged unnaturally from the woman's head, along with her tongue, which fell to rest outside of her mouth. Angry red and purple marks streaked across her neck where someone had squeezed the life out of her. One leg was tucked beneath her at an impossible angle, and an arm cast back over her head as if she had tried to fend off a blow.

Flies swarmed all over the body as it lay exposed in the Alabama heat.

"Come on." Jay nudged Lizzie from her trance. "Let's git outta here."

"But what about her?" Lizzie couldn't tear her gaze away from the dead girl's eyes.

"She's dead! She ain't going nowhere." Jay had started to make her way back up the embankment, and she turned to make sure her sister was following. "Come on," she urged. "We gotta go tell."

Lizzie gave the dead girl one last look and dragged herself out of the ravine. Fear rocked through her, along with the pain from her arm. She struggled to keep up with Jay, afraid if she fell behind, the body would rise and come for her. As she hurriedly made it to the top, a figure startled them, stepping out from behind a large tree.

"Well, looky what we have here," the man said with a sly grin, a worn toothpick stuck between his teeth.

Jay eased Lizzie behind her with one arm. "Look, mister, we don't want no trouble." Lizzie could hear the uncertainty in her tone.

The stranger looked Jay up and down, jangling the keys on his belt loop with one hand. He had on worn jeans, stained with grease and dirt. His T-shirt was tattered and full of holes; sweat stains marked the armpits. He stank of raw onions, a smell almost as strong as the rotting flesh of the dead girl.

"Well, it looks like you've done found it." He laughed out loud and pulled the toothpick from his mouth to toss it on the ground. He glanced down beyond them at the body in the ravine and snickered. "I see you girls met Mary. See, she didn't play nice with me. But you will, won't you."

He took a step toward them, knowing they couldn't back up much more. "Ain't you a purdy little thing." He reached out and tried to stroke Jay's cheek, but she ducked away from him and came back up quickly, hitting him square in the balls. The man bent over and grabbed himself, moaning in pain. "You little bitch."

Pulled hard by her sister, Lizzie ran as best she could, but the man gained on them fast, fueled by his anger and pain. He grabbed at Lizzie's hair, and Jay turned, clawing and pounding at him, causing him to lose his grip.

"Run, Lizzie, run!" she screamed.

The man laughed as Jay continued to try and fight him. Bear-hugging her from behind, he carried her off back into the woods, kicking and screaming.

For a split second, Lizzie stared after them, torn, legs shaking. Pain and nausea tried to make itself known. She glanced down. An unnatural bulge swelled beneath her flesh, and she knew she couldn't fight the man with one arm. Terrified for Jay, she forced herself to run and not look back.

Chapter One

Twenty Years Later
July
Corona County Desert, Valle Luna, Arizona

The victim was male and appeared to be middle aged, gray hair at his temples. He was on his back, the bottom half of his body nude. His genitalia were bloodstained, and a single bullet hole marked his forehead. His hands were already bagged in brown paper bags to preserve any forensic evidence under the fingernails. The bags were sealed just below wrists purple with ligature marks. He had been bound very tightly by his killer.

Newly appointed homicide detective Erin McKenzie pulled off her silver-framed Revo sunglasses and tucked them into the collar of her sleeveless silk blouse. She wiped the sweat from her brow and didn't know whether to blame the desert heat or her nerves for the flush of perspiration she was feeling. It was her first week in Homicide, and she hadn't expected to get assigned to such an important case so soon. She could tell by the silent, wary glances her way that the two male detectives at the scene were in the dark as to what she was doing there.

She had only been briefed a short time ago herself and didn't know the full details of the case yet. Martin Stewart, the older of the men, was staring her down. She knew the overweight detective by reputation but had never been properly introduced. Taking the bull by the horns, she walked over.

"Good to meet you, Detective," she said, matching her colleague's stare with one of her own.

He looked away first and started coughing wheezily. He wasn't happy about her presence, that much was evident. It was a different story with the younger detective. Jeff Hernandez was a friend from earlier days at the Academy and knew she was one of the most credible vice officers in the department.

On his knees next to the DOA, he looked up and met her smile, pulling down his surgical mask to do so. Casting a glance in Stewart's direction, he said, "Just ignore him. He's pissed because you're invading his crime scene and because he quit smoking last week. How are ya, Mac?" He let go of his mask and it snapped back into place.

"I'm not here to step on anyone's toes." She knelt next to him, and they both glanced toward the red-faced man scowling and leaning against the Valle Luna P.D. crime scene van.

"He's pretty much an asshole all of the time," Jeff said. "Don't take it personally."

"I'll watch my step." Erin laughed softly. Stewart was obviously a lost cause, and she didn't want to get into a pissing contest with him over territory. She knew she was being thrown into their turf, and the fact she was female didn't help matters any. She tucked one hand into her black slacks. "So, what have we got here?"

"This poor bastard was one Jonathon Bale. Got I.D. from the wallet we found in his pants over there." A pair of expensive-looking tailored pants lay next to the body, turned inside out with the underwear exposed as if they had been pulled off quickly. "Fifty-two-year-old from Scottsdale, married with two adult sons. Wealthy business owner. One prior for a DUI two years ago."

"Who found him?" Erin put her shades back on. It was two in the afternoon, and the desert sun pierced her eyes.

They both stood and moved away from the stinking body.

"Fourteen-year-old kid was out this morning riding his dirt bike." Jeff yanked the sweltering mask from his face and tossed it into the van, audibly drawing a deep breath of the fresher air. "Looks like number three."

"You do know what he means by 'number three,' don't you?" Stewart asked in a not-so-friendly tone. Without waiting for her to respond, he explained, as if talking to a slow learner, "You do know about the serial killings, don't you? This guy makes *numero tres.*" He held up three stubby freckled fingers just in case she needed to count them in order to understand.

Erin took a breath in through her nose, controlling her flaring temper. She hated assholes like this, who spoke to her as if she were a little girl. "Yes, I am aware of the recent killings."

Stewart puffed out his chest. "Well, then I guess you know that Hernandez and I are assigned to those cases and to this one as well." *Aha. So there it is. Territory. He might as well lift his leg and pee on the dead body.*

"Yes, I'm aware of that, also." She knew what he wanted, complete acceptance from her that they called the shots.

Stewart folded his arms above his belly. It was like a standoff at high noon. Erin almost waited for a tumbleweed to roll slowly by to add to the effect. It occurred to her that Stewart didn't seem to know she'd been assigned to the case as of this morning. From the way Jeff was smiling, she suspected he had some idea. Either that, or he was merely enjoying the banter between his colleagues.

She decided to lay her cards on the table for the both of them. "As of today, gentlemen, I have been assigned to the serial killings as well."

"No fucking way," Stewart erupted. He began pacing like a mad dog and mumbling to himself.

"I need to get up to speed pretty fast." Erin directed her comments to Jeff. "I need to know everything that's entailed in these killings. So I'm counting on you to fill me in on the details."

This stopped Stewart in his tracks. "Well no shit, Miss Fancy Pants! We're all wanting to know everything there is to know!" A throbbing vein on his forehead pulsed at her.

Erin glanced down at her pants. *Fancy Pants?* They were nice pants, but she wouldn't call them fancy. Jeff caught on, laughing at her gentle mockery of the clueless Stewart.

"Look. All I was told is that I'm going undercover on this case," she said. "That's as much as I know at this point."

Stewart stopped pacing and looked from her to Jeff, the slow-creaking wheels of his brain working loudly. "Adams?" he muttered almost to himself.

Some of the color drained from Jeff's face. "No way."

"Who's Adams?" Erin asked.

Stewart laughed heartily. "Holy shit. She'll eat this little tart alive." He walked away toward an approaching black coroner's van, mumbling, "'Bout fucking time."

Jeff stared off into the distance in silence.

"Jeff, who's Adams?" Erin asked him softly.

"Our main suspect in these killings."

Erin was slightly shocked. "A woman?" She looked over at the mutilated body. The killing seemed angry, violent, and very personal. "A woman did that?"

"Yeah, we're pretty sure. And she's flaunting it in our face too. Only we can't get anything to stick to her."

"Well, I have to admit that going in after a woman doesn't sound so bad." Her mind eased a little at the thought. At least she wouldn't be throwing herself at some horrible man who would try to screw *her* while she tried to screw information out of him.

Jeff laughed a little. It was a nervous laugh. "Listen, Mac, this is no ordinary woman. She's as cunning as they get, and I'm betting she doesn't have a conscience bone in her fantastic body."

Erin scoffed at his reference to the woman's body. She had never heard him talk like that about a female.

Picking up on her reaction, he said, "Yeah, she's good looking. Hell, she's gorgeous. And uses it to her full advantage. But there's a cold heart beating underneath that hot package, and if I'm right," Jeff paused on a sigh, "the team is going to send you in as bait."

Erin recoiled at the statement, completely thrown. "Bait?" She shoved her hands nervously in her pockets. "What in the hell are you talking about?"

Jeff grinned. "She's a lesbian."

Erin shook her head. To think, she had kidded herself into believing that she wouldn't have to prostitute herself on this undercover assignment, that she had been chosen for her skills this time. Why did she always have to seduce someone in order to get information out of them?

"This is crazy. How am I supposed to bait a woman?" *What in the world do they expect me to do?*

Jeff eyed her with obvious appreciation. "Trust me, Mac, what you got, she's gonna want."

CHAPTER TWO

Detective Patricia Henderson tapped her pen nervously against her notepad and glanced at the other four detectives sitting in silence around the conference table.

They were waiting for their sergeant to begin the briefing, the first of many that would involve this team and the recent serial killings. A larger task force was in the works, which would likely include the FBI. But as the investigation stood right now, their small team was closest to the case.

Directly across from her, Jeff Hernandez sipped on a cup of coffee. Patricia had trained him at the Arizona Law Enforcement Academy just a few years before, and she trusted him completely. Jeff was hardworking and honorable. He seemed to truly feel for each victim he came across, going out of his way to comfort their grieving families and working whatever hours necessary to solve each case. Her eyes drifted over to Martin Stewart. The difference between the two men was like night and day. Stewart was married, he was from New Jersey, and he was one of the best homicide detectives in the state. He was also an asshole. She liked to think that behind his tough-guy façade there lurked a sensitive, decent human being with a good heart. But it seemed doubtful.

Arms folded, he leaned back in his chair with a toothpick dancing across his thick lips. A pack of gum and a steaming cup of coffee sat on the table in front of him. Apparently, since he had quit smoking, he was popping all sorts of things in his mouth to distract himself from the nicotine cravings.

He glanced over at her, and she quickly looked away and concentrated on the detectives seated directly next to her. Erin McKenzie and Gary Jacobs were deep in conversation, poring over the homicide files. The two had been working closely with Hernandez and Stewart since the third killing, much to Stewart's dismay.

Patricia had been Erin's self-defense instructor as well. Extensively trained in martial arts, she had been assigned to teach at the Academy, something she'd enjoyed doing up until a couple of years ago, when she was promoted to Homicide, a position she had always hoped to achieve. She fingered her small silver hoop earrings and returned a polite smile from Erin. She noticed that the large diamond ring Erin used to wear on her left hand was missing. Jeff had mentioned the young detective's recent separation from her husband. Patricia eyed her own barren third finger and wondered if someday she would wear a ring there signifying commitment.

Shaking the loneliness from her mind, she lifted her gaze to her longtime partner, Gary Jacobs. Gary was a serious, no-nonsense kind of cop, someone who rarely cracked a smile. He was always well mannered and polite, but she had always found it hard to get him to laugh. She grinned as she remembered a time not so long ago when someone had hired a drag queen to come in and sing happy birthday to Stewart. She had been in tears with laughter as the better-than-Cher look-alike straddled a red-faced Stewart and rubbed his bald head while she sang. Gary had sat and watched from his desk with a blank expression on his face, almost as if he were watching grass grow.

Patricia tossed down her pen and rubbed her temples. The headache she had awoken with was not letting up. Sleep had not come easy the night before. She had stayed up late going over the victim files until she knew them by heart. Then, she had studied their main suspect, Elizabeth Adams. With all that she'd read and all she knew, she was worried for Erin McKenzie.

The Homicide Division had pulled Erin from Narcotics, specifically to work on the Adams case. It seemed she had quite a reputation for her undercover work, having obtained the key evidence that put several major drug dealers away. Of course, now she'd have to prove herself all over again in Homicide, and this was what concerned Patricia. A young detective trying to show she could handle herself on a tough new assignment might be tempted to take more risks than she should. Elizabeth Adams was a dangerous target, a skilled seductress who would not only take full advantage of an innocent but would enjoy doing so. And if she suspected Erin was a cop…Patricia didn't want to think about that possibility.

"Good morning, everyone." Sergeant Eric Ruiz marched in with a smile on his face.

Ignoring the unenthusiastic group reply, he slapped a thick stack of files down on the end of the table and adjusted his wire-rim glasses. He was a shorter man, about five eight, with a head full of thick black hair threaded with silver. Despite his modest stature, the overzealous Ruiz managed to intimidate almost everyone, Patricia included. He demanded a lot from his detectives and had a fiery temper with a very short fuse when things didn't go as planned.

"Okay. You all know why you're here, so let's get to it." He rubbed his hands together and began his infamous pacing. The man did not know the meaning of sitting still. "McKenzie, how are you feeling about all this?"

Erin sat up straighter in her chair. "Fine, sir."

"Think you can be ready to roll by Saturday?"

"Yes, sir."

Patricia watched the young detective squirm and doubted that she was as fine or as confident as she claimed. Stirring slightly in her own seat, she directed a question to Ruiz. "What, exactly, is the plan for Saturday, sir?"

He stopped at the question, but only briefly, before resuming his pacing. "We introduce Mac onto the scene at Adams's nightclub, La Femme. And we hope Adams shows an immediate interest."

Visions of the elite lesbian nightclub flashed across Patricia's mind. Adams had owned the popular club for eight years and also operated a small production company known for lesbian-themed films. Patricia's eyes strayed to Erin, and not for the first time, she felt uncertain whether the newcomer was ready or even right for this assignment. Certainly she had the looks. With her shoulder-length light brown hair pulled into a ponytail, exposing high cheekbones and a graceful neckline, she had exactly the kind of sexy vulnerability

Adams found exciting. Oddly, that unsettled Patricia.

She locked eyes with Ruiz. "How far are we willing to let her go on Saturday?"

Erin's face flooded with red, and Stewart about choked on his shredded toothpick. It flew out of his mouth, and he looked around the table like a fourteen-year-old boy talking about porn, an excited grin on his face. None of the other detectives found the question humorous.

"You think we'll need to resolve that now? Adams will move that quickly?" Ruiz pointed the question back to her.

"Absolutely, sir."

"Then what do you suggest?" He tossed the ball into her court.

"Ideally, she should establish trust with the target and permit a credible level of physical contact, kissing perhaps. Some fondling. It will depend on what she's comfortable with, and the circumstances at the time. We just need to make sure she's fully prepared."

All eyes focused on Erin, and Patricia noted the red in her cheeks.

Before Erin could voice her thoughts, Jeff broke in. "We don't actually think Adams would harm Mac, do we?"

Patricia signaled Gary to respond, and he adjusted his glasses before speaking. "At this time we have no reason to believe Ms. Adams would cause harm to Detective McKenzie. Her menace appears to extend solely to males. She has never been known to physically harm females."

"So you're saying Adams will try to fuck Mac senseless, but she won't hurt her?" Stewart was enjoying this way too much.

"In a matter of speaking, yes." Gary remained calm and unamused.

Ruiz stopped pacing, apparently impatient with the discussion. "Right, let's bring Erin up to speed." He tossed several files down on the table in front of the detectives and motioned for Patricia to speak.

Anticipating her, Stewart whipped open the files, displaying grim color photos of the three dead men.

"As you all know, all three of our victims were killed in the same fashion," Patricia said. "All were taken to a private location, a hotel in Mr. Bale's case, where we assume they were promised sexual favors. Then they were injected in the armpit with a tranquilizer." She glanced at each detective. "Our lab has found traces of nylon fibers on the wrists of every victim. It seems they were bound tightly and effectively with nylons, probably to a bedpost, to make the task of injecting them easier."

Ignoring a crass remark from Stewart, she continued, "We have also found traces of the date rape drug, GHB or Liquid X, in all our victims. We all know this incapacitates an individual and in most cases leads to unconsciousness. However, in our victims only a small amount was used. Not enough to render them unconscious. The drug was most likely given in a drink soon after the victims encountered our suspect, just enough to get their guard down."

She paused to sip some water, then wrapped up her part of the briefing. "The injected tranquilizer is one used primarily on horses. It rendered our victims completely defenseless, causing them to lose the use of their limbs and sending them in and out of consciousness." She indicated a picture of the first victim. "Fortunately for these men, the stabbing of the genitalia was postmortem."

Why? Patricia lapsed into thought as Stewart and Hernandez took their cue from Ruiz and picked up the briefing. *Why take the time to mutilate if you don't have the guts or desire to inflict the wounds while the victims are alive?* It was obviously done for a reason, to make a strong statement. The stabbings were either motivated by sheer hatred for these men or they were intended to mislead, to make it appear the crimes were acts of rage. She tuned in as Jeff Hernandez went over the postmortem details.

"Each victim was found in an isolated desert area on the outskirts of the valley, all three within a five-mile radius. Cause of death was an execution-style shot to the head, and ballistics concurs that the same 9mm was used in all three cases. Shortly after death, each victim was stabbed a few times in his penis and scrotum."

Silence descended, broken only by the sound of Stewart chomping on his gum. Wasting no time, he took over from his colleague. "The only things we've found at the scene are the guys' pants and wallets. Robbery was not a motive here. The chick leaves hundreds of bucks plus credit cards in these guys' wallets." He continued smacking the gum and looked around the room at his fellow detectives. "It's a message, people. She's saying loud and clear that she doesn't give a fuck about their money. She doesn't need it or want it."

"I agree," Ruiz cut in. "The suspect knows these men are wealthy. They've all tried to use their wealth and power against her."

"Yes, this is the most important aspect of this case for you, McKenzie." Patricia cast a brief glance in Erin's direction. Light green eyes met hers, their hue startling her momentarily. But Erin didn't seem to notice the unsettling effect she'd had. "The fact that Adams knew each of these men and had verbally threatened them is the main reason she's our number-one suspect."

"How did she know them?" Erin asked.

"All three victims were members of an all-male, high-society-type club that tried to shut La Femme down by revoking Adams's liquor license," Patricia replied. "They also tried to ban the lesbian films she produced from being sold in local stores by claiming they were pornographic. Obviously, Adams became pissed off."

"Enough of a reaction to make her kill these guys?" Erin looked dubious. "It's so extreme. More like something a man would do."

Patricia smiled inwardly, remembering a time not so long ago when she would have thought the same thing. But hundreds of cases, and seeing the worst of people day in and day out, had jaded her. Women were capable of murder, especially crimes that involved killing from a distance. Women were less likely to kill with their hands, avoiding strangulation or stabbing. More often, they shot or poisoned their victims.

"Witnesses in a Valle Luna restaurant overheard Adams threaten the men as they dined with their wives one evening in April," she said. "Apparently she threatened to kill and castrate each of them if they continued to blacklist her."

Erin cringed slightly. "Assuming Adams is the killer, what is it that I'm going in for? You want evidence tying her to the victims?

Or do you just want me to get her talking—strike up a rapport, gain her trust?"

Ruiz stopped walking and leaned on the table, both hands flat in front of him. "Get anything you can. Get her bragging. A confession would be great."

"So, I'm wearing a wire on Saturday?"

With a quick glance at Patricia, Ruiz said, "Yes. However, if at any point you feel it unsafe to wear it, if she gets too friendly, discard it immediately."

"Of course, sir."

"Detective Henderson will also be in the club. She'll be on three-way, so she'll be able to hear you and also communicate with the surveillance team outside if necessary." He stepped back from the table. "You'll be meeting up with our sound guy along with your liaison tonight. It's probably best if they come by your place. That okay?"

"Liaison?"

"To help you prepare for your assignment." Ruiz restacked the files. He adjourned the group until the next briefing on Friday morning, stating the obvious. "Any new information—McKenzie gets to hear about it on Friday. I want her as prepared as possible."

Stewart strolled toward the door. "Guess the next time I see you, you'll be a full-fledged dyke." The comment was directed at Erin, but before she could respond, Patricia moved to stand next to her and stared down Stewart.

With Patricia by her side, Erin said, with a sly smirk, "You better hope so, Detective Stewart. I know you need all the help you can get on this case."

Stewart mumbled a derogatory comment under his breath and eyed both women before stomping away.

Erin turned toward Patricia and gave an audible sigh of relief. "Thanks."

"No problem." Patricia lifted her files. "He's just jealous that you'll get more girls than he ever could."

Erin laughed. "I don't know about that."

Patricia held the door as they exited the conference room. Watching Erin walk ahead, she felt her heart rate quicken. The younger woman was very attractive, with strong, agile legs and a perfectly rounded backside. Not to mention her ample breasts and striking face.

Dragging her thoughts back to the job, she said, "He is one damn good detective, though."

"So I've heard," Erin said doubtfully.

Patricia smiled. Erin McKenzie certainly had a mind of her own. It was an attractive characteristic, something else their main suspect would find appealing.

Erin eyed her vodka and ice. She was already on her second, and she hadn't even been home an hour. At least with this glass she had taken the time to add a lemon twist, unlike the first, which she'd gulped down before it even chilled. She had been drinking more lately, her loneliness becoming unbearable. But she didn't want to focus on that.

She took a sip and thought of her day. It had been a rough one, spent trying to get up to speed on this case and arm herself with information on their suspect. And the night didn't promise to be any more relaxed, with the imminent visit of her liaison and the sound guy. She plopped down on a leather sofa. It was cold on her bare legs and unforgivingly stiff from lack of use. Unable to get comfortable, she stood and tugged at the maroon mesh athletic shorts that matched her gray and maroon Arizona State T-shirt. She decided, instead, to sit on the floor.

The house was brand new and virtually unused, which was especially evident in the new-smelling carpet. She ran her hand along its surface, making a track against the soft grain. The four-thousand-square-foot home contained the finest in furniture and décor, but to her it seemed empty. She hated its coldness and spent as much time away from it as possible.

She fumbled with the remote for the large plasma screen TV. She seldom turned the damn thing on and had no idea how to use the controls. It had been her husband who constantly wanted to replace their electronic equipment with the latest models and insisted they have only the best of everything, regardless of Erin's preferences.

The thought of Mark drew a sigh from her. After he made partner at his law firm, they had seen less and less of each other, until it seemed they were merely coexisting under one roof. Yet he'd still made sure their home and vehicles were top of the line, in case he ever needed to show them off. Mark was all about appearances and Erin had been his trophy, another disregarded possession among many.

They'd managed to stay married for six years, but for the last two Erin had lived in her own room. The new house had provided her with her own wing as well. They'd only lived in it for six months when they decided to separate. Mark had moved out two weeks ago, and Erin still hadn't processed her mixed feelings about her failed marriage. Her job was the perfect distraction; she spent so much of her time on assignment or at her desk, she could avoid thinking about her personal life. It was easier that way. To think about it brought pain and the sting of betrayal. Mark's mistress in Austin was no secret to her. She only wondered why it had taken him so long to decide on a divorce.

Money was the obvious consideration. But for a lawyer, Mark seemed to be taking his time over the property split. He said he didn't want things to get nasty, and he didn't want to hurt her. Erin took another gulp of her vodka. Mark's behavior didn't hurt her anymore. She had simply stopped caring. What got to her was the loneliness, the thought that she was missing out on something truly special, somewhere, somehow. That's what drove her to drink. Was this all there was to life? A career, a meaningless marriage, and a big, empty house?

She mashed more buttons on the remote, and suddenly the DVD she had put in began to play. It was one of the movies Adams's company had produced. Erin had removed a box of them from Homicide, much to the disappointment of some of the male detectives who were enjoying the investigative chore of watching them.

This particular one was titled *Hearts Afire*, and it appeared from the cover to be one of the milder movies. Erin had figured she'd better start off slow and easy. Crossing her legs in front of her, she focused on the screen. She had mentally prepared herself to be shocked by watching two women have sex, but ten minutes into the film her reservations were long gone. Completely engrossed in the plot, she made herself more comfortable by stretching out on her belly and propping her head up onto her fists.

The story was incredible, and she was soon rooting for the two women to proclaim their love for one another. In fact, she became so involved that she found herself on her feet, pacing in front of the TV and laughing giddily when the women finally became intimate. Completely frozen in amazement, she watched as they made love. To her surprise, she was not uncomfortable in any way. Instead, she was intrigued by the spectacle, and when the story came to an end, she hurriedly dug through the box and grabbed another, titled *Leather Lasses*. She slid it into the player and stood waiting for it to begin, but no sooner had the title credits rolled than the doorbell rang.

"Shit." It was undoubtedly her colleagues. Erin had completely lost track of time.

She grabbed the remote and pushed a button to make the DVD stop, but it didn't work. Two women in leather appeared on screen. One grabbed the other and kissed her passionately. Deciding that this could not be left on in front of her guests, she killed the power to the TV, leaving the DVD on and continuing to play. The kissing women disappeared as the screen went black.

The doorbell chimed again, and she ran to the door and yanked it open hurriedly to find J.R. Stanford standing next to an attractive woman. She should have known it would be J.R.; he had worked sound on her last narcotics assignment. He grinned at her in the devilish way that only he could and elbowed the woman next to him to get her to turn all the way around to face the door.

Erin began a greeting, but trailed into silence, startled to find herself staring at Patricia Henderson. The detective's thick auburn hair fell heavily in soft waves onto her shoulders, and she was wearing a green blouse and blue jeans. She looked strikingly beautiful, completely unlike her more conservative work persona. In the light of the setting sun, the eyes that met Erin's were a mesmerizing blue-green, and they shone with something Erin could not read. She felt surprised and excited in a strange way.

Henderson is my liaison? Does that mean Patricia Henderson is a lesbian?

❖

A hand waved in front of her face. "Hello?" J.R. said. "Earth to Mac."

Erin shook her head. "I'm sorry. It's just that I didn't expect to see you." She directed the apology to Henderson.

Smiling, Henderson said, "It's okay. I thought it might surprise you."

Erin motioned for them to come inside. "Why didn't you just tell me today?" she asked, genuinely curious as to why Henderson and Ruiz hadn't enlightened her earlier.

"I asked Sergeant Ruiz not to—not in front of everyone, that is."

They entered the house, and J.R. was once again J.R. "Holy shit, Mac, you dealin' drugs on the side?"

Erin laughed at his complete awe. He was such a character, speaking with a Spanish accent and slight lisp. And he proudly told anyone who asked that he and his mother came from Mexico and that his father was the "Wonder Bread." J.R. was eccentric in every way, dressing worse than a blind man on a good day. This evening's look was tight, faded jeans and a wildly colorful shirt with traffic signals all over it. The loud shirt was unbuttoned halfway down, revealing sporadic chest hair.

"Seriously," he continued, completely oblivious to her eyeing his attire, "I know you was working narcotics and all, but I didn't know you was *working it*." He bumped hips with her and eyed her playfully. "You go, chica."

Henderson also seemed to be taken aback at the spectacle of a home. Erin cringed at what her colleagues must be thinking.

"My soon-to-be ex-husband is partner in a law firm," she said. "That's the only reason I live in a house like this. I could never afford it on my salary."

"Man, I was waiting for fuckin' Lurch to answer the door." J.R. ran a hand over the Italian silk wallpaper.

"Please come in and make yourselves at home," Erin offered, trying to get their minds off the extravagant surroundings. She led them into the living room where she'd been watching the lesbian movies. "Can I get you guys something to drink?"

Henderson shook her head politely, but J.R. wasn't paying attention. Staring past her he said, "Oh man, you got a plasma TV!" and made a beeline for the remote. "I heard the picture is, like, a hundred times better on these things."

Before Erin could stop him, he hit the power button, and the screen came to life just as the two leather-clad women came together in a series of loud, orgasmic screams.

Erin felt her face redden all the way up to her ears.

"Mac, you bad bitch!" J.R. was angling his head as if to better examine the sexual position on the screen.

Henderson laughed. "I see you've been doing your homework." She shoved her hands in the pockets of her jeans, looking a little embarrassed herself.

"Yeah, I don't think Mac needs you," J.R. informed Henderson, without looking away from the screen. "She's learning on her own."

Erin threw her hands up in the air in defeat. "You got me." Inwardly she wanted to die, but she stood her ground, hoping against hope that this would not find its way back to the department. Picturing Stewart's reaction, she winced.

For a moment they all stood in silence and watched as two new women entered the scene.

"Hey, Henderson, you in this one?" J.R. teased.

"Fuck you." Henderson grabbed the remote from him, amidst loud protests. "Just do your thing and get out of here." She stuck it in her back pocket. "We have more important things to discuss."

"Okay, okay." He moved over to his bag of equipment and pulled out some wires and rolls of tape. "There's not much to cover. Mac knows the drill from last time we worked together. But I do need to show you guys how to communicate with each other." He approached them carrying two small pieces.

"Mac, you'll be wired for voice sound. This one is smaller and safer than what we used last time. It fits right in your bra." He motioned for Erin to lift up her shirt and fastened a tiny black device to the center of her bra.

She looked up and caught Henderson watching them, red tinting her cheeks. Suddenly she realized Henderson was not studying J.R.'s wiring technique but was looking at her bare torso. Feeling self-conscious, she glanced down at her black lace bra and fairly toned abs.

Do I look okay?

Judging by the blush Henderson was sporting, Erin thought she must look pretty good. But then again, she didn't know what women liked in other women. Mark had always told her she was too muscular for his taste. She wondered what Henderson thought of her and decided to ask her later that evening when they were alone. She had to make sure she was up to par before she went undercover trying to attract a lesbian.

J.R. had turned his attention to Henderson and positioned a tiny earpiece behind her thick hair, where it was completely hidden from view. "Go in the other room and see if you can hear us," he instructed.

As soon as she'd left, he walked over to Erin and said with a smirk, "Mac has a nice rack."

She laughed and smacked him on the arm.

"Hey, that hurt!" He rubbed his arm. "Seriously, though, what are you carrying…a nice pair of Cs?"

"You know it." She blushed suddenly, remembering that Henderson could hear their conversation.

Apparently J.R. had similar thoughts. "You better be careful being alone here with Henderson tonight. She might try to sleep with you to authenticate your undercover role. This time tomorrow, you could be a butch truck driver wearing horrible flannel shirts."

He had barely finished the last sentence when Henderson came flying into the living room and grabbed him by the front of his shirt, scooting him over to his equipment. "Out, get out now!" She yanked out her earpiece and tossed it to him. "Your equipment works great, now you can go."

"Shit, I was just making sure you could hear us." J.R. straightened his shirt. "Oh man, I think you got some chest hair."

Henderson visibly composed herself, slowly releasing a breath. "I'll take that drink now, please," she told Erin. "Make it strong."

A few moments later, after getting rid of the tactless sound man, Erin returned to the living room, where Henderson was sitting on the couch massaging her temples. "Can I ask an obvious question? Why aren't you the one going in undercover?"

Henderson looked up, her gze intense. She opened her mouth to answer, then seemed to reconsider. "I…I would be recognized," she said after a lengthy pause. "It wouldn't work."

Erin waited for her to explain, but the older detective fell silent, her thoughts obviously elsewhere. Wondering why the topic made her uncomfortable, and suspecting it was personal, Erin framed a question: *Are you a regular at the lesbian nightclub?* It sounded too inquisitive. Instead, she asked, "How bad is your headache?"

"Not so bad. I just need to eat. I haven't had anything since this morning."

Conscious of her empty fridge, Erin asked, "Could you hold off on passing out until a pizza gets here?"

Henderson laughed, her beautiful eyes lighting up along with her face. Erin was suddenly aware that her colleague seldom smiled. In fact, most of the time it seemed there was a trace of defeat beneath her stoic, professional calm. *She should smile more often,* Erin thought. *She's an incredibly beautiful woman.*

"Pizza's fine," Henderson said in a lighthearted tone. "And I promise not to pass out."

"What kind do you want?" Erin picked up the phone and dialed.

"Oh, it doesn't matter as long as it's food."

Erin placed the order for a large pepperoni and hung up. "How's forty minutes sound? I can get two drinks in you by then." She headed over to the bar, grabbed a couple of glasses, and clanked in some ice cubes. "I'm betting you're a scotch drinker."

Henderson stared at her in awe. "How could you possibly know that?" She rose and walked over to the bar.

"Call it a gift." Erin handed her the tumbler filled with twelve-year-old Macallan and refilled her own vodka.

"Thanks, this is just what I need." Patricia rarely drank, but she needed something to help ease her nerves for what she was about to do. It didn't make it any easier that Erin was so attractive. She hadn't been attracted to someone in years. She sipped her scotch. "Those things J.R. said about me…"

Erin looked awkward. "Your private life is none of my business."

"Actually, it's important that you know a little about me. I'm going to need you to trust me and listen to me. That might be difficult if you think I'm going to come on to you."

Erin gulped at her vodka. "I do trust you, Henderson. And I never believe anything that comes out of J.R.'s mouth."

"Thank you. And, please, call me Patricia." She sipped some more scotch and took a deep breath. "I need to talk to you about some pretty personal issues, and it's important that you're completely honest with me. Your life may be at stake. Elizabeth Adams is a predator at the top of the food chain."

"Okay, shoot."

Erin picked up her drink, and Patricia followed her to the couch where they both sat. She squirmed a moment, wrestling with her own uncertainty. It was her job to prepare the young detective for this dangerous assignment. And if she failed, Elizabeth Adams would eat Erin alive. Yet this was far from simple.

"I need to ask you—have you ever been intimate with a woman?"

"No," Erin answered quickly.

"Have you ever kissed another woman?"

Erin looked confused. "I thought I just answered that question. To me, kissing is extremely intimate, and the answer is no."

Patricia sat dumbfounded for a moment. She, too, believed kissing was intimate, but so many people did it casually now, like it was nothing more than holding hands. She allowed her eyes to rest on the woman in front of her and tried not to think about how it would feel to kiss her.

"Listen, I'm not Bill Clinton, here," Erin said. "I don't have anything to hide."

"Thanks for being honest with me." Patricia glanced down at her empty tumbler, wishing the liquid courage would kick in. Bracing herself, she asked, "Mac, have you ever been attracted to another woman?"

The question hung in the air between them. Patricia's blood raced through her temples, but this time her headache was gone. In its place was an excitement and nervousness she hadn't felt in a long time. Adrenaline. Sheer adrenaline was surging through her like a flame catching to gasoline. Why was she reacting this way to Erin McKenzie?

She watched as Erin stood up and began to pace the room. She watched her well-muscled legs as she walked, and mentally traced the smooth lines of her neck as she tilted her head to drink. She had known it the second she found herself blushing at the sight of Erin's bare torso. She was attracted to her. But she hadn't been drawn to anyone in years. *Why now?* Was it that no one had taken the time to notice her feelings in years? Erin had noticed, asking about her headache, paying close attention to how she felt. Was she so desperate that a polite "how are you feeling?" could leave her panting and ready to pounce?

Erin stopped pacing and turned piercing green eyes on her. "I'm not sure what you mean by *attracted*. Do you mean sexually attracted or intellectually attracted or something else altogether?" She began pacing again, flustered and nervous, her emotions obvious in the way she moved.

"Well, I...I guess I mean all of those things. Both of those qualities can lead someone to want intimacy with another. Don't you agree?"

"No, I don't think I agree. I mean, I've had strange and strong attractions to women, but they were never sexual."

Patricia understood the younger woman's confusion. She was trying to identify the nature of her own attractions, a challenge for anyone. Trying to clarify her meaning, she asked, "Did you ever have fantasies about these women?"

"Nothing sexual, no."

"They don't have to be sexual to be intimate, Mac." She paused a moment to let her statement set in. Very softly, she asked, "There were fantasies, weren't there?"

Erin sighed and sat back down on the couch as if defeated. "Yes." She deposited her drink on the coffee table and rubbed her palms on her shorts. "I, uh, I would fantasize about being with them in different scenarios, different situations. But never anything sexual, just being with them."

"Would it be fair to say that you were infatuated with these women?"

Erin reacted as if she had been struck, the blood draining from her face. *Infatuated* was a strong word. Patricia knew she was pushing the younger woman, but there was no other way to do this. If Erin was going to pull off her assignment, she would have to confront this issue and be completely secure in who she was when she walked into La Femme. Obviously, Erin had never explored these feelings because she hadn't had a reason to confront them.

"Mac, it's okay. It isn't always about sex." She slid along the couch and took Erin's hand to comfort her. "This is why I'm here. I need to make sure you're ready for Saturday night. If you've ever had feelings toward women, no matter how innocent they seemed, there's a real possibility that this undercover assignment may open emotional floodgates for you."

"What does all this mean? My fantasies, my wanting these women to respect me and to be with me?" Erin searched Patricia's face, a note of desperation in her voice. "This doesn't mean I'm gay...does it?"

"No, I'm not saying that at all. Let's not jump to conclusions here. I'm trying to get a feel for where you stand on things. If we threw you in undercover right now without exploring these feelings first, you would be in way over your head."

Patricia considered the hand resting in her own. She knew what she had to do, but she suddenly felt like she didn't have the nerve. Or maybe she was more worried about her own reactions than Erin's.

"You've had these infatuations with women for quite some time, right?"

"Since I was a kid."

Patricia turned Erin's hand over in her own with the palm resting up. "And all this time, all those women you fantasized about, none of them ever touched you?"

"Uh, no. Well, maybe a hug or something." Erin's eyes were large and the green had deepened a shade.

Patricia lightly stroked her palm and wrist. Erin's reaction was immediate and evident as she took in a powerful breath and her pupils dilated, erasing most of the green. Patricia knew at once what the reaction meant, and seeing her companion so easily turned on, her own touch the cause, sent hot adrenaline surging to every nerve ending.

"What do you feel, Mac?" It came out as a raw whisper. Choking back a rush of desire, she continued the strokes up Erin's arm. "We need to make sure you're aware of these feelings before you go in undercover. It's okay to feel them, but you must be aware of them so you don't lose control." She looked from Erin's eyes to her rose-colored lips. They were slightly parted, beckoning her. "Because it's so very easy to lose control when you feel desire for another woman."

As she said it, she leaned in closer to Erin, giving in to an urge to taste the other woman and ignoring her screaming voice of reason.

Erin didn't speak. She couldn't. She closed her eyes and instinctively awaited the feel of Patricia's lips. Most of her blood supply was not in her head; instead, her pounding heart was quickly pumping it to her awakening groin. She felt completely out of control, and yet she had never felt so alive, so awake, and so driven. She heard the noise from the garage but didn't register it right away. Her eyes flew open as the noise stopped, and she bolted off the couch when she realized it was the garage door. Patricia jumped up after her, looking mortified.

"It's my husband," Erin said.

Both women gazed as a door opened and a man in an expensive suit walked in, acting as if he still lived there.

"Hi." Mark set down his briefcase.

"What are you doing here?" Erin didn't hide her disappointment. Why did he have to come over tonight of all nights?

Mark gave her a puzzled look. Erin knew her reaction probably came as a shock to him. He was not used to seeing any emotion at all from her these days.

With practiced poise, he smoothed down his tie and put on his best smile. "Hello, I'm Mark McKenzie." He moved toward Patricia and extended his hand.

As they exchanged greetings, Erin wondered what Patricia would think of her now that she'd met the man she'd married. Would she see past Mark's immaculate tailoring and expensive shoes? Erin took in his pale skin, the way his brown hair was graying in an unfavorable pattern. His trimmed goatee sat crooked, flanking his mouth, too much growth on the right side causing his face to look unbalanced. He definitely tried to exude perfection, but he was far from it. Mark had more than a few skeletons in his closet.

She rubbed her face nervously, certain the incredible surge of emotion and desire she had just experienced was written all over her. Irrationally, Patricia's comments about infatuation and fantasies kept playing in her mind. She stole a covert sideways look at her colleague. She was not just incredibly attractive physically, but emotionally as well. Just the kind of woman who could easily become her next fantasy.

Erin's heart rate picked up and she felt her face flush. She was drawn to Patricia. She wondered if it was because she now knew Patricia was a lesbian. The thought excited her, but it seemed crazy at the same time. She wasn't sure what was happening, only that her body cried out for Patricia's touch. Did this mean she was attracted to women? If she was, that meant sex, and sex meant she was a lesbian. No way.

She cleared her throat. "Mark, this is Detective Henderson, we're working a case together."

"I see. Well, I won't keep you, then." He scratched a pink spot just above his eyebrow. One cheek also had some redness to it.

Her thoughts went to his other numerous imperfections, and she realized just how long she hadn't noticed or cared. She moved with him as he took off his jacket and headed toward the other wing of the house. "What are you doing here, Mark?"

He looked over his shoulder and motioned for her to keep her voice down. A guest should never overhear their bickering. "I'm flying out for Austin first thing tomorrow morning and I needed to get some more of my stuff."

Since moving out, he'd been back frequently for various belongings. Erin wished he would just pack up his stuff and get the movers to come take it all. "Oh, another meeting?" She raised her eyebrows. She allowed him to have his fun without interfering, and now she wanted to have hers.

"Yes, several, in fact. What's with the attitude?"

The doorbell rang and she bit back her response.

Mark waited as she paid the delivery man for the pizza, then said, "I'll be out of town for a while. We should talk when I get back."

Erin chewed on her lower lip, trying very hard to bite back the cynicism that so badly wanted to prevail. "Sure. Have a good trip." She gave him a plastic smile and carried the pizza into the living room. After locating some plates, she fished out a steaming slice for her visitor.

Patricia could tell from Erin's erratic movements and strained expression that she was definitely not pleased. "Is this a bad time?" she asked.

Erin shook her head emphatically. "No. It's fine. I just wasn't expecting him."

Patricia accepted a plate and sat back down slowly, willing the wheels in her brain to start turning once again. She knew Erin was married, even if they were newly separated. But in those two minutes of wild desire, she had completely erased this fact from her mind. What was going on with her? She had been attracted to plenty of women, but usually not so quickly and powerfully. She had just come dangerously close to jeopardizing her job with this junior detective, behavior very out of character for her.

They chewed in silence for a while, and she slowly started to feel better with the food in her stomach. She tried hard not to look at Erin's mouth as she ate. Its every movement stirred up the animalistic feelings of wanton desire that hadn't surfaced for years. She felt like a teenage boy sitting next to his first crush.

"Erin, I need to apologize to you for my behavior earlier. I… uh…went beyond what is professional."

That was an understatement. She flushed as she thought about what had almost happened, still perplexed over her loss of control. Erin was young and beautiful and passionate, she rationalized. And…innocent. Characteristics she had yet to find in a woman. She could still feel Erin's instant response to her touch, her startled awakening.

Erin took their plates and set them on the coffee table. "You mean what almost happened? The kiss?"

"Yes, I shouldn't have gone so far." Patricia looked helplessly down at her hands.

Erin sat closer to her on the couch. "I didn't mind," she said softly, then in a rush, confessed, "I liked it. I felt—"

"You don't know what you felt, Mac," she cut in. "This is all very new to you, and it's too soon to draw any conclusions." She swallowed the lump in her throat and willed herself to think rationally.

The situation was just as she'd feared. Erin McKenzie was not ready for this assignment for countless reasons. She was incredibly naïve in terms of her self-awareness and her feelings for women, a potentially dangerous combination when interacting with someone like Elizabeth Adams. How could they ever send her in like this? Patricia had to try to explain the risks.

Even now, Erin was objecting. "Look, this isn't the first time I've had to pretend to be someone I'm not." Her eyes blazed with resentment. "I didn't succeed undercover by being stupid. I had to convince some pretty evil and disgusting men that I was hot for them."

"This is quite different, Erin. It's so much more intense and raw and emotional with a woman. You have to be ready for that." *And you have no idea what you are getting into. Look at the way you responded to just my touch.*

"What makes you think I'm not?" Erin challenged. "You think I'm going to blow it if Adams comes on to me?"

"No," Patricia heard the frustration seeping into her voice. Somehow she had to make Erin understand that it wasn't her professional competence that was in question. "I just don't want you to get in over your head. Imagine being undercover and being attracted to a woman kissing you. Could you handle it? Could you ignore your feelings?"

"I guess there's only one way to find out." Erin's voice softened to a seductive pitch. "Kiss me."

Patricia burned with raw desire. She yearned to take hold of Erin and show her what making love truly meant. But that was two years of celibacy talking. "I should probably go for tonight," she said hoarsely. "We both need to cool our heads and gain new perspective before we do something rash."

"I'm sorry, I'm just not thinking very clearly right now," Erin said. "I hope I didn't offend you."

Patricia took Erin's hands and they stood facing one another. Her chest felt heavy, and with every inhalation she could feel Erin's breath mixing with her own. "You didn't do anything wrong. I understand more than you know."

She placed a gentle kiss on Erin's lips. The warmth from the kiss spread quickly through her limbs, and she instantly craved more. Her body screamed in defiance as she forced herself to withdraw.

"I'm going now. You have a lot to think about." She glanced down the hall to where Mark had disappeared. "Maybe you should talk to your husband about your feelings." She knew they weren't together, but maybe they were still friends. Erin could sure use a kind ear right now.

"Yeah, right. It won't be happening. We're in the process of divorce." Erin looked distraught and even annoyed at the thought. "He lives his own life and I live mine. That didn't just happen when he moved out."

Patricia looked at the beautiful woman before her and thought, what a shame, what a waste of an incredible woman. "I'm sorry," she said softly. "You deserve better."

"We're finally ready to divorce. I think maybe I've just been waiting for my own reason to do so."

"I hope you found your reason, Mac. You deserve happiness."

Erin did not reply, and they walked in silence to the door, those moments of raw emotion they'd shared earlier still tangible between them.

"You're getting your hair cut tomorrow, aren't you?" she asked as Erin opened the front door. Elizabeth Adams liked short hair. Patricia was anxious to see what Erin would look like.

"Yeah, I'll be in after my appointment to go over more information with you."

"Please think about what we discussed, and review the files I brought for you. They'll be your best weapon in dealing with Adams."

"I will, thanks." Erin did not meet her eyes. "Good night."

"Night." Patricia gave a sincere smile and headed out into the warm desert night.

Chapter Three

B y the time Erin reached the Saguaro Park Police Station, she had already somewhat adjusted to her new look. Her hair felt sporty, and she welcomed the newfound freedom in the messy spikes, now lightened to a dirty blond. She was conscious of a fresh confidence and thought maybe she would be able to handle this case after all. While she usually felt completely self-assured on undercover assignments, this one made her unsure and wary. In Narcotics, she'd typically played hard-to-get for some low-life, which meant she had to pretend to be interested and simpleminded in order to secure his trust. It had been easy to zone out and act dumb; the men were so easily turned on and overly confident, allowing her to remain detached and focused on her job.

The new assignment was a different story, especially after last night. She knew she couldn't ignore the feelings that had surfaced with Patricia Henderson. After the detective had left, she'd been too keyed up to sleep, so instead she'd stayed up reading the Adams files. The team had done an excellent job of surveillance, gathering personal details that must've taken months of work.

According to their observations, Elizabeth Adams had a preference for athletic-looking women with short hair, mostly blondes, but she was known to stray to brunettes every so often. She didn't have steady girlfriends, but rather a steady slew of women from whom she could choose at any given time. Erin's task was to be chosen by the nightclub owner, preferably on more than one occasion. She wondered what she would have to do to make that happen. Her stomach burned with anxiety at the thought, and she understood why Patricia had pushed her so hard.

This was not the same as batting your eyes at a man.

She stood before her sergeant's door and took a deep breath. She had to convince him that she was ready for this assignment. How was she going to do that when she had yet to convince herself? She knocked quickly and entered when she heard him call.

Sergeant Ruiz was seated behind his desk, which was covered with neat stacks of files. Patricia Henderson sat across from him, wearing jeans and a blue T-shirt. Her hair was pulled back in her customary ponytail, a sharp contrast to the soft waves the night before. The strap of her shoulder holster pulled the shirt tight across her chest, showing off her ample breasts. She uncrossed her legs at seeing Erin and placed her booted feet firmly on the floor, rising from her chair to help her with the files she was carrying. Her eyes were bright and warm, a good sign considering what had transpired the night before. Erin breathed a little easier.

"Your hair looks great," Patricia said in a raspy voice.

Erin knew the haircut and light color brought out the color of her eyes and the contours of her face. And she could see Patricia was noticing it as well.

She evaded the beckoning eyes and felt her cheeks flush at the attention of her beautiful colleague. Patricia crossed the room with pantherlike grace, muscles moving sinuously under her tight-fitting T-shirt. Watching, Erin felt as if her mind had been given the key to a whole new world. The door had been unlocked and she was seeing what she had never noticed before—the allure of the female body, in particular Patricia's.

"Mac?" Sergeant Ruiz was talking to her.

Erin struggled back from the new world into which she had drifted. "Yes?"

"You okay, kiddo?"

"I'm fine, sir." She willed the blood to leave her cheeks and her breathing to return to normal. She felt dazed, as if she had woken from a trance.

She and Patricia took their seats in silence.

"The hair looks good, don't you think so, Henderson?"

"Yes. Perfect," Patricia said stoically.

"Okay, Henderson, I'll start with you. How did last night go?"

Erin swallowed wrong at the question and coughed as she tried to regain her breath.

Patricia offered to get her some water.

"No, no, I'm fine," she said.

A slight smile. "Last night went well," Patricia answered Ruiz, as if it had been strictly routine. "Mac and I talked a lot, and I have a feel for where she's at in all of this."

"Good. So we're ready to roll for Saturday night?"

"Not necessarily, sir." Patricia maneuvered slightly in her seat. "I don't think she's ready."

Erin, stung by Patricia's words, said, "With all due respect sir, I feel I am ready."

"Mac may believe she is, but I think we should wait until next weekend," Patricia countered.

"Go on," Ruiz said. This obviously wasn't the news he wanted to hear.

"I don't want to get too personal here, sir, but you can't just give a woman a short haircut, dress her a certain way, and throw her to the lions." She eyed them both, stressing her point. "You can't just snap your fingers and make a woman a lesbian. It's the most ridiculous thing I've ever heard."

Impatiently, Ruiz said, "No one's asking her to *actually become a lesbian.* All she has to do is get Adams interested." He paused a moment, steepling his hands. "Saturday is on. I don't want another body showing up because you don't think she can pull off the gay thing. A seduction is a seduction."

Erin cleared her throat. "Look, I can put on a pretty good show. I've done it before and did a damn good job."

Patricia shot her a sideways glance, her expression a mixture of fear, annoyance, and something else. Protectiveness? "No one is questioning your competence, Mac," she said stiffly. "But from what I saw last night, you're just not ready, and it's too dangerous. Adams would see right through it. I think you know that."

Ruiz sighed. "So what needs to be done in order to—"

He stopped talking as Erin rose from her chair and walked seductively over to Patricia, locking eyes with her. Licking her lips, she straddled the baffled detective on her chair, slithering against her. With one fluid motion, she grabbed Patricia's face and kissed her deeply.

For a brief second, Patricia seemed to resist, but just as quickly she conceded and let Erin explore her mouth. All reserve melted away as Erin rode against her lap and sucked on her tongue. Patricia let out a muffled moan of sheer desire and lifted her hands up to Erin's back, trying to pull her deeper.

But Erin withdrew. She had proved her point. Willing herself to maintain the control she was trying to show she had, she detached herself quickly from the other detective. Their lips smacked their objection as their mouths parted. As Erin climbed off, Patricia gazed up at her, eyes dark and smoldering, hungry for more. Erin licked her own lips; the taste of Patricia was hot and sweet. Hurriedly, she returned to her seat and crossed her legs, praying the throbbing she felt between them would soon stop.

She forced a smile at her shell-shocked sergeant. "As I said, sir, I'm ready. I guess we'll have to ask Henderson whether I'm believable."

Patricia's chest rose and fell quickly. Her cheeks were flushed, her lips swollen and dark. Erin's heart raced. Of course she was believable—she was truly attracted to Patricia. But if that much intensity was involved in kissing a woman, she knew she was doomed as far as the Adams assignment was concerned. All the same, she wasn't about to go down without trying. She had never quit on an assignment, and she wouldn't start now.

"She's good," Patricia conceded, her voice strangled.

Ruiz adjusted his glasses and looked as if he was adjusting himself mentally as well. "That's settled, then. Henderson, I'll leave it to you to get things finalized for Saturday night."

"I'm sorry, sir?" Patricia ran her fingers over the surface of her lips in a gesture that seemed completely unconscious. Erin watched her, wanting to do the same. Her own lips were still tingling from the heated kiss.

"I'm suggesting that you and Mac get the hell out of here and get her ready for the weekend."

"Yes, sir." Patricia stood and grabbed some files. She seemed as anxious to escape as Erin was.

In silence, they walked the short distance to a larger room that held their desks, along with those of the numerous other homicide detectives. Erin's desk sat in the center of the room. On it stood two lonely plastic soda bottles, one of them half full with a straw saluting up and out of the opening. A single pencil rested next to a stack of files and a faded white telephone.

She sank heavily into her squeaky chair. "I'm sorry about what happened back there…" God, she could still feel Patricia responding to her. What happened and what she'd felt were one and the same.

Patricia held up a silencing hand. "No need. You proved your point, Mac. Let it go." She rested her hip against Erin's desk and took her sunglasses from the front of her shirt. "We have a lot of work to do, and not much time to do it in."

"Didn't anyone tell you not to buy a black vehicle in Valle Luna?" Erin asked as she climbed into Patricia's full-sized Chevy Blazer. "I burned my hand on the door handle."

Patricia folded the large shade away from the windshield and tossed it in the backseat. She started the car and switched on the air. "Hot is hot. A hundred ten, a hundred fifteen degrees, it's all hell to me. I got black because I like it."

There was a trace of aggravation in her tone, and Erin eyed her carefully. "Are you still upset over what happened earlier?"

Patricia pulled out of the parking lot. Her expression was difficult to read behind her dark sunglasses. "No, not at all. Actually, I'm glad you can perform in front of an audience. You'll need to be able to handle a lot of attention when you're with Adams."

Erin caressed her sore hand and let Patricia's words float around in her mind. She wasn't concerned about Adams and her attention. Numerous other targets had lavished her with attention, attempting to get her into the sack. Gifts, flowers, diamonds. It wasn't anything she couldn't handle. She glanced toward Patricia and wondered what kind of women the elusive detective liked, what it would take to get her attention. The thoughts were ridiculous, but she felt relaxed in the deep heat of the vehicle and allowed her mind the freedom to relive the kiss and to fantasize about Patricia and her blue eyes blazing with desire.

"Do you live alone?" Erin could see they were headed for Patricia's house, although she wasn't sure why. Maybe they needed to talk more about personal issues. That thought made her stomach jump. She hoped Patricia didn't have a live-in girlfriend; the possibility made her feel uncomfortable and surprisingly jealous. She blushed, certain that what she was feeling was written all over her face.

"Yes, I live alone." Patricia paused momentarily. "Actually, that's not quite true."

Erin's heart sank and her stomach flipped. Why did this woman affect her so?

"I do share my home with another." Patricia grinned as she spoke. "Come on in and you can meet him."

"Him?" Erin asked as she climbed down from the truck.

Patricia was ahead of her, walking through her garage to the interior door. The house was in a nice neighborhood on the outskirts of the city. It wasn't nearly as large as Erin's, but it was big enough, with a trim front yard and well-kept rosebushes flanking the garage.

She followed Patricia inside and directly into the spacious kitchen. Deep red Spanish tile and oak cabinets gave the room a warm feeling, and she instantly relaxed in her surroundings. The house was larger than she had expected, with a spacious backyard. Adjoining the kitchen was a sitting room with overstuffed sofas and a moderate-size television.

"Mac," Patricia called from a large living room in the center of the house. She was kneeling in front of a comfortable-looking tan leather sofa.

"What are you doing?" Erin walked toward her.

"This is Jack," she said with a smile.

Nestled on the leather couch, a Jack Russell terrier slept peacefully, curled into a tight ball. Erin smiled involuntarily at the little dog. He had one brown ear that matched his collar, the rest of him being stark white.

"That is the cutest thing I think I've seen in long time," she whispered, careful not to wake him. Mark despised animals, dogs and cats alike, and had forbidden them in the house. "Why doesn't he wake up?" she asked with concern.

"Jack's deaf."

"He's deaf?" Erin shook her head in disbelief. It had never occurred to her that an animal might be stricken by something she had always associated only with humans.

"He usually wakes up by feeling vibrations or by catching my scent." Patricia patted the couch next to the sleeping dog and Jack jumped nearly out of his skin. Quickly, she sat down and comforted him, speaking softly as she rubbed and scratched his back. "I know it's ridiculous to talk to him when he can't hear me, but I just can't help myself."

Jack stretched for a brief instant and gave a Snoopy-sounding yawn before he turned to assault Erin with attention.

"I don't think it's ridiculous. Not at all." In fact, she was touched by the love and tenderness Patricia showed her dog.

Jack licked her palm and then, seeing his owner stand to leave the room, he jumped off the couch to follow the women into the kitchen. Patricia opened a cabinet and removed two glasses.

"Iced tea okay?" she asked as Jack shot out the small dog door in the connecting TV room and bounded into the backyard.

"Please." Erin sat on a tall stool at the counter, watching her pour the tea.

As they sipped, Jack surged into the house like a rocket, carrying a small ball in his mouth. Erin set down her glass and threw the ball for him to retrieve several times.

"You've started something now," Patricia warned laughingly. "You'll have to end it or he'll play all night long."

"I wish I had that kind of energy."

Jack was trotting toward her with the ball in his mouth when he suddenly stopped and dropped it, the hair on his back raising up. Growling, he faced the front door, and a split second later the doorbell rang and he started barking. Patricia scooped him up as she opened the door.

A small cardboard box sat next to the potted plant at the entrance, and Erin heard a delivery truck start up and drive away. "How did he know someone was here?" she asked, amazed by the dog's reaction.

"Probably the vibrations of the truck." Patricia closed the door and made a hand signal at Jack, who wagged his tail and followed her into the kitchen, where she gave him a treat.

"What was that signal?" Erin asked.

"I trained him with hand signs." Patricia placed the box on the kitchen counter and cut open the taped seams with a steak knife. After pulling back the cardboard flaps, she leafed through the contents and pulled out a paperback book, which she set on the counter.

"No kidding? That really works?"

"Sure does. He knows about thirty different signs." She slid the book across the counter. It was *Deep* by Katherine Chandler.

Erin casually flipped the book over to read the back cover, wondering if it was any good.

"Katherine Chandler is a well-known lesbian fiction writer." Patricia said.

"Oh, I get it. More research for me, right?"

Patricia laughed. "In a manner of speaking. Erin McKenzie, you are now Katherine Chandler."

"What do you mean?"

"Did you think we were sending you into La Femme without a believable cover?"

"What about the real Katherine Chandler?"

"You're looking at her."

Erin grabbed the book and turned it over to look at the back cover.

"You won't find a photo." Patricia headed for the living room.

Her mind reeling, Erin followed her to a large oak bookcase. Patricia pulled a good-sized box from the cabinet and carried it to the coffee table.

"I've been writing for quite a while now." She sat down on the leather sofa. "Katherine Chandler is my pen name. The book you're holding is an advance copy of my fifth title. It's not due for release until next month. Sergeant Ruiz and I thought Chandler might be the perfect identity for you."

"Ruiz knows?"

"Yes. He's the only one who knows, though, other than my publisher. I've kept it private." She flushed.

Erin wondered why the topic seemed to make her uncomfortable. It was obvious that Patricia was talented and multifaceted, to say the least. Was she embarrassed by her success, or was it that the books were lesbian—written proof that Patricia must be, too? A fact she no doubt didn't want to get around the department. Erin peered down into the box on the coffee table. It was full of neatly stacked books.

"Why do you keep coming to work?" she asked. "Why not write full time?"

"I love my job. Writing has always been just an outlet for me. Doing it full time isn't an option."

"Are you sure you want to expose yourself like this? If I go with the ID, everyone on the investigation will know." Erin could see that Patricia had worked to build a wall of privacy. Why would she choose to tear it down now?

With a sigh, Patricia said, "Elizabeth Adams has to be stopped, and it won't be easy. She's beyond clever, Mac, she's downright sharp. You need a real identity. Otherwise, she'll catch you, and fairly quickly. You see, when she meets a woman who holds her interest, she goes to any length to find out everything about her. Nowadays it's known as stalking. She always gets her way, and she has a lot of friends in high places who can't seem to tell her no." Patricia hesitated. Her eyes were deep and brooding and deadly serious. "When you go in on Saturday night and she sees you, you may not even see her, but you'll answer your door the next morning to a bouquet of red roses beckoning your return to the club."

"Whoa," Erin said.

"Whoa is an understatement. From the moment you first catch her eye she'll know everything—from where you live to how much money you make in a year to how many pets you have."

"Doesn't all that scare women away?" It sure gave Erin the creeps.

"No, because she doesn't let on to all that she knows. She picks and chooses from the information she has and uses it to her advantage. For example, tomorrow night you'll catch her eye and she'll find out who you are. Katherine Chandler, the writer. She'll start reading your books without letting you know that she knows."

"She's crazy."

"She's something, all right." Patricia rubbed the back of her neck.

Erin could tell from the unconscious gesture that she was tense, troubled in some way by the topic of Elizabeth Adams. She lifted her eyes to Patricia's beautifully shaped mouth, noticing the slight impression of teeth on the bottom lip. She must have been chewing on it slightly. In that moment, Erin wanted to kiss her, to take her soft lips with her own and tell her everything would be all right. She didn't know where the feeling came from, and it took her breath away, overwhelming her, body and soul. The rush of tenderness she felt for Patricia was more powerful than anything she had ever felt for another human being. She knew their roles called for Patricia to reassure her, but the desire to comfort the other woman burned within.

Patricia ran her hand under the front collar of her tight-fitting T-shirt and continued to massage her neck. It seemed obvious that she knew much more about Adams than was on file—and more than she had revealed in her notes.

"I didn't see this kind of information in the files," she said carefully. "How do you know so much about her?"

"You're right. Some of this isn't in the file. I'm telling you because you're the one going in and you need to know."

"So, how did you find out all this personal information?" As soon as she'd asked it, she knew.

"Because I was once involved with her." Patricia confirmed her suspicion.

"Oh." Erin was embarrassed by her own naïveté and hoped her questions weren't opening an old wound.

"It was five years ago, and I'm not proud of it." Patricia made brief eye contact, then looked away while she spoke. "She has a way of sweeping a woman off her feet, making her feel like the only one in the world. She's very impressive, Mac, but you can't forget that she's a predator and she'll do whatever it takes to get the woman she wants."

"If you dated her, how does she not know about the writing?" Surely the nightclub owner-slash-stalker would've found out everything about Patricia if they were lovers.

"I had just started to write when we began dating. I had yet to publish my first book. By the time I did, the relationship had ended."

"I see. So what happens when she gets the woman she wants?" Erin didn't understand why Adams would work so hard to get a particular woman when she seemed to have them by the dozen.

"Conquest," Patricia said. "It's all about dominance for her. She usually only sleeps with them once or twice, then she moves on."

"Is that how it was with you, a one-night stand?" Her stomach turned at the thought. The look on Patricia's face was one of defeat and embarrassment, and Erin realized her question was intrusive. "I'm sorry, it was rude of me to ask."

"No, it's okay. With me it was different. It lasted a few months before I found out she was messing around. I thought she was the woman of my dreams, and when I realized she wasn't the person she'd led me to believe, I got out."

"Why did it last longer with you?"

"Every once in a while she meets a woman who interests her beyond sex. And she sees it as a game. She mistakes lust and the need to control for love. If the woman leaves her, like I did, she freaks out and becomes hell-bent on revenge."

Her face paled and Erin briefly considered moving closer to comfort her. But before she could do so, Patricia dug the books out of the box and handed them over. "You should probably read up as much as you can before Adams beats you to it."

Fear pitted Erin's insides. "What if Adams asks me about a book or a character and I can't remember anything?" Her cover would surely be blown. How could anyone expect her to pull this off as early as tomorrow night?

"That's actually pretty easy to handle. Just tell her you're very private about your writing. Remember, you aren't going to offer her that information. She's going to find out on her own and without your permission." Patricia stood and her tone became hurried. "We need to move on and talk about some other things. Come on."

They headed down the hall and entered a spacious master bedroom where Erin immediately became flustered. An oak wood floor matched the Southwestern furniture and was accented with an Aztec rug. The bed was large and inviting, with goose-down pillows and duvet. Eyes unavoidably drawn to it, she felt her face flush as she thought of the different topics that involved a bedroom. Patricia's perfume lingered in the air, and it stirred adrenaline deep within her once again. She cleared her throat nervously as she imagined Patricia nude in that soft bed, illuminated by candlelight.

Patricia didn't notice her reaction, instead walking into a large closet. She reappeared with garment bags and set them on the bed. "I took the liberty of buying you some clothes to wear to the club." She unzipped a bag and pulled out an outfit. "I thought this would be good for Saturday. Adams is throwing a Wild West party for some business guests from back East. I hope the sizes are right."

Erin eyed the clothing before her, and her blush deepened at the thought of Patricia imagining her in the clothing. The jeans were faded and low rise. They looked to be slightly boot cut, nothing like the flare bottoms that were currently so popular. Next to the jeans was a camel-colored suede vest. Patricia opened up a large shoebox and pulled out a pair of suede cowboy boots to match.

"I hope they fit. I guessed on these too."

Erin eyed the boots, impressed. They were the right size. Fingering the suede vest, she asked, "Where's the shirt that goes with this?" She didn't see anything on the bed that would work with the outfit.

"There is no shirt. It's meant to be worn alone." Patricia looked away quickly, pink spreading across her cheeks.

"I see." Not wanting the other detective to think she was uncomfortable with the revealing outfit, Erin promptly scooped up the clothes and headed toward the master bath. "I better try all these on to make sure they fit."

Patricia shoved her hands in the back pockets of her jeans. "Sure. I'll go scare up something to eat, so feel free to use the whole room."

When Erin returned to the kitchen, she found Patricia bent over, sliding a pan into the oven, her jeans hugging her firm backside nicely.

"Everything fit okay?" Patricia asked.

"Perfectly." Erin sat down at the counter and sipped the iced tea she'd left there earlier. "How'd you know my size?"

"It wasn't difficult." She closed the oven and wiped the counter. "We're about the same."

She seemed uneasy, and Erin hoped it wasn't because the incident in Sergeant Ruiz's office was still on her mind. It hadn't been the most professional way to make her point, and she didn't regret doing so. Nevertheless, she had apologized. Her thoughts strayed to the photos of Adams she had seen in the files, and she bit her lip with a sudden wash of jealousy. Thinking of the gorgeous Adams with Patricia made her blood boil. The suspect was tall, dark, mysterious, and devilishly beautiful, not to mention wealthy, powerful, and extremely sexually confident.

Erin chewed a piece of ice, nervously aware of being shorter, blonder, and completely inexperienced by comparison. She didn't much like her feelings of inadequacy. Even if by some miracle Patricia did find her attractive, they worked together, and somehow Erin couldn't see her carrying on a romance with a fellow officer.

"You want some more tea?" Patricia asked with a friendly smile.

"Sure." Erin smiled back. "So what are you cooking?"

"Lasagna." Patricia refilled her tea. "I'm just reheating some leftovers. I hope you don't mind." She returned the tea to the fridge and then tossed a salad in a large bowl, stirring in a homemade vinaigrette dressing.

"Are you kidding? I hardly ever eat anything homemade."

"You don't like to cook?" Patricia licked some dressing from her fingertip.

"I wouldn't say that. I guess I just never had a reason to. Mark and I were never home much." Erin lapsed into silence for a moment, saddened at the thought of her nonexistent home life. She wished she had a warm, comfortable place and someone like Patricia to come home to.

"So how did the suede vest fit?"

Grateful at the change in subject, Erin said, "It fits, but it's a little snug."

"It's supposed to be formfitting." Patricia smiled up at her as she dished out the salad into serving bowls. "It's an attention getter."

"Ah, you mean girl bait." Erin grinned.

"Something like that. You ready for some salad before the lasagna?"

Erin nodded and helped to carry the bowls and silverware over to the oak table in the small dining room nestled beside the kitchen.

After eating in silence for a few minutes, Erin voiced a concern. "Won't Adams recognize you if you go in the club with me?"

Patricia took a sip of her tea before answering. "Yes. But it won't alarm her. She knows we've been investigating her for weeks. Besides, it would show fear if she turned me away. And Adams never shows fear. It's a sign of weakness."

Erin pondered the information as they finished their salads. The more she heard about Elizabeth Adams, the more she felt a fierce determination to go after her. Patricia returned to the table with dinner plates and a large serving dish filled to the brim with steaming lasagna. She spooned out a hearty portion for Erin before serving herself.

Erin took a bite and let it melt into her taste buds. "Mmm, you are a great cook, Patricia. You can cook for me any time." She chewed gratefully and marveled at how a home-cooked meal could warm the soul.

"Thanks, I enjoy it."

"Feel free to bring any leftovers to the station."

"Why the station? I can just cook for you here." Patricia sipped her drink. "After all, we'll be working twenty-four/seven on this assignment, and there's no need for either of us to starve."

Erin finished another mouthful, relieved that the tension between them had eased. "Those leather pants you got for me—when will I need to wear those?"

The shiny black leather outfit she'd found among the new clothing had fit her like a second skin, and she was very curious as to what event she would wear it to.

"Once a month is leather night at the club," Patricia said. "Adams loves it. Everyone comes in leather dress, the club is darker than usual, heavy music plays, and all the local vampire wannabes venture out of their caves to party."

"Sounds wild." Erin pushed her plate away, her stomach suddenly clenching with anxiety.

"Mmm, it is." Patricia eyed her carefully. "You never partied much, did you?"

Erin pondered the question, weighing whether she wanted to share her past. But seeing as how Patricia had shared some of hers, she decided to do so as well. "Some, when I was real young, like fourteen."

"Fourteen?" Patricia sounded surprised.

Erin sighed. "I got mixed up with some older kids, mostly because I couldn't relate to the kids my own age. I started sneaking out at night and going to parties. This high school guy raped me and I told no one. My pain led to some drug use."

"Jesus," Patricia breathed out.

"So anyway, my folks eventually found out and they sent me away to a clinic for teenagers. I was scared to death in that place and I straightened up real fast, just so I could get out." She looked down at her hands.

"I'm so sorry," Patricia said softly.

"Oh, don't be," Erin said. "It's long over, and I've never looked back."

They sat in silence for a while, then Patricia got up and cleared the table while Erin recuperated from sharing her tale of teenage trauma. Eventually she stood and stretched, trying to clear her mind of the tragic events of those years. She hadn't thought about her past in a long while, and she couldn't afford to think about it now if she wanted to walk into La Femme like she owned the place.

She maneuvered around Patricia, taking a wet dish from her hands at the sink. "Let me clean up. You cooked."

Patricia relented and stepped back with an expression of surprised pleasure. "Just rinse them off and put them in the dishwasher," she said, wiping her hands on a dish towel before pouring a refill of iced tea. "I'll be on the back patio."

Out of the corner of her eye, Erin watched her go and couldn't help but relax a little with the physical chore before her. It didn't take her long to finish, and when she did, she and Jack joined Patricia in the backyard.

Sitting in a deck chair, her boots propped up on another one, she was leafing through some files and appeared to be enjoying the brilliant sunset. Jack bounded through the yard, barking ferociously at imaginary but nonetheless vicious adversaries. Erin smiled at the little white dog and studied Patricia, who was holding some surveillance photos of Adams and staring off into the distance, a faraway look on her face.

"Hey, you okay?" Erin drifted over to stand next to her. The mindless work of scrubbing the dishes had helped to clear her thoughts of the dark clouds, but now it appeared that Patricia might have some clouds of her own.

Intense blue eyes lifted. "I'm fine. A little hot, I guess." She pulled off her boots and socks. "There's someone else I need to talk about with you. Kristen Reece."

She stood and walked over to the pool and sat at its edge. Easing herself into a deck chair, Erin watched as she rolled up her jeans and eased her feet into the blue-green water. The name registered. Kristen Reece was a tall, blond bartender at La Femme and had also starred in some of Adams's lesbian movies.

"What about her?"

"We think she's an accomplice."

Jack ran over and dropped a ball from his mouth into her lap. Erin tossed it across the yard for him. The news about Reece didn't come as a shock. She'd suspected as much just from what she had read.

"You think she's the blond woman the victims were last seen with?" She looked over at Patricia and felt an odd ache at the sight of her, sitting with the pool and the brilliantly painted orange and purple sky as her backdrop.

"Maybe. She and Adams have been involved for years. Adams took her out of an abusive home and gave her work. Reece would do anything for her."

This was all in the file, but Erin let Patricia continue, knowing that what she hadn't yet shared must be important.

"There's only one thing that can come between them. And if that happens, it will be a whole lot easier on us. If we can get to Reece, we'll have Adams hook, line, and sinker."

"So what's the one thing?" She tossed the ball for Jack once again.

Patricia smiled and pulled her feet out of the pool. "Women."

"Women?" Erin scoffed, more than a little nervous at what Patricia was hinting at.

Hair shimmering copper-gold in the setting sun, the detective pulled her knees up to her chest and wrapped her arms around them. "She'll like you, Mac."

"Wait a minute." Erin gulped and nearly choked. Going undercover to bait Adams was one thing, but creating some strange love triangle to bait two dangerous women was a little more than she could handle.

Patricia held up a hand and smiled. "It's simple. When you go in Saturday night, go after Reece."

"What about Adams?" Erin rubbed her hands on her jeans to dry them.

"It'll infuriate her."

"Why?"

"Because she'll want you for herself."

Erin pondered for a moment. "And what will Reece do?"

"Well, let's hope she fights for you and gets pissed off in the process."

Erin couldn't believe what she was hearing. It sounded like two dogs fighting over a scrap rather than two grown women. "So you're hoping that I'll provoke a fight between the two, start to crack the fierce loyalty?"

"Yes." Patricia got to her feet. "You up for it?"

Erin chewed on her bottom lip. Was she? She looked down at her hands and considered her fear of failing. She weighed it against the stigma of quitting and decided to give it her best shot. *What's a couple of dogs, anyhow?*

"Sure," she said. "What's the worst thing that can happen?"

Patricia did a small double take, and they both laughed, sharing a moment of nervous humor. "Okay, let's go over the final plan." She sat down across from Erin and picked up a spiral notebook and a pen. "Saturday night at eight o'clock, we meet at Katherine Chandler's residence."

"Which is where, by the way?"

"I'm taking you there tomorrow morning. Are you packed?"

"Mostly." She didn't require much, and it would take less than an hour to gather her necessities.

"Good." Patricia continued, reading from her notebook. "J.R. wires us and we follow you to the club. I enter the club first. Then ,several minutes later, you enter and head over to the bar, where you approach Reece." She looked up at Erin. "Play hard to get with Adams. It'll intrigue her to no end."

Erin swallowed back some anxiety. She needed to review all the details of this case and her target one more time, and then relax. It was just like taking a big exam. Minutes before the exam, you either knew the material or you didn't, and there was nothing a few last minutes of cramming would help.

"Keep your contact with Adams minimal on Saturday," Patricia said. "Just enough to let her catch your scent and get out. Then we'll go from there."

"Got it." Erin studied the sky. This time Saturday night she would be getting ready to enter the club. After all she had read and been told about this case, there was only one thing she was sure of.

She was getting in way over her head.

Chapter Four

E rin awoke slowly, clawing her way out of a nightmare. Sitting up in bed, she rubbed her face and tried to get a grip on reality. It took her a moment to steady her breathing and slow her heart rate. She'd had the dream countless times before, and it was always the same. She was in that awful place, the place her folks had sent her when she was fourteen. It was deemed a behavioral health center, located at a downtown hospital, but to Erin it had been her own private hell.

The youngest one in the ward, she had also been the one with the fewest problems. The place had been crawling with disturbed teens, violent and suicidal kids as well as those messed up on drugs. That was what her problem had been. Drugs. Marijuana had been her constant companion, along with acid and speed, to bring her up when she got too down.

Her parents had found her stash one day and overreacted as they'd always done, carting her off to the hospital. Any time things didn't appear perfect, they freaked out and overcompensated to fix the problem—anything to get life back to the perfection they worked so hard to achieve. It had been easier not to examine their home life, asking why she might have turned to drugs. Simpler to just void her out, blame it all on her and send her away to get fixed.

"Oh, Erin got mixed up in drugs. You know how kids are with peer pressure and all. You've got to watch them twenty-four hours a day, or who knows what kind of trouble they'll find." Her mother's voice rang in her ears, explaining her behavior away as nothing more than a prank her friends had dared her to do.

She walked into the bathroom and splashed water on her sweat-soaked face and neck, washing away her mother's plastic concern.

She looked at herself long and hard in the mirror and reminded herself that she was no longer fourteen and helpless. She was safe now, and in control of her own life. She leaned on the counter to balance herself as her mind once again flashed back to the dream.

She's sitting on the floor in the center of the room, watching television. It's nighttime and they're running another test on her. She's not sure what it's for, but she's being made to stay up all night with no sleep. There are things stuck to her head to monitor her brain activity. At least, that's what she thinks they're for. Suddenly, a noise comes from behind her. It's one of her counselors. His name is Rick and she thinks he's sick. Sick Rick is what she calls him. Not sick like throwing-up sick, but sick like perverted sick. He's smiling at her, and he moves his pale, gangly body up next to her and squats down.

"Hello, Erin." He winks at her through his thick-framed glasses and swallows. She watches his Adam's apple bob up and down like the fishing bobber her grandfather always lets her use. She looks away and wishes she were with her grandparents. She wishes she were anywhere but here.

Rick's beady brown eyes sweep around the quiet ward before focusing again on her. "How are you?" he asks, sounding concerned. The tone of his voice alerts her to what he wants. He always starts out trying to sound concerned and caring, and his voice gets higher, almost whiny, and she knows what's next. "You doing okay?" He lightly strokes her arm.

She freezes and stops breathing. Closes her eyes and wishes she could leave her body, wishes that the molecules of her soul could somehow float out of the hospital to her grandparents' home, where she feels safe, loved, secure.

"All this testing can be rough," Rick continues. "How 'bout a break?"

Erin shrugs. "I'm fine, thanks." She is always polite, even to Sick Rick.

Rick stands from his squat. "Nah, you can't be fine. Look at you, all these wires. You need a break."

Erin shakes her head in defiance. *"But if I take a break it'll ruin the test, and they'll make me do it again tomorrow night."*

Rick smiles once again, reaching down to lift her up by the arm. "Well then, I'll hang out with you tomorrow night too. And the night after that and the night after that." He lets go of her arm and reaches down to unzip his pants. She tries to run, but the wires on her head have her leashed. "Here, help me." Rick says, taking her hand and placing it on his penis.

"No!" She pulls her hand away.

Rick's eyes get big and he grabs her by the arm tightly. "You do it or I'll send you to the room."

She looks over at the room that stands in the corner of the ward. It's tiny and its walls are covered completely with white pads. She decides her preference is for the padded room rather than Sick Rick and his dick. She draws away from him and opens her mouth to tell him, but she's interrupted by a noise coming from one of the connecting rooms.

A door slams and a loud screaming assaults her ears. An older, pimply boy named Brad is running around the ward, beating his fists against his head as he screams. Counselors give chase, and Rick leans in and whispers in her ear.

"Looks like Brad will be joining you in the room."

The screaming gets louder and louder. It's joined by Rick's deep evil laughter, and Erin can't escape. She falls to her knees and cries. She cries and cries until the real tears bring her out of the nightmare.

Erin dried her face methodically with a soft towel.

"It's over," she said to herself, running her hands through her messy hair. No more hospital, no more Sick Rick, and no more perfection-seeking parents who refused to understand. She had her own life now, a good one, even if it didn't really include her folks.

Forgiving them had not been an easy task, and it had led more to avoidance on her part. She found it hard to sit and talk with them, to listen to how perfect her sisters' lives were and how perfect their own lives were: her father pampering his classic cars and playing golf, her mother traveling and organizing activities with the grandkids. And then, of course, came the questions about the life she'd chosen to live. Why did she have to become a cop? It was such a masculine job and so unsafe. Why didn't she quit and stay home and raise a family? Mark made plenty of money to support that.

She laughed. The light filtering in from the morning sun reflected off her wedding band, drawing her focus away from her parents and onto her fragile marriage. Eyeing the ring, she picked it up and examined it thoughtfully, then returned it to the jewelry bowl on the counter. It clanged around against the surface, ringing in her newfound liberty, then settled in silence in the center. Rubbing her bare finger, she examined it to make sure there were no marks or tan lines. She hadn't worn the ring for a couple of weeks, and yet the bare skin felt soft and smooth, considerably lighter at the absence of the platinum and the ungodly sized diamond. With the first positive feeling of the morning, she smiled and decided to focus on getting ready for the day.

She started the shower and stepped in, letting the hot water wash away the remnants of the nightmare and the negative thoughts that had accompanied it. Patricia was to pick her up at ten o'clock after a meeting with all the other detectives at the station. Erin could've attended, but her sergeant knew she had preparations to see to. After she dressed, she busied herself with what was left of her packing.

Seeing her large duffel bag next to the front door gave her a sense of freedom. She would need to find her own place soon, especially since she and Mark had plans to sell the house. He hadn't been too keen on the idea at first, sounding like he was actually attached to their large, empty home in some way. She didn't understand how he could be, having spent so little time there.

Restlessly, she wandered into the kitchen and opened the stainless-steel refrigerator. She wasn't much of a breakfast person, but she still had an hour left to kill, so she pulled out a cold Diet Pepsi, popped the top, and leafed through the mail as she sipped.

She stopped leafing when she came upon Mark's credit card statement. She didn't usually pay it any mind, having seen its contents before. But she was finally tired of ignoring and pretending, the absence of her wedding band prompting an honest assessment of her life. She tore open the envelope and pulled out the folded papers. Strangely, Mark had never had the statements sent to his office. It was as if he made no effort to hide his extramarital activities. He knew she opened most of the mail—although had she ever questioned any of the charges, he could easily have said he was entertaining a client.

She read through this month's statement, feeling fiercely independent and ready to move on alone. The majority of the charges were from Austin, and that didn't surprise her because they almost always were. But then she came across some charges that completely threw her. They were from baby boutiques, and some were from a baby furniture outlet. She stopped breathing and tried to make sense of what she was seeing. Maybe a client of his was having a baby and he wanted to buy them a nice gift.

The total was almost two thousand dollars. That was one hell of a shower gift. She shook her head and dropped the papers onto the counter. Then it hit her. Mark and his mistress were having a baby.

She covered her mouth and walked like a zombie to the couch. She sat down and stared straight ahead. She wanted to cry but she couldn't. She wanted to scream but she couldn't. All she could do was sit and stare. Time passed; she didn't know how much. The doorbell rang but she didn't move. It rang again after a few minutes, and she finally rose to answer it.

The sun pierced her eyes.

Patricia Henderson stood on the front step. Her smile of greeting faded as quickly as it had formed. "You okay? You look like you just saw a ghost."

Erin laughed a little at the statement, wishing a ghost was all that she had seen. "I'm fine. Let's get the hell out of here." She picked up her bag and walked outside.

Patricia eyed her carefully, closing the door behind them. "Okay," she said as they headed off to her Blazer.

They rode in silence, with Patricia looking over every once in a while, concern evident in the wrinkle of her brow. "Listen, Mac. If there's anything you ever need to talk about, I'm here for you," she said eventually.

"He got her pregnant." Erin kept her gaze fixed on the road ahead.

"What? Who?" Patricia was completely confused by the revelation, judging by her strained voice.

"Mark."

Patricia jerked her head around and looked at her. "He got someone pregnant?"

"Yes. His mistress in Austin," Erin said flatly.

Patricia refocused on the road ahead. "How did you find out?"

"His credit card statement." This time Erin managed to pry her eyes away from the road to look directly at Patricia. "Usually, he spends money on fancy restaurants and flowers and expensive gifts for her. But this time he spent close to two thousand dollars on baby furniture and accessories."

"You're upset," Patricia prompted gently.

"I'm not sure what I am." Erin turned toward the road once more, not wanting to think, just wanting to exist. Sometimes it was easier to just zone out and concentrate on other things. Little things, even. She had briefly studied Buddhism. It had encouraged her to focus on the tiniest of details, and that was what she needed to do now.

Looking out the window, she took in her surroundings. They were in an upper-class neighborhood in the center of the city. The homes were older but very well kept, with most of the homeowners coming from old money. Erin focused on the properties, their well-manicured lawns, and tried to imagine the people that lived in each house. Who were they? How long had they lived there? What did they enjoy doing from day to day? Perhaps it was an older couple. Retired. Yes, they were still in love and they led a peaceful, loving life together in their well-to-do home.

Patricia pulled up in front of one of the smaller places and put the truck in park, summoning Erin back from the deep recesses of her mind. Climbing out of the vehicle, she examined the house before her. It was painted off-white, contrasting nicely with the red-tiled roof. The yard was lush, with green grass and palm trees. A white Honda Accord sat in the driveway. It looked fairly new and she read the tags, knowing that if she entered them into the police database, Katherine Chandler's name would appear.

The sun was warm and mesmerizing, and Erin allowed it to massage her bare arms. Turning back to the Blazer, she picked up her bag and followed Patricia inside, disappointed in having to leave the comforting heat.

The home they stepped into was cool, and she noticed right away that it was furnished tastefully and expensively, with white carpet covering the floors. She immediately became dirt conscious at the sight of the pale room and slipped off her sneakers.

"You don't have to do that here," Patricia said.

Erin held up her hand in protest. "Yes, I do. If I get that carpet dirty, I'll go insane."

Patricia shrugged and pulled off her boots.

"Your socks are very white," Erin said, looking appreciatively at her companion's feet. "Some people's aren't."

Patricia eyed her carefully. "Huh?"

"Sorry, I have this thing about white socks." Erin knew she must sound ridiculous, and she clasped her forehead in disgust. "I know it's weird, and people have teased me about it for years, but I can't stand dirty or dingy-looking socks."

"Uh-huh, so I gather." Patricia stared. "Maybe we should talk about putting this thing with Adams off until next weekend."

Catching the concern on Patricia's face, Erin knew she needed to reassure her, and fast. "I'm fine, really I am."

"Even with all that's going on in your personal life? You need time to deal with it, Mac. You're standing here staring at my feet, for God's sake."

Erin walked over to the couch and plopped down. "Everyone goes through hard times. Even you. And I don't know about you, but the best way for me to deal with them sometimes is to compartmentalize."

"I can see that. But—"

"I need this assignment, Patricia," Erin interrupted. "I need to be able to tuck my problems away for the time being and focus on Adams. Haven't you ever needed something like that? To help you through a bad time in your life?"

Patricia's eyes locked with hers. "I know what you mean. I've written some of my best stuff during the worst periods of my life. But this isn't the same thing as writing a novel. If I even for a second think you're unstable or in over your head, I'll pull the plug."

Erin grinned, relief washing over her. "Deal." It was time to move on to a lighter subject. "This place is great." She looked around the spacious interior.

"It was my aunt's home." Patricia hoisted Erin's duffel bag.

"Your aunt?" Erin followed her down the hallway. "Is she…"

"Dead?" Patricia set the bag down in the center of the master bedroom and shoved her hands in her pockets. "Yes, she passed away last year."

"I'm sorry." Erin hoped she wouldn't be sleeping in a dead woman's bed. The thought sent chills up her spine.

"It's okay." Patricia followed her gaze. "Some of the furniture in the house has been replaced. Including the bed."

Erin breathed a little easier at hearing the news. "She didn't die here, did she?"

"You mean in the house? No. In fact, she hardly spent any time here at all. She spent winters here in Valle Luna, and the rest of the time she was back East or traveling the world."

Erin walked over to the bed and sat down. It was soft yet supportive, and she lay back and spread out her arms, trying to shed some of the tension she'd built up that morning.

"You think you'll be okay staying here?" Patricia fidgeted with a lamp. Erin had the impression the detective was avoiding looking at her sprawled on the bed.

"Yeah, I'll be okay. It's a nice home, comfortable and cozy." She didn't want to talk about herself or her feelings anymore. "Isn't it dangerous, to be so intertwined in the investigation? You know, to have me here living in a relative's house."

"No, we were careful. Very careful." Patricia shifted her weight from foot to foot.

"Were you close to your aunt?"

"Not really. She never could understand why I didn't just find myself a man and settle down." Patricia said the last bit in a Southern accent, no doubt a parody of her aunt.

"Did you tell her why?" Erin sat up and patted the bed for Patricia to join her.

"Yes." Patricia sat down next to her, but not too close.

"And she still didn't understand?"

"She was old and set in her ways. And she expected me to be able to ignore my attraction to women and marry a man."

"Were you ever with a man?" Erin was curious about Patricia's past lovers, no matter who they might have been.

"No!" Patricia flopped back on the bed. "Even if I had tried, I think I would've thrown up from the kissing alone."

They both laughed and stared up at the revolving ceiling fan.

"They're a lot rougher than a woman. It's the facial hair, I think," Erin said. She'd only kissed one woman in her lifetime, but the experience had been earth shattering and very different from a man.

"No, it's a lot more than the facial hair. They always try to stick their tongue down your throat right away."

"How would you know!"

"Hey, I had horrible high school dates too." Patricia sighed. "God, I hated high school. It never failed—every date I went on, the guy always slimed my face with a wet kiss and attempted a rough grope of my breast." She shivered and then laughed. "Except for Barry. Barry could kiss."

"So what happened with Barry? Did it get hot and heavy?" Resting her head in her hand, Erin rolled onto her side to face Patricia.

"No, we never went past kissing. He was the only guy that kissed soft and slow. And we were content with kissing, never anything more."

"Why?"

Patricia laughed. "Probably because we were both really gay."

"Get out! Him too?"

"Oh yeah. He was more feminine than I was." She folded her arms back behind her head. "He was a great guy. Went to prom together and everything."

"What ever happened to him? Are you still in touch?"

"No, we lost touch after high school. But I heard he's out and proud, living in California."

Erin lay in silence for a moment, resisting the urge to reach out and touch Patricia's smooth cheek. "What about now, do you have any close friends?"

Abruptly, Patricia sat up and rubbed her hands on her knees. "I should get going, Mac. I still have a lot of things to go over, and I know you do too."

"I'm sorry, I didn't mean to offend you." She had gone too far with the questioning and she regretted doing so.

"No offense taken. Really. You gonna be okay alone here today?"

Erin walked with her to the front door. "Yes, fine. I think I'll start in on some of your books."

Patricia toyed with her car keys. "Okay. Well, I'll see you later." She opened the door and walked out.

For a few moments Erin stood, leaning her back against the door; then she decided it was time for a drink. Searching the kitchen, she found a bottle of Jack Daniel's and a six-pack of Coke. The house was completely stocked and had everything she might need. She reminded herself that she needed to unpack the photos she had brought. Pictures of her from childhood, as well as meaningless photos of people she didn't know. All of it to help make this home seem like it was really hers.

Drink in hand, she wandered back into the living room and sat down on the couch. Thoughts of Mark swirled in her head, and she didn't know whether she should scream or cry. Why did this upset her so badly? She had known about the affair, even accepted it in a strange sort of way. She'd never confronted him over it. She hadn't cared, so why did she care now?

She took another deep pull from her glass. The Coke did nothing to mask the potent flavor of the whiskey, which she usually avoided drinking. But today she embraced its strength and savored the burn as it seared down her throat. It acknowledged her pain, confronted it head-on, and then numbed it. Numbed it so she could, for the briefest of times, think about it without flinching, work it out without bleeding to death.

Mark. She leaned back on the couch and drained her drink, desperate for it to fight her demons. Where had everything gone wrong? She had grown used to the betrayal, but why? Because she had stopped loving him. The revelation came out of nowhere, and yet it floated in so clearly. She was just as guilty as he was for the failure of their marriage. Had she truly cared, she would've tried harder, she would've insisted he end the affair. But she hadn't. And now this baby, or the hint of one on paper, was a slap in the face. A brutal awakening that her marriage was indeed over, and had been for a long time.

The comfortable groove of ignorance she had been living in had come to a shocking halt. It was time to change, time to make a move. She was now forced to face her failure, and that was what pained her the most. She decided to face it now, before she went in after Adams and while the whiskey was giving her courage. She picked up the phone from the table next to the couch and punched in Mark's cell phone number. It rang for several moments, then his voice apologized for missing the call and asked her to please leave a message.

"Mark, it's me. I really need to talk to you. Can you please call me back as soon as you get this message?" She hung up and lay down on the couch, stretching out her heavy limbs. The stress and the adrenaline had fatigued her, and she closed her eyes and drifted off, the phone clutched to her chest.

She awoke to the phone ringing, its sound coming from far away at the end of a long tunnel.

"Hello." Her voice was like gravel, her eyes still closed.

"Mac?" It was Patricia. "I was just calling to check on you, make sure you were all right."

Erin opened her eyes and tried to focus. "Fine. I guess I dozed off." She sat up slowly, rubbed her eyes, and glanced down at her watch. She had been asleep for a few hours, ample time for Mark to have returned her call. "Yes, I'm okay. Thanks."

"You sure? I thought maybe I could come by later and bring dinner."

Erin thought for a moment, the wheels of her brain not yet awake and slow to turn. "Thanks, but no. I've been asleep, and now I'm behind on my reading. I need to get caught up."

"You sure?" The worry was thick in Patricia's voice.

"Yeah, I'm sure. If I need anything I have your number."

They politely ended the call, and Erin stood and stretched and placed the phone back on its charger. Mark was busy in Austin. Too busy with his new family to return her call. To hell with him and his mistress and their baby. To hell with her past. She squared her shoulders and set her jaw. It was time to get tough. Time to concentrate on the now. Starting with this assignment.

Chapter Five

Elizabeth Adams watched her surveillance monitors with intent. Beyond her private lair, dozens of women danced and laughed, moving like waves through her nightclub. Among them, she would find the next lucky lady destined to be hers for the evening. She could take her pick; no one turned her down. Maybe it was her dark good looks, or maybe it was her money and power. Whatever the appeal, it worked.

Growing bored with what she was seeing, she ran her hands through her shoulder-length mane and decided to continue her hunt down on the dance floor. She took one last look at the multiple screens and came to a stop. A woman in a tight vest and jeans was crossing the parking lot. She was fit, her hair short and light, and she moved with the confident grace of a woman who knew precisely who she was and wanted everyone else to know too. The grainy black-and-white television image did not do her justice, but did enough to whet Liz's appetite.

With a satisfied grin, she murmured, "There she is," and picked up the phone that sat on the counter in front of the security monitors. "The blonde in the vest and jeans. Let her in," she instructed.

Liz didn't know what she would do without her security. She had cameras planted all over the club, as well as a team of loyal personnel. Nothing went on here that she didn't know about—that was the only way she felt completely safe. And, she thought with another smile, good security meant choosing her dates was as easy as selecting a treat from a vending machine.

As instructed, one of her team found the attractive blond newcomer and escorted her to the entrance. With a heated flash of anticipation, Liz strode out of her lair and into the VIP room. Several women turned and eyed her hungrily, their interest obvious, but she ignored them and headed to the railing that surrounded the dance floor. Leaning against it, she watched this evening's prey enter the club. She was even more beautiful than the cameras had promised. Liz considered going after her right away, but thought better of it. She would send Tyson. That always impressed the ladies.

La Femme was large by nightclub standards. Once a warehouse, it was now a state-of-the-art dance club. The renovations had cost Adams hundreds of thousands, and it was rumored that she had every inch of the club monitored by video.

Nervous butterflies flitted about in Erin's abdomen, paying her new attitude no mind. It wasn't just the thought of Adams that made her tummy all atwitter, it was the women. Like it or not, Erin was finding that she had some previously unsuspected attraction to her own sex. And she was about to be faced with hundreds of women, every one attracted to other women just like her. It struck her then that no matter how stoic her attitude, nothing would prepare her for what she was about to encounter. She shoved her hands in her pockets, drew a deep breath, and did her best to clear her mind of Patricia Henderson. The other detective had entered the club just before her, wearing tight faded jeans and a revealing white tank top.

"Good evening, madam." Erin felt a touch to her arm. "If you'll please follow me."

She turned and stared into a monster of a chest in a tight-fitting black polo shirt with La Femme embroidered in pink on the right chest. Looking up, she saw a huge man with a bald shiny head, wearing an earpiece.

Gently cupping her elbow, he walked her past the buzzing women and onto a plush red carpet that led into the dark entrance. This was flanked by two more security guards, both of them large women. He escorted her into an enormous, throbbing party, where he left her staring, completely in awe.

Everywhere she looked, women were dancing. Hundreds of them. Lights, lasers, and strobes flashed down on them, reflecting off their glistening, sweating bodies. The surveillance photos had done nothing to prepare her for the spectacle before her. Apart from the size of the club, which she quickly adjusted to, it was the feel of the place that got to her, the erotic energy. Something primal and electric seized her libido, forcing it up into a lump in her throat. Erin tried to swallow it down, but it didn't budge. Her temperature rose, spreading to her face and loins, awakening her from her standstill.

Looking up, following the lights, she progressed through the room. A catwalk edged the perimeter of the dance floor, where more women stood, some talking, most dancing. Someone bumped into her from behind, jolting her back to her agenda. With new focus, she made her way to the bar.

A song by the Escape Club boomed in her ears, and she smiled, not having heard it for years. Above her, on an elevated platform, a woman danced wearing only chaps and a cowboy hat. A flesh-colored thong covered her most intimate area, and tassels clung to her nipples, swinging in time with the music. She smiled down at Erin and shot her gun in the air, squirting bubbles from its chamber. Several more women, dressed the same, were dancing on other platforms. It was indeed Wild West night.

Most of the women around her were dressed according to the theme, wearing jeans, boots, and hats. Feeling confident in her own attire, she relaxed a little and swung herself onto the one available stool at the bar. Several bartenders scurried about, dancing as they served drinks. Kristen Reece had her back to Erin and was making what appeared to be a cosmopolitan. She was tall and obviously spent quite a bit of time in the gym when she wasn't starring in one of Adams's racy films.

"Howdy." A tiny woman tipped her cowboy hat at Erin and moved in closer.

"Hi," Erin replied, keeping her eye on Reece.

"Buy you a drink?" The woman smiled, showing a prominent gap between her two front teeth. She reached into her tight-fitting Wranglers to retrieve some money.

Kristen Reece had turned and now leaned across the bar to face Erin, her cleavage winking in the tight-fitting tank top. Her thick blond hair was pulled back in a ponytail, making her tilted grin seem even more flirtatious. "What can I get you?" she asked.

Returning the grin and trying to sound confident, Erin said, "Beer's good." She could see why Adams had chosen Reece for her movies. She was very attractive.

"It's on me," the cowboy next to her added, staking her claim.

Reece slid a Corona across the counter, her fingers lingering as Erin wrapped her hand around the cold bottle.

The cowboy tossed down a wad of bills and pushed them toward Reece. "I'll take a beer too."

"Fuck off." Reece pushed the cash back to the tiny cowboy, her eyes never leaving Erin's.

The cowboy wavered as if she might protest, but then decided against it. Gathering her money, she stalked off, back into the crowd of women, her defeat more than evident.

"That wasn't very nice," Erin said playfully.

"Who said I'm nice?"

Erin looked into her sparkling brown eyes and ran a finger around the rim of her beer. "Are you saying you're bad?"

"Oh, I'm very bad," Reece said, taking Erin's finger and slowly placing it in her mouth, sucking the trace of beer from it.

Erin breathed in deep at the feel of the hot mouth tugging at her finger. "So are you gonna buy me the beer, then?"

"Absolutely. Are you sure a beer's all you want?"

"It was, but I'm beginning to think I want something more."

The bartender's eyes blazed with mischief, and she licked her lips. "What are you doing later?"

"Nothing."

Reece kept hold of her hand, softly stroking it. "What's your name?"

"Katherine."

"I'm Kristen." She flashed that grin again. "So, Katherine, how about we hook up later?"

Erin swallowed. Did women always move this fast? "Aren't you going to ask me to dance first?"

Reece laughed. "Sure, we can dance. But I have to work, so maybe we can dance later at my place?"

"Maybe." Erin's voice faltered. Reece's fingers were playing her nerve endings.

The big, bald security guard was back. His voice thundered in her ear above the loud music. "Madam, your presence has been requested upstairs."

"Fuck off, Tyson." Reece stiffened, shoulders thrown back, thrusting her chest out in defiance.

"What's upstairs?" Erin asked, acting bored.

"The VIP room. Ms. Adams herself has asked for you." Tyson reached for her elbow, clearly expecting her to be thrilled and flattered.

"Who's Ms. Adams?" She avoided his hand.

Tyson reared back at the question, as if struck.

"She owns the place," Reece clarified, obviously annoyed at the interruption.

"Oh. Well, thanks but no thanks. I'm fine where I'm at." Erin returned her full attention to Reece, who soaked it up.

After staring a few seconds in disbelief, Tyson adjusted his earpiece and turned his back to the women, saying something Erin could not discern. A moment later, he had his orders.

"Kristen, you've been excused for the remainder of your shift," he said.

"What?" Reece dropped Erin's hand and shot a long look up at a small camera trained on the bar.

Tyson clenched his massive fists, pumping the muscles in his arms. "You're excused."

"Un-fucking-believable!" Reece slammed a cleaning rag down on the bar and jerked a pen out of her back pocket. She reached for Erin's hand and wrote on her palm. "Here's my number. Give me a call sometime." With another scornful look at the camera, she lifted the sectional bar piece and walked past it, slamming it back down behind her.

Erin watched her storm away and head up a roped-off staircase across the dance floor. Were all women that intense? She glanced down at the number on her palm, overwhelmed at how quickly

Kristen Reece had claimed her.

"Madam, if you would step this way," Tyson reminded her politely.

Erin slid down from her stool and nudged past him. "I said no thanks."

She worked her way over to the other side of the bar, away from the looming mass of muscle that was Tyson. She wasn't sure if it was him or the throng of sweaty people, but she was beginning to feel claustrophobic. She turned sideways and wedged herself between two women. A new bartender approached, this one shorter than Reece with jet-black hair. Her face was pierced in multiple places, a constellation of metal.

"Water," Erin said.

"Just water?" The bartender pushed something across the counter to her. "You sure you're not up for something else?"

"Like what?"

"Like a lucky charm." The pierced girl lifted her hand, revealing a small baggie of pills, each one shaped like a four-leaf clover. Erin recognized them as one of the many shapes and sizes that Ecstasy came in.

"No thanks," she said, and taking her bottled water, headed off toward the dance floor as Kid Rock blasted from the speakers.

She spotted Patricia dancing between two women, her left arm wrapped around the woman in front of her while the other hugged the woman behind her, creating an erotic sandwich in which she was the filling.

Sweat laced with desire seeped from Erin's pores. She wanted more than anything to stare continuously, to allow the sensual scene to assault her erogenous zones, awakening the fierce hunger that followed a long hibernation. But bodies crowded hers, blocking the addictive spectacle. She could smell the sweet scent of sweat mingled with perfume and cigarette smoke and took another sip of the cold water before dumping the remainder over her head. Its iciness shocked her but did little to cool her down from the heated sight of Patricia and the sex sandwich. Frustrated, she tossed the empty bottle aside and ran her hands through her wet hair, shaking the water free.

"Hot?" a deep, throaty voice questioned in her ear. A split second later the body followed, pressing up against her from behind.

"A little." Erin glanced sideways, expecting another come-on from a lonely lesbian. Instead she found herself face-to-face with Elizabeth Adams. A thrill rushed through her, and she found it difficult to swallow, though not from nervousness.

The dark-haired woman standing before her was absolutely breathtaking: five feet and ten inches of pure strength and sexuality, a carved icon of beauty and grace, all in one package. She smiled a devilishly seductive smile and easily pulled Erin close.

"Maybe I can help." Her eyes flickered with mischief. They were as light as ice, a shade of blue Erin had never encountered before.

"How so?" Erin reminded herself to remain calm and to act uninterested. But the photos had done nothing to prepare her for Adams's raw beauty.

In a white button-down Western shirt with the sleeves torn off, she looked incredibly sexy. Her jeans were faded and ragged and hugged nicely to her long, firm legs. White and brown snakeskin boots finished off her outfit.

She drew closer, allowing Erin to feel the harnessed power of her body. The alluring scent of men's cologne tickled Erin's nostrils. Adams started to move against her in the same erotic dance Patricia had reveled in, a gentle gyration of legs and hips, arms held firm and fast. Erin loosened her nerve-tight limbs and let them fall into tune with Adams's.

"I could start by offering you a cold drink, somewhere away from all these sweating bodies," Adams whispered seductively in her ear, causing chill bumps to come alive all over her body.

"And where might that be?" Erin asked, inhaling her scent.

"Upstairs in the VIP room," she purred. "I came all the way down here to invite you personally." She pulled back slightly, her arms still resting possessively on Erin's hips. "I'm Liz, by the way."

"Katherine," Erin said. "I met your friend Tyson earlier." She jerked her head in the direction of the huge man now looming by the stairs.

"Yes, he tells me you weren't very nice."

"He did, did he?"

"Yes, he said that you hit on him and then when he refused your sexual advances, you took advantage of him anyway."

Erin laughed and allowed herself to relax a little. "I guess I was a little aggressive."

"Let's hope you're the same way with me." Adams grinned and raised her hand to wipe water from Erin's face.

"So what's upstairs that's so much better than down here?"

The grin widened. "Me."

Erin's heart flipped in her chest. Patricia was right; their target was charming as hell. Tall, gorgeous, powerful in body and in life. Falling for her would be so easy, as it obviously was for countless other women. But Erin was on assignment, and Adams was most likely a killer.

"Maybe some other time," she said, playing her part.

The grip on Erin's hips tightened, moving down to her backside. "This is an offer you can't refuse."

"It's a big deal, huh? Getting a personal invitation?" Erin did her best to act tough, while the temptation to melt into Adams's arms grew stronger, a mere sigh away.

"Most people don't require such"—she leaned in, placing her mouth once again against Erin's ear—"personal attention."

Erin nearly melted on the spot. She clenched her jaw and prayed for control. "Well, I'm not most people, am I?"

"No, you're definitely not most people," Adams said. "And I have a feeling you'll require a lot more of my…personal attention." She took the tip of Erin's earlobe in her mouth and lightly sucked.

Erin shuddered, her grip tightening on Adams's strong arms. The combination of hot breath in her ear and hot mouth on her earlobe was too much to bear. She pushed herself away, suddenly thankful that she had to act uninterested. Breaking their contact would allow her to regain her bearings.

"So show me this VIP room of yours," she said, and ran her hands through her wet hair, sending cool drops down the back of her neck and into her vest, helping to bring her back to reason.

Adams seized her hand possessively. "You got it."

She led Erin through the crowd, brushing past Patricia and her dancing duo. Out of the corner of her eye, Erin saw Patricia observing them, and part of her felt victorious and spiteful at having nabbed Adams. Maybe now it would be Patricia's turn to have to watch while jealousy possessively crawled up her throat. She immediately scolded herself for the thought. They were here to do a job, nothing more. If she felt jealous and possessive of Patricia, that was her own problem. The detective merely perceived her as a coworker, a friend at the most.

She dragged her concentration back to her target, observing the effect Adams had on the women around her. Many stopped dancing to stare as they passed by. But their eyes weren't on Erin—they were on Liz, lustful and hungry. A few hopefuls approached, trying to get her attention any way they could, but she looked past them, through them. It seemed she had acquired what interested her, and now she parted the waters with her trophy in tow.

They headed over to the private staircase where Tyson stood guarding the velvet ropes. He nodded his head at Adams as they approached and removed the rope to let them pass.

The VIP room was darker than the rest of the club, hidden from the strobes and lights of the dance floor. Erin squinted, trying to adjust to the dim surroundings. She was able to make out numerous lounge chairs and love seats where some women sat close and talked while others kissed and groped.

They walked up to a bar on the left side of the room, made noticeable only by a blue neon strip that ran along its edge. A woman stood behind the bar wearing a Western bowtie and a cowboy hat. Her breasts were covered by what Erin at first thought was a tight leather vest, but upon closer inspection realized was painted on with what she could only guess was some sort of body latex.

Instantly intrigued by the all-but-naked woman, she leaned on the bar while Adams ordered their drink, and tried to get a look at what the bartender was wearing below the waist. When she moved,

Erin could see that she had on extremely short cut-off jeans and cowboy boots with spurs.

Adams handed her a screwdriver, and as they walked farther into the room, Erin watched some of the women on the sofas, transfixed by their kissing. One in particular caught her attention, a woman engaged in a threesome, two women licking and sucking on her neck.

Astonished, she asked, "Isn't that—"

"Yes." Adams sounded completely nonchalant about having a prominent Hollywood actress making out in her club.

Desire and disbelief collided in Erin's veins. It had long been rumored that the woman was a lesbian, but it had never been publicly confirmed.

"Would you like to meet her?" Liz offered, gently steering Erin over.

Not wanting to interrupt the kissing trio, Erin said, "No, it's okay."

But Adams forged ahead. "Angie?" The woman continued activity, oblivious to their presence. More loudly, Adams repeated, "Angie."

Angie put up a halfhearted struggle to dislodge her lips from her partner's, but then returned to kissing the woman on her left, their lips connecting with shorter, stronger pulls.

"I want you meet someone," Adams said, this time more forcefully.

Angie seemed to pick up on the stronger tone and pulled away from her kissing.

"This is Katherine." Adams gently pulled Erin forward.

Angie pried herself up from the couch and smoothed down her deep brown leather pants. She wore a very thin white tank top, showing off her ample, unharnessed breasts.

Embarrassed at interrupting the famous woman, and feeling like a little kid meeting her favorite movie star, Erin said, "I'm sorry. I—"

"Hi, Katherine, it's a pleasure to meet you." Angie smiled a thousand-watt smile, her inviting lips bruised and swollen from kissing. She placed a hand on Erin's shoulder, halfway hugging her.

Completely lost for words, Erin felt Angie's breast against her own and mumbled, "I'm a...a huge fan." She immediately felt stupid at having said it aloud. But Angie didn't seem to notice.

"Well, it looks to me like you should be the one in pictures," the actress said, her eyes lingering on Erin's lips.

"Yes, she is beautiful, isn't she?" Adams said. "We were just going to go have a drink."

"Maybe I can join you." Angie's eyes never wavered from Erin's face.

"Some other time," Adams said, and led Erin away.

At a large metal door, she typed in a number code on a keypad, and the door clicked open.

"What's this?" Erin asked.

"My private lair." Adams smiled at her.

Erin hesitated momentarily, gathering her thoughts. Meeting Angie Hartman had thrown her for a loop, leaving her almost giddy with excitement.

The room they entered was large and spacious, containing a lounge area with furniture in light browns and grays and leading into an adjoining room with a king-sized bed. The two huge windows Erin had noticed from the outside provided an incredible view of the Valle Luna nightline.

A bank of security monitors lined the wall behind the bar. She counted fifteen, each capturing a different view of the club, the parking lot, and main entrance. Adams had spotted her before she'd even set foot in the club.

"That's quite a setup you have there." Erin pretended to sip her drink. It looked and smelled like a screwdriver, but she didn't want to risk it. Not yet.

"Security is important to me."

"Don't you mean voyeurism?"

Adams raised an eyebrow but didn't respond. "I hate these Wild West parties," she said after a moment. "But my friends from Philly love them." Capturing Erin's gaze, she began unbuttoning her shirt. "They all think we ride around on horseback and eat tumbleweed." The white shirt parted, and Erin looked away, not yet ready to see the body underneath. Adams bent and pulled off her boots, tossing them across the room where they came to rest with a thud. She eyed Erin hungrily. "Now, how about we take the cowboy off of you?"

Erin didn't respond. She couldn't. Her voice had disappeared along with the courage she was so sure she would have.

Adams stepped ever closer, her head cocked to one side. "Why haven't you ever been to my club before?" she asked, allowing her shirt to flap openly.

"Maybe I have," Erin said, looking at her face, careful not to look at her body. Even so, her eyes were still able to make out a white bra against tanned skin.

"Uh-uh. No chance." Adams ran a hand slowly up the outside of Erin's arm. "I would've noticed you."

Erin's eyes strayed to the well-defined muscles lined up neatly on the taller woman's abdomen. "I don't usually do the nightclub scene," she said.

"Well, then tell me…" Adams stepped closer and lightly kissed her neck. "What do you do?"

Erin inhaled her alluring scent, and heat raced to her loins. She backed away, her heart pounding with want. "Not this." She gave Adams her best stern look. "If you think I'm going to sleep with you, you're sadly mistaken."

"It wasn't sleep that I had in mind." Adams closed the gap between them once more.

Erin wanted to close her eyes and drift into her, but she knew she couldn't afford to get lost in the arms of the dangerous Elizabeth Adams, potentially jeopardizing her assignment. Instead, she placed her hands firmly on Adams's broad shoulders and held her at bay.

"Look, all this may impress other women—the club, the celebrities, your mindless charm. But it doesn't impress me." She held the other woman's stare without flinching. "I'm not out for some quick roll in the hay. This is exactly why I don't do the nightclub scene." She didn't mean a damn word she was saying, but she hoped it sounded convincing.

Adams's face was expressionless, and Erin wasn't sure what she was thinking. Nervous, but determined not to show it, she headed for the door. She could feel the other woman's eyes boring heat into her back. "Thanks for the drink," she said, as she pulled the door open.

"You're welcome." The voice came from directly behind her.

Startled, Erin turned. She hadn't even heard Adams approach.

Adams placed a finger on her lips as if to silence her, then ran it slowly down her neck to the top of her breasts. Erin looked into her fire-and-ice eyes and saw the raw desire churning within.

Careful to steady her breathing, she tore herself away and, without looking back, walked briskly and purposefully out the door, past Angie and her small harem and down the stairs to the crowded dance floor. She wanted to leave, but she knew she couldn't run out of there like a scared rabbit. Instead she grabbed the nearest woman.

The young blond stranger was momentarily surprised by her aggressiveness, but she relaxed quickly and smiled at Erin as they danced. Erin closed her eyes and forced her body to move. The physical exertion did little to distract her from the raging feelings Adams had elicited. She danced hard, grinding her body into the other woman, trying to look like she was having fun.

After two long songs, she gave her partner a wink and nonchalantly exited the dance floor, hoping she had put on a good enough show. Sweat dripped from her body, and her nerve endings and loins were still alive and hungry. She fished out her car keys from her pocket and ran out into the parking lot. The desert night air felt like a furnace turned on low, and it did little to cool her insides down. She cranked up her car and threw it in reverse.

She had done it. The first contact was over, and she had done exactly what was required, maybe even more. She could only hope Adams would remain hooked. She drove several blocks before she pulled over into a grocery store parking lot. After parking in the rear, away from the other cars, she turned off her car and collapsed back against the seat. Her breathing was still rapid, and her heart raced in her chest.

She sat in silence for a while, allowing herself the time to absorb all she had seen and experienced. Would she be able to keep up the charade? Would she be able to successfully and safely interact with Elizabeth Adams next time? That icy stare flashed before her, and she started up the car and put it in drive. As she turned onto Paradise Drive, she rolled down the windows and let the furnacelike heat assault her face, hoping against hope that it would melt Adams's glacier blue eyes from her mind.

Chapter Six

Erin pulled into Katherine Chandler's driveway and shut off the Honda's engine. Before getting out of the car, she glanced up and down the street, making sure she hadn't been followed. Seeing no other vehicles, she locked the car and headed indoors, tossing her keys on the coffee table.

She went through the required routine, checking in with J.R. before she stripped off the suede vest and removed the wire from her bra. She was unbelievably thirsty and strolled into the kitchen. It felt good to walk around the cool house in her bra.

The phone rang just as she began to fill a glass with ice for some tea. Erin answered quickly. It was Hernandez. He and Stewart were staked out in a house close by. They all knew that once Adams ran her license plate, it would be only a matter of time before she tried something intrusive.

"Line's all clear," he said, referring to any phone taps. "And there's been no movement on the house."

"Okay, thanks for the update."

They said good-bye, and she carried her tea back to the living room and took a long sip before pulling off her boots. Once free of their binds, she collapsed back onto the couch, feeling exhausted in a strange way. It was difficult to pretend to be a confident, relaxed human being while having to really be guarded for her own protection. The task was physically and mentally trying, and it hadn't helped that Adams was alluring and devastatingly beautiful. It was hard to look at her and imagine her as a ruthless and sadistic killer. Yet that's how Erin had to see the woman. Her own life depended on it.

She eased back and tried to relax, to find some sort of comfort in finally being away from the club and her dangerous world of make-believe. But her body and mind wouldn't unwind. Her blood was alive and buzzing with sexual energy.

The phone rang again, and she sat up and snatched it quickly. "Hello."

"Great job tonight, Mac. I got killer sound." J.R. seemed just as keyed up as she was. "No pun intended." He laughed at his own comment, not caring if she found it funny or not.

"Good, glad to hear it."

"I knew you would give Adams a boner. And from where I'm sitting, she sounded like she had some hard-on." He sounded muffled and far away, and Erin figured he was driving home and talking to her from his cell phone. "Now all you gotta do is let her fuck you with her big dick, and maybe then she'll tell you that she killed those guys."

Erin rubbed her temples while resting her elbows on her knees. She ignored his crudeness, having heard far worse from him on other assignments. "Yeah, I'm sure it'll be that simple."

He seemed to miss the sarcasm in her voice, or maybe it got lost over the cellular static. "Hey, we all know that sex makes the world go round. Later, chica."

Erin wished dealing with Adams would be as simple as J.R. made it sound. The thought of a sexual encounter with their striking target caused butterflies to flutter about her insides. Erin had to admit, she would gladly fuck Adams to get a confession. The woman was charming and gorgeous, a huge leap from the drug lords she was used to.

She gulped at the last of her iced tea and returned to the kitchen for a refill. The bottle of Jack Daniel's she'd found the previous day sat on the counter, its silent presence speaking to her, promising to bring her down a level and perhaps help her sleep. She picked up the bottle and its misleading promises and put it away, knowing that nothing short of numerous powerful orgasms would ease the sexual charge coursing through her veins.

Images of Adams flashed through her mind. Hair as black as night framed her perfectly carved face, luring Erin in to be held captive in the electric blue of her eyes. Then there was her body. Its strength, beauty, and seduction slinked up, enchanting Erin with its promise of complete and total sexual satiation.

Her mind drifted to Patricia, to the sensual way she had moved between the two women, so erotic…so inviting. She placed the glass back on the counter and glanced down at her bare torso. With fingers still cold from holding her drink, she lightly stroked her abdomen, following the path of blond downy hairs. Her body shivered as she traced her fingers back up toward her bra, where she felt her nipples harden beneath the lace. The ring of the phone startled her and she nearly jumped out of her awakening skin.

Annoyed, she picked it up and demanded, "What?" fully expecting it to be one of her colleagues calling to congratulate her on her success at obtaining lesbian status. At the same moment, the doorbell rang, and she pictured the motley group of detectives standing at the door holding condom balloons and a cake with a dildo in the center and "Job Well Done" lettered in icing.

"Hello, Katherine," a deep sexy voice purred into her ear.

Adams. Shock raced through her, and she eyed the front door. *Could she be here?* She snatched up her vest and slipped it on over her shoulders.

"Uh, hello." She walked as quietly as she could to the door and peered through the peephole. Relief washed through her.

"Do you know who this is?" her caller prompted.

Erin opened the door. "I think I recognize the voice, but I don't remember giving that particular person my phone number."

Patricia entered quickly and remained silent, clearly picking up on the phone conversation. She eyed Erin's open vest and looked away.

"It wasn't hard to get, and besides, I had to call, otherwise I might never have gotten the chance to apologize." Her voice and words were disarming, especially to someone who was easily charmed by her looks and antics.

Katherine Chandler, unlike Erin, was not. "Apologize for what?"

"For my behavior tonight at the club. I was too presumptuous, and I didn't intend to give you the wrong idea."

She was good.

"Mmm. Apology accepted." Erin offered no more; she wanted to make her squirm a little.

"I hope I can look forward to seeing you again."

"I don't know." She tried to sound uninterested.

"Let me make it up to you." Adams was definitely squirming on her end of the line, like a fish trying to hang on to the bait. "Have dinner with me tomorrow night."

"Dinner?" Erin hesitated purposely. "Tell me why I should."

Patricia nodded her approval from the sofa—a good sign considering how well the detective knew Adams, Erin thought.

Adams laughed a deep, throaty laugh. "Because I promise you, it'll be an evening you'll never forget."

"If I agree, will you keep your hands to yourself?"

Adams laughed once again, seemingly enjoying the game she thought Katherine was playing with her. "You have my word. I'll keep my hands to myself."

"Okay, then. I'll have dinner with you tomorrow night."

"Wonderful. I'll have a driver pick you up at seven."

"Wait a minute," Erin protested. "A driver? No, I'm not comfortable with that. I'll meet you at the club."

Adams didn't respond right away, and Erin thought for a moment that she might actually refuse. "The club will be fine. Good night, Katherine." The words were said softly, like a caress.

Erin hung up and sighed heavily. "I didn't expect her to call so quickly."

"You did good," Patricia said.

Erin smiled, then remembered her vest wasn't buttoned up. "I need to go change," she said, heading for the bedroom. "Want to stay for a drink?"

"No thanks. I won't keep you." Patricia raised her voice so she could hear. "I just thought I should stop by to see how you are. Obviously, things went well with Adams."

Erin returned to the living room wearing a black Adidas T-shirt. "She's exactly how you said she would be—arrogant, ostentatious, and unbelievably charming."

"Glad to hear she hasn't changed any."

Erin plopped down on the sofa and propped her feet up on the coffee table. "I did what you said, I played it tough."

"So, how are you? Did she shake you up?"

Rubbing her hands on her jeans, Erin thought about the question. She knew Patricia was just looking out for her, and she knew she had to lie in order to sound competent. "I'm fine." She willed herself not to lower her eyes beneath Patricia's searching gaze. "As for Adams, I got the impression that she's mostly bark and less bite." She hoped she sounded believable, because the truth had her insides knotted and her nerve endings screaming with want.

"That, Mac"—Patricia rose and headed for the front door—"is where you're dead wrong."

The morning sunlight filtered in through the vertical blinds, casting stripes across the bed. Erin opened her eyes and squinted at the sun's greeting. She stretched and felt calm and relaxed. She hadn't slept that well in a long, long time. While the night had been pleasantly free of nightmares, it had brought dreams—dreams that left her feeling warm inside.

She snuggled down into the soft contours of the comfortable bed and closed her eyes, content in the feelings such dreams always left her with. She yearned to return to their tranquil confines. One dream played out in her mind.

It was late and a noise in the hall woke her. Startled, she sat up in bed and looked to the bedroom door as it slowly opened. Patricia stood in silence, wearing the jeans and tank top she had worn to the club.

Patricia walked slowly toward the foot of the bed, her face and body illuminated by the soft light of the moon, her eyes burning a deep midnight blue. Her hands crept seductively to the waistband of her jeans. With great ease she pulled on the buttons, popping them free down the fly of the tight-fitting denim. Slowly, and with obvious deliberation, she moved her hands back up to the tank top, scooting it up to bare her toned torso. In a single fluid motion, she pulled the top up over her head and let it fall to the floor.

Her eyes flashed in the moonlight and lightened several shades, and Erin recognized the fiery, hungry gaze. She didn't know how or why, but Patricia's eyes had changed to those of Elizabeth Adams.

The beautiful woman before her seemed to be enjoying Erin's attention. Her breasts swelled with her breathing, the nipples dark pink and puckering. Her hands moved back to the jeans and inched them down over her bare hips and thighs. Erin's gaze floated up to the nude woman's face. Elizabeth Adams teasingly licked her lips and crawled on the bed.

Elizabeth nuzzled her neck, and Erin could smell the tantalizing scent of her cologne. Reaching for her, wanting to pull her closer, she placed her hands on the warm, strong back. A voice whispered in her ear.

"I'm going to show you how I love." The voice was Patricia's.

A thrill rushed through Erin and she bucked her hips, desperately wanting the feel of the woman against all of her. They kissed warm and deep, Patricia teasing with her hot tongue. The scent on Patricia's neck was arousing and familiar, the scent of Adams's cologne gone.

Patricia's soft, knowing hands explored Erin's nude body, stroking, awakening. She pulled her mouth from Erin's, trailing her way down her neck to her breasts, where she sucked and tugged on the nipples over and over again, causing Erin to pant with need.

She looked up, and Erin realized the face had changed back to Elizabeth Adams. She licked her way to Erin's stomach, pausing just above the pubic line.

"Look at me, Mac." The voice was Patricia's, the face Adams's. "I want you to watch. Watch me love you." She eased her way down with her tongue, and Erin could feel the hot wetness of it lapping at her most sensitive spot. Her head swam. Pleasure came at her in giant waves. Unable to control herself, she threw her head back and came hard against the dark head between her legs.

The morphing of Patricia and Adams seemed strange by the light of day, but in the dream it had seemed completely normal, exciting Erin to the point of no return.

She now understood why she had slept so well. A powerful orgasm had ripped through her body in the middle of the night. She threw the covers back and got dressed in a pair of athletic shorts and a tank top. Trying to clear her mind and her body of the feelings of desire the dream evoked, she padded into the kitchen and poured herself a small glass of orange juice. She had always loved the mouth-puckering taste of the citrus first thing in the morning; it never failed to awaken her senses.

As she downed her juice, she walked over to the front door, curious to see if there was a morning newspaper. Just as she unlocked the deadbolt, the doorbell rang. Startled, she opened the door without first checking through the peephole.

"Katherine Chandler?" A young, thin lad stood partially hidden behind a giant bouquet of roses.

"Yes," she answered, completely taken in by the beauty of the deep velvet red of the roses.

"These are for you." He handed her the enormous arrangement. "Have a wonderful day, ma'am." He gave a quick smile and disappeared.

"Thank you," Erin called after him, dazed.

She couldn't get over the size of the bouquet. It must've been two dozen at least. She set it on the coffee table and fingered the envelope, knowing the romantic gift had to be from Adams. Slipping the envelope open, she pulled out a single sheet of heavy, rippled paper. In the center, a simple message was written in a very neat yet unique hand.

Counting the minutes until tonight,
Liz.

Oh boy. She tossed the card aside and eyed the roses, which took up most of the coffee table. If she had met Adams outside of this investigation, she knew she would have been dangerously affected by the attention; any woman would. Her stomach flip-flopped a little as she realized what the flowers meant. Adams was after her, and now she had to play her cards just right. She had to continue to intrigue the suspected killer without getting too close and, most importantly, without blowing her cover. Could she do it?

A sense of pride washed over her. She had hooked Adams, hadn't she? Maybe she could also get the confession they were hoping for. Even if she couldn't, she wasn't about to go down without trying. She carried the flowers into the kitchen. As she arranged the fragrant blooms, she hoped for her own sake that Adams's behavior would continue to be predictable. It would make her task all the more achievable.

Liz's heart thudded madly in her chest, and she walked with difficulty over to the edge of the cushioned floor. Snatching up her water bottle, she sipped slowly and gratefully as John began jumping over three-foot-high stacks of pads. He cleared them with at least two inches to spare, and he made it look easy. She was always amazed by his agility and grace. It was as if the man had no bones, just limber, agile muscle.

Thoughts of past events flashed through her mind. Men who had caused her grief and pain smiled at her, beckoning her to fail. Her hatred for men as a species ran deep within her bones. Had John not earned her respect, she would've hated him too. But he was one of the only men she'd ever allowed to play a part in her life. She eyed her instructor of two years. He wore loose-fitting gi pants and a T-shirt with a dragon emblem on the front. "Warrior Spirit" was written underneath.

Yes, that's what she was, too. A warrior. Even if she had thought for a brief second that she would collapse as she too jumped over the stacks of pads.

They concluded their workout with punches, John holding a thick black pad in front of his midsection, standing in the center of the room. Harder and faster, Liz punched and pushed until he reached the edge of the mat, then they turned and she punched and pushed him back to the center.

This time she knew he would resist her forward pursuit. She breathed deep and advanced with quick, hard punches, pushing her body weight against him. Slowly, she was able to gain on him, forcing him back to the edge of the mat. Her entire body cried out for her to stop, but she kept pushing, ignoring the pain. John stepped off the mat and lowered the pad.

"Good job." He slipped his hand out from the pad and high-fived her.

Liz resisted the urge to collapse on the floor in sheer exhaustion. Instead, she walked the mat, her hands behind her head, opening up her lungs for much-needed air. After a few rounds, her breathing had steadied and she sat down to stretch. Across from her, John spread out his legs to match hers. With their feet touching, they clasped forearms, and he pulled her toward him slowly and carefully to stretch her legs.

"You know, the police have been hounding me," he said. "They're telling me that you killed some guys. Shot them, mutilated them."

She let the words float around in her brain, trying hard not to get angry. Goddamned cops had been harassing her for weeks, following her, questioning her and her associates. Now they were bothering John. She knew what they were trying to do. They were trying to embarrass her, mark her good name, piss her off.

"Should I keep teaching you, Liz?" he asked as she eased back. "If you're using what I teach you to hurt people, then—"

She broke their grip and hastily stood. "Have you seen me hurt people?" The anger she had tried to force back seeped into her voice. "Have you seen me kill anyone? Mutilate them, shoot them?" She was shaking, but not from the strain on her muscles.

John stood too, his concern and confusion evident "No, but I don't spend every waking hour with you. What am I supposed to think when a bunch of homicide detectives turn up here asking questions?"

"I would think that you know me better than that, John. That you might actually trust me." Feeling upset and somewhat violated, she walked past him and picked up her towel to wipe the sweat from her face. "Tell the police to fuck off."

John watched her in silence, but the tension had left his face. Liz figured her flat denial had settled him. Grabbing her equipment bag, she headed for the door.

"See you later, then?" she questioned over her shoulder.

"Yeah."

She rode back to the club with the air conditioner turned off in her Range Rover. The stereo she blasted happily most days was silent, allowing her thoughts to churn in her mind. Salty sweat secreted through her pores in the stifling heat of the vehicle, but she didn't notice. John's words replayed in her brain, along with her previous confrontations with the detectives.

She never had been able to keep her cool when people said something to upset her. Unable to let criticism slide off her back, she allowed the words to fester in her skin, to irritate her to brash action. She knew the police were counting on that. They were trying to get under her skin.

She pulled up behind her nightclub and sat for a moment behind the wheel, watching the sun shimmer against the silver paint of her Range Rover. The truck spoke to her in its female British voice, letting her know she had reached her destination. Liz glanced at the clock on the dash and realized she only had an hour before Katherine Chandler arrived. Grateful for the distraction from her problems, she shut off the engine and hurried inside to get ready for her date.

"Hi," Erin said loudly to the backside of Kristen Reece.

Reece turned, wearing tight jeans and tight T-shirt with the sleeves and collar cut off, allowing her breasts an ample stage on which to display themselves.

"Hey, you." Reece smiled at her and opened a beer as a gift. "You're back."

"Well, we didn't get to finish our conversation." Erin took a sip of the cold beer and gave her a broad grin.

Reece looked at her for a moment as if thinking. She looked nervously up at the camera in the corner of the bar, then grabbed

Erin's hand and led her hastily away from her workstation.

"Where are we going?" Erin followed behind as best she could, tugged through dozens of lesbians as Reece steered her to the center of the dance floor.

"I figure I only have about thirty more seconds before Tyson comes to take you from me," Reece yelled above the dance music.

"Yeah?"

She wrapped her arms around Erin's waist and pulled her close. "Yeah. So let's dance."

Wedged between moving waves of women, they began to move in rhythm with the dance music. Erin smiled, genuinely enjoying the music and the dance. Although it was obvious that Reece was into her, Erin didn't feel intimidated like she did with Adams. The bartender seemed less intense and more willing to just have fun. A new song melted into the old and the crowd cheered as they recognized the beat. Laughing, Reece and Erin once again joined their moving neighbors in dance.

"Aren't you going to get in trouble for dancing with me?" Erin asked, wondering if she had succeeded in causing tension between Adams and Reece.

"Oh, absolutely." The bartender leaned in to speak closely against Erin's ear. "But I happen to think you're worth it."

They danced close together, grinding with the strong bass of the music. Erin let the beat throb through her veins and raised her arms in the air, feeling completely free.

"Mind if I cut in." The words fell upon them as a statement rather than a question. Erin immediately recognized the deep, smooth voice.

Reece's face turned to stone as she looked over Erin's shoulder and into the eyes of Elizabeth Adams. She released her hold on Erin's hips and leaned in once again to murmur into her ear. "Call me, gorgeous." With that, she shot Adams a cold glare and turned to walk back over to the bar.

"You look amazing." Adams came to stand before her, holding Erin's hands out from her sides and examining her with wicked appraisal.

"So glad you approve." Erin acted bored, all the while trying to ignore how good Adams looked in the black sleeveless shirt and faded jeans.

Adams stepped closer and placed her strong hands on Erin's hips, pulling her in for a dance. Erin swayed a little, overwhelmed by her strength, aroused by her scent. Adams led, slithering her body against Erin's, pulsing with the powerful music. Heat rushed to Erin's cheeks as she allowed herself to move in time with Adams, their bodies meshing, touching, warming. She shuddered and tensed with anticipation as Liz leaned in to breathe in her ear.

"You don't like me very much, do you?"

Startled by the forwardness of the question, Erin shook her head, not quite sure what to say. She decided to be honest. "I don't even know you."

Seemingly satisfied by the answer, Adams gripped her hand more firmly. "Well, let's go remedy that, shall we?" She turned and led Erin through the staring women and out one of the back doors of the club.

Chapter Seven

The sun was bidding the desert good night, casting a warm purple and orange glow across the sky. Erin squinted more out of habit than from the light. "Where are we going?" she asked as they entered the alley behind La Femme.

"For a ride," Adams tossed over her shoulder. Releasing Erin's hand, she climbed onto a sleek black Harley-Davidson.

"Oh." Erin fought the urge to melt on the spot. Elizabeth Adams looked so strong, so alluring, straddling the machine in her sexy outfit and black motorcycle boots. "I thought we were having dinner." She was stalling. She didn't want to climb on the back of the bike. Or maybe she really did, and that was the problem.

Adams smiled and reached back to harness her black mane with a dark-colored bandanna. "I thought we would ride my bike to the restaurant." Tying the bandanna snug, allowing it to mold against the top part of her head, she then reached in her back pocket for another one, which she offered to Erin. "You want one?"

"No, no thanks." She stood still, not moving toward the bike. The thought of sitting so close to Adams, of hugging her from behind, stirred her in ways she didn't think possible.

"Are you scared?" A trace of concern softened Adams's eyes.

Erin knew she couldn't show fear. No matter what kind of fear she was feeling, she couldn't allow this predatory woman to see it. "No, I'm fine," she said and walked over to the bike. "Let's go." She slung her leg over the 600 pounds of machine and rested her hands softly against the thick black belt Adams wore.

"If you're going to ride with me, you'll have to hold on tighter than that," Adams said with a laugh over her shoulder. She grabbed Erin's hands and wrapped them tightly around her abdomen, then reached forward and brought the engine to a roaring life.

Erin tightened her grip as the bike lurched out of the alley with a loud, rumbling growl. She relaxed against the powerful vibration between her legs and looked ahead as they drove off into the evening.

They were headed east, streaking their way toward the promise of night. Erin looked back over her shoulder, where light from the setting sun still lingered. Purple mountains stood along the edge of the valley: tall, brooding, serrated, cutting into the lighter-colored sky.

She didn't know where they were going. All she could do was hang on tight and allow Elizabeth Adams to captain their voyage. The constant vibration of the large bike numbed her legs and crotch, causing her to hold tighter to the strong woman seated in front of her. She tried not to notice the feel of the rippled abdomen muscles moving beneath her hands. Instead, she tried to allow the exuberance of the ride itself to penetrate her entire body. She had never ridden a motorcycle before, and the rush of the wind against her was exhilarating, giving her a sense of freedom that held no boundaries.

They continued east, carving through the mountains that bordered Valle Luna. As they slowed in speed, Erin noted that the mountains no longer appeared purple but different shades of brown, spotted with large magma boulders. Taking in her immediate environment, she could see no sign of a restaurant and suddenly knew they had to be headed to Adams's home.

The dark-haired woman steered the loud machine onto a narrow paved road that wound its way up one of the mountains. Erin held fast to her and looked up at the large house nestled in the side of the mountain. It was close in size to the one she shared with Mark, with the modern look of a newer desert home. Different shades of beige colored its stucco walls, while dark gray tiles covered the roof, blending the home nicely into its desert surroundings.

The bike came to a slow crawl as the ground leveled. A vast electronic gate halted their passage, and Adams stopped and dug in her front pocket for a set of keys. She pushed a button on a tiny remote and the gate slowly swung open, allowing them entry to the long, paved drive.

Adams brought the bike to a stop opposite an enormous front door, then killed the engine and allowed Erin to carefully climb off the back.

"This doesn't look like a restaurant." Erin tried to sound stern. "This your house?" She smoothed down the legs of her jeans and stomped slightly, trying to get rid of the tingling sensation in her ass and thighs. She hoped J.R. could still hear her so the surveillance team would know where they were. She didn't think Adams would harm her, but she couldn't let her guard down no matter how disarming her subject might be.

"Yep." Adams swung with ease off the bike and removed the bandanna from her head.

"I thought we were supposed to be having dinner." Erin followed her up to the front door, reminding herself to act unimpressed.

"We are." Adams unlocked the door and walked in, motioning for Erin to wait on the landing. "I thought we could eat here, in privacy."

"This isn't what I had in mind." Erin folded her arms, acting displeased with the wool her companion was trying to pull over her eyes. A distant beeping sounded from inside the door and Adams punched in an alarm code, then spoke to someone.

She turned back to Erin, wearing a grin. "Can you blame me if I wanted your attention all to myself?" She raised her eyebrow and invited Erin to enter the house.

Erin had to remind herself to stay annoyed as she walked into the spacious home, her arms still folded defiantly over her chest. Adams closed the door behind them and Erin looked around, taking in the expensively decorated surroundings. A growl got her attention, and she looked down as two massive black Dobermans trotted into the room to stand in front of her. They both eyed her, their heads lowered and teeth showing.

Erin stood very still, glad she had arms protecting her chest.

"No, boys." Adams halted next to Erin, her voice deep and commanding. "Friend." Immediately the dogs wagged their tails and circled their visitor in excitement. "It's okay, they won't hurt you."

She scratched them on their heads, and Erin took a breath and let her hands fall to her sides. The dogs licked her hands and tried to nuzzle them, urging her to scratch their short, sleek fur. Her fear fading fast, she gave in to her love for animals and began petting the intimidating pair, asking, "What're their names?"

They walked deeper into the house, the dogs close on their heels. Adams turned and pointed to the larger of the two.

"That's Zeus." The dog ran up to her in response to his name. "And that one's Ares." She patted both dogs firmly on their backsides. "On watch," she commanded and pointed back to the front door. The dogs halted their play and ran off to guard the entrance to their domain.

"You're into Greek mythology, then?" Erin asked as she looked around.

Adams's fondness for the Greeks was evident in more than just the names she'd chosen for her dogs. The house was decorated in whites and light earth tones, with various statues and busts of Greek gods and goddesses. Large tapestries depicted a thriving Athens, while expensive silk drapes hung in layers, framing huge picture windows that allowed for a breathtaking view of the valley below.

"You might say that. How about a drink?" She led them into the kitchen, where she retrieved two glasses without waiting for Erin to answer. She plucked ice cubes from the stainless-steel freezer and looked expectantly at Erin.

"Sure." Erin returned her wandering gaze to Adams. She was in awe of the house and completely confused as to where dinner was going to appear from.

As if reading her thoughts, Adams poured their drinks and said, "Dinner should be here any minute now. I hope you like what I ordered." She filled their glasses with sloe gin and orange juice, topping them off with a splash of grenadine. "Here you go, a sloe screw."

"Very funny." Erin took the drink and sipped at it, enjoying its tangy flavor.

Adams grinned her heart-stopping grin. "I thought you might like that." She walked around the kitchen counter and took Erin's hand. "Come on, I'll show you the backyard."

They walked out through large French doors and into the darkness of the backyard. Adams took a remote control from just outside the door and pushed several buttons, bringing the yard to life.

Accent lights came on, casting the queen palms and other vegetation in a warm glow. A large pool sat in the center of the landscaped yard, the lights bathing the water in alternating colors of purple, blue, and green against the pool's stony sides. A waterfall ran down the slabs of stone between the pool and its adjoining spa. The entire place had the look and feel of a desert oasis, snuggled against the mountainside.

An elaborate chime sounded, and Erin heard the dogs barking from inside the house.

"That must be dinner." Adams handed Erin the remote. "Feel free to find us some music." She went back inside the house, leaving Erin alone.

Erin crossed to the edge of the pool and sat down in one of the deck chairs, examining the heavy box in her hand. The first few buttons were wired to the lighting system in the yard and in the pool. She played around with the lights in the pool before returning to the alternating colors of lights. The next button she tried brought the spa to life with a loud whoosh of the jets.

"Oh no."

The jets shot out with maximum force, causing the water to boil in giant waves. She turned sharply at a different sound and was greeted by two ecstatic Dobermans as they ran toward her from their dog door. After kissing her, the taller one ran over to the spa and tried to attack the water by biting through it.

"Shit!" She cursed at herself, fumbling with the buttons. Finally, she was able to set the jets on low, and she relaxed and eased back in her seat. The dog sneezed and pawed at his snout, trying to get rid of the water he had no doubt inhaled.

Erin noticed then that Elizabeth Adams was standing by the back door looking into the kitchen, where two men dressed in white were working. Absently, she pushed another button, and a noise sounded from the stones surrounding the pool and spa. Small speakers rose up out of the fixtures.

"Whoa." Another button made music softly play. Erin breathed a sigh of relief, thankful she'd finally found the right button and hadn't broken anything. "This place is one big sex pad," she whispered to herself, gazing around the romantic setting. She wondered if there was a button for a pink rotating bed with leopard-skin pillows.

"Ready to eat?" Adams called, and Erin about jumped out of her skin.

She got to her feet and joined Adams at the door, trying not to react to the smoldering look she was getting. The look was definitely one of hunger, and Erin quickly surmised that she was the main course.

One of the gentlemen in white greeted Erin and led the way to the dining room, which overlooked the twinkling lights of the valley below. Tapers on the table and thick candles on some of the surrounding Greek pillars cast a dim light in the room.

"Madam." The man pulled out a chair for Erin, then quickly removed himself after a glance from Adams.

Taking the seat across from Erin, Adams poured them each a glass of white wine and asked, "Do you like lobster?"

Erin took the glass Adams passed her and sipped, savoring the wine's exquisite flavor. "I love lobster," she remembered to answer.

"Good, then we'll start with that."

"We're going to start with lobster?" Erin nearly choked on her wine.

Liz merely smiled. "Relax, it's just a salad."

Erin felt her cheeks redden at her outburst and sipped her wine nervously. The gentleman in white reappeared and Adams gave him some orders, sending him back to the kitchen.

"So, Katherine, what do you do for a living?" A flicker of mischief hinted in Adams's eyes, and Erin knew she'd already had her name checked out.

She toyed with the notion of lying, just to see what Adams would do. "I'm self-employed." She looked away from the piercing eyes and fingered the wineglass.

A different, taller man in white, wearing a chef's hat proudly upon his head, walked briskly into the room carrying two plates. He gave Erin a warm but cautious smile and placed each plate carefully in front of the women, careful to serve Erin first.

"Ladies, this is my chilled lobster salad with basil-lime salsa. It's served atop fresh Romaine lettuce, spicy watercress, and fresh corn. Enjoy." He eyed Adams nervously before walking away.

Erin took a bite of the salad and sighed at the burst of flavor in her mouth.

"How is it?" Adams was watching her intently, eagerly awaiting her reaction.

"Wonderful," Erin replied, a little too excited. She scolded herself, remembering she had to play it cool.

Adams smiled at her, apparently pleased with herself. "Self-employed, huh? You're not going to tell me what you do for a living?"

Erin continued to eat, wishing they could momentarily nix the small talk so she would be free to enjoy the meal with her guard down. "Why should I tell you? You already know."

Adams stopped eating and stared at her. "What do you mean?" Her tone had changed, her voice almost a ragged whisper.

Erin sipped her wine. The intense stare weighed her down like an invisible force, and it made the air thick and hard to breathe. "Please, give me some credit, Liz. You're obviously a very wealthy and powerful woman. And you said it yourself last night when you called me—my number wasn't hard for you to get. Nor was my address, for that matter." She took another slow, deliberate sip of her wine. "So, I'm assuming you took the liberty of finding out everything you could about me. Including my occupation." It was a risk for her to approach the woman this way, and she wasn't sure if she'd made the right decision.

Adams continued to stare, but she did sit back a little in her chair. She moved her mouth to speak, then seemed to change her mind, seemingly at a loss for words.

Erin decided to let her off the hook. "I'm a writer." She let the words penetrate the darker woman's force field as she refilled their glasses.

Adams cleared her throat and placed her palms on the table. "I'm sorry if I offended you by finding out your phone number."

The words were said softly but strongly, and Erin saw the brewing storm clouds in her eyes. It was obvious not too many people called Elizabeth Adams on things, and it seemed a very real possibility that those who did wound up dead.

"And my address." Erin decided to push her just a tad further.

"Excuse me?" Adams was confused, or pretending to be. Or maybe she was also testing whether Erin would keep the heat on her.

"You not only found out my phone number, but my address as well." Erin watched as the clouds vanished from those eyes, replaced by ice.

An uneasy silence stretched between them, as if each was waiting for the other to weaken.

"I'm sorry for all of it." Adams blinked and met Erin's eyes.

The apology was obviously difficult for her to voice, and Erin wondered if this was the first time she had ever backed down this way. She lowered her eyes. Had she pushed her too hard? One of the men returned and took their salad plates. The silence was unbearable, and Erin knew she needed to do something, anything.

"Apology accepted." The ice in Adams's eyes held firm, not cracking. "Am I to assume, then, that you are more than a little interested in me? After all, you went to so much trouble to find me, and now all of this." Erin motioned with her hands at the elaborate dinner setting.

"I'm very interested in you." The ice was finally starting to melt.

"Do you always go to such lengths with women you are interested in?" Erin rested her elbows on the table, cradling her chin with her hands.

"I usually don't have to." Adams sat motionless, her confidence unwavering.

"You're implying that I've been less than cooperative?"

"Something like that." A twitch of a playful grin formed at the corner of Adams's mouth.

Erin breathed deep, thankful that she hadn't pissed the woman off. But just to be on the safe side, she decided that she should try to explain. "I'm a very private person, Liz." She spoke softly but held her tone firm. "And I'm not easily impressed with wealth."

Adams shifted a bit in her chair. "Lesson well learned."

The man returned with their entrees, and they dined in comfortable silence for a while, Erin eating more than Adams, who ate slowly and quietly. She did take the time to refill their wine, and Erin gave her a grateful smile.

"I'm glad you like the food," Adams remarked.

"Like it? Are you kidding? It's the best I've eaten in a long while." Erin knew she sounded more than impressed, but she also knew it would take some work to warm her companion up again. Mindful that she needed to get her talking again, she said, "You're spoiling me."

"It's my pleasure."

"So, why so interested in me?"

Adams put her fork down, the flicker of life returning to her eyes. "Honestly?"

Erin nodded encouragement.

"Well, at first it was your looks. You're very easy on the eyes." This remark was said in a deeper, more seductive tone. "But then, after I spoke to you, it became more."

"More?" Erin felt the heat returning to her cheeks in response to the intense attention. The flattery was affecting her, causing involuntary responses in her body. She took another sip of wine, willing it to release the hot blood in her cheeks.

"You aren't like most women. You want more than a meaningless fling or the flair of money and power. You demand more."

Erin lowered her eyes guardedly and continued to sip her wine. Patricia Henderson had been right. Adams found Katherine Chandler's elusiveness intriguing. Already, she had her pegged and was lifting her game in response. Patricia was turning out to be right about a lot of things.

"I hope I wasn't too frank." Adams allowed her plate to be cleared.

"No, not at all. You were fine." Erin hoped she sounded cool, relaxed, and unperturbed.

"Would you like dessert?"

"Oh my gosh, I don't know."

"Maybe just a bite?"

Erin sighed and laughed. "You twisted my arm."

"We'll share dessert," Adams informed the man. She rose and walked over to Erin, pulling her chair closer to her. "I thought maybe after this we could go for a swim." The suggestion was put out in the air lightly, as if she were treading very carefully with Erin.

"I don't have a suit."

Adams raised her eyebrow mischievously.

"Oh no! No, you don't! Don't even think about it!"

Adams laughed heartily and clasped her hands over Erin's in an effort to calm her. "I'm kidding. I have dozens of suits. Several of them are brand new, never worn."

Erin thought about fanning herself to cool the hot blood that rushed to her face like a flash flood. The thought of skinny-dipping with Liz Adams sent her heart racing and her blood pumping. Images of the woman diving nude into the tropical paradise in the backyard excited her as well as aroused her—two things she definitely should not have been feeling.

This was not good. She was finding that she was way too attracted to the beautiful murder suspect. But she couldn't tell her no, not after she'd pushed her so far over dinner.

"I promise I'll behave. And I've kept my hands-off promise so far. Well, up until now." Adams removed her hands from Erin's.

"Yes, I suppose you have."

"So what do you say?" Adams grinned at her playfully.

"Sure, a swim sounds nice." The boys back at the station were probably getting a real kick out of listening to this. Right about now, Erin knew they were wishing they had hidden cameras in the backyard. She hoped J.R. wasn't broadcasting her attempt at seduction for all to hear.

Before the conversation could get any more embarrassing, the chef returned with a single plate and huge smile. He was obviously pleased that his food had been received so well. Adams had probably threatened to make his life hell if it wasn't. After describing the dessert, a hot apple-macadamia crisp, he left them alone, and Adams took a spoon and scooped up a sizable, steaming bite.

She maneuvered the spoon toward Erin. "Careful, it's hot."

Their eyes locked. Erin's chest was rising and falling quickly, and she was certain Adams could see right through her. She blew on the apple crisp and took a slow bite, careful to wrap her lips snugly around the spoon as Adams pulled it back out.

"Mmm." She kept her eyes locked on the other woman's, knowing the sight of her eating was turning Adams on. "Now, your turn." She picked up the other spoon and dug out a bite. "Careful, it's hot." She grinned and blew on the pastry.

Adams placed her hand over Erin's and leaned in to take a bite. The scene was erotic and captivating, causing butterflies to fly madly in Erin's stomach, despite the meal she'd just eaten.

"How is the apple crisp, ladies?" The younger man stood in the entrance of the room with his hands clasped politely in front of him.

A low growl escaped from Adams as she tore her eyes from Erin's. "Fine. Thank you." Anger laced her words, and the server quickly removed himself from their presence.

She turned to once again look at Erin. "Now, where were we?" She picked up her spoon to scoop out another bite, but Erin stopped her by placing her hand over Adams's.

"I can't eat another bite, Liz. I'm stuffed." She offered a reluctant smile. "But it was very good. It was wonderful." Catching the disappointment on Adams's face, Erin was glad that she wasn't the man who had interrupted them.

Adams rose and kissed Erin's hand with soft, warm, lingering lips. "I'm glad you enjoyed it. Please allow me to wrap things up with our chefs. Make yourself at home."

For a minute or so, Erin waited, physically cringing, preparing herself for the screaming she was sure she would hear after Adams vanished. But when there was no yelling, she relaxed and rose to wander about the house.

She made her way into a sunken living room, which held an enormous gas fireplace and several large, feather-stuffed sofas. She noticed there were no photos of family or friends on the walls, none on the tables. A beautiful oil painting of a woman lounging in the nude hung on the wall. The woman was pale, her skin like cream. Her features were classic and her body curvaceous.

"Do you like it?" Adams had returned in stealthy silence to stand at Erin's side.

"It's beautiful. She's beautiful."

"Yes, she is. Too bad she doesn't exist."

"She doesn't?"

"Not actually, no. That's Aphrodite."

Erin heard clanking in the kitchen and knew the two men would soon be gone and she would be left alone with Elizabeth Adams. The thought made her nervous, but not because she physically feared for her safety.

"Are you Greek?" She tried her best to sound at ease.

"I'm not sure."

Erin recalled that Adams had been raised by an aunt and uncle, her paternity unknown, as were the whereabouts of her mother. "You look like you could be."

"Think so?"

"Yes." Captivated by her beauty, Erin forced herself to look away.

Adams excused herself to see the chef and his assistant out of the house. From the profuse thanks Erin overheard, she guessed they'd been given a sizable tip.

"Ready for that swim?" Adams asked when she returned.

"Sure." Erin shrugged, praying the pool water was cold enough to cool her blood down.

"I'll go get you a suit."

While she waited, Erin wandered slowly around the house, noting how neat it was. Not a single thing seemed to be out of place. She thought about looking in some drawers but didn't want to risk that with Adams in the house. Not to mention the fact that the house was probably wired with cameras, just like the club.

"Here we go."

Erin turned at the sound of the voice to find Adams wearing nothing but a black string bikini. She almost covered her eyes against the sight of the nearly nude, incredibly fit woman standing so proudly in front of her and offering her a bathing suit.

Erin looked away from the sculpted body before her and focused on the two scraps of material Adams handed her. "It's so small." She held it up to examine.

Adams shrugged her shoulders. "I'm sorry. I have others somewhere, but that's all I could find."

The apology sounded hollow, and Erin toyed with the tags on the tiny white suit, debating whether or not she should swim. She could almost hear the guys at the station cheering her on.

"You can change in here." Adams took her hand, giving her no more time to refuse.

Erin followed her to a guest bathroom, noticing her strong, tanned legs and perfectly shaped buttocks. *How can anyone who eats have an ass like that?*

"Come on out to the pool when you're ready." Adams flashed a perfect smile.

Erin watched her walk away, then closed the door to the bathroom and locked it. She made a quick, proficient sweep of the room, checking and double-checking for hidden cameras. Her previous narcotics assignments had left her well trained in the art of planting and retrieving hidden devices, and she knew the numerous locations to house them. The only place she couldn't check for sure was the mirror.

Uncertain what could lie behind it, she walked over to the toilet, out of the mirror's range, and took off her clothes, carefully removing the wire concealed in her bra.

"I'm going to put you someplace where I'll know you'll feel right at home, J.R.," she whispered, standing before the toilet and carefully lifting the lid to the tank. Using the beige-tinted tape that had held the wire to her skin, she secured the small black piece inside the tank and replaced the lid. She then stripped off her remaining clothes and set about covering herself with the Band-Aids and string Adams had so happily provided.

Thank God she managed her bikini line on a regular basis, she thought, standing before the mirror in the tiny white suit. Feeling unbelievably self-conscious, she gave herself the once-over from every angle possible. She didn't look half bad, her body being fit and toned, although nothing like Adams's. That woman didn't have an ounce of fat on her. She was all sleek, lean muscle, and beautifully bronzed by the sun.

Erin took a deep breath. "Well, here goes."

George Michael crooned from the speakers in the backyard. It was now completely dark, the accent lights turned off. The pool light was now purple, and Erin breathed a little easier, knowing that she would be harder to see.

"There you are." Adams was in the pool, resting her hands and forearms on the cool deck at the edge.

The pool changed color, casting a brighter glow on Erin. She hugged herself as if she were cold, and Adams grinned at her like a wet devil.

"I see the bikini fits. Barely." Her eyes burned trails up and down Erin's body. "Are you really cold, or are you just embarrassed?"

She hoisted herself up out of the pool and slinked up to stand in front of Erin. She stood so close Erin could see the water dripping from her hands, her hair, the dark lashes that framed her eyes.

The warm night air shook in her nervous lungs, and she had to cough to clear them. "I'm fine."

She realized she was still hugging herself like a scared fool and let her hands fall to her sides. For a moment, she was afraid Adams was going to touch her, but the woman walked past her and retrieved two glasses off a nearby table.

"I took the liberty of making you another sloe screw."

Erin accepted the drink and thanked her. She sipped at it carefully, afraid to have much more, already feeling the effects from all the wine she had consumed at dinner.

"So, you coming in?" Adams walked past her back to the pool, where she deposited her drink on the cool deck before gracefully diving back in.

Erin crossed to the steps of the pool and set down her drink. The water was warmer than she had hoped for, feeling more like a lukewarm, dark purple bath. She stood on the last step, up to her waist in water, and looked around anxiously for Adams. She suddenly felt very vulnerable, like she was swimming in water full of hungry sharks.

Adams emerged from the water directly in front of her, startling her, causing her to lose her balance and fall from the step. Strong, slender arms steadied her.

"You okay?" Adams asked.

They were standing a mere inch apart in shoulder-high water. The glowing water had changed to a lighter green, and it played in dancing white lines across Adams's strong jawline. Her eyes were alive and bright blue, piercing Erin to the core.

"I'm fine." The words sputtered out like a car that couldn't quite start. Erin tried to back up, but she couldn't move quickly enough.

"Do you like George Michael?" Adams was pressed to her, pinning her against the pool wall.

Thrown by the question, Erin shook her head. "Huh?"

"George Michael. Do you like his music?" The question was like a soft purr, pouring out of those inviting lips.

"Sure, I guess. I haven't really listened to him in a while." She was nervous and rambling, her body screaming for this woman's touch.

"His music gets me hot." Adams leaned in and nibbled on Erin's earlobe.

Blood pounded up to her cheeks, and she felt her skin come alive. Adams pressed further, and Erin had no choice but to wrap her legs around her and cling to her in order to stay afloat.

"I thought you promised to keep your hands to yourself." She was quickly losing control of her body, but she was too turned on to be angry.

"I am." Adams moved away from the wall with Erin still wrapped around her. "I haven't touched you with my hands." She leaned in again and kissed Erin's neck with soft, lingering kisses. "Shh, just relax and listen to the music."

Erin breathed deep and tried to control her senses. The soft kisses, the feel of the strong, sinewy body beneath her, sent her mind reeling along with her flesh. Adams moved her mouth back up to Erin's ear, where she began singing. The words were like velvet, softly playing to Erin's libido.

She gripped Adams harder as the feel of the hot breath in her ear became too much to bear. The other woman took full advantage of the reaction and wrapped her hands around Erin's butt, holding her tight and rocking her body against Erin's as she continued to sing the suggestive lyrics of the song.

The pool, the desert night, even the song lyrics became distant and foggy as Erin felt her blood pump wildly and heavily throughout her body. Adams purred in her ear like a lioness seeking a mate, and Erin couldn't help but move in rhythm with her, trying desperately to ignite the spark that was pulsing between her legs. Adams moved her mouth to Erin's neck and bit down lightly, causing her to buck her hips and nearly orgasm. A raspy groan escaped her throat, smacking her back into reality. She pushed herself away, and Adams reluctantly released her grip.

"What's wrong?" She moved back toward Erin, slinking in the water.

"Uh, nothing." Erin had to think fast. "Restroom. I need to go." *Brilliant, Erin, and so tactfully stated.*

"I'll be right here...waiting." The words floated up to Erin as she climbed out of the pool. "Katherine?"

Erin turned to her as the water once again lightened a shade.

Adams stood grinning in the pool, looking her up and down like a ravenous predator. "You remember where the bathroom is?" The question was a stall, obviously a tactic for Adams to examine her standing there in the white bikini, dripping like a wet dog.

The warm wind blew, puckering Erin's nipples. She looked around for a towel but saw none. "I remember," she said and headed into the house. She was freezing, but it wasn't just the cold that made her shiver as she switched on the bathroom light.

Catching her reflection in the mirror, she knew right away why Adams had wanted her to turn around in the wet swimsuit. The wet bikini was virtually see-through. The fabric molded to her breasts and her dark honey nipples like a second skin. She glanced down at the bottoms and saw the shadow of her hair.

"God damn it." She clenched her jaw as she looked into the mirror. *Whoever said going after a woman would be easier oughtta be shot.* She was angry and she felt incredibly exposed. Frustrated and cold, she sat on the toilet to urinate but found that she couldn't go. She wasn't worried about J.R. hearing her; she knew that he couldn't from inside the tank. At most it would sound like an echo, and he deserved to hear people piss. His mind was always in the toilet anyhow.

She felt pressure like she needed to pee, yet nothing was happening. With a wad of toilet paper, she reached down to wipe out of habit. The paper slid across her and she brought it back up to examine it.

"What the hell?" She was wet. Not wet from the water, but wet with slick juices. She dropped the tissue paper back in the toilet and touched herself with her bare hand. "Oh my God," she whispered to herself. Never before had her body reacted this way, so strongly, spinning such an elaborate web of warm silk. *Is this what it's like to be truly turned on?*

A scratching came from the door, and she jerked her hand away like a teenager caught masturbating. "Uh…just a minute!" She jerked up the cold swimsuit bottoms and washed her hands in the sink. The scratching came again, along with a snort from the bottom of the door.

She dried her hands and yanked open the door. One of the Dobermans stood staring up at her, wagging its stubby tail. "Hi there, puppy." She patted his head and walked out of the bathroom. Looking down the hall, she saw it was empty and tiptoed to the end. Slowly opening the door, she looked into the dimly lit master bedroom. A massive bed sat to one side of the large room, accompanied by lightly stained furniture with dark marble tops. She knew the room was Adams's because she could smell her cologne.

Not wanting to get caught by spying cameras or eyes, she pulled the door carefully closed, knowing that she should return to the pool.

She was just about to turn around when a deep growl came from behind. Turning slowly, she came face-to-face with the larger Doberman. He was showing his teeth at her, just as he had done when she had first arrived. His head was held low, his tail unmoving.

She held up her hands in mock defeat. "Uh, nice puppy. Good boy, Apollo, or whatever your name is."

"Actually, that's Zeus." Adams stepped into the hallway. "And Ares is in the other room."

"Oh, well, they look so much alike." Erin tried to laugh, but it came out in weird squeaks. "Where's that bathroom again?"

"It's down the hall on your left." Her voice was low as she looked Erin up and down again, clearly enjoying the see-through swimsuit.

Erin trotted off past her, cursing herself mentally for almost getting caught. Thank God she hadn't walked into the room. What did she think she would find, anyhow? The smoking gun?

Back in the relative safety of the bathroom, she stripped off the suit and retrieved the wire, placing it in her jeans pocket. Too bad if J.R. couldn't hear. She had to get out of this place and clear her mind. She ran her hands through her hair and exited the room, convinced that Adams would be more than willing to get rid of her nosy new friend.

Down the hallway, a flickering light came from the master bedroom. Adams lay on the bed, wrapped in a towel with the remote in her hand. The footboard of the bed housed a massive flat-screen TV that apparently rose up at the touch of a button. Two women were kissing on the screen.

Avoiding the image, Erin said, "I thought maybe you could take me back to the club now. I'm feeling a little exposed." Her voice was back under control.

Adams pushed a button, and the TV shut off and descended back into the footboard. "I was hoping you would watch my new movie with me and tell me what you thought. It's not every day that I meet a writer, you know."

She was trying to flatter once again, but Erin was too keyed up to let it affect her. "Some other time, maybe." She shoved her hands in her back pockets.

Adams rose and stripped off the towel and black bikini, apparently not caring if Erin saw her naked. "Okay, then. I'll take you back."

Erin looked away from the gorgeous body and stared at the floor. "I had a really nice time tonight. Thank you." She didn't want to end things badly; she needed to keep their suspect intrigued and coming back for more.

"I'm glad." Adams pulled on her jeans. "I hope we can do it again, then?"

"I'm not sure. Things got a little…"

"Exciting?"

"You broke your promise."

"I thought you wanted me to." Adams eased into her black cotton shirt. "You reacted to me. I felt it."

"I am attracted to you, Liz. Physically. But I'm not attracted to your games." Erin brushed past her.

"You think I'm playing games?" Adams caught her arm. Her face was very serious, her cheeks flushed with color.

"I'm not sure," Erin replied.

Adams reached out to stroke her face with a warm hand. "I want to see you again," she whispered. "Please say yes."

Erin hesitated, momentarily overcome with the powerful stirrings of her insides. "Okay."

Adams smiled softly and dropped her hand from Erin's arm. "You won't be sorry."

CHAPTER EIGHT

The ride back to the club was uneventful. The only difference from the earlier ride was the pulse of excitement and wetness that was now beating between her legs. Erin clung to Adams, having no choice in the matter, which fueled her physical flame of desire. Resting her cheek against the other woman's back, she closed her eyes and enjoyed the freedom of the ride.

It didn't take long before she felt the bike slow, and she opened her eyes as they pulled into the parking lot of La Femme. A few lonely cars dotted the parking lot, leaving them virtually alone in the darkness.

Adams drove out to where Erin's white Honda sat patiently awaiting her return, came to a stop, and killed the powerful engine. She quickly stood and turned on the bike to face Erin.

Erin expected her to speak, to slather on some more charm, but instead she tilted Erin's chin gently with her hand, and looking deep into her eyes, lowered her head, planting a warm, lingering kiss on her sensitive lips.

The kiss was soft and gentle, yet completely demanding. Erin knew she should pull away, for the kiss was too warm, too tender, too much for her to handle. But she remained locked, frozen in a world where she herself was melting.

Adams drew back slowly and stroked Erin's jaw with her hand. "I'll call you."

Erin stared into the blue abyss of her eyes and nodded. Then, willing herself to move, she dismounted the bike and went to her car. As she started it up to drive away, she turned took one last look at the woman with the midnight mane straddling her black stallion. Heart dancing in her chest, she gripped the wheel and forced herself to look away. As she drove, her pulse eventually calmed and her mind soon settled. But hard as she tried to erase it, the image of Liz remained.

❖

Kristen Reece had been staring, transfixed, at the security monitors, each one flashing a different location, all capturing the same moment in time. One monitor in particular had consumed her attention for several minutes and she squinted at the grainy image, wishing she could zoom the lens in closer to get a better look.

Liz was straddling her bike, facing the cute blonde Kristen herself had first laid claim to. As she watched, Liz leaned in for a kiss, and Kristen was surprised at how gentle it appeared. Tenderness was not something she had experienced with her dark friend. Sex between them had always been incredible and powerful, an erotic battle. Soft, tender kisses would have no place in that battleground. But it didn't mean that it wasn't something she had wished for.

"Christ." She walked away from the monitors and flopped down on the couch.

Here she was, tense, worried, and panicked, while Liz was off fucking another stranger, another conquest. Why should she be surprised? This was how it always was, how it always had been. She was always the one who was left doing the dirty work—or sweeping up the dirty work of others—while Liz focused on her own needs and kept her hands clean of everything.

She got up and paced the room, too worked up to sit still. She was quickly growing weary of Liz and the way she ruled with absolute power and nonchalance. Kristen knew she was the one who should be running things. She was the one who cared, who thought things through, who paid attention to every last detail. And what did she have to show for it? Nothing. Not a thing. A shitty job tending bar, maybe the occasional bit part in one of Liz's movies. Hell, she didn't even have Liz. And if she was honest with herself, that was what she really wanted, regardless of how unobtainable she knew the woman was. But it was so easy to fall for her, to kid herself into thinking that she was the one who could change her. To get her to settle down, to be the one to finally reach her.

Liz was the reason Kristen had gotten involved in this mess in the first place. Because there was a time, not so long ago, when she would've done anything for Liz. But not now. Now she wanted control, and she wanted out. And she was the only one who could take care of things. Like the cops and the numerous loose ends.

"What the hell are you doing in here?" Liz stood in the doorway, her hands clenched by her sides.

Kristen turned and smiled coyly. "Waiting for you, darling."

"What are you doing in here?" Liz slammed the door closed and walked over to look at the monitors, her gaze focused on the same one Kristen had been watching moments earlier. Whoever the cute blonde was, she sure had Liz's full attention.

"So did you fuck her yet?" Kristen demanded, ignoring the question.

Liz clenched her jaw, her fury obviously growing. "None of your fucking business."

Kristen laughed at the touchy reply and flopped down on the couch, arms folded across her chest. "Whoa, guess that answers my question." She wondered what was going on with the blonde. No one turned Liz down, especially in the bedroom. "Serves you right, you know. Especially since I saw her first."

Liz sighed and tossed her keys on the counter. "I think we're done here, Kris. I'm busy." Her voice was low, a fierce grumble.

"We need to talk."

"About what?"

"What do you think?" Kristen knew her voice sounded as tightly strung as her emotions.

Liz walked into the adjoining room, untucking her shirt as she walked. "There's nothing to talk about."

"The hell there isn't!"

Liz turned, her eyes ablaze, but her voice still low and calm. "Will you quit being a princess and tell me what it is that has you so excited?"

"Oh, well, at least I finally got your attention." Kristen resented how calm Liz was, how calm she always was. If she hadn't felt it firsthand, she would have wondered if the other woman even had a pulse. Nothing ever seemed to worry her. With the exception of her incredible temper and even more incredible sex drive, Kristen had never seen Liz get excited. The more she thought about it, the more it infuriated her. "While you were off playing with blondie, I was stuck here with the cops up my ass!"

Liz walked slowly back into the room, her face tight. "What happened?"

"They were here, asking me questions, talking to some of our girls, some of the customers." Kristen's voice quivered a little as she spoke. "And where the fuck were you? Off on a date? Since when do you *date,* Liz?"

Liz's eyes glinted with anger. "What I do, and with whom, is my own business, and you would be wise to remember that."

Kristen was coming close to lighting a very dangerous fuse, but she didn't care. "It is my business. Especially when you leave me here to cover for you. You think I wouldn't rather be off fucking that blonde instead of answering to the police?"

"Her name is Katherine." Liz seethed visibly.

Why is she so caught up and concerned about this woman? Didn't she hear what I just said? "What's with you? Since when do you give a fuck what somebody's name is?"

"Since now." The statement was a warning.

Kristen studied her carefully. Liz's jaw was set, and a vein in her neck pumped the hot blood of a rising temper. She knew she should tread lightly, but the circumstances had pushed her beyond rational behavior. Even though it was dangerous to act so irrationally, she couldn't seem to stop herself. Why couldn't she just get up and walk out of the room, leave Liz alone to face the demons that were chasing them all?

She remained seated, fear halting her flight. Fear of the police, fear of Liz's uncaring demeanor. Kristen didn't know what it would take to get her to see the seriousness of their situation. Liz was pissed at her, that much was clear. But there was something else there too. Distance. It was as if she were looking right through her, her thoughts somewhere else altogether.

It was that woman. She had never seen Elizabeth Adams distracted like this over a woman. It was as if the police and the investigation were mere gnats, something she could swat at and easily handle. An annoyance in her rosy private world of romance. In the past, Liz's dates had stayed with her at the club or they went out after closing time.

Kristen had never seen her drop everything and escort a woman out of the crowded club. She couldn't believe it, but here she was witnessing it. It was finally happening—Liz was smitten.

"Jesus, this Katherine—she's gotten to you, hasn't she?"

Liz was silent for a moment. "Like I said before, my personal life is none of your business." Her tone made it clear that Kristen needed to back off, otherwise there would be hell to pay.

"Whatever. Just make sure you don't get so far into her that you forget there are things here that need to be taken care of."

"Like what?"

"The police, for starters!"

"They're bluffing." Liz sat down, seemingly bored, and propped her feet up on the coffee table. "They don't have anything on us, that's why they're doing what they're doing. To shake us up."

"I don't give a flying fuck why they're doing it! I want out."

Liz laughed. "Out? Out of what? Jesus, Kris, I really had more respect for you than this. You're doing exactly what they want you to do. Show some balls, for God's sake."

"What about Jay?" The question was asked in a frantic whisper, her voice lowered at the importance of the question.

"What about her?" Liz was still calm but clearly annoyed.

"She's out of control, fucking insane. I just don't even know what she'll do next." Kristen grabbed her temples, her hands shaking, her nerves on edge.

Liz leaned forward, her voice low and completely serious. "Jay will be fine, you will be fine. Just relax."

Kristen shook her head. "I can't do this anymore. I'm bailing." She stood as she spoke.

"No, you're not. You can't."

"Look, I know I made promises and I'll honor them. I'll take care of everything, make it all go away. And then I'll be free to get out."

"You can't, Kris. You won't." Liz stood and grabbed her shoulders, lightly shaking her.

"We'll see about that." Kristen looked her dead in the eye, shook off the restraining grip, and walked out of the room, leaving Liz alone to stare through the open door after her.

Chapter Nine

Patricia Henderson entered the conference room and sat next to her longtime partner, Gary Jacobs. He greeted her with a short smile and pushed a cup of coffee her way.

"Thanks," she said. "We got anything new?"

Gary was busy scribbling notes in his notebook. "A new hair," he replied in his monotone voice.

"Found on our last victim, on Bale?" Excitement lifted her voice, reminding her why she loved detective work.

"Forensics gave us the report on it this morning."

She could tell by his lack of enthusiasm that the hair was not a match to Adams or Reece, their two prime suspects. "So, it doesn't have a source?"

"Not one that we know about." He stopped writing and handed her the report. "The lab says it's a short, dark brown hair, nonpubic in origin, most likely Caucasian, partial root intact."

"But we don't know yet if it's from a male or female." Patricia scanned the report.

"Not yet, but they are going to try to extract DNA. I wouldn't get your hopes up, though."

"That'll take a while." She sighed in defeat and looked up as Jeff Hernandez and Martin Stewart walked into the room.

"Look at it this way," Gary said. "Someone finally screwed up and left us a crumb."

Patricia thought back to the club, to some of Adams's cronies. Could the hair belong to one of them? Was there a third party? None of the evidence they had so far suggested a third suspect. There were only witnesses claiming to have seen the victims with a tall blonde closely resembling Kristen Reece. And then, of course, there were the witnesses who had heard Adams verbally threaten the victims. That was it. That was all they had.

The room was unusually quiet, and Patricia felt like a zombie. Her recent lack of sleep was quickly catching up to her. The previous night had been the worst. She had spent most of it tossing and turning, the kiss between Erin and Adams eating her alive. She cringed as she remembered the tenderness she had witnessed. Jealous bile rose in her throat as she tried to clear the intimate image from her mind. She forced her gaze from the mesmerizing grain of the conference table and focused on Sergeant Ruiz.

"Good morning, everyone." He sounded like another person who had the Monday-morning blues. They all grumbled their replies and he began his usual pacing as he talked. "I've spoken with Mac just this morning, and she tells me that things are going well and as planned."

Patricia glanced down at the briefings before her. Transcripts of the conversations between Erin and Adams played out before her on paper. It seemed Erin had tested the waters with Adams, a gutsy move on her part. And even more surprising was the fact that Adams had kept her cool. But what disturbed her was the story the transcripts didn't tell. Erin had removed the wire to swim with their suspect, and the thought of her alone and nearly nude with Adams made Patricia's blood boil.

Whatever happened in the pool had led to the kiss she'd witnessed in the parking lot. Maybe there had been more kissing in the pool. She shook her head at the disturbing thoughts, knowing she was getting too involved emotionally in this case. She tried her best not to think about Adams seducing Erin and vice versa, but everywhere she turned, she was faced with these scenarios. And more than anything, she worried for Erin's safety and emotional well-being.

"I have some news for you all." Ruiz tossed some photos down on the table. "These are subpoenaed photos from Elizabeth Adams's surveillance cameras in La Femme. If you'll look closely, you'll see Adams is present in all of them. And if you'll note the date and time, you'll see that each photo clears her of the last murder. She was at her club the night Jonathan Bale was killed."

Various curse words were mumbled as the detectives looked at the photos that provided their chief suspect with watertight alibis.

"What about Reece? Was she there?" Gary asked.

"Not that we can see. Which, frankly, folks, is the only goddamned reason we still have a case!" Ruiz threw one of the files down on the floor as his temper got the better of him. "Otherwise we'd have zip! So you better hope to Christ that Reece wasn't in that club on the night of the murder."

"This still doesn't clear Adams of being involved," Patricia spoke up, more terrified that Adams was slipping away from them than she was of Ruiz's temper.

Ruiz had begun pacing again, which he quickly stopped doing to look at her. "We didn't have much to start with, Henderson, and now we have even less! No DA will touch this! We got nothing on that bitch. And she knows it."

Patricia jerked at his high volume. He was right, no one would prosecute on such scant evidence.

"We gotta get one of her girls to talk," Stewart said. "Reece, we gotta go after Reece." His cigarettes were back in his breast pocket, and Patricia wondered just how long he'd been able to go without lighting up. Given the present circumstances, she thought briefly about asking for one herself.

"I agree," Ruiz said, a little more calmly. "But if she doesn't talk, we're screwed. Forensics found nothing on Bale's body, nothing that points to Adams."

The detectives threw out suggestions and ideas while Patricia leafed through some papers until she found the lab reports on Jonathan Bale, their last victim. The autopsy confirmed the presence of GHB and horse tranquilizer, which had also been found in their other victims. Cause of death was the same. Shot in the head with a 9mm. Ballistics confirmed the bullet came from the same gun as the other two. Four stab wounds to the groin. Most likely done very soon after death, given the lack of blood. Very little trace fiber evidence, most of which could be explained, all except for the one hair.

A single strand of dark hair, which didn't match Adams or Reece and couldn't be linked with anyone Bale knew. If she could find the source of the hair, their questions would be answered.

"Okay, what's our plan?" Ruiz clapped his hands together and held them tight before answering his own question. "We go after Reece, squeeze her and hope something drips out. In the meantime, we're watching our two other possible victims, pals of Bale."

Patricia knew he was referring to the two remaining men Elizabeth Adams had threatened: Thomas Rourke and Scott Bartch, both attorneys.

"If the girls go after these guys, they'll have to be invisible for us not to see them."

"What about Mac?" Patricia asked softly, wishing they would pull Erin out.

"She stays under. I've already spoken with her, and she's willing to remain." Ruiz concluded their meeting and the detectives rose, eager and excited at the prospect of going after Reece.

Erin picked up her cell phone and popped in a freshly charged battery. She hadn't realized until today that it had been dead. As it sounded back to life, it alerted her that she had a voice message. She put the phone to her ear and listened to Mark's voice, returning her call. He sounded the same as he always did, concerned but not really caring. He informed her that his meetings in Austin had gone well and he would be back in town sooner than originally expected. But he needed to cover for some colleagues, and he didn't think she would get to see him any time soon.

She deleted the message and set the phone down. She wondered how much of the message was true and how much was bullshit. She never knew anymore. Briefly, she considered calling him back, then decided against it. She didn't have anything to say to him, and she thought back to why she had called him in the first place.

It was funny how quickly her mind had been occupied with other, bigger things since she had first started this case. Mark seemed so trivial to her now, and it had only been a couple of days since she had found the credit card statement. She was simply numb, shut off—like a robot, intently focused on the task at hand. And frankly, she was better off that way. She didn't need to be dwelling on the mistake her marriage had been.

She sat down and picked up her book, Katherine Chandler's latest. Erin quickly found herself engrossed in the emotions of the women and the raw desire they felt for one another. Her thoughts strayed to Patricia and how talented she truly was to be able to create such realistic characters. She could only long to be graced by a passion like the one the fictional women shared. Closing her eyes, she wondered who had elicited such feelings in Patricia. Surely she would have to experience such incredible feelings in order to write about them? Perhaps not. Perhaps Patricia was just like her. Lonely, wanting, needing. She opened her eyes, feeling very alive at the thought of Patricia and what it would be like to be wanted and needed by her.

With a pang of guilt, she glanced down at the flowers on her coffee table. The roses were now accompanied by a yellow bouquet that had arrived earlier that morning. They harbored another simple message from Liz.

Your kiss still lingers on my lips.

The card made Erin unconsciously touch her lips, the kiss from the previous night replaying in her mind. Never before had she experienced such power in a single kiss. Its ability to make her feel so many different things on so many different levels astonished her. The kiss had been tender, warm, sweet. Yet it was teasing and tantalizing, causing desire and heat to flood through her body. She had wanted more, wanted to probe with her tongue, to suck the sweetness from Liz's lips. Her mind roamed to the phone call that had followed the flower delivery.

In her deep, seductive voice, Liz had beckoned her back to the club on Friday night. She wanted to see Erin sooner, but Erin knew she needed to keep her distance while her colleagues attempted to corner Reece. Ruiz had made it clear to her that she was to stay away from Liz until then. So she'd agreed to meet her at La Femme on Friday night, and Liz reluctantly agreed to wait that long. She informed Erin that it was leather night and she couldn't wait to see her appropriately dressed.

The conversation had left Erin sporting another deep blush. She'd hung up much more excited than an undercover detective should be anticipating her next "date" with a suspect.

For the rest of the day, she'd tried to keep her mind off Elizabeth Adams, lounging around and trying to catch up on some much-needed rest. She glanced down at Patricia's book, ready to once again immerse herself in its plot. But before she could read a complete sentence, the phone rang.

"Mac?" It was Patricia, and she sounded worked up. "Don't worry, the boys said your line was still clear."

"Okay. What's up?"

"Has Kristen Reece contacted you?"

The question surprised her. "You mean outside the club?" She sat up a little, the conversation demanding some attention.

"Yes."

"No, why?"

"She's missing. We arrived at her place with a warrant for her arrest before noon, and her place is trashed and she's nowhere to be found."

"What about surveillance? Wasn't someone watching her?" Erin couldn't believe that one of their prime suspects had just disappeared.

"Off and on. It was costing a fortune to keep both her and Adams under constant surveillance, and since they were both at the club most of the time, the team just started solely watching La Femme. Last night Reece left the club just before Adams, and our boys chose to follow Adams instead of her."

"Maybe she'll be back. She's wild. Maybe she went off for fun or—"

"Mac," Patricia interrupted. "There's blood all over her apartment."

Erin sat in silence for a moment as the words played out in her mind. Visions of Reece flashed before her, smiling, teasing, dancing. And now she was missing, her apartment a mess, covered in blood. "Jesus," she whispered, trying to get a handle on all that was happening and what it could possibly mean.

"Listen, J.R.'s on his way over," Patricia said. "Ruiz wants you to go to Adams, see how she's behaving. You up for it?"

Erin cleared her throat to answer. "Yeah, sure."

"Okay, then, I'll let him know. And Mac?"

"Yeah?"

"Be careful."

Erin pulled up at La Femme and cut the Honda's engine. She sat still for a moment, her heart and mind racing. She had called Liz earlier, claiming she couldn't wait until Friday to see her. The nightclub owner had readily agreed to a meeting, sounding more than delighted and extremely seductive.

A chill swept over Erin as she exited the Honda. With a deep breath, she began walking, rubbing her arms to warm herself even though the heat outside was stifling. Liz had suggested they meet at the club and Erin was nervous, knowing the place would be virtually empty and she would be all alone with Elizabeth Adams.

She walked up to the entrance and found the door locked. Knocking, she lowered her arms and glanced over her attire. She had chosen quickly, pulling on khaki chinos and a tight-fitting maroon blouse. She smoothed down her blouse nervously as the door opened.

Liz stood, smiling at her with appreciation. She was wearing a tight black Under Armour workout shirt with black track pants. "Hi," she said, deep and throaty. Her eyes were alive and welcoming. "Please, come in."

Erin did so slowly, her cheeks already flushing from the other woman's intense but approving scrutiny.

"I was surprised by your call." Liz walked ahead of her, leading them farther into the dim and vacant nightclub.

"I know, I'm sorry about that." Erin considered her options, knowing it was vital not to mention Kristen, but also knowing she needed to try and get Liz talking. "It's just that…" She thought for a moment and then lowered her voice, knowing flattery was the way to go. "I can't stop thinking about that kiss."

Liz instantly stopped walking and turned to face her as they reached the stairs to the VIP room. Slowly, with catlike grace, she approached. Erin swallowed with difficulty and hoped Liz didn't notice her nerves.

A sly grin made its way across Liz's face, and she stopped just inches from Erin. "I've been thinking about it too." She cupped Erin's hip with a strong arm, pulling her closer, so close that Erin could feel the warmth of her breath. "In fact, I can't seem to get it from my mind." She leaned in and brushed Erin's lips with her own.

Heat, intense and powerful, claimed Erin, and her mind swam with desire as she melted into the sweet, soft kiss. Her brain screamed, torn between the seriousness of the investigation and the soul-altering feelings she was experiencing with their number-one suspect. Kristen's image floated across her mind as she felt Liz's probing tongue skim across her lips, beckoning permission to go further. Clenching her legs together, forcing herself to stand despite diminishing strength, she took a step back, gently pushing Liz away.

Liz searched her face with intense eyes. "I'm sorry, was that too forward?" The question was asked softly, gently, taking Erin by complete surprise. The woman was so smooth, so disarming. It was hard to believe she was most likely a killer.

"No, it was…" Erin met her eyes, very much aware of the pounding of her blood in her brain and between her legs. "Nice," she finished softly.

Liz smiled and took her hand. "Come on." She led the way up the stairs.

Erin followed silently, taking in the black outfit, searching for the right words. The heat in her cheeks remained as she realized the kiss they had just shared had been heard by all. Why she cared she didn't know, but she couldn't help but feel violated, like her colleagues had just witnessed something very personal.

Doing her best to shake the thought, she stepped inside Liz's private room and closed the door behind them.

"Please, make yourself at home." Liz offered her a seat.

Erin complied and made herself comfortable on one of the sofas. She studied Liz and noticed for the first time that she was slightly damp with sweat. Feeling a tingle of suspicion, and she shifted a little as her mind raced.

"I hope I didn't interrupt any of your plans." She watched the nightclub owner carefully, searching for clues in her reaction.

"Not at all. I was just working out."

"Oh. You work out a lot, then?" Erin asked, her eyes skimming Liz's sculpted upper body under the tight-fitting shirt.

"Yes, especially when I'm stressed."

Erin sat up a little, seeing a way in. She tried her best to look concerned. "Are you stressed today?"

Eyeing her from her position behind the opposite couch, Liz smiled. "I was. But now I seem to be all better, thanks to you."

"Me?"

"Yes, you're a great distraction."

"Distraction from what?"

"My problems."

Erin laughed softly. "You have problems? I seriously doubt that."

The smile remained on Liz's face. "I do."

"Like what?" She raised an eyebrow and kept her tone light.

Liz moved from behind the couch to sit next to her. "Like… problems with the club." She took Erin's hand, lightly stroking it.

"The club is wonderful. It seems to be a big success," Erin countered, her breath shaky and quick from the sensations coming from her palm.

"There's a lot that comes with that." Liz raised their hands, bringing Erin's up against her lips where she breathed softly and deliberately upon it. "Like employees…"

Erin shuddered, her body responding to Liz's hot breath, her mind responding to the words. "You have problems with your employees?"

"Yes." Liz kissed her hand, her lips lightly brushing across her knuckles.

"Your employees seem nice. Especially that bartender." Erin grinned, knowing the words would strike a nerve, but she had to make Liz think she was teasing her, trying to get a rise.

Liz sat back, her eyes suddenly icy and cold. "Kristen? You like her?"

Erin shrugged. "Sure. She seems nice. Why, is she not so nice?"

Liz rose from the couch hurriedly and made her way to the counter, where she poured herself a drink. "Maybe we should do this another time." The words were cold and distant.

Erin squirmed, feeling the chill sweep across the room. Needing to regain some ground, she said softly, "I'm sorry. I shouldn't have said that. I don't like her, actually. I was just teasing."

Liz took a drink of amber-colored liquor and shook her head. "You didn't do anything wrong." Her blue eyes met Erin's, wounded and troubled. "I'm just dealing with a lot right now."

"You can talk to me." Erin probed gently, carefully.

With a sigh, Liz took another big drink and set down her glass. "No. No, I can't." She stared at Erin long and hard, the cold in her eyes softening, warming.

"Of course not, you hardly know me," Erin whispered, looking away as if she were embarrassed. But something else stirred within her, and she found herself truly feeling for the nightclub owner.

"It's not that." Liz ran a hand through her hair, her eyes once again settling on Erin. "It's…highly personal. Something I don't share with anyone."

The revelation startled Erin, and she found herself beyond curious, not just for the investigation, but for her own personal reasons. Drawn by the uneasiness in Liz's eyes, she stood impulsively and approached her. "You are truly troubled, aren't you?"

Shaking her head slowly, Liz said, "You have no idea."

Unable to stop herself, Erin reached out her hand and stroked Liz's face. "If you ever need to talk, I'm here."

For a moment, Liz seemed to be on the brink of saying something, then her face relaxed and she murmured, "Thank you."

Erin gave her a smile and backed away, knowing it would cause suspicion if she pushed any harder. "We'll do this another time, okay?"

"Friday?" Liz asked, looking hopeful once again.

"Friday," Erin agreed.

She left the room and headed back out into the sun. Her insides churned in turmoil, arousal mixed with suspicion mixed with empathy and concern. Shoving her hands down into her pockets, she let the fierce heat massage her coiled emotions before she climbed back into her car. She glanced down at her chest where the wire sat hidden and all-knowing. Although she hadn't gathered much, there was one thing she had learned. There was more to Elizabeth Adams than met the eye. So much more.

Patricia squatted down next to the beige sofa and rested her latex-gloved hand against its side, her eyes focused on the fold in the cushion on the armrest.

"Has forensics swept the couch yet?" she yelled over her shoulder to no one in particular.

Someone walked over and crouched down next to her, but she was too focused to look to see who it was. She held up her digital camera and snapped a picture just as she had done throughout the apartment.

"No, they're still busy in the bedroom." It was Jeff Hernandez, and he was looking at the same fold in the armrest cushion as he spoke. "They did a preliminary sweep of the small bloodstains on the carpet in here, but nothing on the couch."

Patricia backed off a little, not wanting to contaminate the sofa if it hadn't been cleared yet. The bedroom had been their focal point since arriving on the scene the day before. They'd found it in complete disarray, with the dresser drawers pulled out and dumped and the room's remaining contents strewn all about. Accompanying the mess was a large amount of blood, pools of it on the floor as well as splatter patterns on the floor and walls. And whoever had been in the apartment when the bloodshed had occurred had walked from the bedroom to the living room several times, tracking the blood with their shoes and leaving shoe prints. Boot prints to be exact.

Since yesterday, their team had been going over the bedroom with a fine-tooth comb and apparently had yet to examine the sofa. Patricia could understand why. It was beige and showed no obvious signs of tampering. She stood up and retrieved a small baggie and a pair of tweezers from one of their kits, then returned to her squat.

"Jeff, how about giving me some light over here?"

He rose quickly and turned one of their powerful standing lamps toward the sofa. "What've you got?" He bent down, resting his hands on his knees.

"You see that little piece stuck in between the back cushion of the couch and the cushion of the armrest?" She maneuvered the tweezers to the point of focus and hovered them above the reflective piece protruding slightly from between the cushions.

"What is it?"

"Not sure, but it looks"—she grabbed the small, shiny white piece with the tweezers and held it up in front of the light—"like a tooth."

"It sure does." Jeff took a closer look. "And knocked out pretty hard too."

"Mmm." Patricia eyed the tooth. It appeared to be a front tooth, long and thinner than a molar and separated from its source without the root.

She placed it carefully in the plastic baggie. "Hey, guys, we need forensics in here on the couch!" she called into the back room, prompting two white-suited young men carrying tackle boxes to enter the living room. "I found this embedded between the two cushions over there."

"What's your take so far, Jeff?" she asked as the men carefully vacuumed the sofa for any trace fiber evidence.

"She's gone." Jeff looked around. "Or someone sure wants us to believe that."

"Uh-huh. Most likely dead or seriously injured." The blood they'd tested was of human origin and O positive, Reece's blood type. But that didn't mean it was hers, and even if it was, it didn't mean she was dead. But from the quantity, she had to be seriously injured. And now the tooth. Whoever it belonged to had it knocked out of their head at great force.

They both turned and watched as the two men lifted the cushions off the couch, revealing a small splatter of blood on the armrest where the tooth was found.

"If someone did come in here and attack Reece, they confronted her in this room first," Patricia concluded, thinking things through in her mind.

"Struck the first blows. She loses the tooth." Jeff picked up on her train of thought.

"Yes, then she flees to the bedroom, where they have the major confrontation," Patricia finished.

It had been over twenty-four hours, and they still had no leads as to where Kristen Reece was. What was worse was that their surveillance team had pretty much cleared Adams of being around Reece during those vital early-morning hours when she'd disappeared. They had followed Adams from the club to her home back up in the hills, and she had stayed there throughout the night, alone.

"Here, mark it and rush it to the lab." She handed Jeff the tooth and headed for the door.

"Where are you going?" he called after her.

"La Femme."

Patricia walked into the nightclub and headed for the bar. Anger and frustration fed her heart, encouraging it to pump harder and faster, spreading her discontent throughout her tense body.

The place was unusually crowded for a Tuesday night, and she looked around at the mass of women dancing, laughing, embracing. Velvet Revolver pounded from the speakers, paralleling her anger. She came to a standstill behind the group of waiting women, some wanting a drink, some wanting drugs, all wanting a lay. She thought about turning sideways and winding her way through them, but she needed to see who was working the bar before she went up there, entrapping herself in all the women.

She felt a hand on her arm from behind, halting her progress, and she was about to turn to voice her protest when a deep voice sounded in her ear.

"Hello, Patricia." She froze, and her body went frigid and ramrod straight as recognition of the voice took effect. She turned and looked into the eyes that had always been so easy to drown in.

"Hello, Liz." Her voice did little to hide her anger and resentment.

"Let's go somewhere where we can talk." Liz gently took her hand and led her through the crowd.

Patricia thought briefly about protesting, but decided against it. Her anger and determination fueled her confidence, allowing it to burn hot and fierce within her. The crowd soon parted when they saw it was Liz, and they stared and hooted as they always did, casting Patricia glances dripping with jealousy.

They walked past Tyson, who stood guarding the private staircase with his massive arms folded across his equally massive chest. He nodded his shiny, bald head in acknowledgment as they headed up the stairs.

Patricia pulled her hand away and climbed up the stairs without assistance. Liz didn't look back at the break in contact, and Patricia examined her from behind. Worn blue jeans fit snugly to her long, strong legs, while a tight, threadbare white tank top hugged her trim torso and defined, muscular back. She looked away, reminding her libido that Liz was no longer attractive to her. She was a killer, a murderer, even if she had been able to alibi her way out. Liz was smart enough to have figured out how to get exactly what she wanted while at the same time keeping herself in the clear.

They stepped into the dimly lit VIP room, and Patricia was surprised when Liz didn't offer her a seat on one of the overstuffed sofas and chairs. Instead, they continued through the room, passing by a few moaning women engaged in a heated sexual encounter on one of the sofas. Liz led the way to her lair, where she typed in her code and allowed Patricia to enter the private room before her.

"I see the place hasn't changed much." Patricia looked around. Memories of their sexual escapades flooded her mind, and she had to swallow back a surfacing desire.

Liz closed the door behind them. "Why change a good thing?"

"I hope you at least changed the sheets." Patricia was in no mood for light chitchat. She hated what Liz had done to her and how out of control she could still make her feel.

Liz raised a questioning eyebrow at her, the coldness of the remark not escaping her. "Maybe if you had stuck around, I wouldn't have had to change them."

"Hah." Patricia scoffed. "From what I saw, you didn't need me." Her face heated with angry blood as she looked at the bed and remembered walking in on Liz and another woman making love. Hard as she tried, the image of them sweaty and sticky and locked in an uncompromising position never would leave her for good. It lingered, along with the feeling of betrayal.

"Still a scotch drinker?" Without waiting for a reply, Liz walked over to the bar and filled two glass tumblers with ice. "I told you, Patricia, it was just sex. It had nothing to do with the way I felt about you."

"That was the problem, Liz. Everything with you was always just sex. Including me."

Liz opened up an expensive bottle of scotch and filled their glasses. "That's where you're wrong. You know you meant more to me than that." She walked over to Patricia and handed her the drink, then sat down on the sofa.

Patricia sat as far as she could from her former lover, who was braless beneath her tank top. She looked away from the vision of the dark nipples trying to poke through the fabric and sipped her scotch.

"Let's cut the bullshit, Liz. Why are we here?" She needed to stay mad. It was easier to handle Liz if she could hate her.

Liz set her drink down on the coffee table and sat back to cross her legs, resting a black-booted ankle on her knee. "That's what I want to know, Patricia. Why are you here?" Her voice was calm, yet silently demanding.

Patricia rimmed her glass with her finger while she locked eyes with the piercing blue ones across from her. "I just want to get laid like everybody else."

"Now who's bullshitting?" Liz raised an eyebrow. "You and your people have been harassing some of my girls and some of my paying patrons. I don't appreciate it, and I'm asking you to stop."

Patricia laughed heartily. "Tell us the truth about the murders and we'll back off. Until then, we'll be all over you and your women."

"I've already told you, I don't know anything about any murders."

"You're running out of time." Patricia placed her unfinished drink on the table, stood, and walked to the door. "I can help you if you come clean now. Otherwise…"

Liz got up and followed, stepping in close to Patricia, briefly rubbing her scantily covered breasts against the back of her arm while her fingers wrapped around Patricia's elbows. Squaring herself against the detective, she leaned in and murmured in her ear in a raspy, sex-laced voice, "Tell me, Patricia, do you still taste like honey? I can still remember…like warm, sweet honey, right out of the hive."

Patricia shuddered and fought the urge to turn to hit her, knowing that Liz would block the blow and then pull her against her for a deep, passionate kiss. It had happened many times before, but this time she wouldn't do it. She couldn't do it. Liz was no longer just a cheat, she was a murderer.

"I haven't had honey in such a long time," Liz purred. "Let me taste you, let me run my tongue up deep into your hive."

The words waged a battle against her anger, and before they could win, she had to force herself to pull away, to walk hastily out of the door and away from Elizabeth Adams. She should have known better than to go traipsing upstairs with the woman, alone. It had never been hard for Liz to turn her on, to get under her skin. But then again, sex had never been their problem. At least, she didn't think so. But apparently she hadn't been enough for Liz.

Trying her best to clear Liz from her mind and her aching nerve endings, she descended the stairs and stepped down into the dancing wave of women. t.A.T.u. was singing as Patricia pushed and slithered her way through the sweaty bodies and shoved her way up to the bar.

The young pierced bartender slid a drink napkin in front of her. "What can I get you?" Her hair was so black it was almost blue, and as she turned, Patricia could indeed make out a blue streak running down the side of her head.

"Water. And you?"

The girl had bent to fetch the bottle, and she made eye contact with Patricia as she came back up to hand her the water. "That'll be a dollar fifty, and I'm not for sale."

Patricia eyed the studded collar on her neck, the rings through her lip and eyebrows, the black fingernails. "What's your name?" She unscrewed the lid to her water bottle and took a large gulp, hoping it would put out the flame ignited within her by Liz and her words.

"Blade," the girl answered, rolling her eyes.

"Of course it is. Blade is a very tough, scary name. But somehow I don't think you're so tough, and you're certainly not scary."

The girl didn't respond. She just stood, staring, and eventually began to mindlessly wipe the bar.

"I'm Patricia."

"Yeah, I know who you are."

"You do?"

"Yeah, you're that fucking cop who was in here the other night asking questions. I never forget a face." Blade nervously licked her dark lips, and Patricia wondered if the lip ring was painful, or if it, like other painful things, eventually became numb. Ever present, but numb nonetheless, until it was messed with.

Patricia leaned on the bar with her elbows, knowing the nice approach wasn't working. "Let's go somewhere and talk."

"Not interested."

Blade wasn't intimidated by her in the least, but at least Patricia knew she was making her sweat. The girl looked past the bar and toward Tyson. Patricia knew that Liz was probably watching them as well on her security cameras.

"Why not?" she asked.

"I don't have anything to say."

"We don't have to talk. We can do something else." Patricia placed her hand on that of the girl, who immediately stopped wiping the bar and looked at her, completely startled.

"No thanks, you're not my type."

"Why?"

She looked past Patricia for the second time, back toward Tyson. "Because you're old and you're a cop." Her eyes floated back to Patricia's.

"Hey, us cops need to get laid too, ya know."

"I said no. Now fuck off."

Patricia tightened her loose grip on Blade's hand, and the girl's eyes widened. "And I'm saying to you that you will leave with me now without causing a scene, or I'll arrest you right here and now."

"What for?" She remained perfectly still, the vein in her neck giving away her true fear as it pulsed quickly.

"For distributing narcotics, for starters." Patricia removed her hand from Blade's.

Blade opened her mouth to speak, but no words came out.

"You think we don't know about your peddling on the side? We do. But the real question is, does your employer know?" Blade's eyes grew wide once again and she looked nervously around, afraid someone of importance had overheard. "You see, I've noticed that you always sell your drugs over there." Patricia pointed to the dimmer side of the bar. "Away from the cameras. How do you think Ms. Adams will feel about you pocketing all her profits?"

Patricia knew Liz was aware of the distribution of drugs in her club. She also knew the girls gave Liz a majority of the profits. Of course, it was all done so that Liz could disclaim all responsibility. But Patricia knew Liz would be furious if she found out one of her girls was holding out on her and pocketing all the profits.

Blade dropped the bar rag and let herself out. Shoving her hands in the pockets of her baggy black Dickies, she said, "Let's go."

Patricia smiled at her and threw her arm around her shoulder. "Follow my lead."

They made their way through the crowd to the front entrance, where Tyson confronted them.

"Blade, where are you going?" His voice was deep and booming.

"Home," Patricia said, turning to nuzzle Blade's neck.

"Your shift's not over." He pinned Blade with a look.

"Yeah, well it is now." Patricia placed her finger on Blade's chin and tilted it toward hers. "Right, sweetie?" Blade smiled at her and turned back to Tyson. "Right." She wrapped her arm around Patricia's waist and they walked around him and out the door.

Once outside, Blade tried to pull away, but Patricia held her tightly. "Keep your arm around me until we get in the car."

Blade complied and they walked, wrapped around each other, until they reached Patricia's Blazer. "You realize that you probably just cost me my job," Blade said angrily as she climbed up into the truck.

"You're better off." Patricia started the truck and drove out of the parking lot.

"Fuck you, you fucking pig." Blade breathed angrily. "You don't know how bad I need that money. You had no right. This has got to be kidnapping or something."

Patricia drove, completely unaffected by the harsh words. She'd heard far worse over the years. "I know you need the money for art school, and I know you keep that a secret. I guess art school wouldn't do much for your tough-girl act." She kept her eyes straight ahead as she delivered the words calmly.

Blade jerked around in her seat and stared at Patricia, her mouth agape. "Who the hell are you, and what gave you the right?"

Patricia slowed the truck as they approached a red light. "I told you, my name is Patricia, and I have every right to find out everything about you. You work at La Femme, don't you?" She turned to face her defiant passenger. "Well, as you may know, we are investigating the club's owner, Elizabeth Adams, for murder."

Blade continued to sit in silence.

"That gives us every right to find out all we can about her, her club, and her employees."

"But why me? This has nothing to do with me," Blade declared, her voice higher pitched than the meaner, deeper-sounding voice she'd affected before.

Patricia started to drive once again as the light turned green. "Because you might have some information that we need. Information about Kristen Reece, our other suspect."

"I don't know anything. I already told you people that."

"And because your father is a cop back in Minnesota and because he is expecting you to fully cooperate with us."

Patricia heard Blade suck in a panicked breath of air. "You can't do this!" She tried to jerk on the door handle to open the door.

"Relax, it's locked. And if you try to run again, I'll arrest you right here and now for possession of narcotics."

Blade looked at her with her hand held over the lock, obviously contemplating her decision.

"How much E do you have on you right now, Tracy? How much GHB, poppers?" Patricia pulled into a corner convenience store and put the truck in park.

The use of Blade's real name seemed to drain any remaining color from her face. She let her hands fall from the door and into her lap.

"All I'm asking is that you just tell me what you know. What you may have seen or heard. Anything you know may help us."

"And then you'll let me go?"

"As long as you haven't done anything criminal." Patricia noted how young and frail the nineteen-year-old suddenly looked.

"What about the drug charges?" Her eyes were large and liquid as she fought back tears.

"If you cooperate, there will be no drug charges."

Blade nodded, and Patricia climbed down out of her Blazer.

"Where are you going?" Blade asked, obviously afraid now.

"To get you some cigarettes. I have a feeling it's going to be a long night."

"But I really don't know anything," Blade pleaded.

"That you know of." Patricia started to push the door closed.

"How do you know I won't run?"

"Because your name isn't Blade and you really aren't tough and scary. Your name is Tracy Walsh and you're scared shitless."

Patricia shut the door and walked into the convenience store to buy the girl some cigarettes and herself a large fountain drink. She had no idea what the girl knew, if anything at all, but she knew that by taking her, she would make Liz sweat a little more. She would question every last soul in the club thoroughly if she had to. And she knew that this kid in her car, this Blade, was basically a good kid who was possibly in way over her head.

With her purchases, Patricia climbed back into the truck and they drove in silence to the station. Blade stared aimlessly out the window, her hands clasped nervously in her lap. Every once in a while Patricia saw her wipe a tear from her cheek. For a young woman who had never been in trouble with the law, the current situation must be pretty frightening.

They came to a stop in front of the station, and Patricia led the way inside, weaving through hallways and desks until they reached the Homicide Division. She thought about questioning Blade in one of their interrogation rooms so she would be able to smoke, but when she turned and saw her pale and drawn face, she decided the tiny room was out of the question.

"Have a seat," Patricia offered as she sat down at Stewart's desk and set down her drink and cigarettes. She knew he wouldn't mind if Blade smoked.

Blade sat down slowly in the chair across from the desk. Patricia slid the pack of clove cigarettes and a lighter across the desk, and Blade eyed them and took the pack tentatively.

"Are those any good?" Patricia asked as she rose to retrieve her files from her desk, along with a small tape recorder that she immediately turned on.

"They're all right." Blade opened the pack of Djarums with trembling hands and placed one in her mouth. "How did you know what I smoke?"

"I know a lot about you, Tracy." Patricia returned to sit down across from the tough girl wannabe.

"It scares me…that you know so much." Blade lit the dark cigarette and sucked in an appreciative drag. Her shoulders instantly relaxed as the smoke entered her lungs.

"Do you mind if I tape record our session?"

Blade shrugged.

"You have to verbally say yes or no."

"It's okay," she replied softly.

"Let's talk about other things that scare you. Does your boss scare you? Elizabeth Adams?"

Blade shrugged her shoulders and took another drag of the sweet-smelling clove. She wiped her free hand on her white T-shirt, which read, "Take me for a ride."

"Have you ever spoken to Ms. Adams?" Patricia knew the girl wasn't Liz's type and it was possible that the two had never spoken, that Blade could have been hired and supervised solely by Kristen Reece.

"Once or twice." Her eyes were shifty, looking around the desk and avoiding Patricia altogether.

"What did you talk about?"

Blade shrugged her shoulders once again. Obviously she had no intention of talking to a cop about her boss, even under duress.

Patricia looked into the large brown eyes across from hers. "Are you afraid to talk to me for fear of losing your job?'

Blade laughed a little at the question. "Nah, man. I figure I already lost my job the second I left with you."

"Then why so afraid?"

She took another drag, sucking on the cigarette like it was providing her the courage to talk. "All this…murder and everything. I didn't know any of this. I thought she just hated cops like everyone else."

"You didn't know she was being investigated for murder?"

"No."

Patricia sighed and pushed some photographs across the table for Blade to view. "This is why we are asking questions, Tracy. Look at the photographs. These men all had families, people who loved them. And they all had one thing in common." She waited for Blade to look back at her before she continued. "They gave Elizabeth Adams trouble, and she threatened all of their lives."

Blade allowed her eyes to look back at the photos. "What's wrong with them, why do they look like—"

"That's what happens when a body sits out in the desert sun. It cooks."

Blade covered her mouth and averted her eyes. "Put them away, please."

Patricia scooped up the pictures and returned them to their files. "Let's talk about Kristen Reece. How well do you know her?"

"Pretty well, I guess."

"Do you know where she is right now?"

Blade shook her head. "Nah, she hasn't been in to work."

"Have you heard anything about her, maybe from the other girls?"

Blade hesitated. "Someone said that she took off the other night after fighting with Liz."

"They were fighting?"

"Yeah, that night you guys came and questioned all of us. Kris was pissed off and I saw her storm up to Liz's room and that was the last time I saw her. And then one of the other girls saw her leave after that, all pissed off. She said they'd been arguing."

"You don't know what they were arguing about?"

Blade stubbed out her clove in the glass ashtray on the desk. "I just figured they were arguing like they always do."

"How so?"

"You know, like lovers. They were always bitching at each other."

"Tracy, this is important. Have you ever seen someone else talking to Kris and Liz? Hanging out with them?"

She thought for a moment. "Nah, no one."

"Did Kris have a girlfriend?"

"No. She was always hung up on Liz. She had one-night stands and stuff, but no one serious."

Patricia gave an understanding nod. "Have you ever been to Kris's apartment?"

"Huh-uh. What's going on with Kris?" Blade fingered her silver skull ring, twisting it around and around.

"She's missing, Tracy. And we think she's tied to these murders."

"Kris? I don't know, man. I can't imagine her doing that to those guys."

Patricia turned off the tape recorder. Rubbing her temples, she glanced at the vulnerable nineteen-year-old sitting so pale and scared in the chair across from her. The only thing the girl had done was to convince her even more that Adams was involved in the disappearance of Kristen Reece.

Her cell phone rang and vibrated from its place on her belt. She plucked it out of its carrier and flipped it open. "Henderson."

"Yeah, it's Stewart." He sounded excited. "We need you over at Reece's apartment."

"Why, what's up?" She wasn't quite sure if she was finished with Blade or not.

"We found a fucking gold mine, that's what's up!"

"What?" She plugged her free ear with her finger, wanting and needing to hear him better.

"Behind one of her air vents, we found it all. The knife, the tranquilizer, the goddamned smoking gun!"

Patricia felt her blood heat up and pump violently through her body, carrying massive amounts of adrenaline with it. "I'll be right there." She flipped her phone closed and clipped it back to her belt.

"Can I go now?" Blade asked.

"Yeah, you can go. I'll drive you home."

CHAPTER TEN

Erin clawed her way out of a deep sleep to the sound of the doorbell ringing. She lay perfectly still, hoping that whoever it was would go away. But when the ringing of the doorbell gave way to knocking and then pounding, she threw back the covers and slid a robe over her nude body.

"Okay, okay!" She unlocked the door and jerked it open. The bright sunlight blinded her, and she had to shield her eyes before she could make out the figure standing just outside.

"You still sleeping?" Patricia made her way into the house, leaving a slow-moving Erin to shut the door behind her.

"Was, yeah." She followed Patricia into the living room, rubbing her eyes and face, trying to stir up her slumbering blood.

"Sorry to wake you, but we need to talk."

"No problem." Erin made her way to the kitchen. "OJ?" she asked as she removed the carton from the fridge.

"No, thanks," Patricia said, anxiety on her face.

Erin poured herself a glass and walked back over to the couch to sit next to the other detective. "I already know it's serious. Otherwise you wouldn't have risked coming yourself."

She took a sip of juice and studied her colleague, noting how tired and worn out she looked, darkness shadowing her eyes. Her hair was pulled back into a loose ponytail, allowing some unruly strands to fall around her face. Her jeans and polo shirt were covered in dust, and Erin gathered from her hiking boots that she had been out in the desert.

"I made sure you were clear before I came. You know I would never put you at risk."

Erin nodded. "So, what's up?"

"As you know, we went after Reece to arrest her on Monday, and we found her place in disarray and covered in blood."

"Yes," Erin replied, encouraging her to continue.

"In processing her apartment, we found some pretty incriminating evidence."

"The 9mm and the tranquilizer?"

"And the knife as well."

"And does it all match?"

Patricia tucked a strand of hair behind her ear. "Ballistics confirmed the gun match this morning. And the tranquilizer and the knife are matches also."

"That's great news." Erin pulled her robe tighter around her body. She felt cold but couldn't explain why.

"Then this morning at about five o'clock we received a call from the highway patrol. A van was found at the bottom of Pike's Canyon. Apparently it had run off the road and busted through the safety barrier. It landed at the bottom of the canyon and exploded upon impact. We ran the vehicle identification, and it came back as belonging to Kristen Reece."

Erin took in a deep breath and set down her orange juice.

"There was a body inside. It was burned beyond recognition, and we'll be lucky to get anything from it."

"What about dental comparison?" Erin asked.

"We think the van's been there since Monday. And there is evidence of animal tampering. Most of the missing body parts have been discovered not far from the accident scene. But we still haven't located the skull."

"So where does all this leave the investigation?" From what she had just heard, it sounded like they had all they needed to pin everything on Reece.

Erin's stomach flipped as a flare of excitement rushed through her. Elizabeth Adams could be innocent. She looked to Patricia and instantly felt the heated weight of guilt. Why did she want Liz to be innocent? For her own selfish reasons? She glanced away and studied her hands, ashamed at her reaction. This of course also meant that there was no reason to see the nightclub owner again. Suddenly feeling let down and anxious, she tried to find a good excuse to see

Liz one more time.

"The department wants to close the case, pending the positive identification of Reece. We don't have anything on Adams linking her to the murders. We have her threats, but we all know that would get nowhere in court."

Erin sat sideways on the couch, hugging her knees up to her chest as she spoke. "She knew Reece. She could've easily put her up to it."

"Yes, but we can't prove it."

"So what now? Am I out?"

"It's up to you." Patricia's eyes were deep and serious. "I think you should call it quits."

"Why?" Erin searched her face, her own mind unable to piece the overwhelming information together.

"Because this all seems to be falling into place too easily. I think it was just a little too coincidental, us finding all the evidence we needed to blame Reece for the murders. Then we find her body burned, its head missing, making it damn near impossible to positively ID. It's too nice and neat. I still think Adams is involved, and I think she might have framed Reece."

"All the more reason to keep me in." She didn't want to quit now, not when she felt so close to making a breakthrough with the mysterious woman.

"It's not safe, Mac. If she masterminded all this, and she didn't draw the line at killing a woman..." Patricia gestured with her hands to emphasize her point. "Then think how easy it would be for her to do something to you. It's time to get out so the department can wrap this up in a tidy little package and get some positive media for a change."

"But you still think she's guilty, you said so yourself."

"I do. But I don't think you risking your life will bring us anything more than we already have. There's nothing more we can do."

"What does Ruiz think?"

"He's willing to give you one last shot at Adams if you want it. He'll give you tonight, and then he wants you out."

"Okay, then. I'll do it." Erin spoke quickly and confidently, wanting the chance.

"Mac, please. It's too dangerous."

"Will you still shadow me?" she asked, needing to know that Patricia would still be there for her.

Patricia sighed. "Yes, of course. But be careful. She's not happy having me around."

"I'll be fine."

The wind kicked up, bringing with it the promise of dust and rain. Patricia breathed deep, enjoying the raw, earthy scent of a monsoon storm. She looked toward the north, where the dark clouds usually originated. As if on cue, lightning lit up the night sky, showing off the storm clouds, playing tag from one end of the thunderheads to the other. Not wanting to get caught by the blowing dust that would soon follow, she picked up her step and walked quickly to the club entrance.

A horde of leather-clad women gathered around the main door, anxiously awaiting entrance. She made her way past them, eyeing their black leather garb, their dark lipstick, their suggestive stares. Some of the women wore classic S&M outfits: black leather pants, studded collars and bodices. A few wore leashes attached to their collars with no one at the other end. They were hoping against hope that a special someone would choose them for the evening, and then and only then would they allow their leashes to be taken. Looking around, she also noticed that not a single soul had dressed as a dominatrix. That role was saved for one person, and one person only.

"Hey, you have to wait in line!" a large female bouncer yelled to her as she walked through the entrance. "Hey, I said—"

Patricia continued walking, ignoring her until fingers restrained her arm. "Back off." She pulled out her badge. The bouncer dropped her arm and backed away carefully as if the badge were a venomous snake.

Patricia continued on, making her way inside to the heart of the club. Dark techno music thumped so hard it rattled her chest. The dance floor was packed with women, and the usual lasers and colorful lights that shined from above had been replaced by deep blues and purples. She looked around, trying to locate Erin, but it was nearly impossible to make out a face.

She made her way toward the bar, hoping for a better view of the dance floor. Erin had arrived at the club a few minutes earlier, and yet it was already as if she had been swallowed up by the mass of dancing women. It was crucial that Patricia locate the younger detective, and her anxiety wouldn't settle until she did.

The bar was busy with dozens of leather-clad women hovering around it, yelling out their demands. Patricia knew without looking that Blade wasn't there. She had called, earlier that morning, crying, upset because she'd been fired. It was just as well. She didn't belong at the club, working for Adams.

Patricia found a place to stand next to the crowded bar and carefully scanned the dance floor, hoping that Erin hadn't already been escorted upstairs, or worse, somewhere away from the club. She searched for her face, but the task was virtually impossible. A girl with a blond glowing Mohawk caught her eye. Her body was slick with sweat and thrusting in time to the dark beat. She stood in front of her companion, her slick, thrusting arm disappearing into the smaller woman's pants.

Patricia dragged her attention away from the Mohawk girl and her powerful hand job and looked up at the dancing women on the raised platforms—every one of them dressed in various S&M getup—dancing, spanking, whipping.

A movement on the VIP stairs caught her attention. A tall, dark-haired woman was working her way down, slowly, deliberately. Rob Zombie began thumping into the club, feeding the women like blood to a vampire. Elizabeth Adams came into better view and the crowd stilled, watching, waiting for the one.

Patricia knew what Liz would be wearing, having seen it countless times before. Nevertheless, she couldn't help but look. The shiny black pants clung to Liz's legs like a second skin, showing off the muscles underneath as they rippled with her walk. Her black motorcycle boots, heavy, strong, and masculine, were an outward symbol of her strength and power. Her torso was bare, the tanned skin stretching across the etched stack of her abdominal muscles.

She wore a silver chain-front vest, fastened to her by black leather straps. As she walked, the wall of chains swayed, allowing brief winks of her dark, puckered nipples. Her hair was combed back away from her face, and a black leather mask fit snug around her piercing eyes, making her sculpted cheekbones more pronounced.

As Patricia eyed the incredible body in its breathtaking costume, she focused on the leather lace-up guards Liz wore on her forearms, which drove home the overall effect. The outfit was as powerful as it was sexy, demanding attention while it also demanded submissiveness.

Patricia could not tear her eyes away. What was worse was she knew that later, in the privacy of Liz's lair, the tight pants would be removed to reveal the real dominatrix outfit, which was what all these women wanted and wished for.

Patricia had had her, had experienced the powerful sex with their pseudogoddess, and she had to admit that if any of the women knew the sex was even better than they imagined, they would kill themselves trying to get to her.

As it was, they were clamoring at the bottom of the stairs, hoping for a mere glance their way, a smile, or the rare opportunity to actually be chosen for the evening.

Liz walked with graceful confidence through the parting crowd. A few women shouted her name, desperate for her attention. Some moved into her path, and she would grin slyly and grab their leashes, pulling them to her—a breath away from her mouth—and then releasing them with a shove back into the crowd. As Liz teased her admirers, Patricia noticed the swinging red suede tassels of the flogger Liz had fastened to the belt of her pants.

Heated blood rushed to her face and loins as the sight of the flogger brought back images of some of their more intense sexual interactions. Memories flooded back of being lightly restrained on her back on the bed, the tantalizing sting of the tassels against her bare breasts rushing blood between her legs. She remembered Liz straddling her, whipping her. Helpless to stem the flow of images, she braced herself against the person next to her and tried to regain the strength in her legs. She couldn't allow this. She had to get control of herself.

Pushing back the memories of her own heated encounters, she regained her focus on Liz, who continued through the crowd until she came upon a lone blonde standing in the center of the dance floor.

Patricia's throat tightened in recognition. She hadn't seen Erin earlier and wasn't prepared for how she looked. Desire once again ignited her blood as she studied the young detective. Her hair was slicked back against her head. The black leather pants Patricia had purchased for her fit her muscled legs like a tight glove, but instead of the matching black leather vest, Erin was wearing a very revealing black lace bra. The decision to nix the vest and go with the bra alone had obviously been her idea, and Patricia at once understood why she'd done it. The bra was much more revealing and more daring. Definitely something Liz would appreciate. Patricia only hoped J.R. had done his best work in concealing the tiny wire.

With her heart racing with desire and her mind screaming with jealousy and want, Patricia felt sick as Liz approached Erin. In that moment, Patricia hated her former lover with a passion she had almost believed she would never feel again. Whatever happened after tonight, she promised herself, she would make certain Elizabeth Adams never laid her predatory hands on Erin again.

"Hi." Liz's voice was like a purr as she stood before Erin, completely confident and more than a little domineering.

"Hi," Erin said, unable to peel her eyes away from the exposed body before her. The chains were still moving, and she wished they would settle in a position covering the beautiful breasts beneath them. The winks and peeks of the nipples underneath were almost too much for her to handle.

Liz moved her gaze up and down, a grin spreading across her face. "You look better than I could've ever imagined."

"You don't look so bad yourself." Erin tried desperately to downplay how incredibly sexy the nightclub owner looked. She was there for a reason, and it wasn't to lose herself in the feelings Liz aroused.

The crowd around them had once again started to dance, the other women accepting their defeat. Liz moved into her, pressing her warm body up against Erin's. "I'm glad you came," she whispered into her ear. "Dance with me."

Erin shuddered as they began to move in rhythm with the music. She could feel Liz's taut nipples as they found their way through the chains once again. She let her hands rest on the firm planes of Liz's back and willed her body to remain calm.

"Mmm. Your hands feel so good on me," Liz said huskily.

"Hey you two, mind if I join in?"

Erin turned and instantly recognized the movie actress she had met several nights before. She looked equally sexy in the black leather band fastened tightly around her bare breasts. A black patch covered one eye, offering mystique as well as sex.

"Not at all," Erin answered before Liz had the chance.

The actress smiled and moved in close to Erin. Before Erin knew what was happening, the thick luscious lips of the actress had descended on hers with a vengeance. Her hot tongue invaded Erin's mouth, probing and swirling, and Erin pulled away as she felt something else.

She swallowed and half choked at a bitter taste in her mouth. "What was that?" She tried to swallow and wash whatever it was from her mouth.

"Relax, it was only E."

Erin studied her in silence as realization settled in. Not wanting to look the prude, she shrugged as if everything were okay and faced Adams once more, placing her hands on her hips.

"That was quite a kiss." She tried to sound nonchalant, but inwardly she was worried. She had never taken Ecstasy and didn't know how her body would react. She hoped it wouldn't interfere with her plans to seduce their suspect and possibly extract the incriminating statements that would make a case stick.

"Angie's known for her E kisses," Liz voiced, her tone thick with seduction. The actress walked away and they began to dance, once again alone with each other.

"You're right. This beats the hell out of the Wild West party."

Liz laughed. "You have no idea."

"I'd like to find out." Erin looked up into her eyes as she made the seductive yet submissive plea.

"Really?" An eyebrow inched just above the leather mask. "This is quite a change."

"Are you complaining?" Erin asked, toying with her.

Another laugh. "Not at all. Don't tell me leather turns you on… I would never have guessed it from your writing."

Erin tilted her head, curious. "What exactly did you get from my writing?"

"Well, let's see. You're a hopeless romantic and very, very lonely."

The statement startled Erin. Even if she herself wasn't Katherine Chandler, the description still fit. She fumbled for words. "Uh, well, I was hoping you would've gotten more than that from the books."

"Oh, but I did." Liz pulled her closer, tighter. "You write about all that romance and desire because it's what you crave most in your life. True love, idealized romance, and relationships. All of it. You want it all."

"And you think it's not possible." Erin could tell by her tone that she thought true love was unobtainable.

Liz paused for a moment before she spoke. "Not from what I've seen."

"You've never been in love," Erin declared matter-of-factly.

Liz looked into her face. "How would you know that?"

"Because if you had, then you would know that true love is something that you can't control. It just happens. And no reason or sensibility can quell it. It just is." Erin didn't know where the words came from, but they were spilling out.

It was as if Erin had reached a new layer in the depths of Liz's eyes, causing a flood of darker, deeper blue. "The E must be getting to you," Liz said.

"You're afraid. You're afraid to let someone in." Erin said the words softly, the revelation seeming very fragile to her. Liz was a brittle shell, with no emotion on the inside. Those emotions had been hidden safely somewhere else, leaving behind a tough-looking but nonetheless very fragile shell. She could see it all now; it was so clear, and her heart pained for the woman. "It's okay. I understand," she continued softly, searching the striking face. She was so incredibly beautiful. "Take off the mask," she pleaded, suddenly needing to see her face, all of it.

Liz licked her lips at the request. "I…" She looked around, seemingly unsure. "Not here."

She gently took Erin's hand. They began to walk, and Erin took a deep breath, noticing her surroundings as if for the first time. The sound of the music, the different shades of the lights—it all felt so incredible. Amazing. It was all so beautiful. She looked at the women dancing around her. A thin sheen of sweat covered their skin, while the deep shades of blue and purple from the lights accented the contours and planes of their faces. They were breathtaking.

She tripped over someone's foot, causing Liz to turn back to her. "You okay?"

Erin ran her hand over her own forehead, amazed at the sweat coating her brow. In her peripheral vision, she noticed the elaborate movement of the people dancing. She turned to look at them, unable to resist. But the dance wasn't nearly as incredible when she viewed it head-on. At that moment, she knew she was feeling the effects of the drug.

"Fine." She smiled at Liz, truly feeling the smile. In fact, she felt better than fine. She felt fucking fabulous.

Liz led her up the stairs slowly, allowing Erin a wonderful view of her backside in the tight, shiny black pants. She looked at their joined hands. Liz's skin felt so warm, so soft. Erin lifted her hand and kissed it, needing to taste it.

Liz looked at her long and hard, her eyes lightening a shade, blazing with desire. At that moment metallic silver flakes fell upon them from the rafters above. Erin squealed with delight as her attention instantly shifted to the brilliant silver snowfall around them.

The crowd below roared to life and the dancers raised their hands as a Nine Inch Nails song pumped through the sound system.

"This is so much fun." Erin threw her arms around Liz and grinned into her neck.

The full force of the Ecstasy had hit her and she knew it, but she didn't care. She couldn't care; her mind and body wouldn't let her care. She felt Liz tense with arousal next to her. She couldn't help but grin; Liz smelled so damn good.

"What is that, that you wear?" Erin lightly fingered Liz's neck where the scent was strongest.

"It's called Crave, by Calvin Klein." Liz's voice sounded tight and strained.

"Mmm. I can certainly see why it's called that," Erin whispered, meaning every word.

"Are you two having all the fun without me?" Angie was back, and she was standing just slightly between them.

"We were starting to." Liz was clearly annoyed at being interrupted, but her smile remained.

"I believe," Angie said, looking at Liz, "that I owe you a kiss now."

The music was loud and powerful and the words teased at Erin's ears. Looking at Angie and Adams, she suddenly wanted to fuck, and she wanted to be fucked. She wanted to feel someone inside her.

Liz looked past Angie to Erin, studying her face, apparently noticing her arousal. "I don't want any E," she said, sounding distant.

"I don't have any. But I still owe you a kiss." Angie fingered Liz's nipples through the chains.

Erin watched the erotic scene before her. She could almost feel the persistent strokes of Angie's fingers on the dark nipples, as if the actress were stroking her rather than Liz.

"Kiss her," she choked out, needing to see it, but even more, needing to experience it.

Liz stared at her in surprise, her cheeks flushing red at the words. Responding strongly, she grabbed Angie by the back of the head and pulled her close.

"Make me bleed, baby." Angie's plea was deep and throaty, igniting Erin from the inside out. Liz complied, licking her lips, her eyes hungry.

Erin watched with voyeuristic delight as the beautiful women kissed. She could see their tongues battling for dominance. Liz took Angie's full bottom lip into her mouth, tugging at it with her teeth and sucking on it with force. Angie moaned deeply, clinging to her. When Liz finally let loose and pushed her away, the actress fingered her lip, a slight grin curving upward at the feel and taste of her own blood.

Erin swallowed hard, as if she too could taste the blood, heavy and thick with metal, like sucking on a penny. Her nostrils flared, curious to find the scent of it, the scent of sated desire. The kiss had been powerful and hungry, and it had awakened her own need to feed.

"My turn," she let out in a throaty, aroused whisper. She stepped up to Liz and wrapped her hands in the thick hair at the back of her head. The noise of the club receded in a tunneling fog as ravenous need clouded her senses. She could hear her own heartbeat echoing within, rushing her adrenaline-heavy blood to her extremities, to her lips, filling them, darkening them.

She closed her eyes and took Liz into her mouth, sucking in her top lip and rimming it with her hungry tongue. She felt her tremble and then, as if she had regained control, Liz grabbed Erin's back and pulled her closer, groaning.

Erin felt the tongue in an instant, demanding entry, demanding the right to explore and lay claim. Without seeing it, she knew it was longer than her own and astonishingly agile as it tasted her entire mouth in fluid, easy motions. Wanting more, she met the hot forceful tongue with her own, swirling and dueling. She felt Liz's hand at the back of her head, holding her still. Then Liz took Erin's tongue in her mouth and sucked it.

Erin groaned with delight at the sensation, and the flesh between her legs throbbed, demanding to be next. With hunger and need fueling her, she tugged on Liz's hair, wrapping it in her fingers. Liz reacted instantly, standing on her tiptoes, lifting Erin off the ground and wrapping Erin's legs around her waist. "I need to taste you. Now," she said, her throat tight, her voice raspy.

She carried her to the door of her private room, balancing her up against the wall while she typed in her code.

Erin clung to her as they walked inside, the feel of the strong woman between her legs beating reason and accountability hands down. She knew what she was about to do, just as she knew she shouldn't. But nothing seemed to matter to her at that moment except for the need to touch and be touched. Her skin felt alive. Alive as if it were its own thinking being, with a beating pulse and a voracious, insatiable appetite. It craved.

She nuzzled Liz's exposed neck, causing her to shudder. "Take off your mask," she softly demanded.

Liz lowered Erin to the ground in front of the large bed and slowly slid the leather mask from her face.

"That's so much better," Erin said as her fingers lightly caressed the beautifully sculpted features that had been hidden beneath it.

Liz swallowed hard, and Erin noticed. She was noticing everything now. The beauty of the woman before her, the fragility masked by indifference and distance, the delicate pulse that beat just beneath the damp skin on her neck. She was human. And that was something it seemed no one had ever considered before.

"I want you," she said. "I want you to take me."

Liz grabbed at the hand caressing her face. She touched Erin tentatively on her neck.

"Yes, touch me," Erin pleaded. "Before I die."

Liz stepped into her, taking her mouth with dominance and hunger. Erin let the sensual assault of tongue and mouth free her. She felt like flying, and for a second she almost floated away, she almost grabbed onto the string of the pleasurable balloon floating by. Instead, she grabbed at Liz's back, digging her nails in deep, grounding her mind and body.

She heard a growl in her ear as Liz ended the claiming kiss and attacked her neck. Erin shuddered, clinging tight to the muscled back as arousal spread through her heated skin, the hot wet mouth claiming her sensitive skin. She felt warm hands trying to unlatch her bra.

"Wait," she managed, her blood and brain swimming. She pushed herself away, suddenly conscious of the wire she was wearing.

"What is it?" Liz asked, her face hot with the flush of desire. She wanted this woman like she had wanted no other before. Her hands trembled, the need to touch her persistent and powerful. "Katherine?"

Erin turned quickly, making her way to the rest room. "I'll be right back."

Liz stood, unable to move, amazed at how easily Katherine Chandler had charged through her walls, moving right in to stir emotions deep within. Her breathing came heavy and quick, thick with arousal. It caught in her throat as Katherine reappeared, her black bra removed. She stood in the doorway of the bathroom, the air awakening her exposed honey-colored nipples.

Liz remained frozen as the object of her desire neared. "You are so beautiful," she rasped, suddenly alive and driven to touch her. With her breath shaking in her chest, she lightly skimmed her thumbs over the awakening nipples, erecting their thick, hungry buds.

Erin nearly collapsed at the touch and she had to hold tight to Liz's forearms. After a moment, wanting to feel for herself, she mirrored Liz's movements, lightly caressing the dark rose of her nipples through the chains. She watched in amazement as the blue eyes before her became dark, dilating pools.

Liz pushed her hands away. She reached down and unsnapped the other woman's leather pants. As she lowered the zipper, she leaned in and bit possessively on the beautifully exposed neck before her.

Erin gasped at the animalistic feel of the teeth on her flesh. She grabbed Liz's shoulders as her leather pants were removed, one leg at a time. She thought she would feel less confident and more exposed being naked in front of a woman for the first time. But as Liz placed her warm hands on her nude hips and knelt before her, all she could feel was the fierce burn of yearning.

"God, you're already so wet," Liz purred, her voice rich and heavy with want. She licked at the soft inner thigh, wanting, needing to taste the glistening wet of her, already shimmering against her thighs.

Erin clenched her jaw and tightened her grip on Liz's shoulders and in her hair as Liz's tongue moved against her inner thigh.

"Mmm, so good," Liz murmured between long licks. "I'm going to lick up every last drop from you."

"Ah…ah." Strange and inaudible noises were the only response as Liz's tongue continued its path up her leg.

"Look at me," Liz demanded softly.

Erin opened her eyes.

"I want you to watch," Liz demanded, once again lowering her own piercing gaze.

She flattened out her tongue and licked at the engorged flesh.

"Oh…" Erin let out a breathy moan.

Liz continued licking her, one big stroke at a time. Erin's knees buckled and Liz grabbed her buttocks, trying to steady her.

"Lie down," she instructed, easing her back on the bed while she remained on her knees.

The taste of her was sweeter than anything she could've imagined, and it was taking all of her strength to be patient and gentle, when what she really wanted to do was to devour her quickly and aggressively, to give in to the incredible appetite her taste had awakened. But she knew that what she felt for Katherine went deeper than just a need for sex. She demanded more from herself when she was with her, and she wanted their first time to be special.

Feeling her twitch and jerk, Liz toyed with her, teasing her with her breath. "You want more?" she asked as she breathed upon her, her own body screaming its need for more.

"Yes, please. God."

Liz grinned up at her. Then, licking her lips, she eased her mouth back down upon the soft flesh, kissing it deeply, swirling her tongue around the stiff clitoris and then lapping at the nectar that was nature's own sweet arousal.

She felt fingers tighten in her hair and moved her tongue lower, to the source of the sweetness she so hungered for. Finding it warm, wet, and welcoming, she plunged her tongue deep within, feeling the other woman instantly tighten and bear down on her, luring her deeper. She expertly pumped her tongue up and down into the tight warm walls that held it captive.

Erin bucked. "More," she choked out, holding tight to the head between her legs.

Liz thrust her tongue, wanting to milk as much as she could. Persistent fingers dug into her hair and tugged at her head. Knowing it was time for more and unable to be patient, she lifted her head slightly and eased two fingers inside, curling them snug against the patch of skin that she knew was her G-spot.

"Oh my God!" Erin's eyes flew open. Liz was slowly fucking her with her fingers, and she was doing something else inside her. Something that was gripping her internally and causing a warm wash of pleasure to flood up through her center to her belly and beyond. It felt so good, and she was a captive to the pleasure as her body bucked and writhed under the pumping hand.

"Yes, ride my fingers," Liz cooed.

"Oh God, I can't…" Erin tried to lift her head, but she couldn't. She couldn't even focus her eyes. "I can't take any more…It feels so good."

Liz laughed. "Yes, you can. You can take so much more." She lowered her head once again to feed. Once her tongue had stroked around the hard clitoris, she sucked it into her mouth and held it prisoner with her teeth as her tongue resumed its wet, firm assault.

Erin clenched her jaw and threw back her head, pushing herself tightly against Liz's mouth between her legs, arching her back as the waves of pleasure increased and the pressure mounted within her. "I…I'm dying." Her voice was like gravel, and quickly losing strength. Her eyes were clenched shut and she did indeed feel like she was dying, like she was drowning, the pleasure too great.

Liz held fast to her, sucking her flesh and fucking her deeper and faster. She could feel her own excitement building between her legs, and she rocked into her, knowing the pressure from her leather underwear alone would send her over.

Erin let loose of Liz's hair and grabbed at the bed covers, her grip impossibly tight as she awaited the looming tidal wave of pleasure. She began to speak again, but she didn't know what she was saying—the words sounded so unlike her, as if there were someone else inside her, possessing her soul.

"Fuck me! Harder, don't ever fucking stop! Don't…ever… fucking…stop!" She lost all control as waves of pleasure smashed through her over and over again. She clung once again to the dark head between her thighs and held it tightly as her hips bucked and fucked, riding out the stormy waves. A low, throaty howl resounded from her lungs, choking her up, before it eventually faded.

Liz held her tightly until the last of the spasms passed. Then, slowly and carefully, she moved her hand and mouth and crawled up on the bed next to the woman she had just made love to. Never before had she been so moved by the act of sex. Never had she had a woman who was so responsive, so verbal. As she lay down next to her, her own sated flesh gave one last twitch from the orgasm she had experienced on the same wave that had taken Katherine over.

She bent down and stroked the flushed cheek of the woman beneath her. "Katherine." She wanted, needed to look into the expressive green eyes.

Erin heard the word from somewhere at the end of a tunnel, but she didn't respond. The name had no meaning in the world she had entered.

"Katherine," Liz whispered as she bent down to plant tiny kisses on her neck.

This time reality smashed back into Erin's mind at warp speed. "Oh God." She sat up quickly, avoiding Liz's touch and her soft, pleading eyes. They were not the cold eyes everyone had told her she would see. Liz thought she was someone else. She had made love to Katherine Chandler, not Erin McKenzie.

What had she done? Not just to the investigation or to herself, but to this woman? Erin scooted off the bed and hastily pulled her clothes on. She didn't care what anyone said—it wasn't just sex, it had been so much more. She tried to swallow as she jerked on her pants, but her throat felt raw from the strain. Was sex between women always this powerful? She suddenly felt like crying, her emotions dangerously close to the surface after such an earth-shattering orgasm.

"Katherine, what's wrong?" Liz was dressing just as quickly, a look of panic on her face. "Are you okay?"

Erin fastened her bra and reached for her boots. She didn't bother to tie the laces. "I...I'm fine. I just need to go, that's all."

Liz stared at her, obviously baffled and upset by the drastic change in mood. "Did I...hurt you?"

"What? No." She met Liz's eyes and was shocked at the vulnerability she saw there. *Someone was wrong about you, so very wrong,* she thought as she watched the raw emotion play out on Liz's beautiful face. Tears tightened her sore throat, and she covered her mouth with a trembling hand. "I just have to go." She tore away and ran out the door.

Liz didn't chase her. She simply stood and stared after her, too shocked to move. Finally, she took the boot she was holding in her hand and threw it against the wall. "Fuck," she said as it thumped and fell to the floor.

Patricia had been staring up at the top of the stairs since she saw Liz and Erin ascend to the top and disappear. Now, as she stood with a half-empty bottle of water in her hand, she barely had time to process the sight of Erin poised on the landing, wiping her eyes, before the young detective bolted down the stairs and out of the club.

Patricia opened the water and gulped, trying to look natural while her insides were screaming with the need to go after her. But she could not follow immediately without causing suspicion, and this was not the time to blow Erin's cover.

As the minutes crawled by, she made her way to the side of the bar where Liz's cameras couldn't capture her, walked over to the wall, and nonchalantly leaned against it.

"Can I get a code 4 on Mac?" she said.

"Negative. She's on foot."

"Fuck!" Patricia pushed herself off the wall and walked as casually as she could from the club.

No one paid her any mind as she exited. Rain and dust stung her skin, carried by the angry wind. Shielding her eyes, knowing that cameras more than likely tracked her to her truck, she fished out her keys and climbed in. Once inside she cranked her engine, threw the truck into reverse, and drove out of the parking lot.

"Where is she?" she demanded.

"Negative," J.R. replied.

"God damn it, one of you has to have seen where she went!" She scanned the streets while her windshield wipers skidded across the glass, doing little to clear away the light, dirty drizzle.

At the end of the block behind the club, she spotted her, on her knees on someone's front lawn.

"Jesus," Patricia mouthed to herself as she left her truck to face the powerful monsoon wind once more. She ran to Erin's side and knelt down. "Mac! Are you okay?" She frantically checked her for any obvious signs of injury and, finding none, focused on her wet face.

"I feel sick." Erin retched as she said the words, but nothing came up. "I'm so damned thirsty."

"Come on." Patricia slung Erin's arm around her shoulders and helped her up into the Blazer.

She buckled her in, climbed behind the wheel, and drove slowly into the storm.

"Where are we going?" Erin's voice was meek and strained, her eyes hazed and distant.

"Home." Patricia made a turn at the stoplight and steered the Blazer toward her street. She was taking Erin to her home, the place she should've been all along.

CHAPTER ELEVEN

Patricia sat on the edge of the bed and watched the young detective sleep. She looked so peaceful, almost angelic, as the bright morning light haloed her in gold. Her eyelids fluttered and her mouth opened to release muffled words. She threw her arm above her tousled hair and settled back into the peaceful confines of sleep.

Patricia hated to wake her after all she had been through the night before. Jealousy ate at her as she remembered the state Erin was in when she found her. She had been distraught and physically ill, and Patricia knew it had more to do with Elizabeth Adams than it did the drugs she had no doubt ingested. Erin had refused to discuss her encounter, leaving Patricia to draw her own conclusions. Erin had removed her wire. She had been completely alone with Elizabeth Adams for the better part of an hour.

Patricia clenched her jaw as Erin shifted once again in her sleep. Faint red marks dotted the skin on her neck and chest, remnants of a heated and hungry mouth. Visions of Liz and Erin devouring one another flashed in Patricia's mind, and angry blood burned her cheeks. With a cold yet heated shudder, she forced herself up from the bed, suddenly needing to put distance between herself and Erin, as if the detective were tainted.

She almost left the room then, but she had a job to do first. Her insides churned as she recalled her most recent conversation with Ruiz. He wasn't happy. Patricia had told him that Erin had gone dangerously far with their suspect and had put herself at risk by allowing herself to become impaired. Ruiz, clearly frustrated, predictably decided it was time to take her off the case. Patricia had agreed wholeheartedly.

But as she stared at Erin now, she knew it wasn't because she feared for her life, it was because she was jealous. Jealous and angry and bitter, at Liz and at Erin. How could she have let Liz touch her? What happened after she removed the wire? There was only one reason she would have had to remove it—intimacy.

Questions burned her as Erin shifted again in the bed. Like it or not, Patricia knew she had to talk to the young detective. With a deep sigh, she placed her hand on Erin's shoulder and gently shook her.

"Mac?" Her voice was a whisper, strained with angry emotion rather than gentleness.

Erin stirred slightly and moaned. A lump under the covers next to her stirred as well and Jack emerged, stretching as he walked.

"I wondered where you were." Patricia eyed her sleepy dog, wishing things were as simple for her as they were for him. She wished all were well and she herself could curl up next to Erin. But she was afraid that would never happen now, and the probability stung her down deep, nauseating her.

"Erin?" She tried again, suddenly coldly detached, determined to do her job.

"Oh God." Erin groaned and opened her eyes. "I feel like a train hit me." Her voice was not yet awake.

"Yeah, I can see that. We need to talk." Patricia forced indifference, fighting her feelings of attraction.

"Uh-oh. I'm beginning to hate it when you say that." Erin sat up and leaned back against the headboard, rubbing her eyes. "Shoot."

"I have some bad news. It's Mark." At Erin's blank stare, she added, "Your Mark," and saw the color drain from Erin's face. "He was attacked last night. He's going to be okay," she said hastily. "He's critical but stable."

Erin lifted her eyes to meet Patricia's. She sucked in a big, shaky breath as if she had just surfaced from a deep dive. "What happened?"

"He was found in a hotel parking lot, shot and stabbed," Patricia replied, feeling way more than relief at the way things were panning out. Mark was injured and Erin had been found emotionally and physically distraught, not to mention impaired. The combination of factors was more than enough to take her off—and keep her off— the case. Patricia felt good about that, right or wrong.

Erin cupped a quick hand over her mouth. "Oh God." Tears welled in her eyes.

"There's something else you should know." Patricia licked her dry lips, satisfied that Elizabeth Adams would never touch Erin again. "There was a picture of you pinned to his shirt."

"What do we know?" Patricia asked, staring at the stark white of the hospital floor, already drawing her own conclusions.

"We don't know jack." Stewart smacked his gum and searched his pockets for the pack of spearmint. He offered her some, to which she shook her head. "Did you show Mac that picture?"

She knew he was referring to the photo that had been found on Mark. "Yes."

Stewart unwrapped another stick of gum and shoved it in his mouth. "She recognize it?" He chewed loudly and then coughed, evidently having swallowed some of the juice wrong.

"It was the one he kept in his office at his law firm."

"Shit," Stewart mumbled, and Patricia could have sworn she heard the wheels in his brain squeaking as they turned.

"What did the hotel say?" she asked.

"Nada. We're combing through their security cameras as we speak."

"The staff, they didn't see anything?"

"No. And according to their books, he didn't have a room."

She rubbed her hand over her forehead in frustration. "What are the doctors saying? Is he going to wake up soon?"

Stewart jiggled his keys as he spoke. "He's doing okay for a guy who took a bullet in the shoulder, then got stabbed four times in the groin. I guess the anesthetic takes a while to wear off."

"Christ."

"You look like shit," Stewart rasped.

"Thanks." She smiled halfheartedly at him.

"I'll go get you some coffee." He walked off in search of the vending machines, leaving her alone to her thoughts.

Her mind reeled with possibilities, but she was too tired to make any sense of them. All she knew was the hate she had for Elizabeth Adams was growing. With every passing second, she hated her more. Especially when she thought of Erin. She glanced up as Stewart returned, carrying a small steaming paper cup.

"Thanks," she offered, meeting his eyes as she took the cup. She had never known him to be the caring type, and yet she was too damn exhausted to ponder his behavior.

"Hey, even I'm not a total prick." He sat down across from her and rested his elbows on his knees, his jaws working overtime on the chewing gum.

She eyed him and conceded that the obnoxious detective sitting across from her did indeed have a heart after all. "Are you thinking what I'm thinking?" she asked as she sipped at the terrible coffee.

"Sure am. Someone's fucking with us."

"Where's Adams?"

"She's got an alibi."

"Of course she does," she scoffed.

"She's holed up at that mansion of hers in the hills. We've got nothing on her."

"Of course not." This entire investigation was unbelievable. "Did we ID that body yet?"

He shook his head. "Still can't locate the skull, but we did find two more teeth."

She narrowed her eyes. "Let me guess, they match Reece's dental files."

He laughed. "Yep."

"Of course they do." *It's just all coming about way too easily.*

"Do I detect a note of cynicism, Detective Henderson?"

"You're goddamn right you do."

❖

Patricia stood in the hallway outside the open hospital room door. She hadn't meant to eavesdrop on the conversation, but the voices carried out into the hall and she'd heard what Erin had said to her cheating ex-husband. Erin had put a call in to Mark's mistress, letting her know about his condition and requesting her presence. Patricia had been impressed with her nobility and her tact.

"You're a good woman," she said as Erin emerged from the room and closed the door behind her.

"Yeah, well, he deserves to be happy." Erin looked tired, her eyes pained and bloodshot, her face drawn.

Patricia walked next to her, wanting desperately to touch her, to take away her pain, but she kept her hands by her sides, the fear of rejection and exposure of her true feelings winning out.

"So do you, Mac. So do you," she said softly as they walked out of the hospital and into the warm, comforting embrace of the desert heat.

"Mac, you've got to listen to me. Please!" Patricia pleaded.

Erin shook her head and continued to shove her belongings into her large duffel bag. "I said no. I'm not doing it." Her tone was firm.

"Think about what you're saying. You're completely disregarding your own safety."

"I'm not going into hiding, Patricia, and that's final." She shoved the last shirt in the bag without bothering to fold it and tried to zip the bag shut. "Shit!"

Frustrated, she unzipped it and pulled her clothes back out of the bag and onto the bed. As she tossed her belongings around, she was overwhelmed with a sense of failure. Her cover was blown. Elizabeth Adams knew who she was. That thought didn't scare her. Rather, it made her feel guilty and ashamed, knowing that Liz must now think their intimate encounter was just part of Erin's job and meant nothing.

A shudder coursed through her as she remembered the look in Liz's eyes just after they had made love. So deep, so tender, so unlike the woman everyone had warned her about. She shook the image from her mind and tried to get a handle on what she was more upset over—her failure in her undercover role or her exposure to Liz. She knew what she should be more upset over. Elizabeth Adams's feelings should be the furthest thing from her mind. But the woman and her warm blue eyes remained, having claimed her from the inside out.

Lost in her thoughts, Erin watched as Patricia walked over to the bed and folded the clothes neatly before placing them in the bag.

"You know you aren't safe right now," she said. "They know who you are, and they could come after you."

"Then let them." Erin grabbed a shirt angrily and placed it in the bag. "Let Liz or whoever you think will come, come after me. I dare them."

Deep in her heart she didn't think Liz would come for her. She couldn't even fathom the woman being violent with anyone, not after the way she had touched her, had awakened her body. Confusion and desire spilled into her blood, and she wondered if she would ever see the beautiful and mysterious nightclub owner again.

"You think it's Adams?" Patricia asked, surprise evident in her voice.

"I don't know."

Erin hurriedly zipped the bag. Once again, powerful images of their intimacy flooded her brain. She had to see her again; something ached inside of her, cried out for her. She remembered how she had stormed out, how she had run away from Elizabeth Adams and her penetrating eyes, so full of emotion and confusion. As badly as she wanted to see her, to explain things to her, she knew Liz would in no way want to see her again. She was not the kind of woman who would easily forget being tricked. Was the nonfatal attack on Mark a message from her, a cruel vengeance? Erin remembered her tenderness, the gentle, knowing feel of her touch, the loneliness and vulnerability in her stare. It didn't add up. Nothing did anymore.

She headed out of the bedroom and down the hall.

"If you won't let the department put you in a safe house, then at least stay with me," Patricia called after her, fear evident in her voice. "I don't think it's a good idea for you to be alone. And certainly not at your house."

Erin stood still by the front door and gazed at the floor. Even in her jumbled head, Patricia's words made sense. The thought of being alone in her own huge house scared her more than the thought of someone coming after her.

She met Patricia's anxious eyes and lowered her duffel bag. "Okay. But just for a few days."

Patricia sat poised in her desk chair, focused intently on her computer, her fingers flying across her keyboard. She had been writing for close to two hours and was swimming comfortably now, the water warming against her skin as she moved through the sea her words created. She hadn't realized it until she reread her words, but she was writing about Erin.

Lightning flashed brilliantly outside her window, illuminating the office. She looked up, startled, and looked out the window, almost fearing what she might see standing outside. The tree in her front yard bent strongly to the left, submitting to the powerful wind. Rain blew in spurts against the windowpane, smacking at it with large splattering drops. An enormous clap of thunder followed the lightning, shaking the house.

Jack came running into the room and jumped up in her lap, growling at the blowing tree outside the window. She stroked the standing fur on his back, trying to comfort him as he trembled. She couldn't explain how, but her deaf dog could somehow feel the thunder. She looked back to her computer just as the screen went black, along with the desk lamp.

"Damn it." She placed Jack on the floor and busied herself turning off her computer and lamp. She had saved her document and she had a surge protector, so she wasn't too worried about anything regarding her work or her computer. No, she was worried for completely different reasons.

She rose and walked slowly out of her office and down the darkened hallway, making her way into the living room. Erin had placed a flashlight on the coffee table, and Patricia picked it up and clicked it on.

She shone the weak halo of light on the couch, where Erin lay sleeping soundly. "Mac?" She walked to her side and lightly shook her.

Erin stirred. "Yeah?"

"We lost power. I need you to come sleep in my bedroom." With the house shrouded in darkness, Patricia knew she would never be able to sleep unless Erin was right by her side.

She helped her up and they slowly made their way to the master bedroom. Jack jumped on the bed, barking and chasing the flickering beam of light from the flashlight.

Erin lay down on top of the covers, making no effort to pull them back. Patricia walked to the dresser and lit a large eucalyptus-scented candle. Then she turned off the flashlight and placed it on the nightstand. Thunder crashed loudly and the wind surged against the house. Flashes of lightning lit up the room, brightening Erin's sleeping form.

Patricia stood next to the bed, mesmerized by the woman she'd longed to see there. More than anything, she wanted to crawl into bed next to her and curl up against her warmth. She wanted to get lost in the scent of her, to be lulled to sleep by her steady breathing. But she knew she had to double-check the house, she had to keep her safe.

Taking the flashlight, she went off to explore her house, to secure all the doors and windows. As she walked back down the hall, she heard her cell phone ring. She picked up her pace and jogged into the kitchen, where she had left it.

"Henderson."

"Hey, it's Jacobs. You okay?"

"We're fine. Just lost power, though."

Gary's voice was distant and crackling. "The whole city's out. The creek beds are full and we've got some major flash flooding." He was breaking up, his signal weakening. "People trapped in their cars…We've been called out by the mayor…We have to go direct traffic…signals out…looting…You gonna be okay?"

She could no longer make out what her partner was saying. "Yes, we'll be fine." She shouted the words but got no response. "Gary? Gary?" She pulled the phone away from her ear and saw that the signal was gone. She set the phone down on the counter and continued on her quest to check the house.

With her fellow detectives unavailable, there would be no routine drive-by as she had requested. She and Mac were now totally alone, and she hoped she had the stamina to remain alert throughout the night.

Having checked all the doors and windows, she went to her office and collected a spiral notebook and a pen. She returned to the bedroom and propped herself up with pillows against the headboard, careful not to disturb Erin. The room was already stuffy in the absence of the air-conditioning and the ceiling fan—not the ideal environment to try to stay awake in. She thought briefly about opening a window but decided it was too great a risk.

Erin moaned and rolled over onto her back, her face glistening with sweat in the candlelight. Jack had settled down under the covers, too afraid to be above them. Patricia positioned her notebook against her knees and began to write, inspired by the sleeping beauty in her bed.

She wrote steadily for what seemed like hours, milking her mind of the pressure that had built up during the last week. She wrote so intensely and so quickly that her hand throbbed from the strain. Her eyes became heavy with her mind's sweet release, and she fought sleep as long as she was able to. But exhaustion finally won out, and she dropped her suddenly heavy pen and fell fast asleep.

Elizabeth Adams watched the front of the house through the back-and-forth motion of her windshield wipers. The rain was falling heavily, bathing her Range Rover with hard, heavy-sounding drops. She gripped her steering wheel and sat motionless. She knew who was inside. She'd been watching for a while.

A face flashed in her mind. The face that had reached inside her black, desolate chest and squeezed the life back into her heart. Another image stole her breath. The same beautiful face turning from her, the woman she had just made love to running from her, pushing her away and leaving her behind.

Erin McKenzie. She silently repeated the name over and over. *Erin McKenzie, not Katherine Chandler. How did it happen? How did this happen to me?*

Her chest tightened and she could feel her heart bleeding, filling her insides and drowning her soul. She turned off the ignition and stepped out into the cold rain, her jaw set. In a momentary daze, she watched as the water rolled off her skin, unable to penetrate into her very being, unable to cool the fire within. Compelling her legs to move, she walked toward the house.

Patricia opened her eyes and tried to get her bearings. She had fallen asleep and now lay curled against Erin, her face nestled comfortably in her neck. She let the warmth of the moment wash over her and almost fell asleep again.

It was warm in the room, and the heat from Erin's body seeped through her clothes. Patricia turned on her back to let her body cool. The candle on the dresser still burned, but the flame had sunk as the wax melted and now flickered in the barrel of the candle. As her eyes drooped and she began drifting, Jack growled from the foot of the bed where he was peeking out from beneath the covers.

She sat up and reached for her gun, running her hand along under the covers, searching for where she had placed it. Jack continued to growl, and Patricia stifled a gasp as a figure advanced toward the doorway. Frantically, Patricia groped for her gun. Jack jumped off the bed, hopping backward as he barked.

"Shut that little shit up, or I'll kill him." The woman raised her arms, a gun in her hands.

Patricia was almost certain she recognized the voice. She stood and held her hands up, walking slowly toward Jack. "Easy, I'm just going to get him."

Erin awoke and sat up slowly on the bed. "What's going on?"

"Shut up, bitch!" The voice was deeper now, angrier. The intruder swung her arms around, aiming the gun at Erin.

Patricia scooped Jack up and placed him on the bed. "Don't move, Mac," she directed while her eyes remained focused on the figure.

"Watch it, bitch, or you'll eat lead." The intruder moved in, swinging the gun around toward Patricia. Candlelight flickered across her face, confirming her identity.

Patricia sucked in a rapid breath of air. "Tracy, you don't want to do this."

The young woman kept the barrel of the gun aimed at Patricia. Her hair was wet and plastered to her head from the rain. Black eye make-up ran down her face, giving her a demonic appearance.

"My name's not Tracy!" she yelled, the gun shaking in her hands. "It's Blade, bitch." Her voice lowered and she stepped closer to Patricia. "Now back off. It's not you I'm after."

She swung the gun around to Erin, who sat poised on the edge of the bed. She closed her eyes and cocked the gun. Patricia lunged at her just as the gun went off, and wrestled her for control of the weapon.

Erin quickly rose, having thrown herself flat on the bed a split second before the gun discharged. The bullet had pierced the wall over the headboard. She was rushing to help Patricia when another figure entered from the dark hallway. This woman was wet, her short, dark hair shiny in the candlelight. She moved swiftly and hit Patricia on the back of the head with the butt of a small handgun. Patricia collapsed instantly, seemingly knocked unconscious from the blow.

"No!" Erin shouted and she moved toward Patricia.

"Uh uh uh." The woman trained her pistol on Erin. "You stay right there."

Erin stared at her, amazed at the familiar piercing blue eyes.

"I know it's small." The new intruder waved her gun as she spoke. "But you and I both know it'll do the trick. And if it doesn't…" She grinned. "Then I'll use what I prefer to use anyway."

With her free hand she pulled a six-inch serrated blade from her back pocket.

"Who are you and what do you want?" Erin asked.

"Shut up." The woman dragged Blade to her feet and moved behind her, speaking with her mouth right next to her ear. "Now, let's do what we came for." She said the words seductively, and Blade glared at Erin.

Erin held her hands up and walked carefully back to the bed, one unsure foot behind the other. She sat down slowly and watched as Jack pawed at Patricia's motionless body on the floor.

"I don't think I can." Blade had raised her gun, but her hands were trembling.

The woman behind her stroked her arms and kissed her ear. "Yes, you can, baby. Do it for me." The voice was soothing and seductive.

"Drop your weapons, both of you," Erin warned, carefully easing her hand under the covers, reaching for the gun she had felt against her leg earlier. "Do you want to go away for killing a cop?"

"Shoot her," the woman with the knife hissed.

This time something in Blade seemed to go dead. Erin had seen that expression before. Before she could yell a final warning, she glimpsed the telltale movement of Blade's index finger and instinctively dived, raising Patricia's gun and firing through the covers, aiming at center mass as she rolled across the bed.

The bullets tore into Blade's body, dropping her to the floor. Erin scrambled up and hurried around the bed, the gun firmly in front of her, ready for anything. Feathers from the down comforter fell like snow, surrounding the two prone figures on the floor like a peaceful fairytale.

The woman with the knife knelt over Blade, who was breathing with great difficulty. Her eyes were wide and liquid and she spat blood with every agonizing breath.

"Put your hands up," Erin ordered.

Laughter rang out in the stuffy, dimly lit room. Wild, penetrating eyes focused on Erin, and the woman stood, waving her hands in the air, the gun still held tightly in one of them. "You mean like this?"

"Drop your weapon!"

"Well now, which is it? Hold my hands up or drop my gun?" An evil grin tipped the side of her face.

"That's enough, Jay," a deep voice said from the doorway, and Liz walked in.

The woman with the gun looked shocked to see her. "Don't tell me what to do, Lizzie!" She refocused on Erin, shaking the gun at her. "You've grown soft on me, and look at what's happened!"

"You've gone too far this time," Liz said calmly, her eyes fixed on Erin. She stood an inch taller than Jay, but Erin had no trouble seeing the resemblance between the two.

"Ha!" The grin returned to Jay's face and the fire burned brightly in her eyes. "I'll decide when I've gone too far. This little bitch got the better of you, Lizzie, and you know how I feel about people who don't play nice with you."

"I don't need you to do anything for me, Jay." Water dripped from Liz's hair, down the bare skin of her arms.

"I didn't hear you complain."

"I didn't want to believe it was you. I refused to believe it was you. And when I suspected you might be involved, I knew if I made a move to find you, I would've led the police right to you. Can't you see I've been protecting you, just like you claim to protect me?"

"I've always protected you, Lizzie!" Jay shouted angrily, spitting as the words flew out of her mouth. "Who looked out for you when we were kids? Huh? Who?"

"You, Jay. Always you." Liz moved closer until she was right next to her.

Erin took a cautious step back, trying to distance herself from the woman with the wild eyes. But Jay didn't miss a thing.

"Don't you move again, sweet cheeks, or I'll blow your cute little body full of holes. Just like you did my friend here." She used her gun to indicate Blade, now dead, eyes wide open and glazed with fear.

"Put the gun down, Jay," Liz said gently. "This has to stop now."

"First I'm going to kill this bitch who betrayed you." Her voice was low once again, deadly serious.

"I can't let you do that."

"So it was okay for all those other sons of bitches to die, but it's not okay for your little girlfriend here?" She waved the gun again and laughed, amused at herself.

"It was never okay." Liz stared at the barrel of Erin's gun.

"Why the fuck not? We can blame everything on the little vampire girl, Lizzie. Don't take away all my fun."

The power kicked on suddenly and the lights in the bedroom illuminated, startling all three women.

Jay's eyes grew big at the shock of the light and she held the gun out firm, her mouth open. Erin knew she was about to fire.

"No!" Liz lunged at her sister's arm, wrestling her to the ground and muffling the shot.

Erin had dropped and rolled, and she looked up now, her gun aimed at the two dark women on the floor. She breathed deep as adrenaline flooded her veins and she waited to see if she felt any pain, to see if she had been hit. No pain, no bleeding, she was fine. Instantly her thoughts shifted to Liz, and she watched with horror as Jay crawled out from beneath her.

Her T-shirt was covered in blood. "Oh no, no!" She screamed and hunkered down over Liz. "Lizzie, Lizzie, I'm so sorry. Where… where does it hurt?"

A hand to her bleeding shoulder, Liz urged, "Go, Jay. Run."

Jay shook her head defiantly, tears streaming down her face. "No, I won't leave you."

"You have to. If you love me, you'll go. Hurry, before they come for you." Her eyes swung briefly to Erin, and she shoved the blood-covered woman, yelling, "Go, Jay, now!"

Jay fled from the bedroom and Erin stumbled to her feet and followed her. There were no lights on in the hallway, and the rest of the house was still dark as well. She ran as best she could, trying to stay on Jay's heels. She reached the kitchen and tumbled over a chair. Regaining her bearings, she saw Jay sprint from the house through the back door. Erin ran into the yard after her but watched helplessly as Jay disappeared over a five-foot cement fence.

Breathing hard, her eyes still on the fence, she lowered her gun, knowing it was useless to pursue. Besides, there were two other women who needed her attention.

Back in the house, she ran to the bedroom, glanced at Patricia, and rolled Liz over on to her side. Stopping the bleeding had to be her first priority. "Don't move, I'm calling an ambulance." She grabbed the phone off the dresser.

"Wait, please." Liz struggled to stand.

Erin prevented her, phone in hand. "Lie still, you're losing too much blood." She pressed Liz back down and held her hand firmly over her wound.

"Don't call yet." Her eyes were strained, pleading.

"Why?" Erin didn't like the way the color was draining from her face.

"Jay's my sister. You can't tell them about her." Liz gripped her arm in silent request.

"She killed people, I have to tell." Erin was adamant, yet at the same time she didn't want to upset the bleeding woman. She just wanted her to lie still and relax until an ambulance arrived.

"No, please don't. It's not her fault, she's not well. So much happened to her when we were kids. Please. She's all I have. Let me handle her." Liz was begging, pleading, and completely desperate, proving to Erin once again that people were wrong about her. She was far from callous and inhuman.

Nevertheless, she had to do what was right. "I can't do that, Liz."

Liz clenched her jaw and pulled herself back up. Erin tried to push her back down but Liz removed her hand, holding it firmly in her own, demanding that Erin look in her eyes. "Check on Patricia," she insisted huskily, her eyes pained and distant.

Erin once again was nearly lost in the abyss of blue.

Liz reached up and stroked Erin's cheek. "You have to know that I would never hurt you."

Erin felt her skin charge with life under Liz's fingers. She shook her head away from the touch. She didn't know anything about anyone anymore. She lifted the phone and punched in 911. As she waited for a response, she went over to kneel by Patricia, who was still unconscious. Erin checked for a pulse and found it steady and strong.

Relief washed through her as she was connected with an emergency operator.

"Yes, hello. I need a couple of ambulances. I have someone shot and bleeding and someone unconscious and—"

She turned to check on the other woman, but the room was bright and empty.

Elizabeth Adams had gone.

Chapter Twelve

One week later
Not far from Cabo San Lucas, Mexico

She walked slowly on the desolate beach, her feet swallowed up by the cool water with every crunching wave. It was dusk, the time she favored most on the beach. The sun had bade the sea and the darkening sky farewell with one last kiss of brilliant color.

She looked up and spotted the peeking winks of the night's first stars. Up on the softer, drier sand, she eased herself down. Dull pain shot through her from her injured shoulder, but she repositioned quickly, stifling the sensation. She drew her knees up and rested her good arm on them, while her other arm remained snug in a sling.

The bullet from her sister's pistol had torn quite a little hole in her, a painful reminder of Jay's failed attempt to kill Erin McKenzie. Pain of a different sort shot through her as the blond detective's face entered her mind. She had seen the hurt in her eyes, the distrust, the cold distance. She shivered as those images blew in with the sea breeze.

She heard her sister's voice from behind her, calling her name. But when she turned, she found she was alone, the wind playing cruel tricks on her. She stared out at the sea, her mind drifting to Jay, wondering where she was. And wondering still if Erin had told.

As she sat and watched the mysterious sea giving and taking with every wave, she silently hoped her sister was safe and Erin McKenzie had decided to keep her identity a secret, choosing, like the sea, to take it back out with her.

❖

August
Baja Peninsula, Mexico

"*Chicle*, señorita?" a young boy asked, a huge grin on his face.

Liz eyed the large cardboard box of Chiclets chewing gum he carried in front of him with both hands. "Sure." She reached in her khaki cargo shorts with her good arm and pulled out a neat stack of bills.

The boy immediately dug in the box and pulled out two packs of the small gum. He held them out for her and wiped the sweat from his brow. The large box was held secure by a thick piece of string slung around his neck. His Scooby-Doo T-shirt was torn at the collar and his brown pants were two sizes too big, made evident by the giant rolled-up cuffs. She looked down at his bare feet.

"*Es un* quarter," he said with his thick accent.

Liz pushed the gum in his hand away, causing him to look up. She leafed out a fifty dollar bill and handed it to him.

"Gracias, señorita, gracias!" He lifted the string holding the box up over his neck, trying to give her the entire box of gum.

"No, you keep it." She placed her hand on the box, gently resisting. She met his large eyes and smiled at him before walking away.

The boy shouted his thanks after her and she wove her way between people as she continued on her quest through the tiny beachside town.

Tourists walked and talked, stopping to browse at the various vendors selling hand-woven blankets, trinkets, and T-shirts. Many were dressed like her in tank tops, cargo shorts, and sandals. She could smell their suntan lotion as she maneuvered past them, brushing against their fanny packs.

Up ahead, she spotted her destination. Pablo's Fish Tacos stood directly in front of her, and she slowed her pace as she approached the window of the small building.

"*Hola*, help you?" a middle-aged man with silver capped front teeth asked from the window.

The smell of fish was strong, and she pulled off her sunglasses as she ordered, trying to peer into the shady building where the man stood. "*Una cerveza, por favor*." Her Spanish was barely mediocre, but it always got her by.

"Corona?" He held up a wet, icy bottle.

"Tecate, *por favor*," she clarified.

He quickly pulled out another bottle, opened it for her, and slid it across the counter. She leafed out a five dollar bill and handed it to the man, not expecting change. She picked up her beer and wished she had some lime.

"You really should try the shrimp."

Liz turned at the sound of a familiar voice behind her and made her way over to a woman sitting at a table with a bucket full of fresh shrimp on ice. She sat down across from her, placing the sunglasses over her sensitive eyes.

"Help yourself." The woman, Shane Wilson, pushed the bucket toward her and continued to shell and peel the shrimp before popping them in her mouth. The private detective was bigger than Liz, bulky with muscle mass. Liz had known her for years and had hired her on many different occasions.

"No thanks, not hungry." Liz eyed her and crossed an ankle over her knee.

"Mmm, your loss." Wilson licked her fingers. "How's the shoulder?"

Liz took a long tug from her beer, thankful for its iciness. Her shoulder was healing nicely and she no longer had to wear the sling. But she winced as she set the beer down with her injured arm, the dull pain making itself known. She relaxed her face and refused to let the pain win, using the sore arm every chance she got.

"Fine." She answered in the tone that let everyone who valued peace know the topic was closed. Just because she wasn't on her home turf didn't mean the rules had changed. She was still a very private person when it came to her personal life.

"Yeah, well, you look like shit. You've lost weight, you're pale—"

"If I wanted your opinion, I would've asked for it."

"Sorry." Wilson opened her palms in a peaceful gesture. "It's just, you know that I care, and I always sort of hoped that someday maybe you and I…" She leaned across the table and tried to cup her hand over Liz's.

Liz kept her hand out of reach. "Yeah, well, it's not happening."

Wilson sighed and sat back in her chair. Liz figured she was mentally chiding herself for blowing her only chance. She had miscalculated with Liz, assuming from her pale and thin appearance that she was somehow now more fragile and maybe even… vulnerable. But she now knew better. Liz might have looked weaker than Wilson had ever seen her look, but she was still strong and still unavailable.

"Why don't you tell me what you came here to say, what I'm *paying* you to say," Liz demanded, weary of the chitchat.

Wilson rested her elbows on the table, her muscles lined up on her arms and popping out on her shoulders like perfectly shaped pieces of meat resting under the skin. "I found Jay." She fingered her dark beer bottle, peeling at its yellow label.

"Where?" Liz sat back in her chair and pulled her sunglasses off, her eyes never leaving the other woman's. The wind blew in off the nearby sea, rattling the umbrella over their table.

"Where you said she would be."

"Is she…okay?"

"Seems to be."

Liz let out a long, shaky breath and stared past Wilson to focus on the sea. Relief started to wash through her but she wouldn't let it, not yet.

"Anything else?" she asked.

"Yeah." Wilson lifted up her beer bottle and drained it. "No one's looking for her."

Liz sat in silence for a moment, not sure she had heard correctly. "The police—"

"No one's looking for her," the muscled woman interrupted. "No one but you."

This time relief burst through the gates, and Liz grinned.

Wilson sat back and folded her arms over her ample chest, apparently reading this reaction as an opportunity. "So, how about dinner, then? To celebrate?" Liz tugged another sip of her beer and rose from the table. She reached in her pocket and tossed the stack of bills at Wilson.

"I've got a plane to catch." She walked quickly away from the table and back into the crowd of tourists. She pulled out her satellite phone and dialed.

"Yeah, it's Liz," she said into the phone. "Book me on the first flight to Alabama."

She ended the call and continued walking back toward her Jeep Wrangler. She had been traveling through Mexico for a few weeks now, and she was relieved at the thought of finally leaving. Even if it meant returning to her childhood home in the Deep South.

Wilson's words replayed in her mind as she climbed into the Jeep. *No one's looking for her.*

No one was looking for Jay. Not even the police. No one.

She steered her way back out onto the main road. As she drove toward her rented seaside house, the salty ocean breeze ran through her hair, massaging and relaxing, and her thoughts drifted to Erin McKenzie.

She hadn't told about Jay.

Liz thought back to the last time she had seen her. Raw betrayal cramped her stomach once again as she remembered Jay telling her the truth about Erin, the truth about the woman who had somehow reached into her chest and squeezed the life back into her heart. She was a cop, and not only a cop, but an undercover cop pretending to be attracted to her in order to gain information.

It had all been lies. All of it. The feelings, the emotions, the sex. Liz cringed at the thought and hated herself for allowing Erin in.

She made a turn off the main road and onto the dirt road that led to the private beach house. As the Jeep kicked up dirt and fought the road, she wondered if her sister was indeed okay and she wondered the same about Erin. Regardless of the lies and betrayal, she couldn't bring herself to stop thinking of her. Her green eyes sparkling with life, the smile Liz had worked so hard to see, the way that beautiful body had responded to her touch. Could it really have been all lies?

And she hadn't told the police about Jay. What did that mean? Was it a setup? Maybe blackmail? Or was it something else altogether?

She skidded the Jeep to a stop in front of the beach house and climbed out to go pack her travel bag. She didn't have any answers to the questions plaguing her mind. From Jay and her killing spree to Erin and her mysterious behavior, there were so many questions to be answered, so many doors left wide open and unexplored. There was only one thing she was sure of.

The time had come to find out.

Chapter Thirteen

Valle Luna, Arizona

"How are you, Henderson?"

Patricia entered her sergeant's office slowly and sat down in the chair across from his desk. It had been weeks since the shooting, but its toll was evident in her shadowed eyes and pale, drawn face. She knew how she looked. Sleep had evaded her, allowing guilt to eat away at her, reminding her every second of her failure. She had been beaten on her own turf, in her own home, leaving Erin all alone to fight the demons that had come knocking. They were both extremely lucky to have survived, no thanks to her. Patricia cringed at the thought and raised a weak hand to her temple, unconsciously fingering the location of the throbbing in her head. Her tired eyes met her sergeant's and she shifted slightly, realizing he was patiently awaiting her answer.

"I'm fine, sir," she lied, clearing her throat to allow her voice to sound stronger than she felt.

"How's the head?"

Patricia's hand quickly lowered from her temple. "Much better." She offered him a soft smile, determined to hide the frequency of her headaches.

"Glad to hear it." He shifted in his chair and sat up a little straighter as he fumbled through the numerous files on his desk. "First things first. You should know we're ready to wrap up the Adams case."

"What!" Her body grew rigid and her head swam with heavy and blurry thoughts. It was a mistake. It had to be. She had merely heard wrong. "We haven't found Adams yet, sir."

Ruiz's face remained stoic. "We don't need to," he stated flatly. "Walsh fits the bill. She was confused and obsessed and easily controlled by Reece. We have all the evidence we need."

Patricia swallowed with difficulty at her sergeant's demeanor. Her heartbeat thumped into her ears as she eased herself back into her chair. *What are they thinking? Are they crazy?* Yes, that was it. It wasn't her going crazy. It was them. They only needed a little reminding.

"What about Adams?" Her voice was high and agitated, but she didn't care. She couldn't care. "She gets off scot-free?"

No way. Not after all this. Not after what Adams had done to her. A sharp pain shot through her. Adams had done something to Erin as well.

"All the evidence points to Reece and Walsh," Ruiz explained. "We don't have anything on Adams. As bad as we want her, we've got nothing, and her alibis panned out."

While his tone of voice sounded apologetic, it only fed her fury. How could he be sorry? He wasn't sorry. He wanted it closed. They all did. Nobody cared about how bad Adams really was. Nobody but her.

Patricia clenched her fists at her side as her blood rushed through her veins. "She's involved!" Her voice was deep and loud, laced heavily with anger. "You know it as well as I do." She held his gaze, challenging him. She no longer cared that he was her superior. She was right in this and she knew at once what needed to be done. She would have to do things herself. "Give me another week. I'll find her and—"

"Can't do it," Ruiz interrupted, holding up a palm, not willing to wait for her to continue. "The department wants it closed. I have my orders."

"But there has to be some way to get her." She rested her hands on his desk, leaning toward him.

"I'm sorry, Henderson, it's not going to happen."

Patricia closed her mouth and clenched her jaw. Her blood pounded furiously in her ears. She couldn't believe what she was being told. Adams was going to slither through their fingers and get away with murder. Wasn't that the story of that bitch's life? The thought made as her as sick as it did angry. She would be damned if she was just going to let it go.

Ruiz got busy shifting papers, making it clear the subject was closed. "There's something else I need to discuss with you," he said.

Patricia stood very still, her mind racing, her anger flaming like kerosene, burning and raging through her. She knew there was still some forensic evidence to be examined, and she wondered if it all had been processed and she just hadn't been told. The collected evidence had been her last hope of a direct connection to Adams. It must have led nowhere. That's why they were closing the case.

"Go on," she demanded. Her body was on alert, alive with fear, anger, and the desire for vengeance.

"I asked to meet with you regarding Detective McKenzie." He fingered though more files and then, finding the correct one, leaned back once again and mindlessly flipped through it.

Patricia's body hummed as she thought of the younger detective. Erin hadn't been herself lately, and Patricia felt greatly responsible. It was her fault Erin had to go through what she did. Alone. Patricia's heart cried out. She had feelings for Erin that went well beyond protectiveness. Feelings that she could no longer bury or deny.

Ruiz glanced up at her over the file. "Have you spoken to her recently?"

"Some." Her mind swam with the sporadic and short conversations she had with the younger woman. Erin was evasive and cold, locked in her own world of pain.

She had to reach her, some way, somehow. And she was hell-bent on doing so. Now more than ever, Erin needed her.

"I have a recommendation here that Mac be kept on leave for at least a couple more weeks." Ruiz sought her eyes. "A couple of weeks sounds excessive. What do you think?"

Patricia's throat tightened at the thought of Erin returning to work, unable to let the Adams case go. She couldn't allow that to happen. Whatever had gone on between Erin and that woman needed to be put away, kept from Erin's mind. She had to keep Erin away from Adams, to protect and keep her from any more pain. She had to make Mac see that it was she who truly cared about her. Whatever it took.

"I would have to agree with the recommendation," she stated with conviction.

Ruiz tossed the file on the desk and made a steeple with his hands. "Why? You know she's requested desk duty. I really can't see the harm in that. But then again, I haven't spent any time with her. You, I assume, have."

Patricia's mind flew, but her mouth remained closed. The truth was she had seen very little of Erin since the shooting. But she had seen enough to know she shouldn't return to work. Not yet. In fact, she should stay away from anything and everything regarding this investigation. And Patricia would make sure she did. No one knew Erin like she did. No one could see to her like she could. All she needed was time to convince her to forget about Adams.

"She's not well." Patricia unclenched her fists as she exaggerated Erin's condition. She took in a deep breath, knowing that what she was doing was wrong. But she didn't care.

"Not well enough to sit at her desk all day?" Ruiz raised his eyebrows in disbelief.

Patricia shook her head, sounding very serious. "I don't think it's wise. She's not stable. She's jumpy, irrational." *You're lying*, Patricia thought to herself. But still she continued. "She's paranoid."

The word hung in the air, but she refused to feel guilty about it. She was doing this in Erin's best interest. And with the investigation winding down, that would leave Patricia with plenty of time and opportunity to be with her, to show her how she felt. She cleared her throat, ready to voice the final blow.

"She also seems determined to keep going after Adams. No matter what. I don't think she would be willing to back down even if the case is closed. Not in her current state of mind. And we both know what kind of trouble that could bring."

Even if it wasn't true, it was something that absolutely could not be permitted to happen. No way was Patricia going to allow Erin to go near Elizabeth Adams again.

Ruiz looked appalled. No senior officer wanted to think about a loose cannon sitting in their department, just waiting to blow.

Patricia validated his fears. "No sir," she said emphatically, but with a hint of suitable regret. "I think Mac should remain on leave until she gets things back in perspective."

Ruiz sighed and removed his glasses to rub his eyes. "Okay." He slid the glasses back on his face with a frustrated frown. "I'll consider your concerns."

The cool water did little to douse the flames that were burning hot under Erin's skin. She straightened, met her own reflection, and watched as the water ran from her face. After turning off the faucet, she continued to stare, startled at just how much she had changed. It wasn't just her pale, drawn face or deeply shadowed eyes. It was something else. Something deeper; something within. And now with this latest attack on the normal, stable life she was trying to lead, she was hardening even more. She placed her hands on the sink as her mind replayed the words of her superior.

"I'm sorry, Mac, but…"

The department didn't want her. It was the shrink, it had to be. She met her reflection's eyes once again and leaned forward, searching, wishing she could see into the recesses of her wounded mind. Just what the hell happened that night?

A drop of liquid grew heavy on her eyelashes. It fell into the sink and pooled with the remaining water around the drain. Suddenly, an image came. White-hot like lightning, flashing in her brain.

She was looking at her hands. She was on the floor in Patricia's bedroom. She glanced up and over. Patricia lay there, limp, with Jack pawing at her motionless body. Erin cried out but got no response. Her hands were sticky with red. Blood. Somehow she knew it wasn't her own. Her hurried gaze fell to the floor. The light-colored carpet was stained a few feet from where she sat. The lifeless eyes of a young woman stared up into nothingness. Bullet wounds gaped in her chest, leading to horrific holes in her lungs. Blood oozed from the wounds, spreading through the wet fabric of her T-shirt.

Movement from behind her startled Erin back into reality. A woman emerged from one of the stalls and washed her hands. She gave Erin a polite but nervous smile as she hurriedly dried off on a rough-sounding paper towel and then scurried from the restroom. Erin looked into the mirror, knowing somehow that this colleague knew her story. The whole department knew. She only wished she knew as much as they did. Since the night of the shooting, she had only been able to remember flashes of what actually happened. And none made any sense.

Post Traumatic Stress Syndrome was what the tiny woman in the wingback chair had called it. Erin winced. That was why she couldn't return to work. Because she couldn't remember. She gripped the sink in anger. How could they do this to her? She might not be able to remember, but she was fine. She studied the puffiness around her eyes. So she wasn't sleeping well, so what? The shrink had told her that nightmares were perfectly normal. So what was the problem?

She rinsed her face again, determined to make herself look better. For whatever reason, Ruiz and the department thought she was unfit for duty. And true, she did have her problems, but they were not at a level where her work would be affected, certainly not in the desk position she had requested. With the exception of the flashbacks, she was thinking clearly. In fact, she had never been more aware and sure of her surroundings. All that had happened to her recently had been neatly processed and packed away in her mind. Her undercover assignment, the attack on Mark. Elizabeth Adams.

She sucked in a quick breath. Liz. As hard as she tried, she couldn't shake her memories of the woman or their intimate encounter from her mind. *Jesus. The way she touched me.* She shook her head, refusing to let it overpower her. Instead, she clenched her jaw and wiped her face with a dry, stiff paper towel. She had been through a lot, but she was handling it well. Definitely well enough to return to work.

The door to the restroom opened, and Erin breathed deep and stood taller, readying herself for whoever it was. She didn't want to be seen as weak or inferior in any way.

"Mac?"

"Patricia." Relief flooded her. This was her chance. If anyone would see her side of things, it would be Patricia.

"How are you?" Patricia closed the distance between them, placing a hand on Erin's shoulder.

The physical contact shook her, rattling the steady foundation she was trying so hard to project. She cleared her throat as the hand remained, squeezing her slightly. She willed her voice to be strong. "I'm fine."

"I've been so worried," Patricia whispered softly, raising her other hand so she was holding both of Erin's shoulders.

The touch was warm and grounding, yet the close contact was stifling, and Erin felt like she couldn't breathe. The air was too hot. She moved away quickly and pretended to wash her hands. The break in contact calmed her and enabled her to steady her breathing. She couldn't explain it, but she just didn't want to be touched.

Patricia slowly lowered her arms as Erin watched her in the mirror. "Mac, I know what you're going through."

Erin swallowed with difficulty but remained controlled.

When she didn't respond, Patricia continued. "The shooting, what happened...I..."

Erin met her eyes, suddenly understanding. They had done it to Patricia as well. They weren't letting her work. "You too? They're making you go on leave?" It wasn't right, and now Erin knew she had someone else who would fight with her.

Patricia closed her mouth and turned her head slightly, her eyes never leaving Erin's. "No, I'm not on leave."

"Then why am I?" Erin could hear the anger in her voice, making it heavy and strong. If Patricia was fit for duty, then she sure as hell was too. She hadn't even been harmed. Patricia had been rendered unconscious.

"I'm sorry." Patricia took a step toward her.

"Then help me," Erin cut in quickly. "Help me talk to Ruiz."

"I've already tried. They've made up their minds."

A long breath shuddered from Erin as defeat settled in. "It isn't fair." Her voice lowered as her throat tightened.

"I know. But you need to make the best of it." Patricia's hand rubbed up and down Erin's bicep in an attempt at comfort. "Get your life together, recover fully, rest. It's not forever."

Erin felt her eyes well up but she refused to cry. Her face felt hot again, just like it had when Ruiz had told her the news.

"Come on," Patricia coaxed with a gentle smile. "I'll help. It'll be fun. Just think of it as a nice long vacation."

Erin swallowed back her tears. Her body was heavy, her surroundings fuzzy. Defeat settled in around her. And all she wanted to do was melt into Patricia's arms and let someone else deal with her pain and the situation in which she found herself.

"I…don't even think I can handle finding my own place right now. I was counting on coming back to work, getting lost in the case." That was how she had always functioned. By throwing herself into work.

"I understand," Patricia said. "Stay with me."

The words startled Erin as she tried to focus the blur of Patricia's face. "With you?"

Again an image came. Laughter, the pop of gunfire, the smell of spent shells. Blood.

Patricia watched her closely, and seeming to sense her hesitation, explained. "I've had the bedroom completely redone. You won't have to go near it if you don't want to." She touched her face gently. "Things will be okay. I promise."

Erin nodded slowly, unable to speak as the tears crawled up her throat, threatening to consume her.

"Is that a yes, then?" Patricia asked with a smile.

Erin nodded again as relief spread through her like a warm, comforting blanket. The fatigue of the numerous sleepless nights and the stress of reliving her fragmented memory weighed her down now that the fight was out of her. Her body gave in, along with her mind. She was exhausted and suddenly very willing to let someone help. She wasn't going to be alone.

Patricia would be there.

CHAPTER FOURTEEN

September
Arcane, Alabama

Liz reached out to the left of the steering column, fingering for the wiper switch. Thunder ricocheted softly around her, not quite ready to reveal its full fury. Small droplets of rain fell from the blackening sky, dotting her windshield.

Alan Jackson crooned from the radio, proudly singing "Where I Come From." The song was more than appropriate, it so closely paralleled the small town in which she was raised.

She slowed the rented SUV down to a crawl as she approached Arcane and its narrow two-way road governed by a single swinging stoplight. The light changed to green and she continued through her hometown, over the train tracks and up to the abandoned cotton mill. The vast brick warehouse stood where it always had, reminiscent of the town's better days when the mill had been a thriving and important part of Arcane.

Her grandfather had worked his fingers to the bone there, sacrificing his lungs and eventually his life when he could no longer pull in enough air to breathe. Across the street from the mill sat a string of old buildings, most of them vacant as well. A cardboard sign in the window of the old library offered the space for rent. Similar signs adorned several other windows in the town square.

It wasn't a surprise that the town stood beaten and defeated, its pride gone with the mill. It had been this way for at least fifteen years, the remaining residents having to travel ten miles to the closest neighboring town for groceries or a glimpse of civilization.

The Alan Jackson song faded out, giving way to a male DJ who reported that the weather was worsening and the current temperature was 88 degrees. She continued to drive and listened mindlessly as Terri Clark came through the speakers declaring that life was a Catch-22. With the heart of Arcane in her rearview mirror, she drove a little faster, and the small white homes streaked by, many with people occupying the front porches, sitting and rocking with the rain.

She felt their questioning stares and knew that even if she had wanted to wave hello, her greeting would not be returned. She was no longer a recognizable face in the town, and strangers were seldom welcome. She turned off the radio and eased down her windows to smell the rain. If the storm was going to hit with force, it would have to catch her first. For the time being, it loomed behind her hanging above Arcane, randomly dotting her with sporadic sprinkles.

As the small houses became fewer and farther between, they gave way to the lush green vegetation of the Deep South. The summer song of the insects buzzed outside her window as she drove by.

She slowed the SUV and turned left at the sight of an old faded blue mailbox. The name Adams had long since disappeared under the harsh elements of the Alabama seasons. The vehicle left the paved road and continued onto rich, red mud. Although she knew the route, she drove slowly, not knowing it half as well as the road about two miles back, closer to town. The road that led to her childhood home.

She drove carefully, winding her way through the overgrown kudzu looming down over the trees across the road as if it were waiting to envelop her. She was on her way to her grandfather's property, where the private detective had said Jay would be.

After a half a mile or so, the tunnel-like road opened up into a clearing, and she brought the SUV to a stop and killed the engine. The smell of rain hung heavy in the air, though it was not yet falling where she now sat.

She gazed through the windshield at the house before her. It stood just as she remembered it, smaller than the one she was raised in, but a hell of a lot warmer.

Thunder made itself known in the distance as she climbed out of the vehicle and sank her hiking boots down into the lush green grass around her. The ground was rich and soft, giving way to her weight as she walked up to the old graying house. The front porch steps squeaked their protest as she made her way up them and walked between pillars overgrown with more hungry kudzu.

The screen door, equally as old and a little more tattered, stood on loose hinges, and she carefully pulled it open to knock on the door. A dog barked in the distance, somehow hearing her light knock and determined to alert everyone around him. Getting no answer, she knocked again and let the screen door bang closed as she walked to a window and tried to peer in. She cupped her eyes, blocking out the surrounding light, and squinted into the dark house.

From behind, a twig snapped, followed closely by the unmistakable sound of a shotgun cocking, ready for fire. She straightened up slowly and raised her hands before trying to turn around.

"Don't you move an inch," the voice warned from the yard below. "This is private property."

Liz tensed a little, recognizing her sister's voice but worried that Jay had failed to recognize her. "I know—"

"Well, if you know, then I ought to shoot you right here and now where you stand." Her Southern accent had returned full force, reminding Liz of times long since past. Bad times.

"Jay, it's—"

"How do you know my name!" The voice was loud and shrieking, alarming Liz and calling for desperate measures.

She ducked just as a shot rang out and shattered the window behind her. "Jay!" she shouted over the echo of the discharge. "It's me, it's Lizzie!"

Silence prevailed, and she dared not even to look up from her crouch. The steps creaked as Jay ascended them. Liz could hear her reloading the shotgun as she approached. She stared at the muddy boots that came to a halt before her, then raised her eyes very slowly to meet those of a coiled rattlesnake in filthy overalls.

"What did you say?" Jay demanded, but her voice was not nearly as fierce as it had been a moment earlier.

"I said, it's me. It's Lizzie, your sister."

Jay stared at her long and hard, apparently contemplating whether to believe her. She kept the shotgun raised, trained on Liz. Finally, seeming to be satisfied, she lowered the gun a little.

"You come alone?" she asked, jerking her head around to make sure there was no one else hiding in the surrounding woods or sneaking up from behind.

Liz took full advantage of her sister's distraction and sprang up from her crouch to grab the barrel of the gun while sweeping Jay's feet out from under her. Liz quickly unloaded the shotgun and tossed it out onto the grass.

"You've been drinking," she said, placing a boot to her sister's throat, compelling her to stay down. Jay's paranoid behavior worsened when she drank.

"Maybe." Jay struggled for a few seconds before finally allowing her hands to fall at her sides in defeat.

"There's no maybe about it." Liz lifted her foot by degrees, making sure Jay was lucid before allowing her to stand.

She took a step toward the screen door and raised her hand to pull it open, but Jay caught hold of her arm, preventing her.

"What are you doing here, Lizzie?"

"I came to see you." Liz noted how filthy her skin was, her fingernails dark with embedded dirt. She needed to reach her sister soon or she would be lost forever, sucked into the dark abyss of her own mind and held prisoner there for the rest of her life. And it was already happening, starting with the drinking and the personal hygiene, and leading into paranoid behavior.

"Why?" Jay was skeptical.

"Because you're my sister and because I need answers."

"Heh...I knew there had to be a reason. You hate it here."

Liz looked around at the green, rich woods surrounding the house. "Yes, I do," she agreed in a whisper.

"Let's go for a walk." Jay bounded down the steps, not waiting for an answer.

"No." Liz remained firmly on the porch.

Jay picked up the gun and searched her pockets for shells. "You want to talk, Lizzie? Then you'll come with me for a walk." She found a shell and loaded it. "'Sides"—with the shell in place she closed the gun and cocked it—"you ain't still afraid of the woods, are you?"

Liz stared her wild-eyed sister down, ignoring the taunt. "I'll go, but only if you leave the gun."

Her sister seemed to consider the proposal. "You got something on you in case we run into trouble?" Jay asked, completely serious.

Liz nodded, and Jay propped the shotgun up against the house. She then led the way around the back of the house and out to the tiny path that led into the woods.

Even though it was early afternoon, the darkening storm clouds had snuffed out most of the daylight, casting a dark and ominous atmosphere throughout the woods. Liz followed her sister, childhood memories reaching out to her from the wicked-looking tree branches.

"Why did you kill those men in Valle Luna, Jay?" she asked, hoping the topic would help to distract her mind from her current surroundings.

Up ahead of her, Jay stopped walking and turned around. "Cause they was messing with you." She reached up and pulled off a hickory twig and pulled off its leaves. As they continued through the woods, she groomed the hickory.

"You can't just kill people, Jay."

"I did it for you." She flicked the flexible switch, making quick whooshing sounds.

"But can't you see that you made things worse for me, by doing what you did?" Liz tried guilt, desperate to find some way to reach that last grain of reason deep within her sister. And she knew how much Jay loved her.

Jay fingered the switch in her hand as if were alive, a pet that needed comforting. "I thought it would help you. Those men were hurting you." Her eyes grew wide as she spoke, excitement straining her voice.

"What about Kristen, then? Was she hurting me too?" Liz was growing impatient with the ludicrous workings of her sister's mind.

Jay looked away, flicking the switch.

"You have got to stop this. I can take care of myself now." Liz forced herself to speak calmly, hoping to soothe her sister into some sanity. "You don't have to worry."

Jay stared at the ground as if mesmerized by the fallen leaves. "You can't, Lizzie. The bad people are everywhere."

Liz sucked in a quick breath. "Let's go back."

She suddenly knew that she needed to get out of the woods, to get Jay back to a hotel where she could sit her down and talk some sense into her. These woods, they held too much. They were crawling with the ghosts of the past.

Jay raised her eyes slowly from the ground, and an evil grin spread across her face. "No, let's not. Let's keep going." She jogged ahead, laughing as she trotted through the woods. "Come on, Lizzie, just a little bit farther!"

Liz clenched her fists and debated calling the police herself. She was almost willing to do anything to avoid having to follow Jay farther into the woods.

"Come on!" Jay shouted from up ahead.

Thunder growled again and Liz looked up, knowing it was almost directly overhead.

"Jay, wait up…It's getting ready to storm." She jogged after her sister, hoping that the promise of the storm would cause her to turn back.

She found Jay a few yards up ahead, her tracks in the soft mud leading off the path to where she stood atop a large rock, the switch hanging at her side. "You know where we are, Lizzie?" The grin once again spread across her face.

Liz stared down into the ravine. "Let's go back, Jay."

"And miss all this?" Jay waved her stick in the air. "Not a chance. Let's reminisce, Lizzie. Relive our youth," she said in a satirical tone and then laughed out loud at herself.

"Enough, Jay."

"No. I gotta remind you of the bad people. To show you that you still need protecting. Think back, Lizzie, to that day. Remember that day?" She jumped down and pointed her stick down into the ravine's heart, overgrown with ivy, weeds, and bushes.

"I remember."

Liz never knew exactly what had happened to the bad man in the woods that hot summer day twenty years earlier. And whatever the man had done to Jay also remained a mystery. Her sister had never told her. She only knew that from that day on, Jay wasn't the same.

Light sprinkles of rain fell cool on her warm skin. She looked down and ran a finger across the scar on her left arm. An eternal reminder of that terrible day. She met her sister's gaze and felt profound empathy for the young girl who had sacrificed herself in order to protect her. How had she deserved that?

"I'm sorry, Jay," she said. "It should've been me. He should've taken me." She meant it.

Jay laughed and swatted at the rain with her stick. "Nah, Lizzie. It shouldn'a been anybody. Not me, not you…not that poor dead girl."

Liz remembered that the girl had been from a neighboring town, her murder never solved. Not in a legal sense, anyway. Thunder cracked loudly directly overhead, and she stepped away from the ravine, heading back to the house. The electricity in the air pricked the hairs on her arm.

"Lord knows even your worst thoughts couldn't come close to what he did to me," Jay said, seemingly unaffected by the close proximity of the storm. "But that son of a bitch got what was his."

"You mean with Jerry?" Liz asked, startled that her sister seemed to know more about the disappearing man from the woods than she did.

Jay shook her head, a smile spreading across her face. "It was the only time in my life when I can remember that drunk piece of shit doing right by me."

Liz nodded her understanding. Jerry hadn't exactly been the best father figure for Jay and her, but he hadn't been the worst either. He had been a man hell-bent on control and he had ruled their aunt and their home with an iron fist. Always quick to dominate, he took no excuses and offered none either.

"That night, after they had found me and chased him down in the woods…" She tossed her stick aside, suddenly finished with it as she concentrated on the memory. "Jerry come over to Doc Hill's to get me."

Liz only vaguely remembered leaving Doc Hill's that night. Her aunt had taken her to the hospital for surgery.

"Well, Doc Hill told Jerry what all he thought the man had done to me, and Jerry like to have killed him on the spot for saying such things. He grabbed me by the shirt and yanked me outside, the whole time yelling at Doc Hill not to tell nobody. I almost thought he was gonna whip me. But instead he took me out back to the shed. And they had that man in there, all tied up. They were taking turns beating him and burning him with lit cigarettes. I didn't know what to do. I guess I was in shock. I just stood there staring, feeling nothing. And that's when Jerry did it. He handed me his shotgun and told me to shoot him."

"Jesus," Liz whispered as she thought of her raped and battered eleven-year-old sister standing there, gun in hand.

"Yeah, that sick fuck started talking about Jesus. Started begging me not to shoot him, crying and wailing like Dayne used to do when her and Jerry fought. I just stood there watching him, the gun feeling real heavy in my arms. Jerry bent down next to me and asked me if what Doc Hill said was true. I said yes and he said then it was my right to take back from him what he took from me."

Jay paused and breathed in deep, shoving her hands down deep into the pockets of her overalls.

"So did you shoot him?"

"I did," Jay responded, looking at the ground. "I nearly blew his head clean off too."

"My God." Liz wished desperately that she could take it all away and give her sister a clean slate in life instead of the tarnished and scarred one she had been forced to make do with.

They walked in silence for a while, and she tried to make sense of Jay's life. The events of her past had done more than enough to steer her in the wrong direction, as they had Liz herself. But she hadn't ever killed anyone. She wished she could say the same for Jay.

"Jay, will you promise me something?"

"Don't know. Depends on what it is."

"I want you to stop killing."

"But what if—"

"No. No what ifs. I can take care of myself. I don't need you worrying about me."

Jay looked away suddenly, as if the words had stricken her physically.

"Can't you see that it's because I love you that I ask you to stop?" Liz begged. "You're going to get caught someday and sent away to rot in prison. How long do you think it would actually take them to find you here? Not long, Jay. Not long at all. And the only reason they haven't come for you is because I asked Erin McKenzie not to tell."

"And she hasn't?" Jay looked completely surprised. "I didn't think no one would know to look for me here at Papaw's." She said the words in a meek manner, completely oblivious to how obvious the location was. Their grandfather was long dead, but it wouldn't take much at all to find out who his two granddaughters were.

"I can't figure out why she hasn't said anything," Liz confessed. "Maybe they still think I'm responsible, and if you continue to kill, they'll eventually arrest me for the crimes."

"No!" Jay's head whipped around. "I won't let that happen."

"You can't control it, Jay. None of it. Just let it go. Promise me…no more."

Jay didn't respond, and Liz looked up as they approached the house.

"And there's one more thing I need," she said with certainty. "I want you to promise me that you'll leave Erin McKenzie alone."

"She lied to you, Lizzie!"

Liz held up her hand. "She didn't tell about you, did she? And that's after you tried to kill her." She raised her eyebrows, finishing her point. "Promise me."

Jay seemed unconvinced. "The way I see it, I should off her so she could never tell."

Liz stopped walking and looked at her sister. "If you have any respect for me at all, you'll honor this, because I care about her, Jay."

Jay looked around the yard, avoiding her sister's intense stare. "I don't believe it! All the women in the world, and you go and care about a lying cop."

"I mean it." Liz could tell some of the steam had gone out of her sister's rant. "I need to make some things right in my life."

Chapter Fifteen

Valle Luna, Arizona

Hey you," Patricia greeted Erin with a relaxed smile. "How was your nap?" She joined the other woman on the back patio.

"Short," Erin answered with some disappointment.

"Still not sleeping well?" Patricia asked.

Erin shrugged, not wanting to share all the details of her dreams. "I'm still having the nightmares, but I think it's getting better." She looked away from Patricia and let her eyes skim over the thousand waves of sunshine dancing on the surface of the swimming pool.

Patricia seemed to sense that the subject was closed and stood next to her in silence.

"How's the writing coming?" Erin changed to a more comfortable subject. Patricia had been hard at work on a new manuscript, typing away at her computer well into the night.

"It's coming along fine for the moment."

Erin sensed the doubt that came out thick with the words. "You're saying it doesn't always?" Patricia tensed next to her and Erin shifted her gaze from the shimmering pool to study her more closely.

"Not always."

"But it's going well now, right?"

"Yes."

"Then what's wrong?"

"I…" Patricia stared off into the hypnotic dancing water. "I worry that it won't keep coming." She shoved her hands down into her pockets. "I worry that I'll wake up one day and it'll be gone.

That it will never come again."

"You're kidding me, right?"

"No, I'm serious."

Erin could tell she was embarrassed and more than likely feeling exposed at what she had just shared. The realization flattered her. She liked that Patricia trusted her so. It warmed her and made her feel connected to the other woman.

"I've read your stuff," she said. "Not all of it, but enough to know that it's damn good." She waited for Patricia to look up. When she did, she continued with a broad grin. "In fact, I bet you have thousands of fans just drooling with anticipation for the next book."

Patricia blushed. "Thanks, but that doesn't solve my problem. The expectations people have only add to the pressure. I mean, what if I can't give them another one? What if it just doesn't come?"

Erin considered that. Of course, she herself had never worried about such things. But it didn't mean she couldn't understand. And after all the help Patricia had given her, she owed it to her to try.

"That won't happen," she said softly, her mind flying to find the right words. "I'm sure you may have a day or even days when things just don't click, if you haven't already. But they didn't last, did they?"

"No, they didn't last."

"You see, then, you'll be fine." She wished she could sound more convincing.

"This last time, I had stopped for a couple of months because my head just wasn't in it. And the only reason I came out of it was because I found a new..." Patricia trailed off, her gaze in the clouds.

"New what?"

"Muse."

"Oh."

Erin flushed suddenly as she realized the meaning of the word. Patricia had someone? She didn't know why the possibility surprised her, but more than that, she didn't understand why it seemed to strike her down deep.

"Well, whoever she is, you should tell her so she'll be sure to keep inspiring you."

Patricia's response was to stiffen, straight as a rod, and avoid all eye contact. "I need to get dinner started now if I'm going to grill. The sunlight will be gone soon." She headed across the patio to the back door, leaving Erin all alone.

Puzzled, Erin turned back to the well-manicured backyard where Jack lay lounging on the top step of the swimming pool. Patricia obviously didn't want to discuss her muse, and that only made Erin more curious. She thought how lucky the mystery woman would be to have someone as kind, generous, and caring as Patricia was, not to mention romantic.

As the evening sun caressed her face, her mind replayed some of the passionate love scenes Patricia had written. Inhaling deeply, she allowed the scenes to soothe her, to stir her insides pleasantly. She hadn't felt so relaxed in a long, long time. The time off was doing her some good—that much was evident in the brush of bronze on her skin and the lighter shade of green in her eyes. But her memory had not remedied itself, and the nightmares still came, the flashbacks hot on their heels when she awoke.

A face entered her mind, the eyes brilliant and blue, full of fire and desire. She shuddered as she recalled her intimate encounter with Elizabeth Adams. Even though she had been high on Ecstasy at the time, her memory was unclouded. If anything, the drug had heightened her senses, sharpened them to the point where she had craved the physical contact so intensely it seemed every incredible detail was imprinted on her memory.

"Crave." Erin tensed, the sultry voice strumming her heated insides. *"It's called Crave by Calvin Klein."*

The voice continued, caressing her ear, as if the speaker were there whispering to her. She remembered the very moment the words had been spoken. Liz standing before her, a tall, lean, yet powerful-looking female Adonis, her incredible legs hugged by the soft, tight restraint of black leather. Her perky breasts heaving with her every breath under the swaying weight of the mesh vest. Erin clamped her thighs together tightly as the scent of Elizabeth Adams entered her senses. She had always heard that smell was the strongest sense tied to memory, and now she understood why.

Her body instinctively reacted to Liz even though she was nowhere near. Every achingly erotic memory she relived wound her tighter and tighter, and she knew there would be no release, not even self-induced. Nothing, it seemed, could take the place of Elizabeth Adams. Clenching her thighs, her body tense, she shuddered as she allowed the memories to continue.

Liz stood before her in the black leather and chain vest. The mask was gone and she was looking at Erin so intensely, so soft and yet so hungry. Erin felt the pulsing flesh between her legs twitch at the thought of long, talented fingers, of her dark-haired lover playing her, pulling at her from deep inside.

"Wine?"

Erin jerked forward, her eyes flying open in surprise.

"Sorry." Patricia offered a goblet of red wine. Her expression showed she was concerned.

"You just surprised me is all."

Erin rubbed her face as if she were tired, hoping the heat she had been feeling with Liz in mind wasn't as plainly displayed as it was felt. Anxious to erase Patricia's look of worry, she thanked her and took the goblet, sipping at the dark, flavorful liquid.

"Dinner should be ready in a short while." Patricia sipped from her own glass.

Erin's gaze wandered over her face, then froze at her lips, where the wine had stained them full and crimson, vaguely reminiscent of blood.

"Make me bleed, baby."

A hot vision branded her mind, searing itself in. Liz. Sexy, confident, powerful, pulling the beautiful actress into her to feed. Their mouths hungry, Liz sucking and tugging with her teeth. Erin nearly moaned with need. The memory turned her on even now, almost more than it had the moment it had happened.

"You okay?" Patricia moved the goblet from her mouth, her brow creased with concern once again.

"Fine." Erin cleared her throat. "Just memories. Flashes, really."

Patricia's eyebrows rose with what appeared to be hope. "That's good, right? I mean, you want them to come, don't you?"

"I'm not sure anymore," Erin confessed. "I'm not sure I want to know."

She took another sip of wine, hating how the violent flashbacks made her feel. Whatever had happened the night of the shooting, she was sure it was bad, and sometimes she was grateful for not being able to remember every gruesome detail. She had shot and killed someone, a young woman. That in itself was tough to deal with, even without the memory of having done it.

"I don't think you'll ever be at peace until you do remember," Patricia said and walked quietly away.

Erin fingered the rim of her goblet and thought back to what the paramedics had said about that night. They had found her on the floor with Patricia's head in her lap. She had been covered with Patricia's blood, the head wound having bled profusely.

They had tried to speak to her, but she wouldn't answer and gave no response whatsoever until they tried to remove Patricia from her arms. Then she had screamed and cried, convinced that Patricia would soon die, and as they wheeled Patricia away, she had collapsed. The paramedics had sedated her, and when she came to in the hospital the next morning, she couldn't remember the events of that evening.

She pictured herself on the floor, Patricia unconscious and bleeding in her arms. Her heart ached at the thought of Patricia hurt and wounded. She meant so much to her, yet Erin had only known her on a personal level for a short while.

Staying with the writer in her home and in such close proximity seemed to have heightened Erin's deep attraction to her. She was noticing things she had never noticed before, like the way Patricia chewed her bottom lip when she tried to fight back a mischievous grin. Her hearty laugh, her kindness and intellect, her passion with words. Not to mention her body.

Erin bit her own lip as her mind's eye looked Patricia up and down. She thought back to the previous night and how sexy Patricia had looked in a snug gray tank top and matching cotton panties. She had about fainted on the spot as she had stumbled upon her in the kitchen well after midnight, standing there, leaning into the fridge. The refrigerator light lit up her body, showing off firm, ample breasts, a smooth, flat stomach. Her vision carried down to Patricia's panties. She imagined touching her tight ass, running her hands over and down to come forward to her heated center.

What would she feel like?

Her mind's eye traveled from Patricia's panties to her legs, her beautifully muscled thighs, smooth and tan from swimming. She imagined kissing them, teasing them with her tongue, up and down the inner thighs.

Her vision faded with growing darkness, and no matter how hard she tried, she could not return to her pleasant fantasies. Other thoughts weighed too heavily on her mind.

Work. The investigation. Her own current situation. She had been on medical leave for almost two months, since the morning after the shooting, which meant she was excluded from the investigation. She'd heard Tracy Walsh was being pegged as the sole killer. She would've loved to have been a part of it, especially since something gnawed at her continuously, telling her that her fellow detectives hadn't found all the missing pieces. They believed Walsh was responsible for the serial killings and that she might have had help from Kristen Reece, whose murder they also blamed on Walsh.

As for a motive, they'd found evidence in Walsh's apartment that showed she had a strong obsession with Elizabeth Adams. These included pictures of Liz all over her walls, letters she had written to her, and journal entries, as well as stolen items from the club. According to the official police version, this obsession drove her to extremes in order to win the affection and attention of the powerful woman.

Erin gazed into her deep red wine. It was certainly understandable that Tracy Walsh, or any woman for that matter, could become obsessed with Elizabeth Adams. The woman was truly beautiful, one of the most beautiful people Erin had ever laid eyes on.

As her thoughts threatened to turn dark once more, Jack trotted across the patio, his claws clicking against the concrete, a gentle alarm bringing her back to reality. Erin let her hand fall down beside the chair and he happily licked it. His normally stark white fur was wet and dusty from his swimming and running around outdoors. When she wouldn't scratch his back like he wanted, he walked away from her and headed to his water bowl next to the back door.

She smiled after him, always endeared by the little deaf dog. Once at his water bowl, he dug in it with his front paws, splashing the water up on his fur, getting his water cloudy with dirt in the process. Once the water was almost completely brown, he lowered his head and drank from it heartily.

Erin laughed out loud at his behavior, letting the lighter mood relax her body. *Yes, perhaps this time off is doing me some good. I'm here spending time with my beautiful colleague, who just so happens to be a romance writer. Why am I even thinking of Liz? That was a mistake, a one-time occurrence. And I was high.*

"What's so funny?" Patricia asked as she stepped outside with a grill brush.

Erin pointed. "Jack."

Patricia turned and looked down just in time to see Jack try to lie completely down in his water bowl.

"Jack!" she shouted. "You're filthy!"

She walked over to him and pointed, causing him to step out of the bowl. He looked up at her, his tongue hanging large and flat from his mouth, moving in rhythm with his heavy panting. His usually vibrant tail was tucked shamefully between his legs.

"He's hot," Erin said, sticking up for him as she continued to laugh. It felt good to laugh. Damn good.

"Oh yeah? If you feel so sorry for him, then you can be the one who gives him a bath." Patricia bit her lower lip in an apparent attempt to stifle a laugh.

Erin's heart rate picked up at the sight. Instantly, where only seconds before she'd felt a gnawing emptiness, raw, excited emotion swirled. And Liz was moved ever further from her mind.

Nearly light-headed with contentment and attraction, she stood and approached Jack with a large smile. She looked over at Patricia and tipped her wineglass at her. Suddenly she was willing to do almost anything for this woman who had taken her in and been such a good friend to her.

"Fine. I would be more than happy to. You cook and I'll... clean." She looked back down at Jack as he started to dig again at the remaining water, splashing her in the process.

"Done," Patricia said, laughing.

Erin finished toweling her hair and slipped into a cotton button-down sleeveless shirt and a pair of khaki linen shorts. She glanced around her bedroom with a contented sigh. With its double bed and matching light lumber furniture, the room felt more and more like home.

The sounds she could hear as she made her way to the kitchen added to the comforting feeling. The sun had just set, and Patricia had opened the doors and windows to let in the cool night air. The forecast called for rain, and the late-September air had cooled comfortably as the clouds blew in.

Soft jazz played from a small stereo, setting the mood nicely along with the candlelit table, which was set for two. The room, the music, the soft glow from the candles, it all felt so right. Erin smiled as her heart fluttered. As her hand found the pulse beating in her neck, her gaze settled on Patricia walking in from the patio, a plateful of steaming chicken kabobs in one hand.

"Here, let me," Erin said, moving quickly to get the plate.

Patricia could smell the fresh scent of soap and shampoo on Erin and she looked away as she imagined Erin wet. She could see her nude in the shower, soaping her full breasts slowly, throwing her head back into the hot spray in pleasure.

"Thanks," she managed to cough out. She busied herself gathering the food in the kitchen and returned to the table with a bowl of pasta salad and a bottle of wine.

"This looks terrific." Erin sat down and placed a kabob on Patricia's plate and another on her own.

"I hope it's as good as it looks," Patricia said, spooning out the pasta salad for them both before filling their wineglasses. "I'm starved." But what she was hungry for wasn't food. She resisted an urge to gaze at Erin and instead dug heartily into the food, hoping it would, at the very least, distract her.

"It's even better than it looks," Erin said.

After several silent bites, she noticed that for some reason Patricia seemed to be unusually quiet, her eyes never leaving her plate. Unsure as to why, she trod lightly. "Dare I ask where Jack is?"

"He's pouting." Patricia grinned. "He hates baths."

"No kidding?"

Jack had jumped from the tub just as Erin poured the first cup of water over his head. The chase was then on, with him barreling down the hallway and running from room to room, rubbing himself on the furniture and then playfully darting just out of Erin's reach. She smiled just thinking about it.

"And since I had to humiliate myself running all over the house after a slippery dog, you now have to answer me any question I ask." Erin grinned playfully across the table.

"No way," Patricia said, with a soft, embarrassed smile.

Erin noted her modesty and how beautiful she looked even in the worn jeans and faded flannel sleeveless shirt. So incredibly beautiful, and…almost shy. "Yes way," she teased. "Let's see, what to ask." She contemplated as she ate, wanting to come up with the perfect question.

"You're wasting your time," Patricia said. "I never said I would go along with this little game." But she was enjoying the friendly banter. It was good to see Erin being so playful, so relaxed. And there was even the hint of contentment.

"You will."

"What makes you think I will?" *I'll do anything you want. Anything.*

"Because I have powers over you. Superpowers." She wiggled her fingers at Patricia, who found herself frozen, her fingers tightly cupping her wineglass.

The joking words shocked her with their truth, and Erin had no idea. Why would she? How could she possibly know or even understand? It shook her to realize how vulnerable she was at the hands of this beautiful, confused woman. She couldn't let her know.

She had to keep fighting it. Erin had too much on her mind right now to be dealing with such things. But God, how she wanted her. She wanted to claim her as her own, to make love to her so passionately that she would surely forget about Elizabeth Adams altogether. Wasn't that why she really wanted Erin here? So she could have her all to herself?

Patricia rose from the table, needing to distance herself from the younger detective. "More wine?" she asked.

"No, I'm good," Erin said, obviously noticing the change in Patricia's mood. She stood and set about clearing the table. "Thank you for dinner. It was very good." She carried the dishes into the kitchen and piled them next to the sink.

"I'm glad." Patricia moved beside her to start washing the dishes.

"No, let me clean. You cooked." Erin softly wrapped a hand around her wrist.

Patricia stood ramrod straight at the contact. Erin's touch was like a bolt of lightning shooting up through her, charging up every cell in her body to the point of implosion.

"Patricia?" Erin asked. "What's wrong?"

"Nothing." She walked away quickly and headed out the back door. It took all her power not to run at a full sprint out onto the patio. As the door closed behind her, she placed her hands behind her head and stepped out into the yard to gaze up at the stars. She breathed in deeply the promising scent of rain and willed her heart to stop pounding so fiercely.

Maybe it had been a mistake to invite Erin to come stay with her. It was becoming obvious that she had fallen in love and that her emotions were affecting her judgment.

"Christ," she said into the black night. How could she have let this happen?

She had known she was in trouble since that first night when she had helped Erin prepare for her assignment. The gorgeous exterior was one thing, but she hadn't expected to find such a passionate, naïve, and sensual creature within.

Still barefoot, Patricia walked down to the edge of the pool and stepped into the cool water. She should have walked away that first night. She should've wiped her hands clean of Erin McKenzie and the desire she had so clearly felt creeping up within herself. But she hadn't. And now she had contrived to be here alone with her, compromising some of her own ethical ideals in the process. She was gambling their friendship in the hopes of more, and losing the internal battle between patience and desire.

Later, in front of a fire Patricia had lit in the living room, they drank hot chocolate laced with butterscotch schnapps.

Erin stared down into her mug, aware of an awkwardness between them. "Have I done something to upset you?" she asked, feeling bad that after all Patricia had done for her, she must have somehow upset her.

"No, of course not," Patricia replied, but there was a tremble in her voice.

"You sure?" Erin took in the firelight dancing against Patricia's face, her softly glowing auburn hair. Maybe it was just a bad day. She herself had had plenty the past few weeks.

Patricia met her eyes and seemed to shake herself from her mood. Smiling, she said, "Yes, I'm sure. And to prove it to you, I'll even answer that one question you wanted to ask me."

"I was only kidding." Erin hesitated to go there, fearing it might put her friend back on the defensive just as she was relaxing.

But Patricia tossed a pillow at her playfully. "Come on, ask me anything."

Erin blocked the pillow and set her mug down on the coffee table. "Okay, Miss Writer…" She drew in a breath and asked the only thing that came to mind. "Who's this muse you speak of?"

Patricia opened her mouth to speak, but stopped as her eyes met Erin's.

"What is it?" Erin asked softly.

Patricia's eyes burned deep blue, just as they had in Erin's dream. Her cheeks were flushed, and her dark red lips quivered. "It's you," she whispered, her voice tight with emotion.

Erin shook her head. "I don't understand."

"My muse. It's you." Patricia reached out then, slowly, tentatively, and touched Erin's wrist.

"Me?" Erin asked, overwhelmed by the revelation. Desire spilled into her blood.

Patricia's grip tightened. "Yes," she replied huskily. She pulled Erin into her and wrapped her other hand around the base of her neck.

A rush of desire heated Erin's face and lips just as Patricia's warm, wet mouth claimed hers with surprising force. She fell back onto the couch, wrapping her arms around Patricia, bringing her down on top of her. Their tongues danced and dueled and Patricia groaned as Erin took her tongue, sucking it hungrily.

Patricia knew she had lost the control she had been fighting to hang on to all along. Erin tasted so good, too good. She couldn't stop herself now even if she wanted to. Kissing her harder, deeper, she maneuvered herself between her legs, pressing her thigh against her, rocking into her.

Erin moaned into her mouth and Patricia pulled away and looked down at her, gasping for breath.

"Why did you stop?" Erin's eyes blazed with want.

"Is…is this okay?" Patricia asked while there was still time to back off.

"God, yes." Erin needed to feel her, she needed to feel like she had felt with Liz. She could almost convince herself that the encounter would be just like her dream, that somehow Patricia and Liz would morph together. The thought alone caused her to dig her nails into Patricia's back, drawing her down, pressing them ever closer together.

Patricia panted and reveled in the newfound freedom she felt, released from her hidden desire. Her mouth moved downward, starving. Hungrily, she licked and sucked on Erin's neck.

Erin arched up at the sensation and tried to raise her hips to grind against Patricia's firm thigh. The pressure between her legs was unbelievable, and she wanted so badly for Patricia to take her.

As she writhed beneath her, memories of Liz invaded. She clenched her eyes shut, and that perfect face and those piercing eyes seared into her mind. She clung to Patricia, wanting her but knowing she wanted Liz even more.

With her brain and body pounding with hot blood, Patricia almost gave in and pressed her thigh into Erin's warm, searching crotch. But the moment had been so long in coming, she wanted to make it last.

"Wait." She withdrew slightly and pressed Erin back down softly. "We should do this," she traced a finger across Erin's lips and down over her throat, "slowly."

Erin tried to pull her back down again. "Who says we have to go slow?" She grinned, wanting her now, needing her now.

Patricia bent down and kissed her softly, warmly, tenderly before pulling away again. "Since this is your first time with a woman and all, I thought we should take it slow."

Erin bit her lip at the words. Liz burned into her mind once again. She gazed up at Patricia and saw the hunger in her eyes. Her hand moved quickly, working its way down to Patricia's jeans. "I don't want to go slow," she whispered with raw desire as her fingers popped the buttons on Patricia's fly. "I want it now."

She raised up then and took Patricia's lips aggressively into her mouth, sucking and nibbling away any resistance. Yes, she had to have her now. Right now.

Patricia's head swam as her body instantly reacted. Erin's fingers eased their way in with surprising confidence, cupping her hot flesh through her cotton panties. She tore her mouth away, her lips swollen, her body aching.

"Christ," she let out for the second time in mere minutes. But this time the word was nearly shouted out as she shuddered above Erin's hand.

"I want you," Erin cried out. "I want to feel you in me." She took Patricia's hand by the wrist and shoved it between her legs where her flesh pulsed and hummed, painfully engorged.

Patricia felt the desire and hunger conquer her insides with skilled blades and knowing swords, leaving everything in its wake burned, broken, and useless. Erin hauled her down for another powerful kiss, and Patricia worked hurriedly at Erin's shorts as Erin whispered her demands in her ear.

"Yes, please. Hurry. I need you inside." Erin bucked up against her hand. "Hurry."

Patricia yanked down the shorts, and Erin raised her hips and helped get rid of her underwear. "Hurry," she urged Patricia once again. "Fuck me."

As the words crumbled the last remaining gate to her castle, Patricia allowed her desire to conquer her entire body. She crawled atop Erin like a predator who had hunted for years for this one special prey. Their mouths met and battled, followed quickly by their hands. Erin grabbed Patricia's hand again, forcing it down into her wet, hot folds. As soon as she felt the heated flesh, Patricia moaned and plunged her fingers deep inside.

Erin at once arched up off the sofa. "Yes! God, yes." She shoved down Patricia's panties and jeans. "Let me feel you."

Patricia started to stand so she could remove them, but Erin stopped her. "No, don't move. Stay just like that."

Erin couldn't bear the thought of Patricia pulling out of her. She needed her inside, needed to feel her long hot fingers fucking her. Patricia's pants were just below her hips, exposing her glistening flesh under a small tuft of hair. Suddenly desperate to feel her, Erin reached out and nearly choked as she felt how hot and slick she was. Her hunger grew to new heights as she eased her fingers up inside another woman for the very first time. Patricia sucked in a quick breath and moved her hips against Erin's hand, her body clamping down and around Erin's fingers.

"Oh God, yes." Erin closed her eyes, completely overcome with pleasure. She felt Patricia plunge into her then, sending heat up high within her belly. Crying out, she did the same in return, causing Patricia's hips to dance atop her hand. As pleasure built inside of her, she could only think of her dream, deep blue eyes morphing into piercing ice blue, looking up at her from between her legs, somehow knowing her. She threw her head back, the pressure mounting. Then an image of Liz atop her, riding her fingers and groaning with pleasure, sent her over.

Erin cried out loudly, her entire body tensing under Patricia's, her face contorting with intense pleasure. The beautiful sight made Patricia break, a weak cry escaping from deep within her chest. As she rode out the powerful, incredible orgasm, her eyes remained trained on Erin's face—so beautiful, so innocent, so vulnerable. God, it felt so good to be with her, to be the one who gave her such great pleasure, to be the reason she was coming.

Erin bucked several more times, her body milking the last of the pleasure that had rocketed through her. A few seconds later she stopped moving, her breath coming out in short rasps. Patricia eased herself out, and Erin let out a hurried breath at the birth of the writer's fingers. She didn't want to be them to pull out, now feeling literally hollow inside.

"Sorry," Patricia said with a smile. "You okay?"

"Yeah." Erin rested her hand on her forehead, overwhelmed by what had just occurred. Reality came smashing back to her, weighing her down. She maneuvered slightly, realizing she was uncomfortable, and pulled her fingers from Patricia. They ached as she bent them, and she was amazed at how unaware she'd been of the pain.

"It's okay if you're feeling a little strange," Patricia said softly, stroking Erin's cheek. "Sometimes this can be very emotional, especially the first time."

Erin creased her brow, frustrated. She didn't know how she was feeling, much less understand it. "But this wasn't my firs…" Her voice trailed off as she realized what she had just confessed. She gazed into Patricia's eyes and wished she could take back the words.

The statement banged on Patricia's skull, seeking entry. But she didn't want to let it in. "What?" She cocked her head in confusion.

But before Erin could answer, the words penetrated and she released her and stood up, stricken. "Liz? Was it Liz?"

She knew it in her heart, but wanted to believe it wasn't so. *I'm dying inside. Please, tell me it wasn't her.* The pain flooded her insides, and she couldn't bring herself to look at Erin.

"Does it matter?" Erin asked, suddenly defensive. Why did it matter? This wasn't about Liz. She inwardly cringed as she realized that wasn't true. It was about Liz.

"Yes, it matters," Patricia replied. On shaking legs, she took a step closer. "Was she gentle?" Erin stared at the floor. She didn't want to answer, but a part of her didn't want Patricia to think Liz had somehow hurt her—the other detective already thought ill enough of her.

"Yes," she replied and saw the hurt in Patricia's eyes.

"I see." Patricia ran a hand through her hair, trying to hide the trembling in her extremities. *Somebody kill me. Just kill me now. It hurts. Oh God, how this hurts.*

Her body, only moments before bathed in beautiful pleasure, now felt useless and ready for complete collapse. She reached out for the anchor of the sofa.

Erin continued to watch as devastation took hold of Patricia. She didn't understand why. What was the big deal? "I don't see why this matters," she said quickly. "You've slept with her too."

Patricia looked at her with disbelief. *Can't she see? Can't she see why this hurts?* "You're right, Mac," she said, angry at herself for allowing Erin entry to her heart. "Perhaps we should compare notes. Tell me, how many times did she make you come? Did she fuck you so hard you saw Jesus?" Yes, of course she did. Liz was an incredible lover. Unlike anyone else. Incomparable.

"What?" Erin looked alarmed.

"I know what happens on leather night. You can't fool me. Did she tie you up? Make you her little suck pig?"

"No!" Erin shot back, wanting it to stop. "It wasn't like that at all. It was wonderful," she blurted, unable to stop herself from saying what she truly felt.

Wonderful? Patricia stared at her for a moment, then turned and headed out the back door, slamming it behind her.

Erin sank back into the sofa and buried her face in her hands. She had messed up, and badly. Who had she been kidding? Thinking, wishing that being with Patricia would be like being with Liz? She should've stopped herself. She should've just admitted the truth.

That while she was attracted to Patricia, it didn't come close to the feelings she had for Liz. And now Patricia knew that too. She felt a sharp pang of guilt in her gut. What had she done? To her friend, to her colleague? Oh Jesus, this was wrong, so very wrong.

"Fuck," she said, rising from the sofa. "What the fuck is wrong with me?"

CHAPTER SIXTEEN

Valle Luna, Arizona

I t's good to have you back, Ms. Adams."
"Thank you, Tyson, it's good to be back." Liz flipped through stacks of mail. It was seven o'clock, a mere hour before the club would be hopping with revelers, oblivious to the troubles its owner had recently come face-to-face with. "How have things been here?" she asked her head of security.

"Mostly quiet," he replied in his thick, booming voice. "But right after you left, the cops came around asking questions about Blade. They wanted to know if she was involved with you on an intimate level."

"What did you say?" She tossed aside several unimportant envelopes and opened another.

"The truth," he replied. "I had never seen her around you."

"Thank you, Tyson. You've always been a loyal employee, as well as a friend." She met his dark eyes.

Tyson unfolded his massive arms. He looked a little startled at her soft sincerity, a tone her employees didn't hear too often. "Ms. Adams, if you don't mind my asking, are you feeling okay?"

No doubt he thought she was ill. That would certainly explain her thinner appearance, Liz supposed. Maybe even the change in her usually stoic demeanor. She placed the mail aside, having finished going through it.

"I'm fine," she said and walked out of her lair and across the VIP room to stand at the railing, looking down on the large dance floor. Several men worked on one of the large light fixtures, having lowered it from the ceiling above. One of them yelled for the power to be restored, and the lights came to life, swinging and spotlighting, deep blues and purples. She heard Tyson approach from behind as the steel frame holding the lights rose up to its home just below the ceiling.

"Is it true?" he asked. "What they're saying about Blade?"

She continued to lean on the railing, now watching a couple of bartenders readying the bar for the Friday-night crowd. "It seems so."

"What about Ms. Reece?"

"What about her?" She glanced at him, wishing he would leave her be. The topic made her uncomfortable.

"Is she really dead?" he asked softly, obviously affected by what he had heard.

"I don't know any more than you do, Tyson." She was ready to end the troublesome conversation. "Now, if you'll excuse me, I need to attend to business."

She left him standing alone as she headed back into her private room. She had been running La Femme from afar the past few weeks and had done a fairly good job. But now she was back, and it was time to get down to business. She had bills to pay as well as the hiring of two new bartenders to attend to.

With her checkbook in hand, she sat down on the couch and pulled the neat stack of envelopes over next to her at the coffee table. She usually did most of her paperwork at her home in the Valle Luna hills, but tonight she needed to be here instead of alone in her big house. The club and its business were great distractions, and distractions were exactly what she needed tonight.

She glanced at her satellite phone, anxious for it to ring. Erin McKenzie was still first and foremost on her mind, and yet she didn't know why. She should be able to forget about her, just like she had done every other woman she had ever come across.

Was it because Erin had beaten her at her own game? The game of seduction?

She had told Jay that she cared about Erin. Was that true? And if so, what did it mean? She ran a hand through her hair. She did care about her. Hell, she had done nothing but think about her since she had first laid eyes on her.

Impatiently, she dialed her satellite phone. When the private detective didn't answer, she left a message.

"It's Adams. I'm calling about Erin McKenzie."

She opened her checkbook and began the mechanical task of paying the bills. While the work was boring and tedious, she welcomed it, allowing it to free her mind of the young detective who had somehow slipped in under the wire.

When she was done writing away her money, she leafed through several different employment applications. Tyson had attached a Polaroid of each applicant, knowing that she would want to screen her bartenders. Appearances meant a lot to her, especially since the women represented La Femme. Kris had gotten sloppy in the hiring process, and Blade had been a perfect example of that sloppiness.

And ultimately it seemed that Kris had paid the price for her hiring incompetence.

Liz examined each applicant, leafing through page after page. Not a sexy one in the bunch. Tired and frustrated, she stood up and stretched. She looked down at her watch and saw that it was well after eight. Her muscles felt tight and stressed, and she walked toward her bathroom, hoping a shower would help relax her.

She let the hot water beat down on her shoulders and back, pounding the tightness from her tense muscles. She soaped herself and ran her hands down over her body. She had lost weight, giving the muscles in her abdomen a carved look and feel. Her legs had lost some muscle mass, but they still looked and felt long and powerful.

She turned to let the water rinse the soap from her front. Her nipples contracted at the forceful fingers of the water, and a familiar rush of heat twinged between her legs. She hadn't been with a woman in weeks, and her body was finally starting to protest at being ignored. Under normal circumstances, she would've never gone so long, but with things being as they were, she had been too busy worrying about Jay and thinking of Erin McKenzie to care. But now that she was back, there was no reason to continue to starve her ferocious sexual appetite.

In fact, if things went according to plan, Jay would ultimately behave herself and Liz would finally be able to forget about Erin McKenzie once and for all. She just had to see her again one more time before she would will her mind to forget her.

After rinsing completely off, she emerged from the shower and stared at her reflection. Her face appeared pale and tired, a visible reminder that the past few weeks had been trying. She reached up and traced the angry red scar in her shoulder. It was there forever, just like the one a little lower on her forearm. They were scars of the flesh as well as scars of horrible moments in time, never to fade away completely.

She combed through her wet hair and decided to focus on the evening at hand. Perhaps she could get herself interested in some female company. She rifled through her closet and decided on a pair of Lucky Brand jeans. They appeared weathered, with their worn gravel wash, and she chose a featherweight charcoal-colored tee to go with them. The shirt was soft and fit her snugly, hugging her breasts and broad, strong shoulders.

She sprayed on her favorite cologne, laced up a pair of well-worn black Dr. Martens, and gave herself the once-over in a full-length mirror. Her hair was still clinging to the skin of her neck in wet whisks. Her eyes were dark and clouded, a match to the charcoal gray of her shirt. She turned abruptly at the sound of ringing, and snatched up the phone.

"Adams."

"I got your girl," Shane Wilson said proudly.

"Where?"

"She's with your old flame."

"Patricia? Are they…" A knot formed in her throat.

"Fucking?" the PI finished for her with a chuckle. "I don't know, Liz, they look pretty cozy."

Liz ended the call and sat in silence for a moment as her face flushed with heated jealousy, a feeling that had never before coursed through her veins. Its effect was instant and devastating, like tiny shards of crystals invading every cell. She rested her head briefly in her hands, gathering herself. She could not allow herself to think about this tonight. Running her fingers through her bangs, she headed out the door, leaving her troubles behind her.

❖

The VIP room was dimly lit and as her eyes adjusted, she inspected some of La Femme's patrons. The club had a strict policy regarding admittance to the VIP room. A woman had to be one of three things: famous, unbelievably successful, or unbelievably gorgeous. Of course, Liz preferred the guests who were all three.

She passed a few who lacked at least two of the requirements, shook off her disappointment, and made her way to the rail so she could look over the entire club.

A hand lightly stroked her arm. "Hey, stranger."

Liz turned and a familiar face smiled up at her. "Hey yourself," she greeted Angie, who pulled her in for a warm, lingering kiss.

The kiss was tender and unbelievably soft. But then again, Angie's kisses usually were. The famous woman's lips were undeniably the best she had ever kissed. With one exception: there was one woman who had felt better under her lips. She shook the thought from her mind and leaned in next to Angie to survey the crowd below, seeking out an attractive, fuckable woman to take her mind off Erin McKenzie.

"I thought you had a movie to shoot."

"I fly out tomorrow." Angie took a sip of her beer. She was dressed similarly to Liz, in worn jeans and black boots. But instead of a T-shirt, a very tight black tank top fit like a second skin across her large breasts, showing off the black Celtic band tattooed around her bicep.

"Shouldn't you be at home, getting your beauty sleep?"

"Why sleep, when I could be here…fucking."

Liz glanced down at her dancers, the ones she paid to strut their stuff on the raised platforms. It was firefighter night, and all of them wore yellow firefighter bibs, the wide suspenders covering their bare, toned torsos, barely hiding their full breasts.

Bikini Kill thumped in through the gigantic sound system, and the dancers thrust suggestively at the large fire hoses riding between their legs. The scores of women below them screamed, their arms raised in the air as the firefighting dancers turned the valves on their hoses and doused them with water. The cold spray soaked their white shirts, causing the wet cotton material to cling to their erect, dark nipples.

Liz knew she could have any of them. The trouble was, she saw no one she wanted. The woman she wanted was elsewhere. With an ex of Liz's.

"So how 'bout it, hot stuff?" Angie traced a finger down Liz's strong jaw to her neck. "Wanna fuck?"

Liz turned her head and held her gaze. The woman was gorgeous and damn near irresistible, but she had already had her. Many times and in many different ways. Angie wasn't going to be enough for her tonight, and she began to wonder if anyone would be.

"Maybe later," she said, returning her attention to the crowd, her quest to find another woman not yet dead in the water.

Less than an hour later, Liz found herself still alone and being eaten up by the ravenous green monster of jealousy. She dug in her pocket for her car keys, suddenly anxious to leave the pulsating club and all that it held. But a large, thick muscled body stepped in her path.

She knew immediately by the look on Tyson's face that something was wrong. "What is it?" she asked.

"Sorry to disturb you, ma'am, but the police are out front demanding entrance to the club."

"I don't have time for this. They've harassed me enough." Liz walked briskly down the stairs, Tyson alongside.

"They're insisting you come with them, ma'am."

"What?"

They hit the ground floor and she could see a crowd forming at the door. She slowed her pace and walked with stoic confidence.

Agitated or not, she still had to give the impression of being totally in control. A few of her patrons stopped in their tracks to stare after her. She gave them her sly grin and continued with Tyson out to the front entrance. The guards gave way, leaving her to come face-to-face with Patricia Henderson.

Liz should've known. The large-bellied man standing next to her former lover took it upon himself to shove his police badge in her face.

"Relax, detective, I believe you," Liz said softly, almost as if she were talking to a child.

He looked away, momentarily embarrassed, and quickly tucked the badge back into his breast pocket. "Elizabeth Adams?" he then asked loudly.

"Gentlemen...and lady." Liz shifted her gaze to Patricia and slowly looked her over, knowing she was steamed. "You know who I am."

She took several steps forward then, moving the group farther from the club. The last thing she needed was the cops creating another scene in front of her paying patrons.

The two detectives and several uniformed cops moved along with her, confusion showing on their faces. All except for one. Patricia continued to bore holes into her with her eyes. The plump male detective started to speak but then fell silent.

"Put your hands behind your back," Patricia demanded, her tone heavy and firm. Her face remained stern, but Liz still sensed the fire that brewed under her professional veneer. Something was up, and this time it was personal.

"Now what's this all about?" Liz asked, keeping her cool but in no way doing what she'd just been told to do.

"You're coming with us." Patricia took a step toward her, but Liz refused to back down.

Patricia had been harboring anger at her for years, and now it seemed she was finally going to enjoy bringing her down. Liz's heart raced at the realization. It was finally happening. She knew why they were here, and she knew she had to go. But she was determined not to show fear or weakness. Especially in front of Patricia Henderson.

"And why, gentlemen…and lady, would I want to do that?" She returned the detective's stare, her breath and body tensing as she felt her wrists tugged roughly from behind. She countered quickly and without thought, yanking her arms down and away from the arresting cop's thumbs. His grip was lost in a flash, and Liz bounced on the balls of her feet like a caged tiger. "Is this what you want, Patricia?" she accused. "To throw me to the ground and rough me up?"

"If we have to," she responded coldly. "You're resisting arrest, after all."

"Arrest? You never said anything about arrest." She grinned again, knowing she was right, and relaxed her stance.

"You know damn well why we're here."

"You have a warrant?" Liz asked, acting once again like a very cooperative subject.

"Yes, we do." Patricia smiled, and its chill crept through the air and seeped its way into Liz.

She shuddered inwardly, having never seen Patricia so cold. Ever. Doing her best to hide the anxiety that was creeping in along with the chill, she turned to face her head of security.

"Call my attorney. Tell her I went politely with these officers and I'll see her downtown."

"Yes, ma'am." Tyson eyed the group warily before turning to head back into the club.

"Shall we, then?" She extended an arm, indicating they should lead the way. The uniformed cops formed a loose circle around her and the group began to move. "I see you brought the entire department with you tonight," Liz chided, knowing Patricia was directly behind her. "Afraid to do your own dirty work?"

"Oh no. I'm not afraid," Patricia said. "In fact, I'm very much looking forward to getting down and dirty."

Once again, Liz felt the chill, this time creeping up her spine. She clenched her jaw and willed herself to keep her temper in check for now. She knew she had a long night ahead of her.

Chapter Seventeen

Erin hunched over the bathroom sink, splashing cold water on her face. She gasped as its chill seeped into her skin, forcing every pore to awaken and then to shrink into submission.

She straightened and turned off the water. The mirror over the sink told her grim tale. The nightmares held her once-sparkling eyes prisoner, leaving them clouded and obscure, those of a stranger.

It was four a.m., and sleep had refused to visit her. Instead, it had toyed with her and teased her, allowing her to just drift off before attacking her with nightmares. She stared at her weary reflection as her mind replayed the last nightmare, the most disturbing of them all.

It had started off the same as the others, with her in Patricia's bedroom the night of the shooting. But this time she saw a hauntingly familiar face. The blue eyes were icy and fierce, just like Liz's. The hair was as black as midnight, but cut shorter than Liz's. Yet the beautiful stranger was not Elizabeth Adams.

The worst part of the nightmare replayed in her mind. The mysterious intruder attacked Patricia, striking her hard on the head, knocking her unconscious. Then she raised her gun, aiming it at Erin.

Exhausted and frustrated, Erin reached for a towel and patted her face dry. Dreams were almost always fragments of strange and unusual subconscious thoughts or memories. What was the buried truth behind her nightmares? How could she distinguish between a real memory and a figment of her imagination? Her mind had, in recent weeks, become its own worst enemy, and who was to say whether this was another of its cruel tricks?

She padded into the kitchen and made herself a mug of coffee. Then, hugging herself against the early-morning chill, she made her way over to the sitting room, where she wrapped herself in a throw blanket and sat on the couch with her knees pulled up to her chest. She sipped her coffee and picked up the book she had been reading the day before, one of Patricia's. She thought about the woman who had written the beautiful words, and inhaled deeply as she remembered the kisses they had shared, Patricia hot against her skin, burning into her, searing right through her, going straight to her center.

Patricia hadn't said much to her since their brief but heated encounter, and Erin had spent every waking hour wanting to go after her and take her in her arms. She wanted to apologize for her behavior, to explain to her that somehow a new desire had invaded her body like a ferocious virus. She was attracted to Patricia in a way that was almost purely animalistic. Of course, Erin would avoid discussing why her libido had become a ravenous monster. It would only hurt Patricia to hear that since the encounter with Elizabeth Adams, she'd been feeling as if she would implode if she didn't have another woman, and soon. That woman had been Patricia.

Erin was drawn to her words, her beauty, her body. But as attracted to her as she was, she knew for certain that Patricia could never take the place of the one woman who still invaded her dreams as well as her nightmares.

Christ, she was going insane.

She turned the book to the page she had last read, marked with the top corner folded down. To help ease her tortured mind, she focused on the words and allowed herself to be drawn into a world full of sexual innuendo, budding romance, and raging passion.

As if in a trance, Patricia stared through the two-way mirror into the interrogation room. The coffee in her hand had lost its edge long ago, sitting cool and useless in the mug. The woman who had caused her so much pain sat alone at the table, tapping her long fingers against the faux wood.

Patricia winced as she watched those familiar hands. Since Erin's confession, the vision of the two women making wild, passionate love had corrupted her mind, torturing her. It was almost worse knowing firsthand what Elizabeth Adams was like in bed, how powerful and amazing sex was with her. And hearing Erin confess as much had killed her inside. Killed not just her heart, but the hopes and dreams she had for a future with Erin. The worst of it was the word she had used: *wonderful*.

Patricia had slept with Liz many times during their brief courtship, and *wonderful* was not a word she would ever have chosen to describe the sex between them. *Wonderful* made it sound beautiful, even tender. And the way Erin had said the word…so soft, so full of obvious yearning.

The cup in her hand trembled. She dumped out the cold coffee, then breathed deep and allowed a feeling of triumph to overcome her anger and hurt. The forensic evidence had finally come back, and it seemed things were going their way. On the strength of it, Ruiz had agreed to keep the case open and had given the order to bring her in. Patricia couldn't wait to let Liz know she wasn't as smart as she thought.

She squared her shoulders and and entered the small room. As she rounded the table, Liz looked up and smiled coyly. Rage threatened to erupt, and Patricia nearly let it show as she stared at the woman she had grown to hate. Liz had hurt her on so many levels and now, it seemed, she was doing it again by tainting what Patricia truly wanted. Erin.

Patricia wanted to fly across the table and strangle the shit-eating grin right off that exquisite face. She kept the urge at bay by folding her arms over her chest, and instead started in on the questioning, relishing the fact that they finally had some hard evidence against Adams.

"You were there the night of the shooting," she stated, refusing to sit down across from the suspect.

Liz looked surprised. "Where?"

Patricia took a step closer, loving every second, loving that the forensic evidence backed her up. "You bled all over my bedroom carpet, and we have the DNA to prove it."

The expression on Liz's face changed, but only slightly. Patricia knew her words had penetrated, she could see it in the icy flash of her eyes.

"I don't think so," Liz responded.

Patricia saw the jumping vein in her neck and nearly laughed. She had waited for this moment for so long. Too long. "We also found something else of interest." Liz stared off in silence as she spoke. "A fingerprint. Several, actually. All of them belonging to a single, unidentified source. Who is it, Liz? Another one of your loyal followers? Someone else who was stupid enough to believe your lies?"

"You mean like you did?" Liz finally looked at her, the smile gone. Her face was stone, her jaw set. "That's what this is all about, isn't it? You, getting your revenge?"

Patricia wavered slightly, the words getting to her. She had interrogated hundreds of hardened criminals, heard horrible, evil things come from their mouths. But nothing compared to what she was hearing now. Liz could still get to her. She forced her shoulders to relax and reminded herself she was holding all the cards. "It's in your best interest to talk," she said evenly.

"Somehow, I don't think you have my best interest in mind."

Patricia laughed, her body inwardly quaking with anger, jealousy, and the thirst for revenge. Tired of the game, she decided to be truthful. "You're right, Liz. Don't talk. Don't help yourself in any way. We have enough evidence against you to send you away for a long, long time. With or without your cooperation. And frankly, I can't wait to see you go down."

She smiled then and allowed the vengeful feelings to warm her body. It felt good. Ice blue eyes held hers for a long while before Liz looked away. Patricia waited another moment, still relishing her victory, then said, "Have it your way," and started toward the door.

"Wait."

The word came from thin air, and it was said so softly Patricia almost thought she had imagined it. Her hand dropped from the door handle. "Excuse me?" She turned and studied the back of Liz's head.

"I'll talk," Liz said, louder this time.

Patricia walked slowly to the table, her heart leaping in her chest. It was finally happening; Liz was caving. Something she thought she would never see.

"I'm listening." She slipped her hand in the pocket of her slacks.

"I'll talk, but only to Detective McKenzie."

Patricia laughed, completely taken aback. Was Liz trying to get to her again? Yes, that must be it. "No fucking way." Her voice was as hard as her heart.

"Then I believe we're finished, Detective."

Resentment boiled through Patricia at the look on Liz's face. The bitch was messing with her. Somehow she knew how Patricia felt about Erin and was trying to interfere.

"Just what the hell do you think you're doing?" she seethed, hating the woman, now more than ever.

Liz merely looked at her, no readable expression on her face. "I'm trying to cooperate."

"The fuck you are!" Patricia slammed her hand down on the table.

"I said I'm willing to talk, Patricia. But only to McKenzie."

"Why?"

"Do I really have to explain? I think your present behavior explains it all."

Patricia's mouth felt dry and her ears rang. "You can't talk to her. It's out of the question. And if it's me you have a problem with, then I'll go get another detective." She moved toward the door.

Liz shrugged. "It's McKenzie or no one."

"Then I guess it will be no one," Patricia spat. No way was Liz going to see Erin again. No way.

"Then you won't have the answers to your questions." Liz spoke with a bland unconcern that seemed calculated to insult. "And I know you still have plenty of questions. Because I am innocent. And if this goes to trial, I will talk. And I'll make a mockery of you and this whole department."

Patricia's pulse raced. She didn't want Erin anywhere near Adams. But Ruiz was listening, and she knew exactly what he would do. He would bring in Erin. Ultimately, that decision wasn't up to her. Liz had called her bluff and she was going to have her way, as she always did.

White-hot with anger, Patricia turned on her heel and stormed out of the room.

❖

Patricia sat in her Blazer for a few minutes after killing the engine. She stared at her house, knowing who was inside and what needed to be done. Ruiz wanted Erin at the station to talk to Adams. Somehow it had all come down to this.

She exited the vehicle and headed inside. She and Erin hadn't really spoken since the night they'd been intimate. Now she wondered just how intimate it had really been. Looking back, she viewed their encounter as one between two ravenous, horny teenagers, tugging at each other's clothing in order to quickly obtain some release—not the way she had intended things to be. She had foreseen a very different way of making love to Erin, a way she now knew would never happen. Not even if Erin really wanted it. And Patricia doubted that she did.

She dreaded the conversation they were about to have and wished she could put it off. But what had happened at the station with Adams was undeniable. Patricia had lost control, nearly exposed herself. Her feelings for Erin had undermined her judgment, and all for what? They were almost certainly one-sided. The realization hurt, but it was forcing her to get things straight in her mind, once and for all.

She found Erin reading on the couch, looking like she hadn't slept.

"Hi." Erin put the book down in her lap. "Are you okay?" Her eyes ran over Patricia's face.

Patricia sighed and dropped down on the couch. Her hands trembled and her body felt hollow inside. "Not really. We need to talk."

Erin sat up a little straighter. "Okay."

Patricia stared down at her shaking hands for a moment, terrified at what she was about to do. She didn't think she could take any more pain, but she knew it would eventually hurt worse if she let things continue on their present path. With a trembling voice she asked, "Are you attracted to me?"

"Yes." Erin met her eyes before she looked away, seemingly a little embarrassed.

A brief flutter of hope moved in Patricia's belly. But it wasn't good enough. "Is that all it is, then? Just physical attraction?"

Erin didn't look directly at her. "I don't understand," she said softly. Her face had reddened in response to the questioning

Christ, this was hard. But she had to know. "Do you have any other feelings for me, other than the physical attraction?"

"Of course." This time Erin met her gaze squarely. She looked troubled, possibly even hurt by the insinuation. "I care about you a great deal."

Patricia thought for a moment, searching for a way. There was only one question left. She had to ask if Erin felt the same way she did. "Is it…love?"

She clenched her hands, hoping, praying that by some miracle it would be. But as Erin looked away from her, she knew the answer. And while it was no real surprise, the crushing of her hopes and dreams still stung, painfully so.

"I'm sorry," Erin said softly. "I don't think it is. I mean, I would know for certain if I was in love, wouldn't I?"

Patricia fought back hot, biting tears. "Yes, I think you would."

Erin searched her face. "I'm so sorry. I don't know what the hell is wrong with me. I care about you, I'm attracted to you…I wanted you so bad…"

Patricia held up a hand, unable to hear any more. She understood what was happening to Erin. Understood it firsthand, having gone through it herself. "Erin, I think what you're feeling right now is normal," she said gently. "When a woman is first awakened, so to speak, to her sexual attraction to women, she often…"

"Feels like she's going to die if she doesn't have sex with a woman again soon?" Erin finished for her.

Patricia nodded and couldn't help but chuckle a little at the choice of words. "Yeah. I think it's safe to say you're having those feelings, then."

"I guess it's pretty obvious."

Patricia glanced away, deep in thought. It had been obvious, but she had refused to see it. She had been determined to have Erin, determined to live out her dream with her.

"It doesn't mean that I don't care about you," Erin added quickly.

"I know. But I don't think it would be wise for us to act on our mutual attraction again." It pained her to say the words, but she knew that she was saving them both some future heartache.

"So you're telling me in a nice way to keep my lips to myself." Erin smiled slightly at her from across the couch.

"Just from me, yeah." Patricia swallowed some jealousy once again. She couldn't bear to think about Erin with anyone else. Especially Adams. But she didn't want to hurt her feelings either. Erin was confused and going through a rough time. "It's not easy resisting you, you know. I care about you too, which is why I have to do this." She dropped her eyes, feeling extremely exposed.

"I understand." Erin reached out and took her hand. "You've done so much for me. If there's one thing I'm sure of right now, it's that you care. Thank you for that." In a transparent attempt to lighten things up, she added, "That still doesn't change the fact I feel like I'm going to die if I don't have a woman again soon."

As ridiculous as the words sounded, Patricia knew they were true. She'd felt that way herself long ago, after having her first lover. But the woman who was filling Erin's mind with powerful lust and emotion was poison, and Erin was obviously under her heady spell. Now that she knew Erin had been with Liz, Patricia knew it had been Liz, not she, who had ignited such a fierce fire in Erin. The flame was still burning bright in her eyes. She was hungry, wanting, needing…Liz.

Patricia longed to rescue her, but in a flash of insight she understood that Erin was in some ways a surrogate for the self she failed to rescue a long time ago. The younger woman had to figure out who she was and what she wanted all by herself. Even though it pained her to do so, Patricia had to back off, had to let her find her own way.

With a stab of grief, she lowered her eyes, protecting herself. Her feelings were too potent. She would have to distance herself somehow, keep her desires to herself, locked away deep inside.

"What am I supposed to do now?" Erin teased, patting her hand, trying to bring her back from the dark place to which she had gone.

Patricia knew her emotions must be written all over her face. She felt dead inside. An awkward silence stretched out between them until finally, she forced a shrug and said, nonchalantly, "Find some hot babe with an insatiable sexual appetite and screw your brains out."

Erin scoffed and flushed slightly. She looked taken aback by this blunt, almost crude, response. "Yeah right, easier said than done."

"Are you kidding me?" Patricia patted her hand as playfully as she could. "With your looks and charm, you'll be beating them off with a stick." Her words were true, and she smiled through her pain, suddenly very determined to do what was right for Erin, whatever the cost to herself.

Chapter Eighteen

"Are you sure you're up for this, Mac?" Sergeant Ruiz stood next to her, placing a soft hand on her shoulder.

Erin didn't bother to glance over at him. Instead, she kept her eyes forward, focusing on the dark hair of their main suspect. She couldn't see her face from where she stood behind the two-way mirror, only the back of her head and the uncharacteristically slouched shoulders and strongly muscled back.

"I'll be fine," she responded, sounding cold and indifferent.

She was beyond exhausted, her nerves strung out. The fact hadn't escaped her that the very department that had deemed her unfit for duty just a short time ago was now insisting she come in and counting on her to save their ass. She folded her arms as the resentment rose up to bite at her throat.

"I don't know if it's such a good idea," Patricia said.

Ruiz pushed his wire-rim glasses back farther on his nose. "We don't have much choice."

"Why not?" Erin asked in her cold voice, unafraid and uncaring for the first time in years. She felt almost completely disconnected from her body. Like she was a balloon floating high above her physical form. She had no idea what the hell was going on. How could they expect her to do this?

"Up until a few hours ago, Adams was cooperating with us," Ruiz explained. "She came in willingly and she answered most of our questions. But when we asked about the night of the shooting, she clammed up and said she would only talk to you."

"Me?" What did Liz want with her? She must be furious at her for going in after her undercover. Was she planning to have a little revenge, to somehow reveal Erin to her bosses?

"She's waiting for you," Ruiz prompted.

Just then, three other detectives entered the room. Jeff Hernandez gave her a warm, sincere smile of encouragement while Stewart merely glanced her way and coughed in his wheezy manner. Erin moved her gaze past the unsettling sight of Stewart to Gary Jacobs, who was greeting Patricia. The gang was all here. *It's all on you, Erin.*

Breathing in deeply, she grabbed the doorknob and said, "Okay, then."

To her surprise, Patricia moved quickly over to her and pushed the door closed. "Listen, if you get uncomfortable in there…" She gazed at Erin intensely.

"I'll be fine," Erin said with focused determination.

Patricia looked disbelieving, but she moved away from the door.

Erin entered the room and approached Liz from behind, slowly and carefully, trying to get control of her quickly escalating heart rate. Liz didn't bother to turn around.

"Ms. Adams," Erin acknowledged in her best professional tone as she moved past her around the small table.

The memory of hypnotizing blue eyes was fresh in her mind. So much so that she was afraid to look into them, frightened of getting lost again. Willing her nerves to calm, she did the first routine thing that came to mind. She pulled out a chair across from the silent woman and sat down. Only then did she summon the nerve to face her, and in an instant, a powerful shock jolted her body.

"Hello, Mrs. McKenzie." That sexy, deep voice was like a caress.

Erin clutched the edge of the table so hard her knuckles whitened. As she took in the strikingly handsome face and deep voice, the night of the shooting ricocheted through her mind, replaying like a movie in fast-forward.

She saw the evil, dark-haired woman trying to kill her. *Flash.* She saw Adams step in the room. *Flash.* And in an instant, she saw Adams try to wrestle the gun from the woman with the evil laugh. *Flash.* Stifling the shot, saving her life. *Flash.*

She blinked and swayed back in her chair as, in her mind, dark red blood stained her savior's shirt. She opened her eyes wide and let reality hit her under the bright lights of the interrogation room. Adams had been shot. Shot saving her life.

"It…You were there." Erin quickly refocused. The rush of memories left her feeling overwhelmed and slightly dizzy, but she also felt incredibly free. She was no longer a prisoner of her own mind.

"What do you mean?" Liz asked in a cagey tone.

"I remember now," Erin murmured.

She studied Liz thoroughly for the first time, surprised to see how pale and drawn her face appeared. She looked tired and even a little weak.

"What do you mean, you remember now?" Liz met her eyes.

Erin licked her dry lips, her skin burning suddenly in response to that piercing stare. Regardless of how tired and weak she now looked, Liz was still devastatingly beautiful.

"I…" She had to look away from those incredible eyes in order to concentrate. "Up until just now, I had a hard time remembering the events of the night of the shooting."

Liz looked shocked, and the little color in her face seemed to drain down into her neck. "You mean, all this time you just didn't remember?"

"That's correct." Erin watched as Liz's gaze drifted down to the table's surface.

"I see."

Liz felt suddenly sick. Ever since that night, she had thought that Erin had kept her secret out of respect for her, or maybe even because she harbored feelings for her. But it wasn't like that at all. Erin McKenzie had kept her secret, all right, but only because she couldn't remember it.

Hurt beyond her wildest dreams, she clenched her jaw, caught between pain and complete shock. Never before had any woman been able to wound her. Somehow, some way, this young detective had that power, and Liz hated herself for being vulnerable to it.

"I was told you wanted to speak to me," Erin said with a note of uncertainty.

Liz took in the beautiful face before her, noting the dark smudges under Erin's eyes. She repressed an urge to reach out to her. "I did, yes. But now it seems that I have nothing else to say."

"Oh?" Erin seemed surprised and disappointed.

Liz looked away from her then, the hurt too much.

"Let's talk about the night of the shooting," Erin pressed, as if the cop in her was trying to refocus.

Liz could feel the weight of the numerous stares on her back, pressing into her from just beyond the two-way mirror. They were watching her now. Watching and waiting. Excited, expectant, almost like children, wanting her to confess or incriminate herself like some kind of weakling. Well, they were going to be sorely disappointed. She had nothing left to say to the detective sitting in front of her.

"Let's not," she said with conviction.

Erin searched her face. "We have a lot to discuss, Ms. Adams. For instance, my fellow detectives already know that you were present at Detective Henderson's the night of the shooting." She continued to eye Liz as she pressed onward. "Your blood was on the carpet."

Liz didn't respond.

"And now I know why," Erin declared with a note of pride and relief. "You weren't there to kill me or to kill Henderson. You were there to stop the real killer."

Liz stared into Erin's eyes, her heart pounding. "If you remember as much as you say you do, then you'll end this conversation right now."

Erin's head snapped back slightly as if she had been physically struck. Her brow furrowed and her eyes seemed fixed on a distant point. She was deep in thought; Liz could almost see her mind working.

"Your request," she whispered finally, her eyes suddenly bright with comprehension. "That woman..."

"Hush." Liz reached across the table to seize Erin's hand. "Please."

The door to the room behind the two-way mirror flung open as Patricia came rushing into the room.

Erin held up her free hand. "It's okay. We're fine."

"She shouldn't be touching you," Patricia noted coldly.

Erin nodded and reluctantly removed her hand from beneath Liz's. The heat from Liz's touch was almost too much to bear anyhow, and it wouldn't do her career any good to have her fellow detectives see her melt under a suspect's caress. Her mind drifted again to the mysterious dark-haired woman with the familiar eyes and evil laugh. Of course. It all made so much sense to her now. She was Liz's sister. That explained the plea to keep quiet.

So much seemed complicated and confusing. But one thing was perfectly clear. "You saved my life."

"Yes," Liz said softly. "I think, then, that you know what it is that I need to discuss with you."

Erin fidgeted a little in her chair. "I'm not sure I—"

"Please." Despite Patricia's hovering presence near the door, Liz reached across the table to grasp her hand. "I know you will."

Erin stared into Liz's eyes and allowed the heat from her touch to penetrate her blood. She knew what Liz wanted. She wanted her silence. She wanted her to promise.

"Mrs. McKenzie…" Liz stared at Erin with blue flames burning in her eyes.

"Please, don't call me that," Erin said, cringing at the name. "Call me Erin, or Mac, even."

"Erin." Liz seemed to hold the name in her mouth.

In that split second, all Erin could think about was kissing her. She started to shake her head in protest, but the pressure on her hand increased and she looked into the pale, drawn face of the woman who had saved her life. The woman who had fought her own sister and taken a bullet for an undercover cop. The very cop who had invaded her life in order to gain information to peg a serial-murder case on her.

As she realized all these things, her heart opened up and her gaze lingered over Liz's beautiful face and rested once again on her burning eyes. She could feel something tangible between them. Not just a shared secret, but something more.

"If I…" Erin started, but then thought better of it. "I have questions." She withdrew her hand before causing another excited reaction from Patricia.

Liz smiled a tired smile. "I know." She held Erin's gaze, somehow reassuring her that all would be answered. But not here. Not now. "But you remember that I was at Detective Henderson's that night to stop the real killer, don't you?"

"Yes."

The door opened again and Sergeant Ruiz motioned Erin over. "What the hell's going on in here, Mac?" he demanded in a hushed tone.

"She's not your killer," Erin said loudly enough so that Liz would hear.

"Then who the hell is?"

"I'm not totally sure." It was almost the truth. She didn't know the name of the killer or where they might find her. She would ask Liz these questions, and if she didn't get satisfactory answers, she would simply claim that she had suddenly remembered the killer's identity and tell her superior. Until then, the department wasn't going to get the information from her. She owed at least that much to Liz for saving her life.

"What the hell do you mean you don't remember?" Ruiz asked, his temper flaring up. "I thought you said you'd gotten your memory back."

"I remember Adams saving my life, sir. Jumping in front of the shooter and taking a bullet for me."

"But you don't know who the shooter is?" His face reddened.

"I remember the girl, Tracy, trying to shoot me, sir." That much was true.

Ruiz threw his hands up in the air and let them fall to slap his thighs.

Her own temper building on frayed and overtired nerves, Erin moved past him to the hidden room where the other detectives were waiting. Patricia and Ruiz followed her. The sergeant started to speak again, but Erin cut him off.

"No! I'm going to talk now, and you can listen." She'd had enough. Angrily, she said, "Let me get all this straight. First, I go undercover to try and save the department face by getting evidence on the supposed killer. Then, I live through an attack on my life, leaving Henderson injured and another person dead. Then, I'm forced to go on medical leave because I can't remember all of the events of the night in question. So, I go off to try to recuperate, to try to force my mind to remember, because otherwise, I'm out of a job. In doing so, I've had almost no sleep and feel like I'm going crazy. Then, lo and behold, out of the blue, you send Patricia to get me because, guess what, the department decides it needs me again."

She paused long enough to take in the shocked faces around her. Too bad, she thought. After this, they could discharge her, for all she cared. She forged on.

"Being the loyal cop that I am, I came here today for the good of the department. And for some reason, questioning that woman made my memory come back. I'm thrilled about that. Actually, I'm ecstatic. And silly me, I thought my superior and the department would be just as thrilled as I am. But oh no. My memory doesn't peg your girl, so you start yelling at me. Well, fuck that, Ruiz. I can't make the facts fit your theory about who's guilty here. It's not my fault you wasted time and money chasing the wrong person. Adams is innocent. And not only that, she saved my life."

She stopped, her chest heaving, her fists clenched at her sides. Patricia moved quickly to her side and gave her a silencing look, obviously trying to defuse the explosive situation.

"Sir, she's exhausted," Patricia said. "This has been too much."

Ruiz stood perfectly still, staring at his young detective in obvious disbelief.

"Where the fuck did that come from?" Stewart let out before he chuckled. "Damn, Mac, I think going under as a dyke on this case caused you to grow some big, hairy balls."

"You know, Stewart," Patricia seethed, "I'm sick to death of your sexist and prejudiced remarks."

"That's enough!" Ruiz shouted. "From all of you. Now, I know we're all frustrated…"

Ignoring the drama playing out, Erin crossed to the two-way mirror to look at Liz. "How long has she been here?"

Jeff had gone into the room to talk to her, to question her some more, while the other detectives continued to bicker. No one seemed to have heard Erin's question, or they were choosing to ignore it.

With a shrug, she walked back into the interrogation room and, paying no mind to Jeff's questioning look, asked Liz, "When were you brought in, Ms. Adams?"

"Last night."

Erin glanced at her wristwatch. "So you've been here for eighteen hours?"

Her anger exploded into fury. With Jeff on her heels, she marched back into the observation room and slammed the door behind them.

"I want her released," she demanded flatly.

"I don't care what you want," Ruiz said, the shock having passed of his once soft-spoken detective unloading on him. "We're not done questioning her."

Erin knew that it was standard procedure to keep a suspect for hours of questioning. It was one of the ways in which they wore them down. But keeping an innocent woman overnight without rest was ridiculous and Ruiz knew it. He just wasn't ready to let go of the suspect he had invested so much time and money pursuing.

"Well, you may not be finished, but I guarantee you she's finished with you. You have no grounds to keep her and you know it. She knows it too."

"It's not up to you to decide when we are finished with a suspect," Ruiz said coldly.

"I would agree, with the exception of one tiny little thing." Erin moved back to the door and yanked it open. "She's no longer a suspect." With that, she entered the interview room and faced Liz.

"Ms. Adams, I just came back in to let you know that I've finished questioning you." She heard the door open. Ruiz leaned against the jamb, glaring at her. Ignoring him, she said, "And, well…I wanted to offer you my most sincere thanks for saving my life."

She extended her hand to Liz, who slowly rose, then took it in her own. They held each other's eyes for a long moment, and it seemed to Erin that something bright and full of promise hung between them.

"You're welcome, Detective," Liz finally said with a sincere smile.

"Perhaps we can meet up at a later time," Erin offered. "I would love to buy you dinner as a gesture of my appreciation."

Liz nodded, still holding her gaze. "That sounds nice. I look forward to it."

Erin smiled back at her and let her hand fall. Her insides immediately screamed at the break in contact. "Until later, then," she said as she moved to the door.

She could feel Ruiz's heated stare on her back, but she kept on walking.

"So what's going on?" Stewart found some gum in his top pocket. "Is this circus show over or what?"

"No thanks to Mac, it is," Ruiz said.

"That's not true." Patricia knew her frustration with Ruiz was showing. "If we had done our jobs better, then we might have what we need on Adams or whoever else. But as it stands, we've got nothing, and that's not Mac's fault."

Ruiz stared at Adams through the two-way mirror like a man watching the biggest fish he'd ever caught snap the line and swim off. "You were right," he told Patricia. "That woman is involved. She knows something she's not telling us, and Mac all but encouraged her to keep it to herself!"

Patricia hesitated, weighing her words. She didn't know how to explain Erin's strange behavior, but she knew she needed to downplay it or her friend could very well lose her job.

"I don't think Mac's encouraging her," she said carefully. "I think she's just overwhelmed right now with her memory returning, with finding out Adams saved her."

"I don't care if she's saved the world!" Ruiz spat a little as the words came out.

"Should I release her?" Patricia asked. "You know if we hold her any longer, she'll lawyer up."

Ruiz shook his head in resignation. Patricia could tell he was looking for someone to blame for the outcome of this investigation. He was going to take the easy road like he'd wanted to before. This had to look good on paper. They had a dead shooter and a reasonable theory. He was going to hang this on Kristen Reece and Tracy Walsh and wash his hands of any residual doubt. He would have done so already if the forensic report hadn't given them a reason to bring Adams in.

Sure enough, with a defeated hand gesture, Ruiz declared, "We're done here. Cut her loose. This is on Reece and that cop's crazy kid. Write it up and have the report on my desk tomorrow."

Patricia caught a look from Gary Jacobs and shrugged. Every detective in the room knew the case was littered with loose ends and unanswered questions. But the killings had stopped. And so long as they didn't start again, no one was going to care what Elizabeth Adams knew or whether she was behind the killings all along.

Chapter Nineteen

"C an I help you?" a female voice called from the front door. With her heart hammering, Erin thought briefly about just jumping in her car and peeling out of the driveway. But she was too tired to be afraid, too tired to be a coward. Mark was back at the house, something she had insisted on after the attack on his life, and she had to face this.

She stood straighter and looked directly at the pregnant blond woman who had made her way out of the house. Her belly was low and rounded; she was at least six or seven months along. Erin swallowed back the stinging daggers attacking her throat. The deceit still hurt, regardless of her long-dead feelings for Mark.

"I'm here to get my car," she said.

The woman stopped walking and stared like a deer caught in headlights. Erin stood her ground and watched the woman size her up. Her hand came up and lingered at her chest as if she were slightly perturbed.

"Honey, what's going on?"

Erin looked past the woman in maternity clothes to see Mark emerge from the house. He was walking slowly, obviously still healing from the knife wounds. When he saw her standing by her car, his face took on a surprised look, and he greeted her uneasily.

"Hello, Mark." She kept her voice level and unemotional. "I just came to get my car."

"Of course." He gave his pregnant mistress a comforting pat on the shoulder.

An unbearable silence ensued and Erin thought about asking him how he was feeling, but the pregnant woman was shooting poisonous darts at her with every glance. "Well, I won't keep you.

Looks like you're doing well," she said, before climbing into the car.

Digging down under the seat, she found the keys, and when she looked back up, Mark and his mistress were gone. Erin laughed a little hysterically. Mark and his pregnant attack dog were welcome to each other. She genuinely hoped he'd be happy. She put the car in reverse, then backed out onto the road and stared at the house she'd so despised.

Where to now? *I could sure use a drink.*

Erin pulled her BMW into a space near the edge of the parking lot. Night had fallen over the valley, draping it with rich purples and midnight blues that would ultimately darken into the black of night. Leaning back in her seat, she allowed the scent of the nearly new vehicle to fill her insides. The car, like her, had been one of Mark's representations of the perfect life he wanted everyone to perceive he led.

She focused the on reflections off the windshield and decided she would trade the BMW in for something more her. Something a little less showy, maybe an SUV. While she was at it, she needed to find herself a place to live as well. She was ready to shed her former life and start again. She felt much older, suddenly, more herself than ever before.

She looked around at the rows of cars and the cluster of women waiting at the front entrance of the club. She didn't know how she had ended up here, having driven in sort of a daze. But here she was, worn out, defeated, and unbelievably confused. She had told herself she was going for a drink, so maybe that's why she was here—simply for a drink.

She closed her eyes, her heart thudding in her chest. Would she see her tonight? Would they talk? The mere thought of Liz stole the breath from her lungs. She inhaled deeply and tried to relax, but it was useless. Sighing, she clenched the steering wheel with white knuckles. She needed a drink, and nothing and no one was going to stop her from getting it.

❖

"Why would she fake it?" Patricia paced her living room in agitation.

The idea of Erin faking the psychological horror she'd been going through seemed absolutely preposterous, and it infuriated her that Gary would even think she would do such a thing.

"To cover for Adams," her partner said.

"I don't buy it. I've been living with her. I would have known."

Gary gave her a telling glance and sipped his drink. His expression said he'd guessed Erin was more than a colleague to her.

"Think about it," he said. "She acts like she can't remember, so Adams and whoever else have time to tie up loose ends. And maybe she still didn't tell us the whole truth today when she conveniently got her memory back. You were there. You saw how they behaved together. Why do you think Ruiz lost his head?"

Patricia scoffed and walked over to the couch to plop down. She couldn't believe what she was hearing, and worse than that, she couldn't make Gary see how ludicrous his suspicions were. She gazed up at the ceiling, feeling overwhelmed and defeated.

"You're wrong," she finally said. Her heart pounded madly in her chest, and her head hurt from the mental strain.

"Okay. So let's prove it," Gary challenged her. "You said she'd phoned with some story about going out for a drink. One guess where she's headed."

"What makes you so sure?" She studied Gary suspiciously. He'd been cagey with her over the past week, like he was holding something back. Normally she would have challenged him on this, but she had been too busy obsessing over a woman who would never be hers. Aggravated, she said, "What have you got, Gary? We're supposed to be partners, remember?"

He held her eyes for a long moment. "I've been receiving phone calls from an anonymous female. It seems like she could be a credible source."

"Don't tell me…Kristen Reece." She watched him blink as she said the words.

"You know?"

"Looks like we've both been holding out," she said coolly.

Erin slammed the car door shut behind her and headed into the all-women establishment. With her shoulders back and proud, she made her way to the bar.

The soft-butch bartender came immediately to her with a smile. "What can I get you?"

"Kamikaze shooter," Erin replied over the loud music. "Make it three."

"Something scary chasing you, darling?" The bartender tried to touch her hand.

Erin pulled back and dug into her pocket for money. "Just give me the drinks."

"Hey, okay," the woman said.

Erin looked around somewhat impatiently as she waited. Basement Jaxx played seductively in her ears as her eyes adjusted to the darkness of the club. The laser and the lights pulsed across the dance floor, matching the rhythm of the music.

"Here you go." The bartender placed the three shot glasses in front of her in a neat little row.

"Keep the change," Erin said without looking up. She downed the drinks, one right after the other.

As the alcohol warmed down her chest into her belly, she moved away from the bar and headed for the dance floor. The music called to her and she suddenly felt the overwhelming urge to dance her troubles away. Her heart drumming in time with the beat, she reached up and tugged at the stifling material of her flannel shirt. She had worn it to go pick up her car, and until now, she hadn't realized just how warm the material was. Feeling suffocated, she peeled the shirt free of her body, not caring about the buttons in the least. Her attention was on the dance floor, and she flung the shirt to one side.

The thin white tank top she wore underneath was soaked through with sweat, and the air on her wet skin felt remarkable. She breathed deeply in response to the freeing sensation as she made her way to the center of the dance floor. As she began to dance, with her arms held over her head, she closed her eyes and allowed her hungry, lonely soul to be fed by the music.

"What!" Liz yelled as the pounding on her door continued.

She pushed herself up off the bed and staggered across her room. She had finally fallen asleep only to be disturbed by the thundering knocks. With her sleepiness quickly giving way to anger, she yanked open the door.

Tyson stood, looking unsure and more than a little frightened as he read the fury written on her face. "Sorry to disturb you, ma'am," he said.

"What is it, Tyson?" She hoped it didn't have anything to do with the police. As strong as she prided herself in being, she didn't think she had any reserve left to deal with them.

"There's someone here I think you should know about."

"Jesus," she let out with frustration. "So who is it this time? Another fat cop? Another goddamned detective?"

She stalked back into her room and filled a glass with Red Bull. Whoever it was, Liz knew the situation would probably require her presence. Otherwise Tyson wouldn't have bothered her. She chugged her drink, wishing it would feed her cells some much-needed energy.

"Yes, ma'am," he said softly. "A detective."

"Great." She made her way to the couch, where she sat down and propped up her bare feet.

"I thought you would want to know."

"Yes, thank you." She set down the glass. "So what do they want?"

"I'm not sure, ma'am." He eyed her sweatpants and wrinkled T-shirt.

"Well, where are they?" She knew she should have gone home. It made no sense to hang around the club when she needed to get some rest.

"On the dance floor. She's really pushing her way through…" Tyson said with a note of disbelief.

"*Her* way?" Liz abandoned the couch and went over to the monitors, scanning them quickly.

"How long has she been here?" she asked, having to clear her tight throat to speak.

"Not long."

"Has she said anything?" She finally tore her eyes from the monitors.

"No."

Liz had already moved to her closet to rifle through her clothes, tossing a few shirts on the bed.

"Would you like me to tell her that her presence is requested up here?" Tyson turned discreetly away from her as she stripped off her clothes.

"No." She made her way to the shower. "I'll see to her myself."

"Do you see her?" Patricia asked loudly.

Gary shook his head as "Master and Servant" by Depeche Mode blasted through the speakers into the club. On the platforms, women in 1940s apparel moved seductively against one another. One member of each couple wore a zoot suit, topped off with a fedora hat pulled down at an angle over her eyes. Their counterparts in the newsboy hats wore see-through tank tops with suspenders to hold up the wide-legged, high-waisted worker pants. These women busied themselves undressing the suited women, exposing large strap-on dildos beneath their pinstripe pants.

Patricia looked away as the women in the newsboys began sucking on the dildos. Did she really want to put herself through this? She was determined to continue on the case, but going after Erin? It seemed almost crazy to her at that moment as the women danced and gyrated above her.

"To what do I owe the pleasure?" a deep voice asked from behind.

She turned, instantly recognizing the sultry voice. "I think you know why I'm here." She tried hard not to stare at Elizabeth Adams.

"To harass me some more?" Liz queried, raising an eyebrow.

Patricia gave a short laugh. "Harass you? I wouldn't waste my time. You're not worth it."

"Then why are you here, Detective?" Adams had the nerve to look amused.

"Where is she?" Patricia glared at her, looking beyond the muscled arms and the sleeveless blue button-down shirt that so perfectly matched her eyes.

She believed Erin was there, but not because she'd hatched some secret criminal plan with Liz, as Gary had suggested. She thought Erin was there simply out of lust and wonderment, if not to escape her current problems with a drink.

"Where's who?" Liz asked, all innocence.

"Erin McKenzie," Patricia said with hatred in her voice. Liz could act uncaring and aloof with anyone else she wanted to, but Patricia wouldn't let her act that way about Erin.

Liz's face seemed to soften at the name. She looked around the club with what could almost pass as anxiety. "I don't know. I haven't seen her."

"Bullshit!" Patricia seethed. "I know she's here."

"Look, I'm telling you the truth. I haven't seen her. Is something wrong?" Adams's concern seemed genuine. "Is she...okay?"

"Why? You give a shit?"

For a moment Liz's eyes flashed fierce anger, then her face became impassive. "Look around the club all you want. To my knowledge, she's not here."

Patricia threw Gary an angry look. "This is ridiculous," she said as Liz walked away. "I told you Mac isn't involved."

"I don't know. You saw how concerned she got just then. I don't think that's just a coincidence. Mac's probably up in her room as we speak."

"No. She's not here," Patricia said. Gary had it completely wrong. He had mistaken Liz's concern for an instinct of self-preservation. "Adams would never let us look around if she were. I have a feeling that if we asked her, she'd let us up to see her private room tonight. She seems more than willing to cooperate." *Almost too willing.*

"Then let's go ask."

"No. If we go demanding to be let into her private room, don't you think it will set off more alarms in her? If you're right and she does have something to hide in this investigation, then I can guarantee you she's up there right now, trying to figure out why we're here. Adams is smart, way smarter than your average felon."

Gary thought for a moment. "Maybe she's got Mac somewhere else."

"Maybe she doesn't have her anywhere at all. Maybe Mac is somewhere blowing off steam," Patricia said, trying to convince herself as well as her partner.

"I hope you're right. But I don't buy it. I think we should head over to her house in the hills, check it out, see if we get any movement."

"You think she's got Mac stashed there?" Patricia shook her head in disbelief. "If she does, we'll never know it. That place is rigged like Fort Knox, and I'm not about to go and sit outside the gate with my thumbs up my ass all night, just in case." She was tired and frustrated and didn't feel like continuing this wild-goose chase. "So if you want surveillance, I suggest you call in one of the other teams."

"You know I can't do that. The case is closed."

"Yes, so this is nuts! What are we even doing here?"

"You're still a cop, Patricia," her partner said. "You always will be, whether you're off writing best sellers or not. And I know there are things about this case that are eating away at you. Ignoring them won't make it go away."

Patricia groaned. "What are you, a public service announcement?"

"If you're so damned sure she's not involved, what have you got to lose?"

Patricia gazed into his eyes and knew he was wrong about Erin and possibly even wrong about Liz. But still, the phone calls and a few odd facts about Kristen Reece's death nagged at her. As she walked toward the main entrance with him, she realized she was going to get to the bottom of this case, closed or not. But it wasn't because she needed to prove anything to Gary. She needed to know the truth. Whatever it was.

❖

"They're here looking for that cute blonde, right?" Tyson asked.

"Yeah," Liz said, watching the detectives cross the dance floor.

"I heard them saying she went out for a drink."

"So far you're batting a thousand, Tyson." Her patience was wearing extremely thin. "Now tell me your point, because I know you have one."

"Well, after hearing that, I took the liberty of calling over to Chasity's."

She turned toward him, her interest piqued. Chasity's was the only other lesbian nightspot in Valle Luna. Located just down the street, it was a tiny establishment with just a bar, a small dance floor, and a room with a pool table. With La Femme's size, budget, and popularity, no one else seemed to want to compete. But Chasity had opened her place fifteen years ago, well before La Femme, and she still had her regulars.

"And?"

"She's there."

Liz stood straighter at the revelation, instantly ready to go.

Tyson continued. "Chasity said she's already cut her off. She's drunk and barely able to walk, much less dance. I asked her not to kick her out."

"Thanks." She gave him a sincere smile. "Will you please escort the detectives around while I'm gone? Including my private quarters, to show them that she's really not here?" She was already walking.

Ahead of her, Tyson reached Patricia and her male counterpart just before they hit the door.

"Excuse me, Detectives." His thick voice boomed out, getting their attention. "I've been instructed to show you around the club. Anywhere you wish to go, I will make sure you have access."

They exchanged a look. "Thank you, I think we'll take you up on that," the male detective said.

Chapter Twenty

Liz pulled her Harley-Davidson to a stop behind the small bar just a few blocks down the way from hers. As she killed the engine, she could hear the loud music drifting out through the door, which was always left open just a crack during business hours. She dismounted the black-and-chrome machine and walked the short distance around the white brick building.

A sign was mounted by the entrance, warning that no one under the age of twenty-one would be admitted. But as she pulled open the door, no bouncer stood to check ID. Only the eyes of the few patrons turned to examine her as she walked in.

"Hey, Liz!" Chasity called out from behind the bar.

Liz made her way over to the tall chairs and shook the older woman's hand. "Chas, long time no see."

"No shit, man." Her friend's brown eyes were warm. "So how you been?"

"Better," she responded, offering no more.

Chasity brushed self-consciously at her 1950s diamond-patterned button-down shirt. "I'll bet." She looked past Liz to the dance floor, where Erin swayed to the music with her eyes closed, obviously lost in her own little world and very intoxicated. "This is hers." She handed over a flannel shirt from behind the bar.

Liz took the garment and ignored the questions in her old friend's eyes. Instead, she made her way to the dance floor and stepped in front Erin.

"Hi," she said.

Erin opened her eyes and focused blearily. She, and one other, appeared to be the only dancers on the small floor. "Hi yourself." She offered a sloppy grin and, poking at Liz's chest with a finger,

slurred out, "Wait a minute! I'm not at your club, I left your club."
She looked around hastily. "What are you doing here?" She stepped
closer to touch Liz's arms. "Are you real? Or are you just a figment
of my imagiation…imagination."

"I'm real." Liz steadied her with a half hug. "And you're
drunk."

"Ohmygod really?" She laughed hysterically.

"Come on, let's go." Liz tried to steer her off the dance floor.

"Where to?" Erin asked, dragging her feet. "I wanna dance."

"You've danced enough."

"I wanna dance some more." She stopped in her tracks, resisting
as Liz tried to guide her toward the exit. "Gah," Erin let out as she
looked up into Liz's face. "You are so fucking gorgeous, ya know
that?" She reached up to touch her.

Liz grabbed at her hand, stopping her before she most likely
poked her eye. Then quickly, and with relative ease, she hoisted her
up and over her shoulder.

"Hey!" Erin yelled, weakly slapping at Liz's back. "This isn't
dancing!"

Liz carried her to the bar, where she tossed a hundred dollar bill
on the glossy wood counter and apologized.

"Nah, man. She wasn't any trouble. Entertaining, maybe, but
no trouble." A few of the other patrons at the bar voiced up and
agreed with the bar owner.

"Then, for your hospitality, drinks are on me," Liz said, refusing
to take back her money.

They left the bar, and Erin found herself on her feet again next
to Liz's Harley.

"You all right?" Liz asked.

"Fucking fabulous." Erin grabbed her forehead as a wave of
dizziness surged through her. Closing her eyes, she leaned into Liz
and swallowed back some nausea.

"You up for a ride, dancing queen?" Liz asked, looking down
into her face.

Erin stood on her own once again and watched as Liz bent
down to start the bike. "I don't think I can," she said over the roar
of the engine.

"Sure you can." Liz swung her denim-clad leg over the bike. "You can ride in front." She scooted back on the seat and motioned for Erin to climb on in front of her. Having little choice in the matter, Erin shrugged, then climbed onto the bike.

"Here, put on your shirt." Liz helped her shrug into the warm flannel.

Too drunk to think about anything serious, Erin let the shirt warm her skin and concentrated on the feel of Liz pressed up against her from behind. Strong arms confined her as Liz grabbed the handlebars.

She grinned uncontrollably as her skin awakened, loving the feel of the thighs encasing her, the breasts pressing into her back. She inhaled Liz's scent, which immediately triggered erotic memories. As they drove off from the small lesbian bar, she leaned back into Liz, closing her eyes, loving the feel of the wind, and the feel of the beautiful woman behind her.

They hadn't traveled very far when she felt the bike slow down and they pulled into a corner convenience store. Liz parked and cut the engine before she quickly and easily dismounted.

"Why are we here?" Erin asked, blinking away her impending headache.

"I'll be right back." Liz gave her shoulder a gentle squeeze.

As she waited, Erin rested her hands on the tank of the bike. She swallowed back more nausea while listening to the drone of the traffic behind her. She rubbed her temples and thought that perhaps she shouldn't have had the sixth shot after all, not to mention the two vodka chasers she had insisted upon.

With the thought of alcohol making her sick, she tried instead to concentrate on the beautiful and mysterious woman who had surprisingly shown up to rescue her. She had no idea why Liz had come to get her, but drunk as she was, the idea of being with her once again instantly excited her, encouraging her to sober up.

"Here," Liz said with a soft smile as she returned to the bike.

Erin took the brown paper bag. "What is it?"

"Stuff that will help."

Liz climbed back onto the bike and Erin held fast to the bag as they roared back into traffic and headed away from the heart of the city.

Before long, the night air became cooler. They drove until they hit the mountains to the north of Valle Luna. This area, in the heart of a desert preserve, had yet to be developed, and Erin recognized the protected park as they climbed up the paved road. She had never been to the top of these mountains and was awed by the breathtaking view of the valley below.

Liz slowed the bike as they came to a large level area overlooking the city. She parked parallel to the drop and cut the engine. "Turn around," she said.

Erin reluctantly stood, hating to be out of Liz's arms. Still holding on to the bag, she repositioned herself on the bike, looking directly into the beautiful face of Elizabeth Adams.

"Go ahead, look in the bag," Liz suggested.

Erin pulled out a twenty-ounce bottle of Coke, some aspirin, and two small bags of potato chips. "What's all this?" she asked, instantly craving the Coke.

"My own little hangover prevention kit," Liz said with a smile. "Thought you could use it."

"Thanks." Erin unscrewed the bottle top and took a swig.

"I know it's a little unconventional, but the Coke always helps to settle my stomach and the chips always sate my salt cravings."

"Sounds like you've had a few wild nights."

Liz chuckled. "One or two."

"Uh-huh." Erin took another sip of Coke before looking back up into Liz's incredible blue eyes. "So why did you come get me? How did you even find me?"

"Your two detective friends came to see me tonight at La Femme."

"Who? Patricia?" Erin was suddenly sober.

"And some guy," Liz confirmed.

"Why?" Surely Liz was not being harassed again. "I told them that you didn't do anything, they should leave you alone."

"They were trying to find you. Patricia seemed upset and I thought you might be in trouble, so I came looking for you."

"Why would I be in trouble?" Erin's stomach churned with anxiety. She had no idea what was going on with Patricia.

"Well, considering the condition I found you in, it's a good thing I took the time."

"I just wanted a drink." Thrown by the idea of her colleagues coming to La Femme to look for her, she asked, "Why was Patricia so upset?"

"I don't know. And when I told her I hadn't seen you, she got more upset, like she didn't believe me."

"She probably didn't." Erin knew how much Patricia despised and distrusted Liz.

She had told the other detective she needed some time on her own. Why the search party? She felt in her back pocket for her cell phone and flipped it open. One missed call from Patricia, and there was no message. It certainly wasn't anything to cause great alarm. If something were really wrong, wouldn't Patricia have kept trying to reach her? Wouldn't she have left a voice message? Puzzled, she closed her phone and slid it back into her pocket.

"You know, I felt bad tonight when I saw you like that. I feel like it's my fault," Liz said. "That maybe you're all torn up inside over what you did for me in front of the cops you work with."

Erin shook her head. "I did the right thing by you." She met Liz's eyes. "I won't lie to you and tell you that it hasn't caused me some grief and possibly more in the future. And that does upset me. But I guarantee you that it's not the only thing troubling me right now. It's a lot of things."

"Your life."

"Yes. We all have trouble in our lives, don't we?"

"Some more than others," Liz said quietly.

Erin caught a glint of sadness in her eyes and reached out, gently placing her hands on Liz's. "Talk to me."

Liz nearly trembled under the warm and caring touch, the gesture almost too much. She was quickly losing the battle within herself over Erin McKenzie, her dark and desolate soul surrendering to light and love. She looked away, hating how emotional and easily moved she was. How could this have happened? How did this woman do what no other ever could?

Gathering her nerve, she eased her hands from Erin's, the warming sensation spreading like a virus in her blood. "I need to tell you about Jay," she said, almost in a whisper.

Erin touched her hand again. "What do you want to tell me?"

"Jay is messed up." Liz wanted to withdraw, but she needed Erin's strength. "She's got it in her head that she needs to protect me like she did when we were kids."

"Have you spoken with her since all this happened?" Erin asked.

Liz shook her head and let out a shaky breath. She was never this emotional, not even about her own sister. It was Erin McKenzie and the way she sat looking at her. With warmth, caring, and unconditional understanding. Things she had never seen in anyone's eyes before, things she knew she would forever be drawn to.

Looking away, she finally managed to continue. "I told her to leave you alone, and to stop the killing."

"Do you think she will?"

"I hope so. I just can't figure it out. I've never known her to be violent. I don't know where this is coming from." She looked back to Erin. "I've got a private investigator following her to make sure she doesn't do anything she's not supposed to. But last I heard, she'd left Alabama, and now I don't know where she is."

"Alabama?"

"That's where we grew up."

She felt Erin squeeze her hand and she swelled with emotion deep within her chest, wanting to tell Erin everything. From her horrible childhood to her countless lovers, she would tell her all of it, because for once in her life, she knew she had found someone who would understand. She also knew Erin would accept nothing less than noble behavior from here on out.

"The detective doesn't know where she is now?" Erin asked gravely.

"I haven't heard yet."

"Why haven't the police found her? I don't remember reading anything in your file about a sister."

"That's probably because there's not much to find. Jay's my half sister. We were both illegitimate. My mother breezed into town after she'd had us, saying she couldn't care for a baby. So my aunt took us."

"She just dropped you off and left you? Never saw you again?"

Liz nodded. "We were raised and schooled by my aunt. I, for the most part, didn't even have a medical record until I broke my arm and needed surgery. And after a certain traumatic instance, Jay pretty much lost her sense of reality and wouldn't even stray far from the house. Not many people knew her."

"My gosh. I'm so sorry."

"Don't be," Liz managed, her throat tight. "It's something I got over a long time ago."

"Thank you for telling me."

"I said I would. And I'll tell you more as I know it. In regards to Jay, my private detective will make sure she doesn't hurt anyone else. I just don't want you to go crazy over all this."

Erin leaned closer across the seat of the bike. Her eyes were no longer unfocused as she gazed at Liz. "What I'm going crazy over is you." She reached out and lightly touched her cheek.

Liz breathed deeply at the warmth of the touch and clasped the hand that elicited such powerful reactions in her. Turning it over, she lightly kissed the palm. She finally knew some of the reasons why Erin moved her so, but she also knew that she would most likely spend eternity trying to discover the rest.

Erin shuddered across from her. "You don't understand how much I think about you," she whispered breathlessly. "I'd never been with anyone…"

"I was your first?"

"Yes." Erin looked embarrassed.

Liz sat in silence, dumbfounded. "Why didn't you tell me?" she asked, fearing that maybe she had rushed the encounter or been too aggressive.

"What was I supposed to say, exactly? Besides, nothing happened that I didn't want to happen."

"So, you didn't just sleep with me for the sake of the case?"

"No, of course not!" Erin sounded almost insulted. "I may have been undercover, but I wouldn't do that."

Relief washed through Liz. It felt good to know that what she had felt was most likely mutual. "But that was weeks ago," she said under her breath, silently reliving the wonderful encounter in her mind. "There's been no one since?" A dull, heavy sensation fell upon her insides as she thought of Erin with another woman.

"Once." Erin's eyes pleaded for understanding. "It was a mistake. I thought I could...I don't know, erase you. But every time I closed my eyes, I saw you."

Liz lifted Erin's chin to look into her eyes. She remembered how crazy with lust she had been after her first experience with a woman. And it seemed that Erin, like her, was having difficulty in erasing their encounter from her mind.

Swallowing emotion, she said huskily, "I understand. And I want to see you again. Soon."

"I want to see you too," Erin replied.

"Call me. Any time." Liz took a pen from a small satchel on the side of the bike and gently wrote a phone number in the very palm she had just kissed.

Then, with slow deliberation, she tilted Erin's face and kissed her. She had to fight the urge to take in more of her, to conquer Erin's mouth with her own. She felt so good, unlike anything she had ever known.

They pulled apart slowly. Erin's eyes gleamed with tears. "I don't want to let you go," she said.

"Hey." Liz cupped her beautiful face. "I'll see you again soon."

"I know." Erin made a visible attempt to pull herself together. "I think it's just everything. It's all getting to me."

Liz stroked her hair away from her face. "It's going to be okay. I promise it'll all work out."

A tear rolled down Erin's cheek. "I hope you're right."

"I'm always right." She kissed Erin's forehead. "Now let's get you back to wherever you're staying so you can get some rest."

Erin awoke the next morning to find Patricia staring at her from the end of the bed, a coffee mug in her hand. Sleep, heavy and cloudy, pulled at her consciousness, making it difficult to focus.

Bright sunlight cascaded through the window, casting a warm glow across the sheets. Squinting, she forced herself to sit up.

"Did I wake you?" Patricia sounded barely awake herself.

"No. I'm used to people staring at me while I sleep." Erin offered a tired smile but got none in return.

"Where were you last night?" Patricia asked bluntly.

"What?" Erin was not sure she'd heard correctly. The look on her friend's face was one of distress, and her question didn't seem to fit with the pain in her eyes. "I went out for a drink. Like I said."

"Were you with Adams?"

Erin hesitated, truly thrown. "For a little while." Alarms penetrated the fog in her mind and she was suddenly fully awake. "Why? Is something wrong?"

"You tell me, Mac." Patricia's voice was thick and scratchy.

What the hell? "I don't know what you're saying." Erin didn't like the tone of Patricia's voice, and she certainly didn't like where this was going.

Why was Patricia making it her business to discuss something that could only be hurtful? Erin wasn't an idiot. She knew Patricia had feelings for her, and it was no secret how she felt about Liz. Obviously, Patricia was having some problems letting all this go. Why else would she be so upset?

"I'm asking you a simple question," Patricia said in a taut, hard tone Erin had never heard her use.

Shaken and upset by the questioning, Erin matched the unpleasant tone as best she could. "I went for a drink, just like I told you I was. Liz showed up. She said you were in her club looking for me, so she got worried and came looking herself. We went for a ride in the mountains, then she dropped me back here. Satisfied?"

Patricia stared at her like she'd lost her mind. "Do you have any idea how bad this sounds?"

"Why would it sound bad? She's not guilty of anything."

Contempt replaced any remaining concern in Patricia's expression. "Are you really so naïve you believe that? Or is it something more? Are you involved with her?"

Erin hesitated over the question. Was she involved? Technically, no. Not yet. And maybe never. But that was her business and no one else's. "What does it matter if I am?"

Her response seemed to trigger something in Patricia. The ice melted from her stare, and fiery anger blazed. "Do I have to spell it out for you? She's still a murder suspect. The fact that she saved your life only means she didn't want *you* killed! It doesn't prove a damned thing about her role in the other killings."

"You're saying she's still under investigation?" Erin thought of the sergeant and his determination to nail Liz any way he could. Was it only Ruiz who wanted her to go down? She stared at Patricia, and her heart thudded madly in her chest. What was her real agenda? Could she trust her at all?

"I'm saying you are implicating yourself." Patricia's chest rose and fell with her heavy breathing. "There are people who think you're involved with her and you've been covering for her."

"That's not true." Erin's mind raced. How could anyone who knew her believe that? "What do you think, Patricia? Do believe what they're saying?"

"Of course not. And I've been trying to tell them. But frankly, Mac, I can't keep it up. Especially when you're off secretly meeting her. Maybe if you stopped seeing her, I could better plead your case."

"No." Erin was not going to allow herself to be manipulated this way. She threw off the bedcovers and swung her feet to the floor. "I will see who I want, when I want. To hell with all of you." She grabbed her jeans and felt around for her keys, then remembered she didn't have her car. "Fuck." She fumed as she headed for the bathroom.

"Mac, wait," Patricia urged. "This is important. It could destroy your career. Please stay and talk to me. I can help you work this out."

Erin paused in the doorway. "No, Patricia, you can't. Because whether you believe it or not, there's nothing to work out. I haven't done anything wrong."

She struggled over the words because she absolutely knew that withholding the information about Jay was wrong. But for reasons she didn't quite understand, she couldn't bring herself to tell Patricia, or anyone else for that matter. With a sharp sense of betrayal, she turned and walked out the door.

Chapter Twenty-One

Erin sat staring at her phone. She opened her palm and eyed the phone number written on it in black ink. It was faded but still legible. She wouldn't have let it wash completely off before writing it down.

Sighing and sitting back against the couch, she looked around her new home. It was a modest, well-kept townhouse, small enough to be cozy, but large enough for her to breathe. It hadn't taken her long to find one she liked, and when she'd offered a large amount of cash to move in immediately, she quickly found herself with a set of keys and her own covered parking space.

She gazed down and ran her hand over the soft fabric of the sofa. The living-room furniture had just arrived the day before and she could still smell its newness. Lucky for her, she had found a store that delivered quickly, ending her nights on the uncomfortable air mattress. Last night she had slept on her new sofa, and her new, large bed would be delivered the next day.

She turned her hand over and eyed the phone number again. Patricia's words rang in her ears, but to be on the safe side, she knew she shouldn't see Liz. She didn't understand why the department had suspicions about her, but she didn't want to add any fuel to their fire either. She eyed her phone again, brand new and sitting on the table next to the couch. Maybe Liz would have some answers. If not, she should at least warn her that the police were still looking at her as a suspect. So much so, that they were now willing to tie in one of their own as an accomplice.

She cringed at the thought. Was it because they now knew about Jay and knew she had failed to tell them about her? Whatever the reason, she had to talk to Liz. She picked up the phone and stared at the numbers on the buttons. Who was she kidding? She could try to convince herself that the reason she was calling Liz was to talk about the investigation. To warn her, even. But the real reason had nothing to do with the police or anything associated with them. She was calling because she couldn't get the dark beauty out of her mind for even a second.

She pushed the talk button and dialed the number. As she waited for it to ring, she briefly wondered if she was being watched. She had checked for a tail yesterday and today and hadn't seen anyone, but that didn't mean they weren't there. Her telephone had been connected just that morning and she figured they couldn't possibly have a trace on it yet. Confident in that, she waited for the voice she needed to hear.

"Hello."

"Hello, Liz." Erin felt strangely unsure and shy all of a sudden.

"Erin?"

"Yes. Yes, it's me."

"I'm so glad." Liz sounded genuinely happy to hear from her, and still so damn sexy with her deep throaty voice.

Feeling like a smitten schoolgirl, Erin said, "Me too."

"How are you?"

"Fine," Erin said quickly, trying to convince herself as well as Liz.

"I don't believe you. You said that too quickly."

"No, I am. Really." She smoothed out her shirt nervously with her free hand, as if Liz could somehow see her. She looked down and eyed the shirt, silently wondering if Liz would approve. Along with the townhouse and the furniture, she'd purchased new clothing.

"I guess I'll just have to wait and see you to judge for myself," Liz cooed, instantly making her blush. "How about dinner tonight?"

"Yes." Erin stumbled over the word, the conversation moving so fast. She hadn't even had time to ask Liz how she was doing in return.

"Wonderful. How about my place? You remember how to get there?"

"Yes. Uh, Liz?" She had to speak quickly, before she was sidetracked with more alluring dinner-date conversation. "I think the police are still watching you."

Silence.

"Is that all?" Liz asked.

"Well, no, but I really don't want to discuss it over the phone."

"I understand. But just so you know, this is my satellite phone. I use it for all my private calls."

"That is somewhat of a relief." Erin relaxed a little.

"If they are still watching me, is that going to present a problem for you tonight? Coming to my place?"

Erin thought for a moment. She had thought of nothing else the entire previous night, tossing and turning on her new couch. How would it affect her if the department knew she was still seeing Elizabeth Adams?

"I don't care if they know."

"In that case, it doesn't bother me either. I've grown used to their watching my every move. One more night of their pathetic surveillance won't make a difference."

"Liz?" Erin blurted out. "Why do you trust me? I mean, how do you know that I'm not still working undercover for them?"

"I guess I don't know that for sure. I hope you're not, but not for the reasons you may think. Not because of Jay or anything like that."

"What, then?"

"Because if you are working for them, then I would know that this…your feelings toward me were just a charade. And that would devastate me."

Erin fell silent, her mind sending no words to her mouth.

"And besides, I've already discussed Jay with you, and if you were really still working for them, I suspect she would already be in custody and I would be charged with obstruction and conspiracy and anything else they could pin on me."

"True," Erin said.

"So, you still up for dinner? Sounds like you could use a nice meal with warm company."

How warm are you? I'd love to find out. She blushed at her own thoughts. "Absolutely."

"Great. How's seven sound?"

"I'll be there."

Erin walked up to the enormous front door carrying an expensive bottle of wine and a ferociously hungry attraction for the woman she was about to dine with.

On the drive over she had tried to calm her nerves and her butterflies, but to no avail. She was nervous, yes, but not just because of Liz, who would no doubt be drop-dead gorgeous and as warm and charming as ever. What made her more nervous was the fear that her own overwhelming attraction and feelings toward her would cause her to do or say something stupid and completely embarrass herself. In short, she didn't trust herself.

She waited on the doorstep, already hearing the deep barking of the Dobermans. Liz knew she was there, having opened the gates that gave access to the driveway. Erin hastily looked down at herself, yet again examining her choice of outfit for the evening. She rubbed a sweaty palm on her jeans and smoothed out her tight-fitting black V-neck shirt. She had worn her new black boots to match.

She heard Liz call out to the dogs, beckoning their silence. Then she was in the doorway, smiling as she unabashedly looked Erin up and down. "Wow. You should definitely wear black more often." She motioned for her to enter.

Erin felt her face redden at the obvious appraisal.

"And she blushes." Liz chuckled. "You're something else, Erin McKenzie."

"Stop," Erin begged. "I'm just…"

"Embarrassed?" Liz closed the door behind them, her eyes roaming Erin's body the way her hands would.

Cheeks burning, Erin said, "Well, yes."

"You're not used to compliments." It was stated matter-of-factly.

"No, I guess I'm not."

"Well, that's something we'll have to remedy now, won't we?" Liz stepped in closer and placed her hands gently on Erin's hips. Then she leaned in and placed a very soft, warm kiss on her lips.

"I'm glad you're here," she said.

Erin was almost afraid to move for fear that her legs would buckle. Rattled, she finally choked out, "Thanks for the invitation. This is for you." She held out the bottle of wine and tried not to stare at the smooth skin of Liz's chest.

The shirt Liz had on was smoky gray and unbuttoned down below her breasts, offering a teasing and tantalizing view every time she moved. Feeling her face flush yet again, Erin focused instead on Liz's worn jeans and bare feet.

"Thank you." Liz inspected the wine. "It will be perfect for later tonight." She moved past Erin and headed for the kitchen. "Make yourself at home," she said over her shoulder.

Erin followed her down the tiled walkway into the kitchen, as did the two obedient black dogs. Their claws clicked against the tile, and their stubby tails wagged with excitement at their guest.

"I didn't know you could cook," Erin said as Liz sliced some red pepper and zucchini.

"I don't do it very often, but I do know how." She scooped the veggies up and dropped them in a wok. They made a sizzling noise as they hit the aromatic sesame oil.

"Smells great."

"I've got a white wine chilled, would you like some?" Liz moved over to the stainless-steel fridge and pulled it open, exposing more alluring flesh beneath her open shirt.

"Yes," Erin breathed out huskily, actually referring to the soft, creamy flesh of her breasts.

Liz busied herself pouring the wine, seemingly oblivious to Erin's reaction.

"Here you go." She handed over a glass. "Start in on that while I finish up dinner."

Erin took the wine gratefully and adjourned to a small sitting room where she could watch as Liz moved around the kitchen like a seasoned chef, adding oils, sauces, and spices to the stir-fry.

Sipping the chilled wine, she tried to relax under the curious stare of the two Dobermans. She remembered her previous visit to this large home and how anxious she had been. The nervousness she felt now was different, more hormonally based than before. Her previous visit had had her shaking in her boots, fighting her growing attraction to the then murder suspect while trying to do her job. She no longer suspected Liz of anything, no matter what Patricia wanted to imply.

"I thought we would eat in here instead of the dining room." Liz set their meal down on a low coffee table and took two large cushions from the sofa, placing them on either side of the table. "You mind dining from the floor?"

"No." Erin rose from the couch. "Is there anything I can help with?"

Liz had already moved quickly back into the kitchen. With a sly grin, she said, "No. Just sit there and look beautiful."

Erin made herself comfortable on one of the cushions, her heart beating wildly in her chest. As she glanced down at the food, she realized that in spite her budding excitement and desires, she had no appetite for food.

"Hope you're hungry," Liz said.

She set the serving bowls down along with her wine and spooned Erin a hearty portion of the steaming stir-fry and then served herself. She settled down on the cushion lotus style and handed Erin a pair of chopsticks.

Erin fingered the sticks uncertainly, a smile on her face. She watched Liz expertly lift noodles and vegetables with the chopsticks and slip the utensils into and out of her mouth. The sight was completely erotic.

"Your turn," Liz said, apparently noticing she had yet to take a bite.

Erin met her eyes and then fessed up, feeling completely foolish. "I, uh, I'm not sure how."

Liz immediately scooted over to kneel next to her. "I'm sorry. I shouldn't have assumed." She gently took Erin's hand in her own and positioned the chopsticks. "There, you see, you use this finger as a base and this one to move your main stick."

The hot blood pounding in Erin's ears made it difficult for her to comprehend anything she was told. Lust washed through her body as Liz's skin brushed hers. Unable to concentrate, she asked, "Can't we save us both some grief by letting me use a fork?"

Liz laughed and Erin felt her breath shorten as the deep and seductive sound played in her ears. Everything about the woman was turning her on. She imagined the same deep, throaty sounds pouring out of her in the throes of passion.

"Sure, I'll get you a fork," Liz said, completely clueless to Erin's lustful imaginings. "But first I want to see you give it a try."

Erin was sure her desire was displayed all over her face. Her skin burned under Liz's intense gaze, and with her hand trembling, she held the chopsticks and grasped a drooping bite of slick noodles. She moved her hand quickly to her mouth, feeling the noodles start to slide. Leaning forward, she attempted to shove the food into her mouth before it fell, but she didn't quite make it, dropping noodles on the table as well as on her chin. As she chewed, she sucked in the wayward noodles.

Liz chuckled next to her. "It takes practice. Here." She lifted a stranded noodle, inviting her to take it.

Erin opened her mouth and Liz placed the tip of the noodle on her tongue. Slowly, she sucked the noodle in, wishing instead that she could suck on the fingers feeding her.

"Can I ask you something, Erin?" Liz lowered her hand, a thoughtful look on her face.

"Sure." *Please ask me to eat you now.*

"Earlier today when you asked me why I trusted you—well, I guess I'm wondering the same thing. Why do you trust me?"

Erin finished chewing, a little surprised by the question. She had no problem answering it truthfully. "Because you saved my life."

Liz stared at her and then smiled, the answer obviously satisfying her. "Thank you for telling me."

"You're welcome." Erin smiled in return. "By the way, this is really good," she said, pointing to the food.

"Glad you like it." Liz remained next to her, pulling her own cushion and bowl closer. "I seem to be fresh out of forks, so it looks like I'm going to have to feed you." She grinned a devilish grin before picking up another bite for herself.

Erin laughed. "Next you'll be telling me you're fresh out of swimsuits again."

"Now that you mention it…" Liz laughed again and pinched out another bite, offering it to Erin.

She took the mouthful seductively, lightly sucking on the sticks as they were eased from her mouth.

Liz stared, obviously affected. "Before I forget," she said, "or better yet, before I get carried away and forget, what happened with Patricia that got you so upset? That is, if you don't mind my asking."

"No, it's okay." Erin answered softly. "They think I'm covering for you."

"Covering for me how?"

"They think I've been conspiring with you all along," Erin said. "Leading them away from you as a suspect."

"They think that about one of their own?" Liz asked, her dislike for the Valle Luna Police Department and its male heads clear.

"Apparently so. I guess they want you so bad they're willing to throw anyone in the pot with you."

"My God. I'm sorry, Erin. I never should've asked you to keep quiet about Jay. They don't know, do they?"

"Patricia didn't say. But if they don't know, they will eventually. Maybe not tomorrow or even next week. But I can't see them letting this go any time soon. Someone will always be at it, and as long as they are, they will eventually discover your sister."

"What happens to you when they do?"

"Lucky for me, I can simply claim that I didn't remember."

"No," Liz said adamantly. "You shouldn't lie. Not for me or anyone else. It was wrong of me to even ask. I love my sister, but I won't see you go down for this. I'll tell them everything."

"Don't," Erin said, placing a hand on hers. "They'll spin it any way they can to see that you're punished to the full extent of the law. They hate you, Liz. They want to see you burn for these murders, one way or another. I couldn't bear to see that happen. You didn't kill those men, Jay did."

Liz looked down at the hand resting on her own. "I should've stopped her as soon as I suspected it was her. I was just so afraid that I would lead the police right to her, and I wasn't convinced she'd done it. It's not like her to hurt people. She's too damn afraid of people to hurt them. She's so disturbed from what happened to her when we were kids."

"What did happen to her?" Erin asked after a long pause.

Liz took several moments to form the words. Finally, looking steadily into Erin's eyes, she said shakily, "She was kidnapped and then raped and tortured by a murderer when she was eleven."

"Oh, my God," Erin let out, truly horrified.

"Jay saved me that day. She told me to run. She let him take her instead of me."

Stunned into silence, Erin watched Liz virtually crumple in front of her. The bond between the two sisters was still very much in evidence, and the guilt Liz felt was obvious from the strain in her voice.

"You feel that you owe her," Erin said calmly, truly feeling for her.

"Yes. She protected me, and now I have to protect her. Even if…even if she killed. I have to get her help. No one will ever understand her like I do." She lapsed into thought, then said, "I was willing to protect her at any cost to me or anyone else. But I won't see you get hurt in this."

"But she's your sister. You hardly know me."

Liz shook her head. "I do know you. I don't know how it's possible, but I do. And I would do anything to protect you as well."

Erin was shaken by the words. She wanted to protect Liz too. And she would, as long as she could. "Liz, I can promise you this. I won't say anything about Jay as long as she continues to live in peace. But if I suspect that she's involved in more violence…I will have to tell."

"I understand. I feel the same way. As soon as I get another update from my private detective, I'll fill you in."

With a deep sigh, Liz lifted Erin's hand and placed a soft, warm kiss across her knuckles. "Now, let's think about more pleasant things. You up for a swim?"

"That depends." Images of their last pool encounter flooded her mind as well as her loins. Letting her raging libido give her confidence, she said, "Are you fresh out of swimsuits?"

"I am," Liz responded in a deep voice laced with innuendo.

Erin tried not to shudder at the sight of Liz's shirt moving against her breasts. "That's too bad," she countered.

"Is it?" Liz rose to her feet and unfastened the remaining buttons of her shirt.

Erin watched, completely mesmerized, as the last button was released, exposing a muscled abdomen and the promising curves of rounded breasts.

Liz seemed to relish her delight in the striptease. "Your turn," she said.

Erin looked down at herself. "No fair. I don't have any buttons."

"Well, that's not good enough."

Erin grinned. Bending over, she pulled off her boots and tossed them aside. Then she pulled off her socks and stood beaming at her dinner companion. "Your turn."

Liz trailed her fingers down her exposed skin as she watched Erin study her. When she reached the waistline of her jeans, she unbuttoned them and inched them slowly down over her hips. The shirt she wore was rather long, covering her most intimate area, but not before Erin saw the lack of underwear.

As her face and body burned with pure desire, she continued to watch with voyeuristic delight. Liz pulled the jeans down past her ankles, tossed them across the room, and stood before her, nude, save for the shirt seductively covering her erogenous zones.

Erin gulped at the sight but tried not to show how shaken-up she really was. Instead, she gave a half grin and lowered her hands to inch up her shirt. She pulled it up with agonizing slowness, watching Liz's face as she went. She could see the bold desire in Liz's eyes, and she found that the exhibition was turning her on tenfold. Her skin felt unbelievably sensitive as the shirt, along with her fingers, maneuvered up and over her body. She let the shirt fall down next to her and stood before Liz, breathing heavily in her black lace bra.

Liz sucked in a quick, hot breath of air as she again was treated to the sight that had haunted her for weeks. She stepped closer, reaching out to grab hold of Erin's jeans. "You're behind. I think I need to help you catch up."

She yanked Erin closer and unbuttoned her jeans. As she lowered the zipper, she watched Erin's eyes flood with a darker shade of desire. With her own blood throbbing angrily between her legs, she pushed the denim down and off and took in black panties, a sculpted torso, and full breasts. Erin was the most beautiful thing she had ever seen. No other woman could ever compare.

With slow deliberation, Liz drew open her own shirt. Their eyes locked and Erin reached up and ran her thumbs across the taut nipples, her fingertips rimming Liz's aching breasts. Sensation shot through Liz like hot fingers, moving from her breasts and igniting her very core. Liz choked back a near cry of desperation as her shirt fell to the floor and she was exposed, more so than she had ever felt with anyone.

Erin eyed the beautifully carved body before her. She was unbelievably gorgeous. Near perfect in almost every way. From her sculpted face and high cheekbones, to her broad strong shoulders and arms, to her creamy rounded breasts with the dark rose centers and her exquisitely etched abdomen, right down to her long, strong legs. Of course, Erin thought as she ran a light hand down to the thin patch of dark hair between those legs, she had saved the most delectable morsel for last.

Liz shuddered once again and grabbed Erin's hand, halting its pursuit to the nucleus of nerve endings. "Your turn," she gasped out.

Erin stared at her lips, wanting so desperately to kiss them. She was unable to move, completely mesmerized.

Liz stepped ever closer and ran her hands up and down Erin's sides, awakening her skin instantly. Shuddering, Erin braced herself on Liz's shoulders.

Liz felt her nostrils flare as she leaned in and inhaled the skin of Erin's neck. She at once recognized the scent of her and clenched her legs together against the mounting pressure between them. Then, as she allowed the scent to swirl in her brain, she reached around and unhooked her bra, bringing it forward across her shoulders and then letting it fall as it freed her ample breasts.

"My God," she breathed out before she even realized it. She looked into Erin's burning green eyes as she touched the puckering dark honey nipples. "You are so beautiful."

"Ah…" Erin clung to her wrists and moaned, her head tossed back. "If you don't stop…" She caught her breath. "I'm going to come." Every stroke against her nipple felt like a hot stroke between her legs. She couldn't understand it, but it was happening. Almost like magic.

Liz growled in response, and with obvious reluctance she lifted her hands from Erin's breasts. Erin tried to regain control of her breathing, but it was difficult. She could still feel the hot fingers playing on her nipples. As she breathed deeply, she focused on the fierce blue eyes and loosened her grip on Liz's wrists, letting her hands once again fall to her sides.

Liz moved closer, this time resting her hands on the black lace panties. As she lowered herself to remove them, Erin stiffened. Hot breath struck her nipples and she nearly came on the spot.

"Oh God. I think you better leave the panties to me."

"You that excited?" Liz looked up at her, an eyebrow raised.

"You have no idea," Erin said huskily.

"I think I might."

"If we're going to make it to the pool, we better go now." Erin was not sure if she could even walk.

Liz grinned and took her hand. "Let's go, then."

As they stepped outside, Erin realized she was nearly nude and instantly covered herself.

Liz walked unabashedly to the pool ahead of her. "There's no one around to see," she offered as she dipped a foot in to test the water. "I don't have any immediate neighbors. And if you're worried about air voyeurs, the sun's just about completely gone."

Erin glanced to the west and saw the last finger of sunlight bidding the earth good night. She relaxed a little and dropped her arms, enjoying the feel of the warm night air on her aroused breasts.

She watched as Liz descended into the pool, one step at a time, before diving in at the last step.

She surfaced in the luminous water, looking like she had just stepped out of a magazine. Erin watched as she ran her hands back over her wet black hair and looked up at her, eyes blazing nearly the same shade of blue as the pool.

"You coming?"

Erin laughed, thinking just how close she had been to doing just that moments before. *Christ, yes.* She slowly ran her hands down over her body until she reached her panties. Then, while holding Liz's gaze, she carefully inched the panties down over her hips and thighs to her ankles. She stepped out of them and kicked them into the pool and dove in.

The water felt cool and refreshing. As she surfaced, she wiped her eyes and searched for Liz. She was gone. With the sunlight quickly descending into night, it was difficult to locate her right away. The lights in the pool changed color, and she could see no sign of her under the water. Just as she was about to turn to look behind her, she felt a warm body press against her back.

"I'm right here," Liz breathed in her ear.

Erin gulped as hot hands ran up and down the sides of her body. She tried to turn, but Liz inched her hands up to her breasts, where she firmly grasped her nipples. Erin cried out as wonderfully erotic sensations flooded through her. Liz nibbled on her ear and then moved to her exposed neck, which she bit and sucked while pinching and rolling Erin's nipples with her fingers.

"Oh, God. I'm going to come." Erin squeezed her eyes shut, trying desperately to ignore the overwhelming flames burning in her nipples, burning between her legs.

"No," Liz whispered, pulling away from Erin's neck. "Not yet." She let go of her nipples and turned her around. "I want so badly to take it slow with you, but I don't think I can," she confessed breathlessly.

"I don't want you to take it slow. I want you so bad it hurts." Erin cupped Liz's face with her hands. "Kiss me," she demanded, pulling her into her.

Liz closed her eyes and kissed Erin. At first the kiss was soft, tender, and warm. She felt Erin's tongue lick her lips, tasting her. And then she heard her moan and pulled her tighter as the kiss became deeper, hungrier. Erin's tongue claimed her mouth with a vengeance, fueling her desire, shattering her control. She kissed her back with all her might, devouring her, conquering her. She held the back of Erin's head and walked her backward in the pool until they reached the steps. Once there, Liz slowly withdrew from the powerful kiss, breathless and dizzy.

"Don't stop," Erin pleaded, trying to pull her back down to her mouth. "I can't go any farther," she said as she looked behind her, feeling the steps against her legs.

"Yes, you can." Liz grasped Erin's hips and buttocks and lifted her. Head thrown back, Erin clung to her shoulders and wrapped her legs around Liz's waist as she carried her up the stairs.

"Oh my." Liz set her down on the top step. "I can feel you. You're unbelievably wet." She ran a finger down Erin's chest to her belly before inching lower, where a thin veil of manicured hairs swayed gently with the ebb and flow of the water. "And this"—she maneuvered her fingers carefully into the folds—"is something I've got to have right now."

Erin's eyes widened at first in response to the words and then in response to the touch. She shuddered and melted as she grabbed Liz's shoulders, leaning forward to rock against her fingers.

Liz groaned as she felt the abundance of hot silk in her hand. Letting Erin move forward, she eased her fingers up deep inside and carried her away from the stairs, back into the pool, supporting her with her free hand.

Erin moved in waves, ground down against the incredible feel of the long hot fingers inside her. She clung to Liz's shoulders, digging her fingers into her skin, unable to keep her eyes open for any length of time. She pursed her lips and arched her back, the sensations unbelievable and still coming in new and overwhelming swells.

"Feels so good," she said, opening her eyes to look at the woman who was unlocking the doors to such pleasures.

"Does it?" Liz wanted more of her. She eased her free hand up her back and held her shoulder down from behind. Then, with strength and grace, she pulled her back a little, curling her fingers up deep inside her.

Erin bit down on her lower lip and groaned. "Fuck me." She was deadly serious. "Harder." She tried to bear down on the fingers, needing more, craving more, almost willing to kill for more.

Liz moved her back against the wall of the pool, ready and willing to do anything for her, anything to please her. She eased Erin off her and positioned herself before her, reaching down in the breast-high water to open up her legs.

"Hold on to me," she said huskily as she plunged back into her.

"Oh God!" Erin cried out, clinging to her.

Liz drove into her hard and fast, feeling her tighten and grip from the inside. She bent down and bit her neck, needing to consume her in every way possible. Erin's voice became deeper and strained, and with every sound she choked out Liz could feel the orgasm looming. Erin clung to her now, arms wrapped around her back, her short nails digging in.

"God, don't stop," she rasped out. "Give it to me."

Liz added another finger and bent her knees for more leverage. She pumped Erin harder and fuller than before, drawing out slowly before pushing back in. Erin went from speaking her demands to biting down. Liz could feel her skin give beneath the clamp of Erin's teeth, which excited her even more. She knew it was time; she had to release Erin before she herself burst with orgasm. Reaching up with one hand to grab hold of the edge of the pool, she braced herself to fuck with all her might. With Erin still clinging to her for support, she placed her thumb over Erin's engorged clit while her fingers fucked her.

Instantly Erin responded to the pressure and pulled her mouth from Liz's shoulder to throw her head back and groan like a wild animal. Liz reached up deep within her, curling her fingers while stroking the excited flesh of her clit. Looking into Erin's eyes, she slammed into her. She rocked her hard and deep and fast.

Chanting unintelligible words, Erin knotted her hands in Liz's wet hair. Her insides were on fire and her toes were curling as her feet dangled freely in the water, her entire body centered on the thrusting fingers. She closed her eyes as their heat seared into her, while the strumming of her clit made her bite her lip so hard it nearly bled.

Insurmountable pleasures rocked her body, consuming her, possessing her very soul. As heat invaded the last cell, lighting up her body from within, she opened her eyes wide and focused on the beautiful face of her lover. She felt the heat and light explode inside her and opened her mouth to cry out, but her voice was too weak and strained to shout. Instead, she jerked and rocked with the orgasm in silence as the heat escaped her body in a million invisible pieces.

Liz felt her come but heard nothing until finally Erin managed to choke out a strained cry just before she stopped spasming. She collapsed against Liz's shoulder, her whole body limp and resting on her three fingers, still deep inside her.

"Wow," Liz said in Erin's ear. "It was definitely good for me too."

Erin groaned and raised her heavy head. "Yeah?" she asked with a lazy grin.

"Oh God, yes." Liz could still feel her insides throbbing.

"Did you…" Erin asked hoarsely, "did you come?"

"No." Liz carefully withdrew her hand from between Erin's legs.

"Good," Erin said, somehow finding the strength to stand.

"Why is that good?" Liz asked.

"Because I'm hungry." Erin cupped the cluster of excited flesh between Liz's thighs, causing Liz to nearly jump out of her skin with excitement.

"Oh yeah?" Liz asked playfully, holding fast to Erin's wrist, so very close to orgasm.

"Yeah," Erin said confidently. "And you're just what I've been craving."

Liz shuddered, so close to going over, so close to losing control. "We'll see about that."

Chapter Twenty-Two

Erin studied the beautiful woman stretched out on her belly, propped up on her elbows. Liz seemed almost like something from a dream. The warm candlelight flickered upon her rhythmically, like the soft, steady breath of a sleeping child.

As she let her eyes play upon the nude skin of her lover, Erin found herself overwhelmed with emotion. Leaning forward from the headboard of the bed, she cradled Liz's face in her hands and placed a lingering kiss on her warm lips.

"Mmm. That was nice." Liz grinned as Erin sank once again back against the headboard.

It was nearly three a.m., and as relaxed as she was from their hours of lovemaking, Erin wasn't yet tired. Unable to move her gaze away from Liz's body, she reached over to the nightstand for the bottle of red wine she had brought earlier that evening as a gift and refilled the single glass they now shared. As she sipped, she once again eyed her lover lying amidst the rumpled sheets on the king-sized bed.

"I wonder," she said aloud, "how many women have been in this bed." *How many women have sat where I do now, taking in your incredible beauty after making love?*

Liz stared at her a moment and pushed herself up into a sitting position before she responded. "To be honest with you, I usually don't bring women here."

"You don't?" Erin was surprised.

"No, I don't. My past lovers were just that. Past." Her eyes sought Erin's. "They didn't mean anything to me."

"Yet you slept with them." Erin was curious about her sex life. It was hard to believe that someone who had loved her so passionately for hours on end could separate herself emotionally from the lovers she took.

"It was just sex."

"Just sex?" Erin relived how Liz had ravished her that evening, sometimes gently and tenderly, sometimes aggressively, but always with great emotion and passion. Maybe there was more to loving women than she understood. She knew for certain that she couldn't make love like that to a complete stranger just for kicks. But maybe that was just her. Maybe other women could do it. Obviously Liz had done so.

"It was different with you, Erin," Liz said, as if she was searching for words to explain something foreign to her. "I have feelings for you. What we just did…It wasn't just sex, it was so much more."

Even as she made this confession, Liz realized she had never felt like this about anyone. But Erin made her feel comfortable and accepted, and she knew she could speak her true feelings without fear of judgment or rejection. She could finally open up to another human being. She trusted Erin enough to be vulnerable in a way she had found impossible for most of her life.

"Liz?" Erin lightly stroked her leg. "Why did you forgive me?"

"Forgive you for what?"

"For misleading you, for going undercover and letting you think I was interested in you."

"You were just doing your job. You didn't know me. For all you knew, I could've been the killer."

Erin sat in silence, feeling her heart swell in her chest. She felt almost undeserving of the kind and gentle love Liz was offering, but at the same time she was thrilled. She felt the same way toward her.

"Besides," Liz continued, "you didn't tell them about Jay. And as risky as that was on your part, there must've been some reason why you did that for me."

"I suppose there was," Erin admitted. "I think I've been drawn to you all along."

"The feeling is mutual." Liz leaned in to kiss her.

"Tell me something else, Ms. Adams," Erin demanded lightly as their lips parted.

"Anything."

"When you made love to all those other women…"

"Oh God." Liz dropped her head in her hand.

"Did you allow them to make love to you?"

Liz peeked at her through the fingers held over her eyes.

"Because," Erin said, pulling the hand away from her face, "I'm still waiting my turn." She lightly caressed her, starting at her shoulders, moving down her arms to her hands.

"I've never really let anyone do it." The words were said so softly she barely heard them.

"Never?" Erin gently probed.

"I always got off more or less by giving."

Erin was completely dumbfounded. "Will you…let me?" She longed, more than anything, to physically lavish Liz with the same pleasures that had overwhelmed her not long before. With each powerful orgasm, she had tried to do something in return, but Liz had been too strong for her physically and had easily wrestled out from underneath to dominate her once more.

Liz stared into the warm green depths of Erin's eyes. She could feel fingers awakening her sensitive and starving skin. "I'm not sure if I can," she confessed, truly wanting to, but not certain how she would react.

She had always been highly sexual, and it had never taken very much for her to climax. The real question was whether she was finally willing to give the control she so desired to another human being. Was she ready to let someone love her? Physically as well as emotionally?

"Then we are quite the pair," Erin said, offering her a smile. "Because I have no clue what I'm doing, so I'm not sure if I can either." She laughed a little, hoping it would help ease her lover's guarded state.

But Liz didn't laugh, she just sat looking at Erin. "It won't take much," she whispered, holding her hand. "What I feel for you is so powerful, it nearly does it on its own."

Erin moved in to kiss her before the tears had a chance to well up in her eyes. Not in a million years had she thought she could experience the emotion she felt for this woman. All her life she had heard about love, first in fairy tales and then in the girly giggles of her schoolmates. When she'd met and married Mark, she had convinced herself it was love because it was like her parents, a partnership based on a friendship. It was what everyone did. They settled down and went about their daily lives. But it wasn't love. She knew that now. She knew it because that was what she was finally feeling. Love.

"Lie down," she said softly and gazed down in wonder as Liz lay naked on her back in the candlelight. Lightly, she ran her fingers up and down her firm, smooth body, watching as the nipples tightened in a cluster of deep rose.

"What would you like me to do?" she asked, wanting to give her the utmost pleasure, but a little unsure as to what she might want most. With all the wild stories she had heard about Elizabeth Adams, she hardly recognized the confident nightclub owner lying so vulnerable beneath her fingers. And then she remembered that the wild stories were all one-sided, that Liz herself had rarely been touched, and suddenly she knew that Liz probably had no preferences. She just wanted to be loved.

"Anything you want," Liz replied huskily from the soft pillow.

"I think…" Erin said, letting her hand trail down to the dark strip of hair, "that I would like to taste you."

Liz shuddered beneath her and clenched her legs together in response to Erin's touch. Erin moved her body down alongside Liz's as she carefully and gently urged her legs apart. She could hear Liz's shaky breaths as she positioned herself between her legs and ever so softly kissed her inner thighs. Liz's skin was warm and unbelievably soft, and she found herself lost in a whole new world as she continued to kiss and taste her way along the strong legs. In the far-off distance she could hear Liz moaning and sucking in quick breaths of air, but she was so immersed that she hardly paid any mind to the sounds of pleasure.

"Erin?" Liz rasped out, lifting her head off the pillow.

"Hum?" Erin looked up, just as content as she could be, and not yet even to the most wonderful part of her new world.

"It feels so good," Liz breathed out. "You better hurry, I don't think I can last much longer."

"But I haven't even touched you there yet," Erin protested, not anywhere ready for Liz to climax yet.

"Doesn't matter." Liz collapsed back onto the pillow.

Erin watched her in silence, unsure what to do. She looked down at the mound of clustered satin just below her mouth. As she exhaled, she could see Liz respond. She realized Liz was so sensitive and so ready that a breath alone would send her over. She had to act soon if she wanted to have any fun at all. With her eyes riveted on Liz's face, she carefully extended her tongue to touch the tip of her clitoris. Then, with slow deliberation, she lightly massaged the soft skin. She didn't know what she had expected a woman would feel like under her tongue, but nothing could have prepared her for what she was experiencing.

The mound of flesh was soft yet firm, giving and twitching as she pressed the length of her tongue down upon it. She marveled at its warmth, reveled in its quick movements, devoured its satiny texture. But what she found the most exciting and fascinating was not the heated silky skin under her tongue, but Liz's reactions. With every wonderful manipulation, Liz let out strangled cries of erotic bliss.

Erin watched her intently, enjoying the splendid display of her powerful muscles rippling under the dampened skin of her torso as she coiled and stretched, jerked and twitched with every lick. She had never experienced such an erotic encounter, had never witnessed such an incredible display of raw pleasure with her at the helm, captaining the velvety voyage. The scenario was nothing short of miraculous, and she never wanted it to end. She could bestow pleasures upon this woman for eternity and never tire.

As Liz writhed beneath her, she settled down more comfortably atop her, adding more weighted pressure to her strokes. She knew that whether she wanted her to or not, Liz was dangerously close to climaxing. Savoring the feel and sweet taste of her, Erin swirled her tongue all around the swollen tissue, placing pressure on the edges while lapping at the center, trying to drive Liz mad with intense pleasure.

As her own skin burned brightly with lust and pleasure, Erin braced herself as Liz came beneath her, nearly bucking her right up off the bed. She could never have been prepared for the intensity, the sheer physicality of pleasing another woman. The reaction was so raw, so incredibly animalistic, and yet so intensely personal and intimate on every level. She did her best to hold on, to remain in her position, but Liz was convulsing and bucking so much that when she finally did stop, Erin's mouth was swollen and stinging, her lips swollen. It was as if she had tried to hold fast to her lover with her mouth.

She licked at her tingling lips and lay between Liz's long, powerful legs, watching and listening to her breathe.

When she finally stilled, Liz asked, "Did I hurt you?"

"Hurt me? Are you kidding? I've never experienced anything so incredible before."

"Come here," Liz said softly.

Erin pushed herself up from the warm confines of her legs and crawled slowly to her side, nestling in the soft covers.

"Do you have any idea how good you make me feel?" Liz asked, gazing languidly into her eyes.

"If it's anywhere near as good as you make me feel, then I do have some idea." Erin snuggled up close to her, feeling relaxed and wonderfully content. She closed her eyes and felt her breathing slow and match that of her lover, their bodies' own sweet lullaby.

She didn't know how long she slept or even if she truly had slept when the deep sounds of the Dobermans barking pricked her ears. With the noise not quite registering, she lay motionless in Liz's arms, certain the dogs would soon calm down. It wasn't until Liz stirred beneath her that she opened her eyes and sat up. The barks resounded like thunder throughout the house and were accompanied by a pounding at the front door.

Erin looked around wildly, her eyes trying to adjust to her dim surroundings. "What's going on?"

"I don't know." Liz jumped out of bed and into her jeans. "Whatever it is, it can't be good." She moved quickly over to the bed, where she cupped Erin's chin in her hand for a gentle kiss.

"Wait, I'm coming with you," Erin insisted. She bounded off the bed and hurried into her jeans and black shirt.

As they walked out of the master bedroom and stepped into the hall, the pounding continued on the large front door.

"What the hell?" Liz muttered.

Red and blue lights flashed through the windows, announcing a police presence. Erin felt the color drain from her face. Liz was right—whatever it was, it wasn't going to be good. She reached out and gripped her lover's hand, making a silent vow that whatever it was, they could handle it together. She jumped as the pounding resumed.

"Police! Open up!"

Liz unlocked the door, looking into Erin's eyes one last time before she pulled it open.

"Elizabeth Adams?" a gruff overweight detective asked, just as he had done countless times before.

"What's this about, Stewart?" Erin stepped in front of her lover, making her way just outside the door.

Stewart stared openmouthed, the shock of seeing her at the house apparent on his meaty face. Erin looked past the dumbfounded man to several other detectives, who were shining flashlights in and around Liz's Range Rover.

"What the fuck are you doing here?" Stewart whispered in his wheezy voice. He had turned his back to Liz and stood so close Erin could smell the thick stench of cigarette smoke clinging to him in an imaginary yellow layer of nicotine.

"Never mind my personal business," she said. "What are you all doing here?"

A chill swept over her skin. Was this Patricia's doing? Revenge for Erin's hasty departure from her home? They hadn't spoken since. She watched helplessly as numerous police personnel scurried about the Range Rover, wearing plain clothes and navy blue bulletproof vests with *Police* written in yellow across their backs.

"Detective." Liz looked intently at Stewart. "I hope you have a damn good reason for being on my property. And how the hell did you even get in here?"

"Through the gate." The two women turned at the sound of a woman's voice.

Patricia stood in front of them, her expression unreadable.

"You broke it?" Liz's eyes flashed with anger.

"No." Stewart scoffed. "It wasn't even on, Your Majesty. All we had to do was give it a push."

"Not on?" Liz looked startled.

"Where were you tonight, Ms. Adams?" Patricia asked as she turned off her flashlight.

"Here—" Liz started before Erin gripped her arm to silence her.

"She's not answering any of your questions until you tell us why you're here," she demanded, locking eyes with the woman she'd thought was her friend.

"There was a fire tonight, Mac."

As she spoke, a giant floodlight came to life behind the Range Rover, illuminating the front of the house.

"What does that have to do with Liz?"

"The house that burned was your former residence. Mark's house."

Erin took a small step as a wave of dizziness washed over her. "Mark's?" She felt Liz's strong arms wrap around her for support just in time.

"Did anyone get hurt?" Liz asked.

"Like you give a shit," Stewart bellowed out next to her.

Erin shot him a look of warning, and he shut his mouth.

"No. Fortunately, they got out in time," Patricia said.

"That still doesn't answer why you're here," Erin said, regaining her strength and standing on her own once again. "If you came to tell me—" She broke off, realizing they hadn't expected to find her here, so that ruled out the "delivering bad news" option. Something else was going on. There were too many of them, and they appeared to be searching with a purpose. What were they looking for?

"We have several witnesses who claim that a dark-haired female was seen leaving the house in a silver Range Rover seconds before the fire started," Patricia said.

Erin felt Liz stiffen. "So? It could've been anyone."

"We came to question Ms. Adams about an hour ago," Patricia continued. "And upon our arrival, we looked in through the back window of her Range Rover and saw accelerant."

"What?" Liz's voice rose.

"Several large cans, along with rags and boxes of matches."

"Bullshit!" Liz shoved her way quickly over to her truck and stood next to several men, one of whom was taking pictures. She peered into her truck and went completely rigid.

"What is it?" Erin hurried toward her ashen-faced lover.

Four red gasoline cans sat in a neat row along the back cargo space of the truck. Liz checked the latch.

"Something's wrong," she said. "I never leave my truck unlocked. Somebody put that stuff in there."

Patricia approached before Erin had a chance to make sense of all Liz was trying to say. "If you give us permission to search your truck and your property now—"

"No," Erin declared adamantly. "Tell everyone to back off."

Patricia shrugged. "In that case we'll wait here and snap pictures of what we can see until we get a warrant."

Erin knew the drill. They were just biding their time until a judge granted a warrant first thing in the morning. She looked up into Liz's eyes and said, "Call your lawyer."

"I need to just tell them the truth," Liz whispered wearily. "Someone's messing with me. It has to stop."

"No." Erin gripped her arms. "Call your attorney. They're going to want to question you about your whereabouts tonight. Don't say anything. If someone is setting you up, then they've gone to an awful lot of trouble to do so. And the police aren't about to believe you no matter what you say."

"So, where were you tonight, Ms. Adams?" Patricia asked for the second time. Her face was cold and professional.

Truly afraid for her lover, Erin said, "She was here all night."

"Are there any witnesses to back that up?"

"Yes," Erin said. "Me."

Stewart whistled when he heard the statement. "How do we know you ain't in on it with her? After all, it's your ex's house that got torched."

"What about my gate?" Liz asked. "Don't you find it a little strange that it isn't working?"

"You probably cut the power to it," Stewart responded with a shrug.

"Why would I do that?"

"To disable the front cameras."

Liz turned to Patricia. "It's obvious someone did all this to set me up."

"Or you did it to cover your own ass, knowing full well the cameras would be seized by us for viewing," Stewart wheezed.

"If she went to all that trouble, then why would she leave her truck out in plain view with the accelerant still in it?" Erin asked, facing off with him.

"Maybe she got a little tied up with her accomplice," he said mockingly, shaking his head at her. "I always heard dykes like to fuck a lot. Maybe you two just couldn't wait."

"You son of a bitch!" Erin took a step toward him, wanting to beat the shit out of him right there on the spot.

Liz's hands clamped down on her shoulders, stopping her before she could take a swing at him. "Shh. Easy now. It's not worth it."

"We're going to need you to come downtown with us for questioning, Ms. Adams," Patricia said with patent satisfaction.

Erin placed her palms on Liz's chest. "Go," she whispered. "But promise me you won't say anything. I'll find a way to make them believe."

Liz kissed her forehead and nodded in silent agreement.

"You two looked pretty cozy earlier," Patricia said as she watched Erin pace outside the interrogation room.

Erin glared at her. "This isn't right. She was with me all night. You have no grounds to hold her for this."

"We do," Patricia said calmly. "We got that warrant, and the first thing we found was a pair of boots in the Range Rover that matched a print left at the fire. Not to mention the cans of gasoline and kerosene, the same accelerants that caused the fire."

"That's not possible," Erin breathed out. "Someone is setting her up."

"Who?"

Erin shook her head. "I don't know." *Jay?* She thought to herself. *But why would she?*

"I think you do know," Patricia said. "You see, I believe you when you say that Adams had nothing to do with this fire. The evidence…It's all a little too easy for me. But I think you're hiding something for her. Question is, what? And why?"

Erin looked up as the door to the room opened. Two of her colleagues emerged, followed by Liz. She was handcuffed, and Erin sucked in a quick breath at the painful sight.

"What's going on?" she demanded.

"They've arrested me," Liz said in a surprisingly calm manner.

"But you didn't do it," Erin proclaimed in a high-pitched voice. "They won't listen to me." She looked around at her former friends, wishing someone would hear her and release her lover. But no one met her eyes. Like mindless, heartless robots, they led Liz along the corridor en route to the holding cells. Erin walked at her side, desperately trying to come up with a plan. Her own credibility was obviously shot. No one was treating her with any respect, and she'd overheard Stewart mutter something about her psych assessment.

"There's a way to prove it," Liz whispered to her at the elevator. "I just didn't know if you would be willing to show them."

"What? I'll do anything, just tell me."

"The tapes. The security tapes from my house. The ones in the back of the house hopefully weren't damaged or affected by the power outage. If they were working, they should have us on them."

"Okay." Erin was ready to go and get them as quickly as possible.

"Wait," Liz whispered a little louder. "Watch them first. And if you still want to use them, give them to Cynthia, my attorney. She'll handle it."

Two days later, Erin stood waiting once again at the police department. As she killed time, she looked around at the place once so familiar to her. A place where she had spent countless hours poring over files, following up leads, or doing mindless paperwork, all of it an attempt to distract herself from her lonely, mundane life, her unhappy marriage. Now the place felt foreign to her, almost uncomfortable. She tried to sit down but found that she couldn't stay still. Her nerves were edgy, preventing her from relaxing as she waited for the word on her lover.

She had gone back to the house in the hills the day before to retrieve the security tapes only to be turned away at the door by her colleagues. The place had been under siege, with police personnel searching every last inch of the expansive property, convinced they finally had Liz for something, even if it wasn't the serial killings.

Erin had pitched a fit at first and demanded entry, but when her former friends threatened to arrest her for interfering with an investigation she had walked away. Temper boiling, she then called Liz's attorney and informed her about the tapes. That was the last she'd heard until an hour ago, when Cynthia had called her, letting her know she had the tapes and they proved Liz was home at the time of the fire. She was planning to show this evidence to the police.

As Erin waited, she paced and watched her feet. She didn't know exactly what was on the tapes; she had no idea where the security cameras were positioned. But they had to show some activity in the yard during the hours in question. Envisioning the usual distant, grainy security camera images, she hoped the picture quality was good enough for them to ID Liz conclusively.

A door opened and several male detectives walked past her, eyeing her the whole way. She heard their snickers and knew that it was probably all over the station that she had shouted at Sergeant Ruiz and was some kind of basket case.

"Hey Mac." She turned as J.R. walked up behind her. "Are you crazy? You shouldn't be here."

"Why not?"

"Why not?" He looked past her to the male detectives. "Because you and Adams are the hottest thing out there right now."

"What?"

He cupped her elbow and led her away from the stares and the snickering. "The tapes, man. It's all over the department. Everyone's dying to see the Mac and Adams pool porno."

Erin nearly collapsed on the spot. "Oh God." That was why Liz had wanted her to watch the tapes first. "Have you seen it?" she asked, wondering who all had.

"Nah." He shook his head. "I tried like hell, though."

She ignored his playfulness, far too concerned about the seriousness of her present situation. "So everybody knows?"

"'Fraid so."

She sighed and finally took the seat she had been avoiding, dropping her head into her hands. She had been so thrilled to think that Liz had an alibi, she hadn't even considered the content of the tapes. "There is good news, though." J.R. took the seat next to her. "That video is one hot little get-out-of-jail-free card."

"It better be." If her career hadn't been over already, it would be now.

Two more men walked by, both of them staring openly at her. "Is that her?" one asked. "Man, she is hot," the other said.

"Hey, fuck face!" J.R. yelled out. "You gotta problem?" He stood up, puffing out his chest like a pigeon. The two men walked quicker, eager to get away from the crazy man with the accent. "That's what I thought," he called after them. "Fucking assholes." He sank back down into his chair.

Erin choked back tears and whispered, mainly to herself, "What am I going to do?"

He rested his arm around her slumped shoulders and said, "Hey, it's gonna be all right. Look at it this way—porn pays a hell of a lot better than police work."

"Thanks, J.R." She couldn't help but laugh. She was too tired and overwhelmed by the situation to do much else. "You're a real pal."

"Don't mention it. Now, I gotta go get to work. But the next time you girls wanna make a video, call me. I heard the sound on that thing was terrible." He jumped away from her as she swung at him.

❖

"Why did you do it?" Liz asked as they left the police station a short while later.

"I didn't get a chance to view them," Erin said. "They wouldn't let me. So I told your attorney to go ahead."

"Are you insane?" Having seen the tapes for herself, Liz could only imagine what they would do to Erin's reputation in the department. She was more than outed and would never escape the gossip.

"I think I may be." Erin's laughter sounded nervous. "They were that bad, huh?"

Liz wrapped her arm around Erin's shoulders and pulled her in closer as they walked. If the situation hadn't been so difficult for Erin, the heated scenes in the pool and the spa would've definitely turned her on. "Let's just say that you are one hell of a responsive lover, Erin McKenzie."

"Great."

"I'm so sorry," Liz said, feeling incredibly guilty about the whole situation. She cringed as she realized how much Erin had suffered throughout this whole ordeal. And it wasn't over yet. Jay had to be found before anyone else got hurt, Erin especially.

"Don't be sorry." Erin looked up at her, eyes bright with emotion. "The tapes freed you. That's all that matters."

"You're unbelievable, you know that?" They stopped at the car. "Sacrificing yourself like that for me."

Erin started to say something but then stopped.

"What?" Liz probed, gently cupping her face in her hands.

"I love you," Erin confessed softly, her eyes searching Liz's face. "I know it seems so soon to be saying such powerful words, but...it's what I feel."

With her heart bursting, Liz placed a gentle, lingering kiss on her lips. Holding Erin's gaze as she drew back, she said, "I love you too."

❖

"Where's Kristen Reece?" Patricia stood in front of her partner's desk, her anger barely under control.

"I don't know," Gary said. "She's in hiding. She says Adams tried to have her killed and got someone else by mistake."

"So we could cut a deal. Her testimony against Adams. In exchange, she does time on a conspiracy charge. Ruiz could talk the DA into that." Frustration pounded in her temples. She needed for this to be over once and for all. She needed to move on. Get her life back.

"You're still sure Adams is involved?"

"She has to be."

Gary gave her an odd look.

Patricia returned one of her own. "Are you saying you're not?"

He shrugged. "You know me. Evidence is what counts."

"Then I had better find some before Ruiz pulls the plug on us."

"Someone framed her for that fire," Gary pointed out.

"Or she set that fire and framed herself, knowing she had that tape to prove her innocence!" Patricia shot back. Her temper was showing. She hated feeling so out of control. But she wouldn't put it past Liz to hatch a scheme like that. She'd probably sent one of her cronies in to do the dirty work while she fucked a cop in her pool. That sounded just like the Liz she knew. And as far as alibis went, they didn't get any better. Patricia stared off, her mind racing. So if Kristen Reece wasn't the crony this time, who was?

She searched her mind for answers, and finding none, she said, "I think it's time I took a trip to Alabama."

"What's in Alabama?" Gary sounded lost.

"Adams spent her childhood there." They had briefly searched the run-down town after the shooting, thinking she might be hiding there. Turning up nothing, they had retreated. Now Patricia wasn't so sure that they had looked hard enough.

"And you think there's something there we've missed?"

"There's a piece missing, Gary. And whatever it is, it's not here." She headed for the door, certain in her gut that she was right about this.

"When will you be back?" Gary called after her.

"When I have something more than I do now."

Chapter Twenty-Three

Arcane, Alabama

The smell of decaying flesh was unforgettable. Patricia recognized its unique aroma as she stood before the unkempt house Elizabeth Adams had grown up in. The day was warm and humid, and the air hung heavy, holding fast to the rotting smell of death.

Delaying the inevitable, she kicked at a stone buried in the thick green grass and contemplated her options. She hadn't introduced herself to the local sheriff yet, a discourtesy that might be held against her. Too bad, she decided, breathing through her mouth as she climbed the rotting steps to the porch. She had come for answers, and answers she was determined to get.

She was glad she had worn her boots, because she had to kick in the front door. The body that had alerted her of its presence with its smell wasn't hard to find. After checking to make sure the place was empty, she put away her gun and entered the front room, where the body sat propped up in an old, worn recliner facing the front door, a twisted greeting to whoever stumbled upon it. The cause of death was pretty evident as well—a dime-sized bullet hole piercing the center of the forehead.

At first she wasn't able to tell if the body was male or female. Its state of decomposition was so advanced that the body was grotesquely bloated, blown up like a balloon by trapped gases. It wasn't until she approached it cautiously that she saw the woman's ID lying open in her lap, as if on display.

Patricia read the ID without touching it. Shane Wilson, a thirty-five-year-old private investigator from Valle Luna, Arizona. She recognized the name at once as that of a former cop she knew. That fact, coupled with the overpowering smell, sent her reeling backward to the porch, where she heaved the contents of her stomach over the side.

She spat out the bitter taste, called in her discovery, and retreated to her car to wait for the local sheriff. What was Wilson doing in Arcane, Alabama, and who had killed her?

She didn't have to wait long for the first deputy to show up, a light-haired man with a thin, downy mustache. He seemed unimpressed with her. A Yankee. Sniffing around in their backyard.

After the introductions, he said, "You seen anyone else since you been here?"

"You mean here at the house?"

He nodded.

"No."

He looked her up and down. "You a friend of the Adamses?"

"Not exactly. I'm investigating a series of killings. This address came up in our inquiries."

"I own property just up over the hill there." He pointed, but she didn't bother to look. "That's how come I got here so quick."

"So you know the Adamses."

"Well, I know for a fact that Jay Adams didn't appreciate people snooping around on this property."

"Well it's a good thing he's dead now, isn't it?"

"Shoot, Jay Adams ain't dead. I seen her just the other week."

"Excuse me? Her?"

The deputy looked at her like she was the dumbest thing he had ever come across. "Yes, her."

"Who is Jay Adams, exactly?"

His brow creased and he squinted at her suspiciously. "Maybe you better just go on and lead me to the dead body before Sheriff Bowman gets here."

"Wait a minute," she said. "When you say Jay Adams, do you mean Elizabeth Adams?" For a brief moment she thought that the two might very well be one and the same.

"No. I haven't seen Lizzie in years. I'm talking about Jay." He cast a guilty look toward the house, as if the words were some sort of secret.

"And who is Jay?" She tried again, a little softer. She even batted her eyelashes and readied herself to act stupid. "I only know Elizabeth. She's a good friend of mine and, well, I'm just curious to know who Jay is. I would love to meet her while I'm here."

The deputy stood a little straighter and sucked in a big breath of air, pushing his small chest up and out. "Well, I guess it won't do no harm. Jay is Lizzie's sister. But best I know it, she hightailed it outta here last week."

"Miller!" Another car rolled into the driveway, and big, brawny Sheriff Jimmy Bowman made his way over to where they were standing. "What's going on here?"

"I was just telling this lady about Jay, sir. She's a friend of Lizzie's and—"

"Jay?" he snapped, his eyes growing wide.

"Yes, sir."

"We don't know nobody named Jay."

"But sir, the detective here's a friend of Lizzie's."

"Miller, go inside and tape off the scene."

The deputy gave Patricia an unhappy glance before he scurried off like a scared rabbit.

"According to your deputy, Jay Adams is Elizabeth Adams's sister."

"No, ma'am. Miller is confused."

"But he seems to know her."

"Look, I don't know who the hell you think you are. I've known the Adamses for a long time. Since before you was even born, I would suspect. I knew Lizzie's Uncle Jerry and Aunt Dayne well. Hell, I even remember the names of their dogs. And I'm telling you that there ain't no Jay Adams. Never was. You ask your friend Lizzie. She'll tell you, she ain't got no sister."

"I see."

The guy was lying through his teeth, but Patricia had a feeling she'd just gotten exactly what she'd come for. She now knew what Adams and Mac had been hiding. Her name was Jay.

Valle Luna, Arizona

Erin stared down at the letter in her hands with utter disbelief. It was a certified business letter informing her that she had been released from duty…indefinitely. She read it over and over, convinced that it was a mistake. That her mind was once again playing cruel tricks on her. But there it was. The words remained.

She let the letter fall from her lap onto the floor. A slight squeak escaped her mouth, and she raised a trembling hand to cover it. The department had let her go. They no longer wanted her. The letter said it was partly due to her medical condition and partly because she had compromised an investigation.

She stared straight ahead as her eyes welled up with tears. The sobs tried to come, but she choked them back, hating the way her throat burned and tensed. The day she had been sworn into the department had been one of the happiest of her life. And now that was gone. She had been written off. She was no longer good enough to wear a badge.

It wasn't right. There had to be something she could do. There had to be someone who would listen. Patricia. Yes, Patricia would understand. Wouldn't she? She gazed at her phone, and it stared back, dead and cold. She had left it off the hook on purpose, tired of the harassing phone calls.

Since the night of the fire, Mark and his colleagues had bombarded her with angry accusations. They thought she was after his money. They thought she wanted to have her cake and eat it too. She was no longer the woman scorned, to be pitied but ignored. She was a lesbian. The fire wasn't about revenge. She wanted to claim half the insurance. At least that was the theory.

A knock at her door startled her. She jumped up, angry, ready to scream at whoever it was. To tell them to fuck off and leave her alone. She yanked open the door and sucked in a big breath of air.

"Hi," Liz said softly. "I tried to call but I kept getting a busy signal."

Erin nearly choked at the sight of her. The warm, knowing look in her eyes, her gorgeous face, framed by midnight hair. It was truly amazing how a human being could look so incredible standing there in jeans and a thin gray tank top.

"What's wrong?" Liz asked.

"I…uh…" Erin tried to fight the burning betrayal she felt rising up in her chest. She tried to fight back the stinging words from Mark, from the press. But as she looked into the face of the woman she loved, she caved. All of it came erupting up out of her, exploding like a powerful volcano, leaving her insides hollow and crushed.

"Oh, baby, what is it?" Liz immediately embraced her, kicking the door shut behind them. She walked Erin over to the couch and sat her down, stroking her tear-streaked face. "Shh. It's okay, tell me what's wrong."

Erin looked into her eyes. "It's…it's everything," she sobbed out, sucking in quick jerky breaths of air. "It's Mark, the press…"

Liz watched her, listening carefully. She knew that Mark had been bothering Erin. The man was furious and rightly so. He had nearly lost his life and his unborn child in the fire. But he was wrong about Erin. If he knew her at all, he would know that she could never do such a thing. As for the press, they were hungry vultures feeding off a scandalous story. She had made some calls to have it stopped, and she felt good knowing that she at least still had some pull in this city.

As she studied Erin's drawn face, the far-off look in her eyes, she mentally chided herself for staying away from her so much the past few days. She shouldn't have spent so much time at her house putting it back together again after the mess the cops made of it. Instead, she should've had Erin over. But she had been worried for her safety, knowing that for whatever reason, someone was fucking with her, and she didn't want her lover to get caught up in that.

She'd thought Erin would be safer at her own place. At least for the time being.

"But that's not the worst of it," Erin hiccupped. She picked up the letter and plopped it in Liz's lap.

Liz read it carefully, the heat rising to her cheeks as she finished. "They can't do this," she said. "They have no right. We'll sue!"

Erin collapsed against her. "I don't know what I'm going to do," she said meekly.

"Don't you worry. We'll handle it." She cupped Erin's face, wanting so badly to make everything all right. To take her away from all that plagued her. Some day very soon she would, but right now she needed to take care of her immediate needs. "You hungry?" she asked.

"No, I can't eat."

"You sure? I can go get us something. Feed you in bed, just like I did the other night."

Erin gave her a tired, quick smile and rose up off the couch. "I'm sorry, I just don't feel like eating." She held out her hand. "Come lie down with me?"

Liz took the warm hand and walked with her into the bedroom. They lay down side by side in their clothes on top of the bed. Liz reached down and pulled up a light blanket to cover her defeated lover. In no time at all, they fell fast asleep, snuggled comfortably into one another.

Erin awoke in her lover's embrace. Darkness was all around, blanketing her surroundings. She eased herself up, careful not to wake Liz, able to tell that she was asleep by her breathing. She rubbed at her eyes and focused on her bedside clock. It was after eleven.

She yawned and climbed down off the bed to head into the kitchen. Sleepiness had given way to thirst, and she padded to the fridge. After grabbing a chilled bottle of water, she turned and shut the fridge, but not before its light spilled out into the living room. Blue eyes stared at her from a shadowed face, and she yelped and dropped the bottle.

"Gosh, honey, you scared me," she said, grabbing her chest and feeling the fool. "I thought you were still asleep." She bent down and picked up her water. Standing back up, she watched the figure and waited for a response. When it didn't come, fear shot through her and she nearly dropped the bottle again. "Liz?"

The figure stepped closer, and Erin at once knew it wasn't her lover. The woman stood shorter than Liz, and Erin could smell her. She smelled foul.

The silent woman raised an arm at her, and Erin stood completely frozen to the ground.

"What's going on?" Liz asked as she flipped on the kitchen light. She walked toward Erin and then stopped, noticing her unwavering stare. She turned her head as she approached, blinking her eyes in the bright light.

"Hello, Lizzie," Jay said as her arm remained still, pointing a handgun right at Erin.

"Jay," Liz breathed out in shock. "What are you doing! Put the gun down!" She went toward her sister, but Jay swung the gun around at her.

"Don't do it, Lizzie! Or I'll shoot you dead where you stand." When Liz stopped her advance, Jay continued, "You don't seem happy to see me, sister. Y'all really should lock the door if you don't want company so late."

Liz stood still, her mind spinning. She cringed as she realized she hadn't locked the door behind them earlier, too worried about Erin at the time. She stared at her sister with wide eyes, trying to think of a way to reason with her.

"Why, Jay?" she asked, truly hurt and stricken by her sister's actions. She had to try to get her to talk, to stall her before she did anything rash.

"She's bad for you," Jay said, wiping her nose with her free hand. She wore the same filthy overalls Liz had seen her in more than two months before. She hadn't bathed recently; Liz could smell her stench. "That fire was set so she would have to go to jail."

"Jesus, Jay." She couldn't believe her own sister was doing such things. "What you did was wrong. You know that, right?"

"It was done for you."

"For me? You almost killed two innocent people! One of them almost nine months pregnant. Not to mention the fact that the cops found evidence pointing to me as the culprit."

"You?" Jay asked, her voice a higher pitch with obvious surprise. "No, it was supposed to look like she did it."

Jay glared at Erin once gain.

"Then why did you put the gasoline and the boots in my truck?"

Jay shook her head and started to speak, but she couldn't. Instead she waved the gun harder at Erin.

"No…no, it was her. It was supposed to look like it was her. She's bad for you. She's bad!" she screamed.

"No, Jay," Liz said, doing her best to sound calm. "She's good for me. I love her."

Jay shook her head violently and then grabbed at it, clutching her hair. "No. No, you don't mean that!"

"And I love her too," Erin said, stepping up to stand by Liz's side.

"No…no…" Jay pulled on her hair and took wild, unsteady steps, first toward them and then back, pointing the gun at them as if it were an accusatory finger.

"I mean it, Jay. I love her. You wouldn't hurt someone I love, would you?" Liz could tell her words were getting to the disturbed woman. Almost as if they were penetrating her shell, forcing her to see reality. She watched her sister, holding her breath, feeling Erin's hand slip into her own. They stood still, watching and waiting, a united front against anything and everything that threatened their relationship. Just as they had done days earlier when the police had come calling after the fire. Just as they would do for all eternity.

"I would," said a voice from behind Jay. Liz stood staring, completely stunned as Kristen Reece stepped in from the darkness of the hallway.

"Kris," Liz breathed, gaping at both women in complete shock. Jay filthy and mentally unstable, Kristen looking very healthy and well kept. "You mean…"

"That's right, it's been me all along."

"You? I was going to say...you're alive." Words weren't coming easy to her. The situation before her was overwhelming, and she desperately tried to make sense of it all.

"Alive and well. I look good for someone who was burned beyond recognition in a car crash, don't I?" She looked down at herself and straightened her shirt.

"If it wasn't you, then who?" Erin asked softly as she thought of the remains found at the site of the wreckage. The remains that never had been proven to be those of Kristen Reece.

"No one anyone will miss, rest assured. And all it took was a little dental work on my part."

"I can't believe this." Liz rubbed her forehead with her free hand. Words from the past rang in her ears. Kristen telling her that she wanted out. That she would make everything okay and then disappear. And now it all made sense to her.

"Miss me? I missed you, darling." Kristen laughed, staring at Liz.

"But why?" Liz shook her head. She couldn't understand why Kristen would do it. All along she had thought that Jay had been responsible for the killings, that Kristen knew about her suspicions and was trying to help her stop Jay.

"Why? Why? I did it all for you, sweetie. Like some pathetic, lame-ass fool who thought if I did, that you would love me. But no...you only wanted to fuck me. And boy, did you do that well." She paused, eyeing Erin, sizing her up. "But that was okay, because I had all but convinced myself that you couldn't love." She looked back to Liz. "That maybe you just weren't capable. But then this little bitch came along and proved my theory wrong. And now, I'm so fucking fed up with you and your new bitch that I'm ready to kill you both. Her first, of course, so you have to watch her die."

"No, Jay. You can't. We talked about this, remember?" Liz looked past Kristen to her sister, pleading with her.

"Oh, you're right. She can't. She's weak. Crazy and weak. But she has been good for most things. She's been a great getaway driver and a wonderful silent witness. She and Tracy were the perfect little helpers. Both of them were so enthralled with you that they were willing to do anything once I convinced them they were helping you."

"Jay, don't listen to her. Why did you ever listen to her?"

"She told me those people were bad," Jay responded in a childlike voice, looking back and forth between Kristen and her sister. "That they were hurting you."

Kristen laughed wickedly and walked over to stand next to Jay. "You see? My perfect little puppet. She'll do anything I ask, and all for you, little sis." She stroked Jay's face, looking back to Liz.

"Jay, did you kill those men?" she asked, needing to know.

"They were bad," Jay answered, sounding a little less convinced. "Kris said they were bad and she drugged them up and I drove."

"Did you kill them?" she asked again.

"I—"

"I told you she's weak," Kristen interrupted. "She couldn't even stand to look at them after I shot them. And she nearly threw up when I stabbed them."

"Jesus," Liz whispered, suddenly realizing that her intuitions about her sister had been right. Jay hadn't killed. She couldn't.

"Now it's time to end this little game," Kristen said, regaining their attention once more. "It's time for me to say farewell to all this. To kill both of you, to pin all of it on you, Liz, and then I'm off to retire in the tropics." She grinned.

"You'll never get away with it," Erin declared with disgust.

"Oh, but I will. You see, no one knows the truth other than our little circle here." She looked to Liz. "Your little private eye found me, though."

"No." Liz remembered that she hadn't heard from Shane Wilson in days. Too long.

"Oh yes. She was so easily seduced. All I had to do was let her fuck me, and she told me all I needed to know about you two."

"Where is she?" Liz asked, already fearing the worst.

"She's fine. In fact, I left her sitting in your uncle's old chair. All nice and comfy." Her wickedness escaped her again in shrill laughter.

"You bitch!" Liz shouted with rage as she lunged at Kristen with Erin tugging on her, trying to hold her back.

"Yes, I suppose I am," Kristen said with another evil grin. She raised the gun and fired a shot at Liz, tearing a hole through her arm as the bullet passed through and embedded in the refrigerator.

"Fuck!" Liz screamed out, immediately staggering back, gripping her arm.

Erin rushed to her in panic, shielding her from further bullets as they both sank to the floor. It was all too much. The ambush, the gunfire, the shrill laughter. All of it so reminiscent of the other horrible night that she had lived through not so long ago.

"Did that hurt?" Kristen mocked in a high-pitched voice. "Oh I'm sorry. I must've missed. But this one won't." She raised her arm again to fire. Erin tugged on Liz's arm, and they both crawled quickly farther into the kitchen, trying to hurry before Kristen fired again.

"No!" Jay shouted as she tackled Kristen's arm.

Kristen wrestled with Jay, unable to get a shot off. She freed the hand with the gun and coldcocked her with the butt of the gun. Jay fell to the floor in a daze, trying to gain the strength to stand back up and fight Kristen.

"Shit," Kristen said, eyeing her. "Goddamn little hillbilly!" she shouted as she kicked Jay in the gut, then watched with pleasure as she doubled over.

Jay coughed and wheezed as her lungs screamed. She scurried away from Kristen as best she could, unable to handle another assault.

Erin had been shielding her lover in the corner of the kitchen, trying to stop the rapid loss of blood. Liz was trembling, her face ashen. Erin had managed to grab a large knife from the kitchen counter while Kristen was busy with Jay. She stood now to face off with Kristen Reece. She squared her shoulders and waited, careful to place herself between her lover and Kristen. She wasn't about to leave Liz to save herself. She was going to try to fight for them both, or die trying.

"Now I'm going to have to kill all of you." Anger shook Kristen's voice as she watched Jay scamper away from her. She cocked her head in thought and then continued in a lighter tone of voice, looking toward Liz. "Actually, that works out better for me. Detective Jacobs knows I'm alive, and this way I can wipe my hands clean of it all. Blame it all on you, Liz, and your crazy sister. Make it look like Jay killed you and then herself." She finished her thought with a smile.

She laughed again as she saw Erin approach her with the knife. "I suppose you're going to tell me to drop the gun and fight you fairly?"

"You don't have the guts to do so," Erin responded through clenched teeth. She heard Liz groan behind her, heard her moving, but she wasn't about to turn her attention away from the woman who threatened their lives, their love.

"You're right, she doesn't," Liz whispered as she staggered to stand beside Erin.

"Such harsh words." Kristen laughed as she clutched her chest. "You're breaking my heart."

"I'm sure we are," Erin replied, her gaze shooting daggers into Kristen. "Because she doesn't want you. She doesn't love you."

"Shut up, you little bitch!"

Erin had struck a nerve and she kept on, taking a step closer as she spoke. "She loves me, not you."

"Fucking whore," Kristen spat.

"How could she love you, Kristen? You're evil. You killed all those people and then tried to frame Liz. How could she love you?"

Kristen glared at her. "That's right, I did. And I'm going to get away with it too."

Liz raised her good arm back over her shoulder just as Kristen finished the words. She yelled for Erin to get down.

Erin flung herself to the floor as Liz yelled, and watched as a knife turned end over end as it flew through the air with rocket speed. She covered her eyes, not looking to see if the knife hit its mark.

A shot rang out. Then another. Erin flinched, waiting to feel the pain, but none came. She opened her eyes slowly and looked around. Kristen lay in a twisted heap on the floor. The knife wavered in her chest as blood ran out from two holes beside it. Erin looked back toward her lover, unsure where the other two holes had come from. Liz stood bracing herself against the kitchen counter, holding her arm. She looked to Erin and nodded that she was okay. Erin heard someone moving behind Kristen and pushed herself up into a crouch, ready to react if she needed to. She watched the kitchen door intently as someone stepped into view.

"You two okay?"

Erin looked up and nearly collapsed with relief when she recognized Patricia. The detective nudged Kristen's lifeless body with her boot and then lowered her gun.

Erin immediately went to her lover to make sure she was all right. Liz was trembling, but okay. Erin turned to Patricia. "We need an ambulance."

Patricia nodded and flipped open her phone.

"I need to go check on Jay," Liz said softly. Erin nodded as Liz passed her and walked unsteadily over to her sister.

"Jay?" she whispered, reaching out to touch her arm. Jay stood suddenly, almost as if she were afraid. She looked around wildly and touched her head. A large knot had already formed where Kristen had hit her.

"Jay?" Liz tried again, needing her to focus.

Jay looked at her sister and saw the blood oozing down her arm. "I'm sorry, Lizzie. I'm so sorry."

"Shh. Never mind." She looked back to Erin and Patricia and then dug in her pocket. "Here." She shoved a large folded stack of bills into her sister's hand, then took her by the hand and led her into the bedroom, where she snatched up her satellite phone from the night table. "Take it," she said, handing it to Jay. "Take it and go."

"What?" Jay said, shaking her head in confusion.

"Go, Jay. Get out of here now."

"But—"

"No!" Liz said, a little louder. "Get out of here. Go to Mexico. I'll call you on the satellite phone to make sure you have what you need."

"But after what I done—"

"You didn't kill. You only did what you thought was right." She looked back toward the kitchen and saw Patricia and Erin bent over Kristen. "The police won't understand that, Jay. They'll lock you away forever."

Jay stared at her in silence.

"Just promise me you won't ever let anyone talk you into doing anything bad ever again. No matter what." When Jay nodded, she said, "I'm going to get you some help, but not here. You'll never get it here. Now go."

She motioned for Jay to go out the patio door from the master bedroom.

Jay took a step, then hesitated. "I love you, Lizzie," she choked out.

"I love you too, Jay," Liz whispered as she watched her sister slip out the door and into the night.

Erin moved her hand from Kristen's neck. "No pulse."

She looked at Patricia, who appeared as shaken as Erin felt. "Please tell me you heard what Kristen said."

"I heard enough."

They both stood, and Erin nearly sobbed with relief. "What were you doing here?" she asked, grateful beyond words, whatever the answer might be.

"I needed to talk to you both about Jay. But your phone was off the hook and I got worried."

Erin started to voice her profound thanks but stopped short when she saw Liz stagger back in from the bedroom.

"Oh my God," Erin exclaimed, running to her. "Lie down," she insisted as she eased Liz down to the floor. "Just relax. They're almost here," she encouraged her softly.

Liz looked up into the face of the woman she loved. She felt cold and weak and she couldn't quite focus on Erin. "I love you," she whispered just before her vision tunneled into blackness.

EPILOGUE

Two months later
Utopia, Arizona

Patricia leaned against the redwood railing on the deck of her new vacation cabin. It was a cool, crisp November morning up in the pines. She snuggled her thick terrycloth robe closer to her body as her lungs filled up with the fresh mountain air. She looked down at her deck chair. A notebook stared back at her, her favorite pen clipped to it. It held the manuscript she was writing, a novel based on the events of the serial killings and the people involved. Only unlike the real events, the book was fiction, something people could enjoy as entertainment.

She sipped her coffee as those events replayed in her mind. She almost wished the misery she had lived through *had* been fiction. Fiction was a whole lot easier to deal with. But then, she supposed, that was why she wrote. To help her deal with life and the curveballs it threw her way.

She looked down into the ravine that ran below her cabin. A young deer stood perfectly still, as if it sensed her presence. Then, as it gained confidence, it began to move once more. As she watched the deer continue to walk through the ravine silently searching for its breakfast, she thought about Jay Adams.

The police still had no idea of the woman's whereabouts. Patricia was convinced Elizabeth Adams knew exactly where her sister was, but she also knew she would never tell. While Patricia didn't approve, she could understand her reasons.

After the shootout with Kristen Reece, Erin and Liz had told the police everything. It seemed that Jay, along with Tracy Walsh, had been manipulated by Kristen, but it still didn't excuse her of wrongdoing. She had a lot of questions to answer, and the department would continue to search for her.

Erin had been cleared of any charges and given only a slap on the wrist for withholding the information about Jay. Patricia suspected the department was avoiding bad press by playing down her behavior. Losing her job was seen as punishment enough.

Patricia drained the last of her coffee. A pang of loneliness pierced through her as she thought of Erin. As the deer ran off, frightened by her movement, she realized that she hadn't heard from Erin lately. She hoped, with all her aching heart, that she was happy.

The Aegean Sea
Just off the Isle of Lesbos, Greece

Erin stood staring out at the incredible teal green sea. It was late afternoon and the breeze was blowing cool. She hugged herself and focused on the Isle of Lesbos in the distance. They were due to dock there that very evening. They had been on the chartered yacht for days now, and while she found comfort in its secluded safety, she was looking forward to setting foot on solid ground. While she felt safe on the water and secure in the arms of her lover, the nightmares still came, somehow finding her out at sea. As hard as she tried to put all of the negativity behind her, its darkness still festered, a black lump in her gut. Would she ever be okay? Would she ever be able to deal with all that had happened?

She hoped with all she was that it was possible. A smile found its way to her lips as she thought about her beautiful lover. The woman who loved her so passionately. The woman who had taken her away from all that troubled her. Protecting her, adoring her.

She was grateful for all that Liz had done for her. She couldn't imagine her life without her now. She gripped the rail of the yacht as memories floated in off the waves. So much had happened. She could barely sort it out in her head. The last month had been trying, but she and Liz had still managed to emerge hand in hand and ready to start their new life together. The police were finally leaving them alone, finally accepting that there was no case against either of them. She had lost her job, but after all that had happened, she knew she would never choose to go back even if she could. She was scarred now, and resentful. The department would never look the same in her eyes.

She ran a finger over her left hand, rubbing where her wedding ring had once rested. Her divorce from Mark still wasn't final, but they were no longer fighting over the settlement, which meant it was only a matter of time.

"Hey, beautiful," Liz said as she walked up behind her. "Cold?" She slid her white blouse off and placed it on Erin's shoulders.

Erin hugged the shirt to her and inhaled her lover's wonderful scent, a scent that always sent shockwaves of lust through her no matter how often she smelled it. Her thoughts instantly strayed to the things Liz had done to her just that morning, and she blushed as she slipped the shirt on.

"You look beautiful," she said, watching the wind toy with Liz's hair. She smiled at the color on her cheeks, brought on by long days in the sun and wind. She was so breathtaking, Erin knew she would never tire of looking at her. Lightly, she touched the angry scar on Liz's bare arm, and tears formed in her eyes. The hauntings from that night returned, the night she could've lost her.

"Hey…it's okay." Liz could read her so well. She stroked her cheek and hugged her close.

They had both needed to get away. On the yacht, they were surrounded by water, not people. Eventually the nightmares would stop. Eventually, Erin would feel safe again. She knew Liz would see to that.

Erin tilted her head to gaze up at her. "I love you so much," she said, her eyes filled with wonder. "I never thought I could feel like this."

"I'm glad." Liz kissed her again. "Because there's something I want you to have." She reached into the pocket of her white linen pants and withdrew a deep red velvet box.

Erin immediately placed her hand over her mouth and watched, eyes wide, as Liz opened the box to display the diamond ring inside.

"I love you, Erin McKenzie," she said, her voice thick with emotion. "I want to be with you always. I will protect you and love you for the rest of my life." She took Erin's hand and slipped on the ring. "If you'll have me."

Erin threw herself into Liz's arms, completely overwhelmed with emotion, and kissed her long and deep. Liz groaned against her and pulled Erin into a tight embrace. When they finally paused for breath, she reached up and fingered lips that tingled after the hungry kiss.

"I take it that's a yes, then?" she asked with a raised eyebrow.

"Absolutely." Erin tugged on Liz's white tank top, drawing her closer. It was going to be okay. All of it. She had Liz by her side, now and forever. Together, they could get through anything.

"You know…" Liz leaned down to bite Erin's neck. "We still have another hour before we make port at Lesbos. What do you say you and I go inside and celebrate our honeymoon a little early?"

Erin shuddered under her warm mouth. "Mmm. Only tonight," she said, rubbing her thumbs across Liz's nipples, "it's my turn."

Baja Peninsula, Mexico

Jay sat in the white thick sand, staring out at the sea. As the waves crashed against shore, she thought about her sister and all the wrong that had been done in her name. She reached down and ran her hand through the soft grains. She still felt guilty about letting Kristen manipulate her to do things to hurt Lizzie. But there was nothing she could do about it now, and her sister was safe and off cruising the world.

She stood and wiped the sand from the backs of her legs. Yet again, Lizzie had helped her escape. And as long as she promised not to hurt anyone else, she would remain free. As she walked back up the beach, she renewed a silent vow to her sister. If anyone ever tried to hurt Lizzie again, like those men did, or like Kristen…she would be there. She would be there to protect her. Always.

About the Author

Ronnie Black lives in the desert Southwest, where she pursues writing as well as many other forms of creativity. Learning, reading, traveling, and playing sports are a few of her other sources of entertainment. She also relishes being an aunt and thoroughly enjoys the quality time spent with family and friends. *In Too Deep* is her first novel. She also has a short story in the new Bold Strokes Books anthology *Stolen Moments: Erotic Interludes 2*.

Books Available From Bold Strokes Books

Force of Nature by Kim Baldwin. Wind. Fire. Ice. Love. Nothing for Gable McCoy and Erin Richards seems to go smoothly. From the tornado that sets its sights on them to the perils they face as volunteer firefighters, the forces of nature conspire to bring them closer to danger—and closer to each other. (1-933110-23-6)

In Too Deep by Ronica Black. When undercover work requires working under the covers, danger is an uninvited bedfellow. Homicide cop Erin McKenzie embarks on the journey of her life…with love and danger hot on her heels. (1-933110-17-1)

Stolen Moments: Erotic Interludes 2, edited by Stacia Seaman and Radclyffe. Love on the run, in the office, in the shadows…women stealing time from ordinary life to make passion a priority, if only for a moment. Fast, furious, and almost too hot to handle. (1-933110-16-3)

Course of Action by Gun Brooke. Actress Carolyn Black desperately wants the starring role in an upcoming film produced by Annelie Peterson, a wealthy publisher with a mysterious past. How far is Carolyn prepared to go for the dream part of a lifetime? And just how far will Annelie bend her principles in the name of desire? (1-933110-22-8)

Justice Served by Radclyffe. The hunt for an informant in the ranks draws Lieutenant Rebecca Frye, her lover Dr. Catherine Rawlings, and Officer Dellon Mitchell into a deadly game of hide-and-seek with an underworld kingpin who traffics in human souls. (1-933110-15-5)

Rangers at Roadsend by Jane Fletcher. After nine years in the Rangers, dealing with thugs and wild predators, Sergeant Chip Coppelli has learned to spot trouble coming, and that is exactly what she sees in her new recruit, Katryn Nagata. But even so, Chip was not expecting murder. The Celaeno series. (1-933110-28-7)

Distant Shores, Silent Thunder by Radclyffe. Ex-lovers, would-be lovers, and old rivals find their paths unwillingly entwined when Drs. KT O'Bannon and Tory King—and the women who love them—are forced to examine the boundaries of love, friendship, and the ties that transcend time. (1-933110-08-2)

Hunter's Pursuit by Kim Baldwin. A raging blizzard, a remote mountain hideaway, and more than one killer for hire set a scene for disaster—or desire—when reluctant assassin Katarzyna Demetrious rescues a stranger and unwittingly exposes her heart. (1-933110-09-0)

The Walls of Westernfort by Jane Fletcher. All Temple Guard Natasha Ionadis wants is to serve the Goddess, and she volunteers eagerly for a dangerous mission to infiltrate a band of rebels. But once she is away from the temple, the issues are no longer so simple, especially in light of her attraction to one of the rebels. Is it too late to work out what she really wants from life? (1-933110-24-4)

Change Of Pace: *Erotic Interludes* by Radclyffe. Twenty-five hot-wired encounters guaranteed to spark more than just your imagination. Erotica as you've always dreamed of it. (1-933110-07-4)

Fated Love by Radclyffe. Amidst the chaos and drama of a busy emergency room, two women must contend not only with the fragile nature of life, but also with the mysteries of the heart and the irresistible forces of fate. (1-933110-05-8)

Justice in the Shadows by Radclyffe. In a shadow world of secrets, lies, and hidden agendas, Detective Sergeant Rebecca Frye and her lover, Dr. Catherine Rawlings, join forces once again in the elusive search for justice. (1-933110-03-1)

shadowland by Radclyffe. In a world on the far edge of desire, two women are drawn together by power, passion, and dark pleasures. An erotic romance. (1-933110-11-2)

Love's Masquerade by Radclyffe. Plunged into the often indistinguishable realms of fiction, fantasy, and hidden desires, Auden Frost discovers a shifting landscape that will force her to question everything she has believed to be true about herself and the nature of love. (1-933110-14-7)

Beyond the Breakwater by Radclyffe. One Provincetown summer three women learn the true meaning of love, friendship, and family. Second in the Provincetown Tales. (1-933110-06-6)

Tomorrow's Promise by Radclyffe. One timeless summer, two very different women discover the power of passion to heal and the promise of hope that only love can bestow. (1-933110-12-0)

Love's Tender Warriors by Radclyffe. Two women who have accepted loneliness as a way of life learn that love is worth fighting for and a battle they cannot afford to lose. (1-933110-02-3)

Love's Melody Lost by Radclyffe. A secretive artist with a haunted past and a young woman escaping a life that proved to be a lie find their destinies entwined. (1-933110-00-7)

Safe Harbor by Radclyffe. A mysterious newcomer, a reclusive doctor, and a troubled gay teenager learn about love, friendship, and trust during one tumultuous summer in Provincetown. First in the Provincetown Tales. (1-933110-13-9)

Above All, Honor by Radclyffe. The first in the Honor series introduces single-minded Secret Service Agent Cameron Roberts and the woman she is sworn to protect—Blair Powell, the daughter of the president of the United States. First in the Honor series. (1-933110-04-X)

Love & Honor by Radclyffe. The president's daughter and her security chief are faced with difficult choices as they battle a tangled web of Washington intrigue for...love and honor. Third in the Honor series. (1-933110-10-4)

Honor Guards by Radclyffe. In a journey that begins on the streets of Paris's Left Bank and culminates in a wild flight for their lives, the president's daughter and those who are sworn to protect her wage a desperate struggle for survival. Fourth in the Honor series. (1-933110-01-5)